Harriet's
Eternal Tears

Best wishes

Dave

David John

www.harrietseternaltears.co.uk

Harriet's Eternal Tears

Published by The Conrad Press Ltd. in the United Kingdom 2023

Tel: +44(0)1227 472 874

www.theconradpress.com

info@theconradpress.com

ISBN 978-1-915494-70-2

Typesetting and Cover Design by: Charlotte Mouncey, www.bookstyle.co.uk

The Conrad Press logo was designed by Maria Priestley.

Printed and bound in Great Britain by Clays Ltd, Elcograf S.p.A.

Profits from book sales of *Harriet's Eternal Tears* will be donated to the charity Combat Stress. They help ex-servicemen and their families cope with post-traumatic stress.

At 5 a.m. on July 10, 2016, I was waiting for the sun to rise over Mametz Wood. My great-uncle had done the same thing, in very different circumstances, one hundred years to the minute before. Beside me stood an incredible woman. She is beautiful, intelligent, fiercely loyal and devoted to her boys (all characteristics shared with Harriet). Kathy, you have helped so many people over the years, including me writing this book. I am the luckiest man alive.

About the author

David John was named after his great uncle, who died at Mametz Wood, on the Somme. He worked as a GP, in North Somerset, for thirty-five years, and is now a tour guide at the M Shed Museum, in Bristol. *Harriet's Eternal Tears* is David's first novel and is based on an unforgettable conversation with his grandfather. David is currently writing a sequel, which starts in Bolshevik Russia in 1920.

April 1918

In an ordinary terraced house, the blood drained from Harriet's face when she heard her daughter's wail-like scream. 'Mam. There's a letter. Jesus Christ, there's a letter.'

There could be little doubt from the tone of the young girl's voice, exactly what she meant by a letter. Harriet rushed out and grabbed it from Evelyn. She frantically tore it open. It surely couldn't happen again.

France April 1918

Family of 7647 Private Emrys John. 11th Corps Cyclist Battalion.

I am sorry to inform you that your son is reported as Missing in Action. The battalion was in action in an area that is now behind enemy lines. Much of the battalion was reported missing, including Major Davies, who we believe was taken prisoner. We have unfortunately had no similar report about your son.

You will be proud to know that the battalion performed so well that day that we received personal thanks from Field Marshall Haig himself. Your son's sacrifice has therefore not gone unnoticed.

With regards.
Lieutenant Collins
Acting Commander Cyclist Battalion

Evelyn looked up to see the grey sweating face of her mother. Harriet slumped into a chair, clutching her chest, while her daughter began to panic.

'Da. Da. Come quick. Mam's ill.'

1

Rehoboth Chapel, Briton Ferry, South Wales, February 1915

Harriet John couldn't concentrate.

She stared absent-mindedly at the plain walls of Rehoboth Welsh Baptist Chapel as if they might talk sense to her. Some sort of sense in a sea of nonsense.

All she had heard about that morning, while silently waiting for chapel to begin, was which of the young boys had joined up and how exciting it was. It was making her sweat with anxiety. Grasping her daughter's hand, she stared over at her elder son, David.

He was tall, in everyone's opinion good-looking and clever, everything a mother could want. He had only recently turned nineteen and despite her protestations, Harriet secretly knew that it was just a matter of time before he would join the throng of young men answering Lord Kitchener's call.

She returned to reality just in time. Her younger son was standing facing the tightly packed congregation, open Bible in hand. Harriet knew that, unlike his brother, Emrys was going to find this difficult. The young boy stuttered as he began to read.

'Exodus 32 Verses 25 to 29

And when Moses saw that the people had broken loose - for

Aaron had let them break loose to the derision of their enemies-then Moses stood at the gate of the camp and said 'Who is on the Lord's side? Come to me.'

And all the sons of Levi gathered around him. And he said to them 'Thus says the Lord God of Israel. Put your sword at your side, all of you, and go forward, from gate to gate, throughout the camp and each of you kills his brother and his neighbour.' And the sons of Levi did accordingly. And that day about three thousand men of the people died.'

Harriet leaned over and patted Emrys on the knee, as he sat down next to his sister. That had gone surprisingly well. Now for the sermon. What would that bring this week Harriet wondered with some trepidation. The Reverend Hughes began with a roar, index finger pointing at the congregation.

'Who is on the Lord's side? Come to me.'

He stopped for a moment for his words to sink in.

'Some of you will have read the words of that great man, that great Welshman, Mr David Lloyd George, in his speech at the Queen's Hall in London.

This is what he said. 'We have been too comfortable and too indulgent, many perhaps too selfish. The stern hand of fate has scourged us to an elevation, where we can see the great everlasting things that matter for a nation. Honour, Duty, Patriotism and the great pinnacle of Sacrifice.'

The tall pastor stopped again this time to regain his breath.

'Mr Lloyd George wants to see a Welsh army in the field. He should like to see our nation give a good taste of its quality, in this struggle, for Europe.

So I agree with Mr Lloyd George when I say I envy you

young people your opportunity. For most generations, sacrifice comes in the drab weariness of spirit. It comes to you today and it comes today to us all, in the form of a great thrill and glow of a great movement for liberty.

You will go with my blessing but more importantly His blessing.'

Harriet's sense of anxiety and foreboding had multiplied as the sermon progressed. David's job as a rollerman in the tinplate works was vital to the war effort. She told him so on almost a daily basis. However, she knew her eldest son well simply because so much of herself could be seen in him. Honour, fairness, and above all leadership.

She knew that now that the first casualties were appearing, David's sense of loyalty would mean that even she would have difficulty persuading him to stay at home. She also knew that if David joined, many of the other boys in Rehoboth that morning would also be unable to resist. And they were just boys. Thank God Emrys was only seventeen.

Her mind returned to the half-registered sermon. She didn't feel comfortable or indulgent and certainly not selfish. Life with her husband Josiah had certainly not been comfortable. She had become a mother, father and breadwinner. Josiah was no longer the dashing miner she had married against her father's wishes. He spent most of his day, sitting in his corner, coughing up copious amounts of foul-smelling black phlegm.

Harriet looked at the front pew where the Roberts family normally sat. M.G. Roberts had given her a part-time job, at the big house, working in the kitchen and serving at table. Despite the glint in his eye, M.G. Roberts had always been a gentleman. More than could be said for some of his friends, especially those who occupied the front pews of the numerous churches and chapels.

She realised just how much they had come to depend on David since he had begun working. Harriet had once dreamed that her clever, unassuming son would have the opportunity to make something more of himself. She had even dreamed the impossible that he would get an education and become a teacher or even a doctor.

She was however a realist. So, David and Emrys and their descendants would be condemned to hard physical labour, breathing in toxic red fumes, just a different colour from those that had destroyed their miner father.

She was being selfish, but couldn't help it. She had heard that Mr Lloyd George also had two sons. They would, surely, be going as well. Serving at table, she had heard M.G. Roberts' friend, Sir Alfred Mond, saying that he had taken in some Belgian refugees and how distressed they were. That, of course, was immediately before he furtively grasped her thigh.

Harriet wandered through the crowd outside Rehoboth Chapel looking for Emrys. He was so very different from his brother. To get him to read so well that morning had been a minor triumph.

They might now have more food on the table, but their previous poor diet had left its mark. His teeth were ragged and red from decay. He smiled frequently which only increased Harriet's embarrassment. People would say that she was a bad mother. Today, the left of his face was swollen. He had done well to finish the reading and then not fidget during the lengthy, self-indulgent sermon.

Harriet shivered in the cold wind outside the entrance to

the chapel, deeply troubled by the euphoria inside. It seemed so unbecoming in a place of worship. She looked with concern at her youngest son's face.

'How does your mouth feel, Emrys?

'Hurts.'

'Come home and I'll get you some arrowroot.'

Emrys moaned.

'Mam, it just makes me feel dizzy. Anyway, I have to take yesterday's paper up to M.G. Roberts. He has been away in London.'

Harriet knew that it had only been as a favour to her that M.G. Roberts had employed Emrys as a part-time messenger boy. He had even given him his own son's discarded bicycle, a heavy wooden thing with a hard iron seat. She was pleased that Emrys had taken this job so seriously. Then again she knew that none of her children would ever let her down. Harriet answered quickly.

'Emrys, today is the Lord's Day. I'm sure M.G. Roberts doesn't want you to work on Sunday.'

Emrys laughed.

'I'm not working. I'm only taking him his newspaper and post. Anyway, the factory is open today. The Reverend said we all need to do our bit towards the war and M.G. Roberts is important.'

Harriet knew how important M.G. Roberts was, certainly for her family. He employed all of them except for Evelyn and Josiah. Harriet in the house, David in the tinplate works, and Emrys doing all sorts of things. Harriet inwardly smiled at the change in her youngest son since being taken on by M.G. Roberts. He was becoming such a nice boy. If only he would calm down a bit.

Emrys dashed the few yards back to the small terraced house and through the unlocked front door. Behind him loomed a bitter world of fire, noise and smoke, the lumbering dragon-like monoliths of the Albion Steelworks, belching the red dust. He picked up a pile of papers from the small downstairs bedroom which he shared with his brother and ran out into the tiny backyard.

Emrys began cycling up the street and accelerated along Neath Road. He quickly passed Rehoboth Baptist Chapel on the right and the rival Jerusalem Baptist Chapel on the left. He started to sweat as he began the long haul up the slope to the large house, Bay View, overlooking the harsh industrial landscape on the riverside below. He crossed behind the Town Hall and through an impressive pair of iron gates, swerving to avoid the simple horse-drawn cart blocking the front of the main door.

He could see M.G. Roberts's son, Matthias Roberts, supervising the unloading of several large cases. Emrys had heard that Master Roberts was returning by train, from boarding school, that day. Despite being the same age they had never spoken. Why should they?

As Emrys began to help with the cases, M.G. Roberts appeared to greet his son on his return.

'Good chap, Emrys. Take that one upstairs. Ivor will show you where it goes.'

Emrys struggled up the wide staircase with the heaviest case and then returned to collect the newspaper from his bicycle to give to M.G. Roberts. M.G. Roberts clapped him on the shoulder.

'Thank you, Emrys. Now off you go. I know your mam will

want you home on a Sunday. I'll see you at eight o'clock sharp tomorrow at the dock gates. You are going to have a busy day.'

As Emrys prepared to leave, M.G. Roberts continued.

'Have you and your brother thought about joining up yet? You need to think about it. Matthias would love to go, but his sisters want him to finish school.'

'I'm not old enough, Mr Roberts, and you couldn't do without me.' smiled Emrys.

M.G. Roberts laughed.

'Cheeky bugger. No. If you want to go I'm sure I can help you.'

Emrys free-wheeled down the steep slope, which had been such a struggle on the way up. He was deep in thought.

Things seemed to have settled down. Harriet sat mending one of David's socks in the back room of their small house. It was such a simple task that she was able to lose herself in thought.

The house was unusually quiet. None of her children was at home. The only noise, apart from the clicking of the knitting needles, was the snoring from the corner of the room. When Josiah wasn't smoking he was sleeping. Maybe things weren't so bad after all, however. All week nothing had been said about the sermon. Maybe David had taken notice of her protestations about how important his job was.

Her thoughts were disturbed by the front door slamming shut. Her daughter, Evelyn, must have returned ahead of time. That would be nice. She looked up to greet her pretty daughter. Instead, she was met by an ugly grin staring down at her. It wasn't Evelyn. It was Mrs Margaret Eynon and judging by her face, she had something unpleasant to say. Mrs Eynon wouldn't be there if she didn't have something unpleasant to say.

'He's in the queue.'

Harriet looked confused waiting for the beaming busybody to continue. Who was in what queue?

'David. He's joining up. He's in the queue outside the town hall.'

The blood drained from Harriet's face. The town hall housed the recruiting centre. She was through the front door a few seconds later, grabbing for her shawl as she went. A jubilant Mrs Eynon chased in her wake.

The hall was only a few hundred yards up the road just past Rehoboth Chapel but she needed to get there quickly. Get there before it was too late. She breathed heavily with relief. It wasn't too late. Sweating from equal measures of fear and anger, she could see her elder son's upright stance and broad shoulders, waiting patiently for his turn. She would have one last opportunity to talk some sense into him.

David looked up from his deep conversation with a friend, to see the maelstrom about to hit him. His red-faced mother was running towards him, holding her long dress up, to avoid tripping. Harriet screamed at him as she ran.

'What in God's name do you think you are doing? You have a job that's vital to the war effort. You don't need to go and can keep your head held high. This family has just got back on its feet and you will ruin everything. Anything happens to you, it will finally finish for your poor father.'

Harriet suddenly became aware of the sniggering crowd, looking on in amusement. They were just relieved that it wasn't their mams berating them on the side of the road. Her anger turned on them effortlessly.

'And don't you bunch of wasters look so smug.'

She gazed up at her son. His look of horror and embarrassment had turned to one of deep affection. His reply sounded kind but firm. He wasn't going to be pushed around, even by his mam.

'Mam, I'm sorry but I have to go. Nobody is going to call me a coward and they will. You know they will. Job or no job. Anyway, M.G. Roberts says by the time we are trained the war will be over.'

Harriet could tell that her efforts weren't working. Her son was standing firm. She had only one more card to play. It was something she was able to do deliberately but only used when in desperate need. Her face twisted into a grimace and tears began to roll down her cheeks. This surely must work. They had reached the steps to the front door of the town hall. A recruitment poster was plastered to each of the pillars which flanked the doorway. Lord Kitchener himself stared maliciously at them.

A recruiting sergeant looked down pityingly at her and David. He must have witnessed this exact scenario so many times over the previous few months. A weeping mother desperately trying to stop her son from going to war. His voice was quiet and sympathetic.

'I think you should go home now, Madame. He's a big boy you know. Big enough to make his own decisions.'

Harriet blurted out through her tears.

'He's my big boy and it's a stupid decision.'

She looked blankly in disbelief as David disappeared through the doorway, not daring to look back. Then she was alone. Alone with the recruiting sergeant and the line of boys, all too embarrassed to meet her eye. She stood there waiting. Waiting for a miracle. Waiting for David to come out smiling, saying that he had changed his mind.

She could stand it no more. She turned away, tears still pouring down her cheeks. Real tears this time. If she had wiped away her tears and looked more carefully, she might have witnessed a pair of legs disappearing through an open window around the side of the hall. Those legs belonged to her other son, Emrys.

Emrys had not dared to join David in the queue. He would have rapidly been sent home. Even if he had managed to avoid his brother's gaze, somebody would have spotted him and reported it to his mam. Finally, if he had miraculously made it to the front door he might not have convinced the recruiting sergeant. He looked far too young. His solution was simple. Get through the window and take his chances from there.

He knew the window belonged to a small office with a door leading to the main hall. It wasn't normally locked but perhaps he would not be so lucky this time. Maybe he would have no alternative but to clamber back out of the window, his plans for some excitement away from Briton Ferry foiled. He silently sighed in relief as the door opened just a few inches.

He peered at the scene inside the hall, weighing up his options with minute care. This might be his only opportunity for years to get out of this bloody town. Out into the real world where he could make his fortune. A fortune and a life that would be denied to his perfect brother, who would undoubtedly return to the steelworks after the war was over. If his courage didn't desert him, there would be a choice of two tables at the far end of the hall.

The first had a large sign in front of it. 38th Division

Cyclist Company. Sitting behind the table were three immaculately dressed people. First was a young lady, with a long nose and green hat. She held a pen in one hand, waiting to spring into action as a scribe. Next to her sat a very young officer. There could be no doubt from his features that he must be related to the young lady. A brother or a cousin, maybe. Along the table again was an older officer with an opulent black moustache.

Behind them stood someone who was well known to Emrys, from his work at the tinworks. Sir Alfred Mond. His mam was always careful not to explain why she didn't like Sir Alfred. M.G. Roberts seemed to like him, though, and he was a Member of Parliament, whatever that was. Anyway, if he was good enough for M.G. Roberts he was good enough for Emrys. There seemed precious few people interested in being cyclists, however. The front of the table was empty.

The second table showed a marked contrast to the first. The Royal Welch Fusiliers. Dozens of young men, unable to keep their excitement in check, teamed around it. In the centre stood David at last smiling. Emrys ducked behind the door to make sure that he would not be discovered and marched back home by his brother. He peered out again when an eerie silence fell on the hall.

The group of men was standing with their right hands dutifully raised. Emrys watched enthralled as the men proudly broke the silence and began to recite, their faces wreathed in joyful grins.

'I swear by almighty God I will be faithful and bear true allegiance to his Majesty King George the Fifth, his heirs and successors and that I will, as duty bound, honestly and faithfully defend His Majesty, his heirs and successors, in person, crown and royalty, against all enemies, according to the condition of my service.'

Emrys peeped out of his hiding place in a combination of awe and jealousy at his brother who was shaking hands with the recruiting sergeant and then hugging one of the other recruits. He couldn't wait for David to disappear through the front door. He could imagine the welcome their mam would have for his brother. It wouldn't be pretty.

The group of men finally began to file out. At last, it was safe for Emrys to emerge from the tiny office, confident that he wouldn't be immediately evicted. Which table would he present himself at? He loved cycling for M.G. Roberts but surely he should join the same regiment as his brother. They could go off to war together. The Royal Welch Fusiliers it would have to be.

Despite the cold room, Emrys was sweating from a sickening combination of excitement and anxiety. He knew that he shouldn't be there. He was too young. He knew that at any moment he might be being paraded down the road, to face the wrath of his mam. On the other hand, as M.G. Roberts had said on several occasions, this might be the only opportunity for him to see the world. The world beyond Briton Ferry.

He smiled at the same sergeant, who had shaken hands with David. The sergeant roared with laughter.

'Jesus Christ, Sonny, you must be bloody joking. You've got a mouth like a syphilitic whore and you're bloody aged about twelve.'

Emrys was taken aback for a few seconds. He was not used to being talked to in that fashion in his God-fearing community. The sergeant continued.

'Fair play for trying though, Sonny. Now, bugger off back to your mam.'

Humiliated, he began to trudge towards the front door, forlornly gazing at his feet. He wasn't bothering with the window this time. He knew that everything was bound to be reported to his mam in minute detail. He could only imagine her reaction.

He looked up to find his way blocked by the short, rotund figure of M.G. Roberts. He felt himself being gently guided by the arm towards the table with the young lady behind it. The cyclists.

'Miss Mond, I have a recruit for you. This is Emrys. He works for me so I can vouch for him.'

Emrys was very aware that this young lady, in the elegant green dress and hat was of a class that wouldn't normally even notice him. Today and here, it didn't seem to matter. He beamed at her broadly exposing her to a full frontal of his so-called syphilitic whore's mouth. She immediately recoiled in horror.

'Oh my God, Henry, I think I'm going to be sick.'

The young lieutenant next to her roared with laughter. Emrys's face turned puce with embarrassment. A second rejection despite the efforts of M.G. Roberts and, to make matters even worse, a disdainful laugh from the lady. That was before M.G. Roberts angrily raised his voice to the third person behind the table, the smartly dressed officer with a prominent black moustache.

'Captain Davies. I would be indebted to you if you could take control of your two colleagues. This young man has put himself forward to serve his King and Country. Please treat him with the consideration that he deserves.'

Emrys had a feeling that this stern-looking man might just show a little more sympathy. He certainly didn't seem amused. The captain looked up at Emrys and examined him carefully before beginning his questioning.

'Right my boy, let's see what we can do for you. Firstly, can you ride a bicycle?'

M.G. Roberts answered the question before Emrys could even open his mouth.

'Emrys cycles for me as my messenger boy.'

'Thank you. Secondly, what do we do about your teeth?'

The young woman sniggered, but to Emrys's surprise, it was her father, Sir Alfred, appearing from nowhere, who replied.

'I will pay for his teeth to be fixed by a dentist if he can get to Swansea.'

Captain Davies looked up at him with renewed interest. Emrys hadn't realised that he had such powerful friends.

'I guess the last thing is your age. You certainly don't look nineteen. Do you think your family will agree to you going?'

M.G. Roberts smiled knowingly and replied for Emrys who was yet to utter a single word.

'Now that, Captain Davies, is where you might have a problem. The formidable Harriet, his mother. Maybe I can help you there, but don't put any money on it. Come on, Emrys, let's go and have a chat with your mam.'

David sat at the table still not daring to look at his mam. She was glumly studying her feet. She was silent. She had said enough already. Only Josiah seemed in good spirits. To Harriet's annoyance, he had glowed with pride when David had returned from the recruitment centre.

The silence was broken by a loud knock on the door. They looked at each other in surprise. Nobody knocked. They just let themselves in through the unlocked door. Evelyn shot out of her chair before anyone else could move. She was just relieved to leave the bitter acrimony even for a brief moment. Harriet heard the door open and then her daughter shouting out from the tiny hall.

'Mam. M.G. Roberts is here and he has Emrys with him.'

Harriet called out, automatically.

'Good God. What now?'

Harriet couldn't believe that she was walking back down Neath Road, rushing to reach the recruitment centre before it closed. M.G. Roberts was to one side and an unusually quiet Emrys on the other. He obviously couldn't believe what had just happened either. She still had time to change her mind but she knew she wouldn't.

Both her sons would be going to war. Sir Alfred's offer to get Emrys's teeth fixed was just too good to turn down. Even if it meant him joining up. She vividly remembered the parents of poor Martha Richards, after she had died from blood poisoning caused by a mouth infection. Well. It wasn't going to happen to Emrys. Not if she could avoid it. Added to that, M.G. Roberts had said that the cyclists were just like messengers and Sir Alfred would certainly be doing everything he could to keep his own son away from the fighting.

Evelyn had been in tears but Josiah and David had nodded encouragingly. Harriet eventually wordlessly shrugged her shoulders. She just hoped and prayed that it was a sensible decision.

At the doorway to the town hall, M.G. Roberts ushered them straight past the same recruitment sergeant who had talked to Harriet earlier. They were soon in front of the cyclists' table. Everyone was laughing now. Everyone except Harriet. Sir Alfred smiled at her, knowingly. M.G. Roberts insisted that Emrys would make an excellent servant over in France, for Lieutenant Mond, Sir Alfred's son. They laughed again.

Harriet could stand it no more. She rushed back past the recruiting sergeant and towards the only place where she knew she might find some solace. The clearing in the woods. The beautiful woods which came down almost to her back backyard had always been her sanctuary.

2

Harriet waved Emrys off on his journey to Swansea for the visit to the dentist, promised by Sir Alfred. She would have liked to have gone with him but money was short. It was a luxury that they just couldn't afford. At least he wouldn't be alone. He was meeting another of the Cyclists there but the appointment was at a very strange place. The Metropole Hotel.

Instead of paying for a train, Harriet discovered that Emrys had managed to hitch a lift on the milk boat, collecting milk from the far side of the River Neath. Asher Crocker, the young dairyman was, like seemingly everyone else in Briton Ferry, a good friend of Emrys's. From there it would be a pleasant cycle along the Tennent Canal. Typical Emrys. Never do anything the simple way.

Emrys rushed to the impressive modern entrance to the Metropole Hotel. He was late and Ted wouldn't be impressed, but the journey had taken longer than he had expected. The towpath of the canal was normally empty but today had been a hive of war activity. He ignored his friend's glare. He was sure the dentist would have plenty of time for them.

Without saying a word, he walked straight through the ornate, double doors into the vestibule hall. He stopped still, appropriately open-mouthed. They had expected a small waiting room with a few people sitting sedately. Instead, it was a huge reception area, complete with a high, golden ceiling. Scores of men sat patiently waiting their turn for the free dental treatment. Interspersed several more, who had already been butchered, moaned quietly from bloody mouths.

The two boys pushed their way to the reception desk. The boys had imagined that they would be the only ones. What they hadn't known, until that moment, was that Sir Alfred was paying for a whole battalion to have their teeth sorted. They would have to make themselves comfortable. It could be a long wait.

Two hours later Emrys was slowly climbing the ornate staircase to the rooms above. He heard Ted laughing from his seat directly below. Ted hadn't been laughing half an hour earlier when he had descended the stairs, sucking on a bloody rag. Now, Ted was just relieved that while his own ordeal was over his friend's was just beginning.

Emrys stopped, his bravado deserting him just momentarily. He wasn't a baby but where was Mam when he needed her? Then he remembered. He remembered the girl, in the recruiting centre, laughing at him. He would get his teeth done and go off to war. Nobody would dare laugh at him then.

He arrived at room 3 and knocked gently before entering. He had not known what to expect. After all, he was the first of his family to have ever visited a dentist. Blacksmith with tongs was the normal thing. In the far corner, a semi-conscious man lay in a bed with blood dribbling copiously down his chin. Emrys's confidence began to ebb once more. In front of him was a strange-looking chair covered in green leather. To one side stood a table containing various, evil-looking instruments. On the other side was a pleasant-looking man wearing a grey waist waistcoat talking to a very large orderly in overalls.

Emrys sat down in the chair and gave his name to the

orderly. He closed his eyes and tentatively opened his mouth. The pleasant-looking man quickly prodded his teeth, intermittently saying 'Oh Dear'. Finally, an age later, the dentist gave his opinion.

'Right, my boy. It's a little bit of a mess I'm afraid. This is what we can do for you. The bottom ones aren't too bad. We only need to remove two on the left and one on the right. The tops are all completely gone. All except your middle incisors. That's your four middle ones. But we might as well remove the lot.'

Emrys took a moment to reply. This man couldn't be being serious.

'Remove all my teeth. How will I bloody chew?'

The dentist smiled patiently.

'Look, my boy, none of your upper teeth are working at all. They're no use. They will cause you even more problems soon. Big problems. You need to get rid of them and I can do it now.'

'Can I still go to France?' Emrys asked. He didn't want to be left behind.

'Only if we get you a good denture. You will need to have a denture to use one of the new gas masks.'

Emrys wished he could ask his mam. Before any major decisions, he always asked his mam. He then recalled again how the girl in the green dress had laughed at him. He simply nodded his head and closed his eyes again. He felt a soft mask being placed over his face and choked on the volatile liquid, as it was poured onto the layers of gauze.

The dentist had explained that the trick with using anaesthetics in dental cases was getting the level just right. Too little and he would struggle in pain. Too much and there was the risk of the breathing stopping or inhalation of the copious amounts of blood and saliva. In truth, not very reassuring. Emrys didn't have the time to change his mind, however. He started to feel tired and the last image he had, before falling asleep, was the door opening and a young nurse walking in with a bowl full of hot steaming water.

When he began to wake up, he was lying on the bed in the corner of the room. At some stage, unseen, it must have been vacated by the previous occupant. The nurse was sitting next to him, gently mopping the blood from his mouth. He could hear the grating sound of a drill from the chair. The next victim was already being attacked. The female voice calmly spoke to the dentist.

'Poor thing is coming around at last.'

There was a tinge of relief in the reply.

'Thank God for that. I thought he'd never wake. Once he's fully round give him the painkiller and get him downstairs.'

The nurse added, her voice laced with compassion.

'Is he really going to France? He's only a baby.'

Emrys would normally have objected to being called a baby even by this kind lady, but his mouth was so painful. He fell asleep again only to be immediately woken as some bitter medicine was poured into his mouth. He swallowed hard, the medicine diluted by copious amounts of thick blood. He felt himself being sat up. At that moment, he opened his eyes. The dentist was tugging at the next victim's mouth with a large glistening instrument, whilst the huge orderly held his head firmly.

'I'm going to throw up,' Emrys shouted.

The nurse quickly reached for a china bowl and Emrys began to wretch.

'For God's sake get him out of here.' growled the dentist.

Emrys staggered along the corridor supported by the nurse. He had the stairs to negotiate and was beginning to feel unsteady. The chandelier, above him, seemed to revolve, violently. If only he could reach the crowded vestibule on the ground floor without falling. With no more steps to trip down, he collapsed into a welcome chair. Ted rose from his seat and joked.

'Where have you been? You've been bloody ages. I nearly went home without you.'

The nurse stared at Ted, like a schoolmistress. Emrys was barely capable of hearing the conversation, as he battled with dizziness.

'Are you taking him home?'

Ted replied.

'No. He's cycling.'

The nurse didn't sound amused. She didn't have time for jokes.

'Very funny.'

Ted insisted.

'No. Seriously. He came on his bike.'

She threw up her hands in exacerbation.

'Well, I can tell you one thing for sure. He's not going back on it.'

Emrys collapsed further into his seat, not caring how he got home. He just stared up at the chandelier which had momentarily stopped revolving. The nurse whispered patiently.

'Emrys, you have to come back in a week. You're not listening, are you? Right. I'll write it all down, for your mam.'

The next voice was Ted's.

'Miss? How do I get him home?'

Ten minutes later, Emrys felt himself being pushed towards the railway station by a fat orderly, in an ancient wheelchair. Ted trotted, dutifully, alongside, pushing the precious bicycle. The wheelchair had seen far better days. Every bump in the pavement jolted through Emrys's jaw, like an electric shock. He barely noticed that the railway station was just a few hundred yards away. He was beginning to become dizzy again.

He opened his eyes in time to see a miserable ticket collector, waving them straight through. The ticket collector threw up his hands in horror.

'Jesus Christ. Not another one. What have you got up there, a butcher's shop?'

Poor Emrys was laid down on a wooden bench, while the orderly disappeared back towards the Metropole, taking the rickety torture chamber of a wheelchair with him. Almost immediately, a portly, bespectacled army officer was peering down at him. He was no ordinary army officer, however. He was wearing a dog collar. Despite his uniform, he had to be some form of a clergyman. Emrys opened his eyes again and surveyed the figure in front of him before whispering painfully.

'Mr Hughes.'

The clergyman whispered back.

'Emrys. Good to see you. Perhaps not in this condition, however.'

By good fortune or, as Emrys was a true Baptist, by God's will he had stumbled upon the Reverend Levi Gethin Hughes, son of Reverend Hughes of Rehoboth Chapel. He was an army chaplain home on leave. Emrys never did discover what the Reverend Hughes had been doing in Swansea. He was however catching the same train back to Briton Ferry, where he happened to be staying for a few days.

Emrys shook violently as his lips began to turn blue. Levi put his briefcase under his head and took off his officer's tunic, which he draped over the recumbent figure. He joked.

'You've just been promoted, Emrys. You're now a lieutenant.'

Emrys fell into a welcome drug-induced sleep until he was woken to be laboriously helped on board the train by Levi and Ted. Even though he had often been woken by the goods trains rattling through the night a hundred yards from the room that he shared with David, this was the first time he had travelled on one. It was not going to be the exciting event that he had always imagined.

The train jolted to a start and nausea returned, once more. Lying across the wooden seat, he could resist no longer. Copious amounts of blood and bile were projected all over the floor and Reverend Levi Hughes's left leg. Levi looked over at Ted, who had begun to giggle, and laughed too.

'If I wasn't a clergyman, I would swear! I might swear anyway.'

The rest of the journey was uneventful if everyone ignored the wrenching, vomiting and moans of pain. The train soon slowed to a halt at Briton Ferry station. Now the next problem. How was Emrys going to get to 11 Neath Road, more than a mile away? He was in no condition to walk even with help. There would be no wheelchairs available here, even dilapidated ones. He heard Levi Hughes ask.

'Right, Ted. Can you ride a bicycle?'

Despite his condition, Emrys thought it a silly question to ask someone who had just joined the Cyclist Corps. He listened, without comment.

'Of course.'

'Well, off you go to his house. What number is it, Emrys?'

'Eleven' Emrys whispered painfully.

'Eleven Neath Road. Near the end. Off you go and get some help.'

Fifteen minutes later, David, Ted and two other men came running toward them. About one hundred yards behind, also running, came Harriet. Another hundred yards back again was Evelyn. His da had probably decided to stay in his usual place, the corner of the back room, smoking a cigarette.

Emrys felt the four men lift his dead weight onto their shoulders, like pallbearers carrying a valuable corpse. Harriet and Evelyn clucked around the men, unnecessarily telling them to be careful. Levi Hughes walked behind, covered in vomit and blood. Levi smiled at Harriet, as they entered the front door, and took back his tunic. Harriet whispered her thanks, as he wandered back through the crowd towards Ritson Street.

Four weeks later, Harriet stood on the pavement opposite the hated Jerusalem Chapel waiting for the parade. Next to her, Evelyn snivelled as she tried to hold back her tears. Josiah stood on the other side of the young girl, grinning with pride. His youngest boy would be in the parade marching to the train station for the first leg of his journey to join his brother in the training camp, somewhere in North Wales. After that France.

The last week had been the worst. David had left a few days before and she had promised Josiah that this time she wouldn't cry. It was a promise that she knew she wouldn't keep. The tears began well before they had even caught sight of her son. It only took the sound of the brass band marching toward her.

Josiah's glare alternated between Harriet and Evelyn. They both knew that he considered any sign public sign of emotion as a demonstration of weakness which he wouldn't tolerate. They would be made to pay for it later.

At last, the boys appeared, marching haphazardly to the joyful martial music. Emrys was in the centre grinning a toothless grin and waving to everyone. Then he saw his family. He and his four friends Ted, Albert, Gwyn and Emlyn waved even more furiously. Harriet suddenly realised that her son might only be happy now that he was going off with his friends.

A cold shiver shot down her spine. Which of those five would she never see again? She wanted to run out into the road and give each of them one last hug, but she couldn't. What would people say? What would Josiah say?

She stood rooted to the pavement for several minutes after the boys had disappeared towards the station. Josiah had already left and Evelyn was tugging on her sleeve. Keeping Josiah waiting, when he was in this sort of mood, was foolish but Harriet felt a vital need to collect her thoughts. The crowd lining the road was breaking up quickly, everyone clapping each other on their backs and shaking hands.

She only then noticed on the opposite side of the road two people standing motionless, hands tightly clasped. She had never dared speak to the pastor of Jerusalem Chapel and his wife. Unlike Rehoboth's Reverend Hughes, the Reverend Powell was renowned for preaching against the war. That was why Jerusalem Chapel was known by some of her friends as The Kaiser's Temple. The two of them were at the parade. But why? Surely they wanted peace, not war. Then Harriet understood. Their eyes were firmly closed. They might be against the fighting but it wasn't going to stop them from praying for the young men marching to war.

Harriet silently closed her eyes and joined them in prayer, before Evelyn began pulling her down the road.

3

December 1915

It was the letter that Harriet had been dreading for months. While her boys were training in Rhyl, in North Wales, she knew they were safe. Once they were moved to England, then it would only be a short time before they would go to France and her worries really began. She had read it twice before handing it to Evelyn, who studied it seriously, intermittently looking up at her mother's ashen face.

Winchester December 1915

Dear Mam,

Sorry I haven't written for a bit. We have been very busy with things. We came here to Winchester from Rhyl. We have seen some wonderful things already. The train went through Oxford which is where all the rich English go to college. Then last week Lieutenant Mond led us on a long ride on our bikes. We went to Salisbury. There is a church there like you never seen. It's bigger than Albion Steelworks. Then we went to a circle of huge stones built by the Druids. Lieutenant Mond knows around here because this is where he went to school.

I am glad that M.G. Roberts had a word with Lieutenant Mond. I am definitely going to be his servant when we get over to

France. I will get an extra penny a day's pay so thank you, M.G. Roberts.

It's great news about David. What a twentieth birthday present for him to be made a sergeant. Da must be so proud. I haven't seen him for a while. I don't know whether his battalion is still in North Wales.

A funny thing happened. Sir Alfred Mond has sent us some equipment. You would have laughed when you saw it. It was ten bugles and ten drums. He must think we are going to have a concert.

It is great to be here with all my pals. Emlyn, Albert, Ted and, of course, Gwyn send their regards.

Da will be proud of me too. I have learned to become a boxer. Our PT in Rhyl was a huge man who Da will have heard of. He is Bombardier Billy Wells, a heavyweight boxing champion. He says that I have talent and should take up boxing when this is all over.

Yesterday we had to be up early. The whole division had to parade for Queen Mary and Princess Mary. The Queen looked as miserable as Mrs Eynon. The reason we done that we now know is that we are sailing to France tomorrow. We are going on an old rust bucket paddle steamer called The Maggie.

Mam, I know this is useless for me saying but don't worry about me. I have seen so many things already that I wouldn't have seen in the Ferry. I have good pals looking out for me. I also have Lieutenant Mond and Sergeant Marshall making sure that I am safe.

Look after Evelyn and Da until we get home.

Your loving son Emrys

Evelyn was still reading when she felt a sharp tug on her sleeve. She looked up as her mother said.

'Fetch your coat.'

Josiah also looked up, removed the cigarette from his mouth and asked.

'Where are you two off to, in such a hurry?'

Harriet replied firmly.

'Our boys are going to war. Evie and I are going to war. Don't try and stop us.'

Josiah made no effort to rise from his armchair as the two women marched out of the room, leaving him alone to finish his cigarette.

Harriet and Evelyn strode purposefully down Regents Street and into the yard in front of Taylors Foundry. Harriet had walked past it many times but this was the first time she had ever gone in. In front of them was a much larger building than she had appreciated from the road. It was built from rough stone with seven bays, each with brick surrounds. The central arch was bigger than the rest and contained the main door. There were windows above each of the bays also brick lined. Above the central bay was a further large opening with a pulley above.

Tentatively peering through the open door, she was hit by the ear-piercing noise, followed by an intense blast of heat. How could anyone work in such a place?

She was determined, however, to do her bit to help her two boys. As everyone knew if Harriet wanted something enough, she normally got it. Circumstances might be in her favour. She knew that at the beginning of the war, Taylors had been transformed for the production of artillery shells. Not only had

Taylors suddenly needed an expansion in the workforce, but many of their men were answering Kitchener's call. So they were desperately trying to recruit. Harriet had heard that they were even taking on women.

They looked around at the hard-working machines. Dozens of perspiring men laboured away, but the occasional young woman was also struggling manfully with the heavy weights. Perhaps they would have a chance. Harriet had hoped that one or both of the Taylor brothers would be there. She was known to both of them and they might be sympathetic. Glen Taylor in particular was a frequent visitor to the Roberts' house. She couldn't see either of them.

Instead, she saw one of their managers, Mr Francis Newman. Her face dropped. Mr Newman was also well known to Harriet but for entirely different reasons. Knowing the Taylors she was surprised that they were employing him. He had become infamous for his comments about women workers. Their hair or petticoats might get caught in the machinery. He was also well known for his wandering eye and, if the female was young and pretty enough, his wandering hands.

Harriet stood before Mr Newman with Evelyn a step behind her. She knew that the work was very physical and she might be considered as being too old. Perhaps, Evelyn might be thought of as too young and small. Although Harriet was doing all the talking, Mr Newman's gaze seemed to frequently drift towards Evelyn. Harriet felt herself holding her breath with increasing unease. She was about to say something that she might regret. She just managed to stop herself as Mr Glen Taylor appeared through the doorway.

'Harriet. What are you doing here?'

Harriet's praises had been sung frequently by M. G. Roberts.

'Look, Mr Taylor. Sir. Our boys are going to be in France. We want to do our bit. We want to make shells that might just save their lives. We want to work for you. We want to make shells.'

Mr Taylor was silent for a few seconds, carefully studying the two women. He would know that Harriet would be hard-working. He also must know that she wouldn't be at all militant. Trade Unions were not a thing for Harriet. What you got was someone who would punch in on time, work hard and then go home to look after her family. Evelyn might be a different matter. Malnutrition earlier in her life had left her appearing delicate. Perhaps Mr Taylor had also heard a few unpalatable whispers about Francis Newman and Evelyn had undoubtedly inherited her mother's good looks. Harriet had read Glen Taylor's mind.

'Mr Taylor. Evie is a good girl. A hard worker. She's much stronger than she looks. And I promise you that I will keep an eye on her every minute she's here.'

Harriet looked him straight in the eye. There could be no doubt in Glen Taylor's head about what this mother meant. Should he take the risk?

'Look, Harriet. We would love to have you. I know you will work hard. Your daughter, however. Evie. I just think you're a bit young. Maybe next year when you are bigger and stronger. If the war is still going on of course. God forbid.'

Harriet had anticipated this.

'Mr Taylor, sir. I'm afraid we come as a pair. You either want both of us or neither of us. I'm sorry if that sounds like blackmail, but that is how it is. And we don't work Sundays. If you could just see yourself giving her a two-week trial.'

Blackmail it undoubtedly was but it must have amused Glen Taylor. Harriet had banked everything on Taylors being short of reliable workers.

'Right then. We will take the two of you on if the hours are satisfactory. You and Mr Newman can discuss it and come to an arrangement. You do know that we can't always give you shifts together.'

Glen Taylor looked from Francis Newman to Harriet. There could also be no doubt that Harriet again knew exactly what he meant. She said nothing.

'Good. You start tomorrow.'

Evelyn responded immediately.

'I do work on Sundays.'

The following day they walked the two hundred yards down Regents Street to their new place of work. They were anticipating their first twelve-hour shift at Taylors with some trepidation. Mr Newman had made his well-practised facetious comment about long hair and petticoats. The petticoats were just a mean insult. No one looking for a job at Taylor would ever have enough money to own a petticoat.

So, they wore their hair tied up in brightly coloured scarves. Harriet was wearing a tight dress, whilst Evelyn an old pair of Emrys's trousers. They certainly weren't glamorous. Emrys being Emrys, they had needed patching many times. They were also slightly too big and baggy, held up by an old belt. They were, however, immensely practical. They were unlikely to get caught in the machinery. The job was dangerous enough without risking that. They also might not attract Francis Newman's wandering eye.

They went through the central bay, leading from the yard, at ten to eight, in plenty of time for the 8 o'clock start. As Glen Taylor had anticipated, Harriet was not going to be late. At five past eight, Evelyn was running back up Regents Street, sobbing loudly. Mr Newman had sent her home for dressing inappropriately.

'Men wear trousers. Young ladies wear dresses. At Taylors, we have standards. Go home and dress properly. No pay until you're back. Not a very good start, girlie.'

Harriet was going to have to keep a close eye on Mr Newman. She looked down at the rudimentary shell case passing along the conveyer belt in front of her. A brief moment of profound guilt swept over her. Was this shell going to be the harbinger of grief for some poor mother? Some poor mother, just like herself, far away in Berlin or Munich.

4

Northern France, April 1916

It was a talent that Emrys had inherited from his mam. It was possibly a surprising talent considering that she was so fiercely honest. She was excellent at listening to other people's conversations without being noticed. Now in this hell hole, called Givenchy, he was using that talent to its full. He was sitting with his back to a wall of sandbags, with his eyes closed unnoticed in the dark. Ignoring the scratching of rats in the background and the occasional explosion, he began listening with growing interest to the two officers. They were discussing Lieutenant Mond.

'Henry's pretty intense for one so young. He can only be seventeen.' said Lieutenant Parry.

Captain Davies seemed to wait for an age before replying.

'Well he's got a lot to prove, hasn't he? Not only is his father half German, but he's Jewish, as well.'

Lieutenant Parry sounded as surprised, as Emrys. They all had seen Henry Mond praying during their church services.

'Henry is a Jew?'

Captain Davies explained.

'No. Henry was brought up Church of England by his mother. But his Grandfather was a German Jew. Doesn't bother me, of course, but it seems to bother Henry. That is why he is always volunteering for some madcap idea. He'll either get awarded a VC or get killed, along with half his platoon.'

Emrys was discovering that, despite the cold wind, he was beginning to perspire. This explained a lot. He couldn't understand how Lieutenant Mond, let alone Sir Alfred, could be German. It did explain, however, why their platoon always seemed to be given dangerous jobs. The extra penny a day that he had boasted about to his friends seemed less good value. Being close to Lieutenant Mond as his servant, suddenly, seemed a dangerous occupation. Despite that, Emrys liked him. He secretly liked how the lieutenant had started calling him 'Boxer' after his exploits with Billy Wells, in the boxing ring. It made him feel special.

They were finishing their six-day stint in Givenchy the next day. They had done nothing more dangerous than filling an endless supply of sandbags. Even Lieutenant Mond seemed pleased to be leaving. There would be no glory, in Givenchy. There was just the continuous spectre of death or injury combined with the endless sea of thick, purulent mud.

Emrys was just looking forward to a few days of getting cleaned up. Perhaps he might even have just a few hours away from being at Lieutenant Mond's beck and call. It might not be home, but Essars sounded an admirable place to rest after this shit hole.

The next day, Emrys was holding Lieutenant Mond's bicycle for him when they finally arrived in Essars. He couldn't wait to be allowed to leave. He just wanted to wash for the first time in six days. With luck, there might even be the prospect of a bath to get rid of the lice.

For the time being, however, he could only stand at the back of this group of officers while they discussed their evening's entertainment. Next to Captain Davies stood a stranger. Captain Jones. Wearing jodhpurs he must be some visiting cavalryman. Captain Davies seemed to have known him from school and Captain Jones like everyone knew Lieutenant Mond's father. Lieutenant Parry was next to be introduced, to which Captain Jones howled with excitement.

'Your brother was at Dulwich with me. Capital fellow. Played inside Harold Gillian in Evans's year. I remember the game against Bedford. Must have been in 1912. Score twenty-eighth all. Best game I've ever watched. Capital fellow.'

Emrys was still waiting to be dismissed by Lieutenant Mond. He was astonished once again at how these rich people all seemed to know one another. They seemed to have always played cricket, football or rugby against each other at school. Lieutenant Parry enthusiastically pumped Captain Jones's hand.

'Listen, Paul. We're having a concert for the men, tonight. Would you like to join us? Not sure what's on the bill yet. Chap plays the piano pretty well.'

Lieutenant Jones roared his appreciation.

'Capital. Capital. Wouldn't miss it for the world.' Then addressing Henry Mond. 'Henry. A smart chap like you should be doing a turn.'

Henry Mond seemed to think about this. Normally the acts were done by enlisted men. He did however have a tiny secret that he now reluctantly revealed.

'Well, I do write poetry. I could read one of my poems. They're a bit sombre I'm afraid.'

'Capital. Capital. Officers have got to keep their end up you know.' said Captain Jones.

Later that evening, they crowded, into the old barn. The front row was a line of straw bales, reserved seats for the officers. Standing behind the packed enthusiastic lines of enlisted men included Emrys, Gwyn and Ted. Emrys was pleased to see the ancient piano to one side. He loved sing-songs. When Captain Davies stood up to ask for silence, he was received by a cacophony of jeers. They all knew tonight was one night when military discipline, just to a tiny extent, might go out the window. The captain patiently waited for silence before he began.

'This is Private Smith from the 1st Welch. He is going to play the Number 2 Rhapsody by Liszt.'

Emrys groaned along with most of the audience. They wanted music hall, not classical music. A beautiful flowing sound floated from the dilapidated piano. Emrys instantly fell mesmerized and unusually silent. This gorgeous sound seemed so out of place just a few miles from the mud and horror. It, finally, came to a crescendo and finished. It was followed by a few seconds of stunned silence and then by a tumult of cheering and whistling. The officers, led by shouts of Capital from Captain Jones, called for an encore.

Captain Davies stood to make his request. There were no jeers this time.

'Marvelous, private, what can we induce you to play next?'

'Marche Militaire by Schubert, sir.'

'Very appropriate.'

Captain Davies sat down and Private Smith began again. Quickly there were tears in eyes. Emotions were high.

'Soppy bastard,' Ted said to a weeping Emrys.

Emrys wiped away his tears, noticing that Lieutenant Mond was beginning to look nervous. He was surprised because his officer was normally so brash and confident. Perhaps he hadn't realized the standard of the other acts. Lieutenant Mond certainly wouldn't want to look a fool next to an ordinary soldier. Emrys closed his eyes again silently hoping that it would go well. He knew who it would be taken out on if it did not. Lieutenant Mond coughed to clear his throat before beginning.

'War. By Henry Mond

Distantly clear in the oceans and continents
Murmurs of war mumbled and groaned
Rattle of guns and clink of accouterments with crowds, bloodily toned
Stripped for battle and drunk with armaments
Clamouring contest a nation enthroned
Death and his breath swept slowly through the fields
And at the farmyard, lying in sunlight on a peaceful land
In at the cottage door
Sighed chill upon the heat of unfought war
Down the deserted side streets of the town
That echoed faintly to the distant crowd
Thronged in the Main Street
Pale as the breath of icebergs through a ship
Against the hearts of women grown
Solemn and cold but wonderfully proud'

There was stunned silence again. The normally reserved and loyal Sergeant Marshall whispered at the back.

'I think I'll go out and hang myself.'

Clapping started from the front row, quickly followed by cries of 'Capital. Capital.'

Then to Emrys's relief, everyone joined in. After all, thought Emrys, it did rhyme in places. A few seconds later everyone was cheering.

At last, Private Smith returned to the piano. He was going to lead the sing-song. Emrys had hoped that the men would request music hall numbers. He knew however that they would want the hymns they knew so well from the chapel. They had frequently sung together over the past months but tonight seemed a special night. They sang as if there was no tomorrow. Then again there might not be. The harmonies seemed perfect. The back row put their arms around each other's shoulders and swayed to the music. Maybe, this was better than music hall after all. In the front row, Captain Jones looked at Captain Davies in admiration. There was only one thing he could say.

'Capital.'

The billets for the men in Essars were damp and cold. The officers would be infinitely more comfortable living in local homes. The compensation for Emrys however was the proximity to the town of Bethune.

It was with relief that he, Ted and Gwyn were able to walk rather than cycle the mile and a half into Bethune. Even Emrys was sick of their long rides on heavy unmanageable bicycles. They crossed the small bridge over the canal that divided Essars from Bethune. Emrys was very keen to try out the rudimentary French, which he had picked up listening to Lieutenant Mond.

He was delighted when two Mademoiselles sitting at the

side of the road called out to them. At least one looked like a Mademoiselle but the other appeared more likely to be a Madame. They wore the lowest-cut dresses that he had ever seen. There certainly weren't many dresses like those back in the Ferry especially in the chilly wind. Emrys started enthusiastically.

'Bonjour, Mademoiselles. Comment allez-vous?'

Ted tugged on Emrys' sleeve to usher him away. Emrys was having nothing of it, smiling again, before continuing.

'Je m'appelle Emrys. Comment appellez vous?'

Ted tugged at him even harder as the two women burst out laughing.

'Come on Emrys, you silly bugger. What are you playing at?'

Emrys couldn't understand the fuss, as he was ushered around the corner. After all, hadn't Mam told him to talk to the local people? Ted shouted at him through tears of laughter.

'For God's sake Emrys, were you born yesterday? They're bloody whores, you idiot. They're prostitutes.'

Emrys looked at Ted and Gwyn in shock.

'Are you sure? They seemed very nice.'

His two friends just kept laughing.

'Emrys, boy, I really think you need an education.'

The three friends had walked into the main square of Bethune. A huge rectangular space, the size of two rugby pitches, was dominated by an ancient and elaborate belfry. The buildings around the marketplace were narrow three or four-story, medieval structures, each with steep pointed roofs. Each ground floor sported a shop front, overflowing with exorbitantly priced goods. Each one vied for the custom of the hundreds of British servicemen, milling around.

Mainly undamaged by the war, Bethune was an oasis, in the middle of a morass of horror. They could ignore the sound of gunfire, in the distance, and seek out normal pleasures, for a few hours. Normal pleasures came in many forms, as Emrys had just discovered.

They were looking forward to using their few spare coppers to buy some proper bread instead of the hard tasteless stuff supplied by the army. As they walked, still laughing, Emrys noticed a familiar figure walking towards them. It was his brother David, whom he hadn't seen since Kinmel Camp in Rhyl six months previously. Both stopped dead in disbelief and then grabbed each other ferociously. Emrys was surprised to hear his perfect brother swear.

'Well, I'll be damned. What the hell are you doing here?'

David shook hands with the other two cyclists and then returned to hug Emrys once more.

'It's good to see you, brother.'

It had surprised Emrys how pleased and relieved he was to see David. They had always been a bit distant at home. David decided that Mam would want him to treat his young brother to lunch. Still hugging each other they walked away. David said that the place to go was just around the corner. Even Emrys had heard Lion D'or, an old-fashioned hostelry, complete with old beams and stone floors. It would be filled to the brim with British NCOs and officers. It was not a place for mere privates.

He held his breath as his brother quietly smuggled him into the back room. David must have frequented this place many times before. A small six-year old girl, with tousled hair, approached the table. She surprised Emrys when she opened her pouting mouth.

'Bonjour, David.'

David's reply surprised Emrys even more.

'Bonjour Annette. Une bière s'il vous plait. And what do you want, brother?'

'A fizzy water please.'

David continued.

'Bien. Une bière et un Perrier. Et puis deux plats de jour. Merci beaucoup, Annette.'

Emrys waited for the little girl to disappear before commenting.

'You're drinking beer, David. That's new.'

'I don't think God will mind too much with all that's going on here if I have the odd glass of beer. Or something stronger for that matter. I'm sure if Reverend Hughes saw what we are seeing even he would agree. Or Mam for that matter.'

Emrys smiled silently. He wasn't sure that he agreed about Reverend Hughes.

'If Mam was out here, she would have got it so bloody organized that we would have won months ago.'

David laughed.

'I expect your right. Did you know that Mam and Evelyn are working at Taylors? Probably riskier than being a cyclist just peddling around miles behind the front.'

The next fifteen minutes were spent in a combination of gentle banter and reminiscing. Fifteen minutes as brothers, not soldiers. They were interrupted by the arrival of a sulky sixteen-year old girl carrying two plates. David greeted her.

'Merci, Agnes.'

'Mon plaisir David.'

Emrys looked down at the food in front of him. It was

nothing like anything he had ever seen before.

'David, what the hell is this?'

'This, brother, is liver in red wine sauce. Don't worry about the red wine. The alcohol is boiled out whilst it's cooking. Good health or should I say Bon appetite.'

Emrys tentatively tried this unaccustomed delicacy. What a wonderful taste. Almost as good as Mam's cooking. He loved it even when David told him it was horse liver. The next hour seemed to pass in a second. Emrys had noticed the pronounced shake of David's hand. He also noticed that the shake seemed to have been cured by the third glass of beer brought by Agnes.

They made their way back to the square where they would go their separate ways. Emrys knew he would be late for the evening parade but didn't care. Even the prospect of Lieutenant Mond's wrath wasn't going to rush him. They hugged once more. Before parting, David gave his brother some advice.

'Listen. Mam wrote to me about Lieutenant Mond. He's trouble. If you're not careful he'll get you killed. Try to stay away from him.'

Emrys trotted back towards Essars. He didn't know when or even if he would see his brother again. Through his tears, he didn't even notice the girl in the low-cut red dress calling out.

'Bonjour, Emrys. Comment ça va?'

5

Despite David's dire warning, there were advantages of being with Lieutenant Mond. When they returned to Givenchy there was none of the backbreaking digging and filling of sandbags for Emrys. Each night, his friends returned from their labours, at the front line, with every muscle aching. He stood up straight and laughed. All he had been doing was sitting next to his officer with a pencil and paper.

He had followed Lieutenant Mond and an engineer captain to the entrance to the sap trench. This sap trench was different. It was a hole in the ground with a ladder descending into the darkness. They were going down a tunnel. Emrys recalled some of the stories his miner father had told them when he was small. They generally involved collapsing tunnels and crushed miners. He had been terrified of confined spaces ever since.

The engineer led the way, with Emrys nervously bringing up the rear. He descended into the dimly lit darkness. The passage seemed a mile deep and to run right underneath No mans land towards the enemy line. In the semi-darkness, he could see that the roof was supported by feeble wooden beams. Every ten yards a cursory oil lamp, barely lighting the way, produced eye-watering toxic fumes.

At last, they reached the far end of the passage. A cramped gallery contained a table and three chairs. Emrys didn't know how long he would manage to stay. Blind panic would surely make him flee to the freedom of fresh air.

On the table stood a complicated electrical machine with two earphones attached. The engineer sat down and summoned Lieutenant Mond to join him. Emrys stood grasping the back wall and willing his feelings of panic to somehow miraculously disappear. The engineer began.

'Okay, this is my baby. At least this is my French baby. The Frenchies have had these for months. They've given us this one for free.'

The engineer continued.

'The Germans have had them for even longer. We captured one near Armentieres, last month. They call it a Moritz.'

Emrys noticed that Lieutenant Mond looked distinctly uncomfortable. Perhaps, Lieutenant Mond didn't like dark places either. Then Emrys remembered. Sir Alfred Mond's name over his factory door. His middle name was Moritz. Perhaps this German wonder machine had been invented by some distant or not-so-distant cousin of the Lieutenant. The engineer continued.

'This is how it works. We've got wires running along from here in both directions. If their telephone wires are badly insulated, the ground will be the medium of transmission. So we will pick up the signals on our wires. This little beauty is a three-valve amplifier that will do what it says on the tin, amplify the sound. So we can listen with the earphones.'

Lieutenant Mond butted in.

'What's the range?'

'That's variable. Depends on the amount of water. Lots of water around here is good. The range is three or four hundred yards for speech and maybe a mile if they are using bleeps. We haven't managed to work out the bleep system they use yet.

Lots of bleeps mean something is up. That's it in a nutshell. That's why we need German speakers.'

Emrys had lost interest. Nobody at home even had a telephone. Nobody he knew anyway. Nobody except M.G. Roberts. All he knew was that he would be stuck under No mans land for hours on end looking after the lieutenant. He now did understand why they were there. Lieutenant Mond could speak German. He jumped as he heard loud banging, raising his rifle nervously. The engineer laughed.

'Settle down, private. Some mining is being done somewhere. Might be us. Might be Gerry. Can't tell. Sound transmits for miles. Don't worry. All we need from you is to keep the battery charged. See that handle? Pull it up and down twenty times once an hour. The dynamo keeps the battery charged. The easiest job you've ever had.'

It was not quite as simple as the engineer had thought. He had not factored in Lieutenant Mond's continuous and exorbitant demands. Where's my tea? Concentrate. Don't fall asleep.

It was, even so, an easy time compared to his friends outside. There were no filling sandbags, no night guard duties and no worrying about snipers. He did discover what claustrophobia was and that he suffered from it. The ground shaking from every mortar bomb which exploded made it worse. Apart from waiting on his officer and keeping the battery charged, however, all he had to do was note down translations of the German telephone messages.

After the first two days, he had gotten used to it. Even the darkness. There never seemed to be anything of interest. It was just another waste of time. An easy waste of time. To relieve the monotony Lieutenant Mond began talking to him.

'Well, Boxer. What are you going to do when this is all over? Are you going to be a boxer like Billy Wells suggested?'

Emrys had been thinking about this for a while. Everyone expected him to become a rollerman in the hot tin plate works, like his brother. He answered carefully. This was the first time he had talked about it out loud. His friends would just laugh.

'Definitely not, Lieutenant Mond, sir. I've had enough of people trying to knock my head off. And I'm not going to the Tin Works, either. I'm going into business on my own. Like M.G. Roberts. I'm going to make carbonated water. I'm going to have my own factory.'

Lieutenant Mond seemed to look enviously at him. The lieutenant, himself, would have no such dream. His destiny would be without doubt his father's business.

On the third day, Emrys was in a melancholy mood. He knew that the cyclists were to be relieved that very evening. They would be going back to Essars to clean up and rest. No more mud or rats for a few days. Lucky them. He was not so lucky. He had just been told that he and Lieutenant Mond were staying for another boring week. German speakers must be in demand.

As he bent down to enter the tunnel and follow Lieutenant Mond down into the low passage he silently cursed David. What was the good of advice if there was no possibility of following it?

As usual, some muddy engineers were working on the tunnel constantly shoring up the roof. Their glum looks turned to smiles. They were delighted that the cyclists had arrived. It meant that they could make their way back to the fresh air.

The first job for Emrys was to recharge the battery using the dynamo. As he sat down Lieutenant Mond switched on the amplifier and began to listen to the crackly sounds.

Things were different. There was an immediate flurry of German messages. Emrys could see the anxious frown on the lieutenant's face. A wave of relief swept over him when he was ordered to make his way back and find Captain Davies. Anxiety and claustrophobia were a toxic mix. He was in desperate need of fresh air. He only managed to breathe two deep breaths, however, before being plunged back into the darkness followed by Captain Davies. Davies enquired.

'Henry, what have you got for me?'

Emrys noticed how concerned Lieutenant Mond sounded when he replied. Yes. David had been right.

'We are not sure. They're definitely up to something though. Could be they're just changing battalions. It's certainly not like yesterday. Listen to this. Reserve platoon to arrive at eleven and take cover in dugouts. Can't believe they are going to raid on a clear day like this. I tell you though, Percy, they're up to something.'

Captain Davies thought for a second.

'Thank you, Henry. I think this is too much for us. I'll ask for support from the infantry. Keep me informed.'

Emrys and Lieutenant Mond sat tensely for the next few hours. Messages quietened down for a while making Emrys feel gratefully redundant once more. He was relieved to see the lieutenant calming down. A false alarm no doubt. There was a sudden further flurry. Lieutenant Mond began to sweat nervously. At that moment, Sergeant Marshall appeared out of the darkness.

'Lieutenant Mond, sir. This lad has been down here long enough, sir. He needs a rest. He needs some fresh air. With respect, sir.'

Lieutenant Mond squinted at his Hunter watch. To Emrys's surprise, he agreed immediately.

'Quite right, sergeant. Right, Boxer. Charge up the battery for me and get out. I want you back in thirty minutes prompt.'

Sergeant Marshall hadn't finished.

'With respect, sir. You need a rest too.'

Lieutenant Mond responded firmly.

'Thank you, sergeant. When I need your advice I will ask for it.'

Emrys accompanied Sergeant Marshall back up the passage towards the welcome sunlight visible at the far end. Despite the return of claustrophobia, he felt strangely guilty for leaving the lieutenant on his own.

Suddenly, a series of small explosions rocked the tunnel. The two cyclists stood still and looked at each other. What could be happening? A huge roar shook the whole tunnel so violently that it would surely collapse on top of them. All the lights had blown out and they were pitched into darkness. Emrys felt something heavy strike his arm.

He was just relieved to be still alive. These tunnels were perhaps not so safe after all. The two of them choked and coughed in the thick smoke. Emrys knew that Sergeant Marshall was the very best person to be stuck down here with. He might have a foul temper but he always seemed to know what to do. He was relieved by a few seconds of light as the sergeant struck a match. The match quickly extinguished itself in the putrid air. They were plunged back into darkness. Emrys heard the sergeant say as Emrys himself was scrambling towards the distant light.

'I think the tunnel has collapsed. We have to see if we can dig the lieutenant out.'

Sergeant Marshall must have somehow got a lamp relit because he now angrily bellowed after Emrys, who was racing down the passage.

'Come back. That's bloody cowardice. You'll be on a charge. You could be bloody shot for that.'

Actually, Emrys thought that he had had considerable presence of mind. He turned around clutching the spade that he had happened to notice earlier propped up against the tunnel wall. It must have been left by some careless engineer. He looked up at the sergeant who had blood trickling down the side of his head.

'Thought this might come in useful, Sarg. Do you know you're wounded?'

Marshall wiped the blood away with his sleeve before pointing to Emrys's arm.

'Do you know you're wounded, too? Come on. We need to find the lieutenant.'

Emrys barely had time to look down at his arm, which dripped blood through his tunic. If the lieutenant was entombed in mud, they only had a few minutes to release him before he suffocated. It also sounded as if there was a lot of activity above ground. Mortar shells could be heard bursting. They knew that it was only a matter of time before the heavier stuff opened up. That might be a problem.

They made their way on all fours down the partially collapsed tunnel. It turned out to be far easier than Sergeant Marshall had anticipated. They hadn't needed to use the shovel at all when they arrived at a place that Emrys immediately recognised.

It was about ten yards from the gallery where the lieutenant had been working. They were met by a wall of mud. The tunnel had completely collapsed. It was a hopeless cause. Lieutenant Mond must have been crushed to death. Above them was a tangle of twisted metal and splintered wood. The roof was in a precarious state. A large vibration from a nearby mortar shell might bring the whole thing down on them. The two men looked at each other. They needed to get out. It was only then that they looked down.

On the floor of the tunnel partially covered by a collapsed beam and with his foot caught under the wall of mud, lay Lieutenant Mond. He was unconscious and bleeding profusely from his face and chest. He was however very much alive. He must have been making his way back along the passage when the large explosion had occurred. Whether he had taken notice of Sergeant Marshall's advice or had been made wary by the preceding small explosions, they could not tell.

Emrys set to work with his spade to free the trapped foot. Out of the corner of his eye, he could see Sergeant Marshall applying a field dressing to the lieutenant's face. Emrys was worried. If he wasn't careful, he might bring the whole, bloody lot down on them.

It proved easy to release the foot. They had been lucky. The heavy beam had not actually fallen on the lieutenant. That would have been a problem. Emrys heard a muffled moan. Lieutenant Mond was definitely alive. Now, all they needed to do was get him out. They dragged him clear of the beam by the arms and collapsed on the floor. There was a remarkable lack of rats. They had obviously come to the reasonable conclusion, that this was a risky place to be. Looking around Emrys agreed with them.

'Come on, Emrys.' Emrys was surprised to hear the sergeant using his Christian name. 'Let's get him out of here. Help will be coming soon.'

They grabbed the lifeless body by the shoulders again and began to pull it down the passage. They had to avoid the frequent, vicious obstacles, but that proved to be impossibly difficult. The passageway was barely waist high. Lieutenant Mond seemed, in the mean time, to have regained consciousness. He was staring, eyes fixed into the distance, a dead weight unable to help them.

Emrys felt exhausted, as he flopped to the floor again. His arm had begun to throb. He knew that he couldn't continue. Even for Lieutenant Mond. Sergeant Marshall quietly took control.

'Right. I'll stay and look after the lieutenant. You go and see if help is coming. Take the lamp with you. And be quick.'

Emrys needed no second bidding. His da had talked about roof collapses in the mine and said that one was always followed by a second. The sooner he was out of that passage the better. He crawled his way toward the entrance. He could see a faint movement in the distance. Crawling towards him was the help that Sergeant Marshall had promised. The help came in the form of Lieutenant Parry. Emrys shouted.

'We need help. Lieutenant Mond and Sergeant Marshall are back there, wounded. We can't wake the lieutenant up. He's just staring. We need help.'

Lieutenant Parry was remarkably calm.

'Calm down, soldier. We're here now. Off you get to the trench. Report the situation to Captain Davies and make sure we have some stretcher bearers by the entrance. Now off you go.'

Emrys emerged from the narrow entrance into the daylight. Captain Davies was peering down, looking anxiously. At least he was acting anxiously. You could not see his face as it was covered by a gas mask. Everyone seemed to be wearing gas masks. Emrys had left his own somewhere down that black hole. Captain Davies shouted excitedly.

'Stretcher-bearers. Here. Now.'

He then had time to glance down at Emrys and kindly whispered.

'Well done, soldier. Now get to the rear and get that arm seen to.'

When he eventually had time to think about it, Emrys was surprised by his own calm reply. After all, he had just emerged from a hell hole, had blood on his arm and he'd lost his precious gas mask. Any sane person would have taken up the captain's order in a heartbeat.

'I need to attend to Lieutenant Mond when he comes out, sir.'

Captain Davies didn't reply. He had more important things on his mind.

Emrys sat down in the mud with his back to the trench wall, close to the entrance to the tunnel. At least he still had his rifle strapped to his back. Losing his weapon would have been an even more serious offence. On top of his gas mask. Despite all the panic and confusion around him, he closed his eyes. He was going to stay until Lieutenant Mond was brought out. He owed him that much. He didn't need to wait long. Sergeant

Marshall was first out and even smiled at Emrys.

'You still here? I thought you would be long gone.'

Emrys, taken aback by the sergeant's easygoing nature, answered frivolously.

'Thought I would wait for you, Sarg. We can have a quiet stroll together, back to the dressing station.'

Sergeant Marshall laughed.

'No stroll for me. That was a mine down there. There must be a bloody great crater out there. Gerry might be along soon. Off you go and put your bloody mask on.'

At that moment, Lieutenant Parry and Corporal Jones appeared through the dark entrance dragging a muddy, blood-spattered figure. A bloody field dressing was firmly pressed against Lieutenant Mond's jaw. Mond was still staring upwards, the dark roof of the tunnel replaced by the cloudy sky. He muttered incoherently, strangely oblivious to his injured face. Emrys bent down until his ear was just a few inches from the Lieutenant's twisted lips. He thought he might be able to make out the words through the blood and anguish.

'Boxer. Boxer. Boxer.'

Captain Davies put his hand on his friend's shoulder as he was carried away by two grim stretcher-bearers. He turned once more to Emrys and pointed to his arm.

'You go with them. You could do with a bit of care too. Looks like you might have booked some leave yourself. And put on your gas mask.'

Emrys, quickly, trotted after the stretcher, which was already heading in the direction of Windy Corner and, then, on to the regimental first aid centre. He just hoped that none of the other officers would notice his lost gas mask.

Emrys sat down, on the ground, next to Lieutenant Mond's stretcher at the first aid centre. It had begun to rain lightly. Even the raindrops didn't seem to make the lieutenant blink. He continued to just stare open-eyed at the sky.

It seemed a long time since the stretcher-bearers had carefully deposited their load in front of the medical tent. He hadn't had the heart to turn down the cigarettes they had given him. He said that he was saving them for later.

Now, even he could see that Lieutenant Mond was getting worse. He was frighteningly pale and had begun shivering violently ten minutes previously. He continued to mutter quietly.

At last, the help that they desperately needed finally arrived. A short bespectacled man stood over them. He was wearing a long white coat, the front smeared with blood. Underneath was the uniform of a captain. Next to him stood a tall corporal with a notebook and a stub of a pencil in his hand. The captain only looked down at Lieutenant Mond briefly. He appeared to be too busy to even touch him. He turned to the corporal.

'Head injury. Chest injury. In shock. Semi-unconscious. No hope I'm afraid. Try and get a dose of morphine into him, a blanket if we have any left and some shelter from this bloody rain. We'll be burying the poor sod by morning.'

The doctor turned and walked quickly toward the next wounded soldier. Emrys stood up in shock. They were leaving Lieutenant Mond to die. It couldn't be true. Surely, they couldn't. He rushed past the corporal and tugged on the captain's sleeve. The captain swivelled round in anger, opening his mouth to shout at the mutinous upstart. Emrys got there first.

'Please, captain, sir. I'm so sorry, but please have another look at my lieutenant. I'm sure you doctors can save him. Please look at him.'

Emrys was glad to see the angry look leave the captain's face as quickly as it had arrived. This man must have some compassion.

'Look, Sonny. Your lieutenant is dying. All I can do is give him as comfortable death as I can in this bloody place. I'm truly sorry.'

Emrys was persistent.

'With respect, captain. If you knew who he is you might look again.'

The captain was beginning to lose his temper again.

'I don't care if he's Jesus Christ just cut down from the cross. He's almost dead and there's nothing you or I can do about it.'

Then he must have thought again. Who, in fact, was this young lieutenant guarded by an even younger private? He looked quizzically at the filthy, blood-spattered individual giving Emrys just enough time to speak.

'This is Henry Mond. His father is Sir Alfred Mond. He's something in the Government.'

The captain was considering the situation carefully. On the one hand, the lieutenant looked on his last legs. On the other hand, Sir Alfred was known everywhere. If the captain made a mistake here his whole career might go up in smoke. Emrys, sensing that the captain's resolve might momentarily be wavering, pleaded.

'Please, captain sir. Please take a quick look at him. Then we all, including Sir Alfred, can say that everything was done.'

Shrugging his shoulders the captain bent down to examine

Henry Mond, while Emrys exhaled gratefully. The captain looked up at his assistant.

'Right. I've been persuaded. Get him inside and warmed up. We've no intravenous fluids so we'll have to see if he can take fluids orally.' Turning to Emrys, he continued. 'That's where you come in, boy. Keep your officer warm and see if you can get some drink into him. Carefully, mind. The corporal, here, will try and find an ambulance. If we don't get him to Bethune quickly we'll have wasted our time.'

Emrys sat patiently for the ambulance, despite his throbbing arm which nobody seemed interested in. Lieutenant Mond lay next to him still staring at the roof of the tent and jabbering away.

'Boxer. Boxer. Boxer.'

He hadn't got any tea into his charge without him choking. He daren't try again. Maybe Lieutenant Mond would be helped by a cigarette. It might even calm him down. Emrys took one of the cigarettes out of his tunic. He lit it and carefully placed it between Lieutenant Mond's lips. It was a mistake. A sudden deep breath led to a paroxysm of violent coughing. Emrys quickly grabbed the cigarette hoping that no one had noticed.

What should he do with the cigarette? A deep drag, by himself, also induced a spasm of coughing. The second drag didn't. He did indeed feel something course through his veins. He somehow knew that this wouldn't be his last fag. He closed his eyes trying for a few seconds to forget about this hell hole of a tent full of blood, death and screaming.

A moment later his prayer was answered. He was, soon, trotting alongside the stretcher toward a van. It was the ambulance that seemed to have appeared from nowhere. Emrys studied it carefully. It certainly wasn't one of the broken-down excuse for a medical vehicle that he had seen bouncing along the road twenty minutes previously. Despite the mud, the radiator seemed to gleam brightly and the cross on the side was a vivid red. It was almost as if an especially comfortable mode of transport had been conjured up for this illustrious patient.

'Wouldn't be surprised, knowing Sir Alfred.' muttered Emrys to himself, only half in jest.

He left his charge momentarily and wandered over to the bored driver, leaning against the wheel arch waiting for his admirable vehicle to be loaded. The driver was probably keen just to get his vehicle away from this bloody place before it was scratched. Emrys spoke needing, just for a moment, to talk about something other than the war.

'This is nice.'

The driver laughed.

'It ought to be. It's a bloody Rolls Royce. You'll never get another chance to ride in one.'

Emrys was elated. Despite Captain Davies's comment, he had expected his arm to be bandaged and then be pointed straight back in the direction of the front line.

'Do you mean that I'm coming too?'

'Didn't they tell you? Typical. I need someone in the back to look after the patients.' Snorted the driver. 'And you are that someone. I'd get back there if I were you. I'm not hanging around for you.'

Emrys dashed to the back, in time to see the last stretcher being loaded and jumped in just before the doors were slammed shut. As the light disappeared and they were left in the dark, claustrophobic box, he heard the driver receiving his instructions.

'Bethune. The College.'

This was the first time that Emrys had been in a dark, confined space since the hell of the tunnel. He felt his heart begin to flutter and nauseous panic return to his throat. From one of the four stretchers rammed into the confined space came a scream.

'Boxer. Boxer. Boxer.'

Lieutenant Mond was having a similar reaction to himself in the darkness. Emrys swallowed hard to fight back his over-whelming nausea and grabbed the lieutenant's hand. Holding an officer's hand. Who would have believed it? It seemed to work, however. The screams disappeared to be replaced by the continuous eerie whimper.

The ambulance might be a Rolls Royce but it didn't save the occupants from the potholes. Hitting a particularly deep one made the rear end fly into the air with a crash. The occupant of another stretcher shrieked and started to gurgle. A sudden jet of vomit hit Emrys. He shook the nauseating fluid off his hands. He was covered. He had, by necessity, let go of the lieutenant's hand. He grabbed it again as the screaming returned.

'Boxer. Boxer. Boxer.'

Ignoring the acrid smell of bile and blood covering him, Emrys clung tightly to the hand, closed his eyes and prayed for the first time in months.

The ambulance seemed to be going faster. It wasn't hitting potholes anymore. Perhaps they were on a proper road. That could mean that they were already in Bethune and would be stopping soon. Emrys could not wait to jump out of this coffin.

Suddenly, he ducked as something slammed against the side of the ambulance just above the lieutenant's head. Everyone screamed in terror. Everyone except the driver, who shouted.

'Fucking kids.'

The ambulance ground to a sudden stop and in a flash the door was open. Emrys was out. He wasn't staying there for a moment longer than he needed to. He stood stationary in surprise. To one side was a group of young boys, laughing loudly while kicking a heavy football. On the other, a group of nurses was rushing towards the ambulance. A sign over the door said College Saint-Vaast. The driver had also got out and was angrily making his way toward Emrys.

'Little buggers. They always do that. Kick their bloody football at the ambulance. Bloody ridiculous putting a Casualty Clearing Centre in a school.'

He looked at Emrys, for the first time.

'Christ, mate. What the hell has happened to you?'

Emrys looked down at his tunic. He was covered in blood and black tarry slime. He turned to look back into the ambulance. Blood was everywhere. On the doors, the floor and the four stretcher-bound patients. Lieutenant Mond must have died whilst Emrys was holding his hand. Then Emrys heard it. A tiny whisper.

'Boxer. Boxer. Boxer.'

He was alive. On the stretcher above was a deathly white motionless figure. Emrys hardly registered the driver speaking.

'Poor bugger. Bled to death during the journey. Now I'm left with this fucking mess to clear up.'

Emrys didn't reply. He was too shocked to reply. He watched Lieutenant Mond being carefully unloaded and began to walk alongside the stretcher toward the front door of College Saint-Vaast. A nurse, who despite her blood-stained tunic seemed to Emrys to be ridiculously young and attractive with vivid blue eyes, barred his way.

'Where are you going, soldier? I hope all that blood is not yours.'

By some miracle, Emrys had already recovered his frayed wits. He knew that his best chance of getting home was by staying close to Lieutenant Mond. He stretched out his injured arm with the torn sleeve towards the pretty girl.

'Sorry, Miss. I am looking after Lieutenant Mond. I have to stay with him. Captain Davies orders. I just have a scratch on my arm.'

The nurse smiled back at him.

'We're looking after your lieutenant now. Whatever Captain Davies said. And you need to be cleaned up. Cleaned up so that I can take a good look at that arm. It's me and the doctor who decides whether it's a scratch. My name is Nurse Allsop but, when we're alone, you can call me Beatrice.'

She gently led him into a small side room, with two large sinks against one wall. White tiles covered the wall above them. Beatrice Allsop continued more professionally.

'Get all your clothes off and get washed. Quickly, now. This washroom is meant for the school and we're not supposed to use it. So, no dawdling. And get that arm cleaned up.'

She threw a plain blue set of overalls at him.

'Put these on. They're the best I can do I'm afraid until I can get that lot clean. Sit on the chair outside. Here are a couple of cigarettes. Have a smoke while you wait for me. I'll take a look at that arm and see what we can do.'

Emrys was in no position to argue, but there was one thing he still wanted to know.

'Lieutenant Mond. Is he going to be all right?'

Beatrice Allsop smiled.

'I promise I'll find out. When I come back to see to that arm, I'll let you know. Now. Chop chop. Get clean.

And then she was gone leaving Emrys alone in the draughty washroom.

He was sitting outside the College, smoking the fourth cigarette of the day. In fact, it was the fourth cigarette of his life. He understood instinctively the damage they had helped do to his da's chest. He also didn't dare think of his ma's reaction. But then she had never been in a Casualty Clearing Centre next to a pile of clothes covered in blood.

When he had removed his tunic, he had been inconsolable. His cut was so mild. Not much more than a scratch. Just a little bit worse and Captain Davies's promise of home leave would have come true. As it was he was sure that cleaned and bandaged, he would be on the way back to the cyclists and the front in the morning. He was just glad for the opportunity to sit peacefully watching the young boys playing football. He disappeared back into another world, where he and David were kicking a ball in the lane next to their house in Briton Ferry.

A soothing female voice caught him unawares.

'Are you called Boxer? The Lieutenant seems to want you. He keeps on screaming for you. The doctor thinks you might be able to calm him down. He needs to go for surgery straight away. So, the doctor needs him calm.'

Nurse Allsop was already walking back into the College

without waiting for a reply. Emrys stubbed out the half-smoked cigarette against the wall and chased after the figure disappearing down a long corridor. Even before the nurse could manage to open the door he could hear the screams.

'Boxer. Boxer. Boxer.'

Emrys barged his way into the large, crowded hall. In the good times, this must be a wonderful building. The walls were covered in dark, finely carved oak panels. Now it was filled to the brim with blood and despair. In the far corner, three figures were vainly trying to hold down a struggling figure.

'Boxer. Boxer. Boxer.'

Emrys rushed over and pushed an attendant out of the way. He grabbed a flailing hand and shouted.

'Lieutenant Mond. It's Boxer. I'm here. You're going to be all right.'

The lieutenant didn't look all right. Despite his screams, he looked deathly pale and had begun to shiver once more. Emrys looked pleadingly at the doctor who was finally able to let go of his patient. Emrys's welcome arrival had successfully reduced the screams back to a whisper. The doctor started speaking directly to Nurse Allsop, ignoring Emrys.

'Nurse. This man will need some blood before we can operate on him. He won't survive without it. Have we anyone who might give some?'

The nurse had a sign of resignation in her voice.

'No, doctor. We have nobody left. Most of the patients need their blood as much as he does. There's nobody.'

What trouble was Lieutenant Mond going to get Emrys into now? He spoke up loudly, interrupting the doctor as he began to speak.

'There's me. He's welcome to a bit of my blood if it will do him some good. Not too much mind you.'

The doctor looked at him for the first time. The cut on his arm was still undressed and smeared with blood.

'Young man. You have been wounded, yourself. You will be needing that blood.'

Emrys looked over at Beatrice Allsop.

'Nurse said it's only a scratch. Can't have bled much.'

The doctor shrugged his shoulders and looked earnestly at Emrys.

'Look, private. You have to realise that it is an experimental procedure not normally done in British Hospitals. I'm, as you may or may not have guessed, Canadian. The thing is that there is a risk of your blood not suiting Lieutenant Mond. It could even kill him. It's just that without it he will certainly die. Still up for it?'

Emrys nodded his head solemnly. Yes. David was right, again. Lieutenant Mond was definitely trouble. Nurse Allsop patted him on his uninjured arm and then began to roll up the sleeve.

'We are going to put a needle in your arm and a tube will take the blood over to the lieutenant. Just keep him calm if you can. He seems to listen to you.'

He winced as the needle entered the front of his elbow, but was fascinated as he watched his blood pouring into a large jar. He suddenly felt nauseous again and began to sweat. He certainly didn't want to make a scene in front of this young girl. In fact, he realized that if she hadn't been around he might not have volunteered, in the first place. Just before he looked away he saw the doctor using a tube with a syringe to pump his blood from the jar into Lieutenant Mond's arm. His blood. Fixing his sight firmly on a large crack in the ceiling plaster, he began to talk.

'You're all right, Lieutenant Mond. You'll feel better soon. You're going to go home to your mam and da. Sorry, I mean Sir Alfred. Don't know what your mam's called.'

Nurse Allsop interrupted him to his delight, using his Christian name.

'Are you all right, Emrys? You look horribly pale. Maybe just a few minutes more and then we'll stop.'

He was determined not to faint in front of the girl. He stopped talking as overpowering nausea overtook him, once more. His vision was going in and out of focus. Then nothing. The last thing he heard was Nurse Allsop's shout.

'He's going. He's going to faint. Lie him down straight away.'

He was unsure how long he was out for. When the needle had been put into his arm it had still been light. When he opened his eyes only darkness came through the window. He was on a bed still in the large hall with wooden panels. He no longer seemed to be attached to any tubes, which was a small blessing.

He began to focus on the figure in white at the end of his bed. Perhaps it was an angel. No. He was very much alive and looking at the nurse. The nurse with nice eyes. What was her name? Nurse Allsop. Yes. Beatrice Allsop. She was laughing at him.

'What sort of soldier do you call yourself? Fainted at the first sight of blood.'

Emrys laughed.

'Only at my blood. I'm fine with other people's blood. What time is it?'

Beatrice Allsop spoke more sympathetically this time.

'Middle of the night. You must have been exhausted. Stress and everything. Straight after coming round from the faint, you fell into a deep sleep. We didn't want to wake you. Now, here's a cigarette and I'll go and make you a nice cup of tea.'

The nurse stood to go, but Emrys stopped her.

'Miss. Lieutenant Mond. Is he alive? I mean did he get enough blood? I just felt so unwell. I wish I could have given more.'

Emrys closed his eyes because the nurse looked so serious.

'Now look here. Firstly, I told you to call me Beatrice. Secondly, you did well. Better than most, I can tell you. We were about to stop the transfusion anyway, so your fainting didn't make a scrap of difference. Just caused a bit of a stir. As for Lieutenant Mond, if I'm honest he looks better than you. He's had his operation and they stopped the bleeding. Still not speaking though. Now, you need that tea. And something to eat, if I can find anything at this time of night.'

Emrys took another drag on his cigarette, coughed and, then, spoke again.

'Thank you, Beatrice. I just feel so tired. I suppose I will be going back to the cyclists tomorrow, though.'

Beatrice Allsop turned and smiled.

'I had forgotten. You don't know. You're not having a lie-in, tomorrow, but you're not going back to the front either. You're going to Boulogne. Lieutenant Mond has broken his jaw, so he's going to the specialist ward in the Hospital there. That's where all the face cases go. Given who his father is. That's caused a bit of a fuss I can tell you. Given who his father is, the doctor has ordered you to go on the Red Cross train with him. To look after him and things. You never know, you might have to go all the way home with him. Now rest while I make that tea. After that, I'll clean that wound, for you.'

Emrys gave his cheekiest grin.

'I'll look forward to it.'

Beatrice Allsop grinned back.

'I really don't think you will.'

6

Harriet jumped when she heard the shriek of excitement from her daughter at the front door. She had become increasingly nervous lately.

'Mam. Mam. There's a letter from Emrys.'

As she tore open the envelope, Harriet was nearly as excited as Evelyn. Even Josiah looked up from his chair. David's letters were always so precise telling them in detail about his work. Her younger son, however, never seemed to write about the war. They were full of all the antics which he got up to with his friends. The letters were both fun and funny.

She unfolded the plain brown paper that Emrys always used as writing paper. Her heart missed a beat and the blood drained from her face. She hadn't even gotten past the address.

Facial Ward. 13th Stationary Hospital, Boulogne.

God. No. He had terrible injuries to his face. Harriet closed her eyes in prayer before reading on with increasing panic.

Dear Mam.

I am in a hospital in a place called Boulogne. You do not need to worry. I'm not injured. I am just here looking after Lieutenant Mond, who is bad I think.

Harriet put down the letter for a moment, in relief. Her

prayer had been answered. She whispered with a trembling voice before reading on.

'He's fine. Nothing to worry about.'

I am just here looking after Lieutenant Mond, who is bad, I think. We come into the docks in Boulogne on the hospital train. It stopped so close to the ships that I thought we were coming home. But we got put into an ambulance which was more like a horse and cart. So. No. I'm not coming home. The ambulance took us up the cliff to the hospital.

Along the road are the biggest houses you have ever seen. Even bigger than Bay View. But you know what. Nobody lives in them. They are all boarded up because of the war. What a waste. The seaside is lovely. Blue water. Not like the mud we got in the Ferry. The sun is shining. No wonder the rich French come here for a holiday.

The hospital is not such a great place. It is in a whole load of wooden warehouses. We are all right now, but they must be cold in the winter. Lieutenant Mond is in a little room at the end of the building on his own. The main ward is a terrible place. Men with terrible injuries to their faces covered in bandages. The suffering is pitiful.

Mam. You said in your last letter that Evelyn is thinking of coming over here as a nurse. Mam. Don't let her. The things she will see are really awful. Our family has given enough already to this war. She is doing enough by working at Taylors. And knitting me socks, of course.

Sorry, it hasn't been a happy letter. The next one when I get back to Gwyn and the boys will be much happier. Love to everyone, especially Da and Evelyn. Love Emrys.

Harriet handed the letter to Josiah. Poor Emrys. He had had to grow up so quickly.

Emrys was pleased that he had finished writing the letter. He hadn't gotten around to writing, for a few weeks and would post it later. He was sitting on the floor of Lieutenant Mond's room with his back to the wooden wall. The Lieutenant was in a deep undisturbed sleep for the first time. He seemed to be a bit better. He had, even, drunk a little tepid soup patiently fed to him by Emrys using an old wooden spoon. Maybe Emrys might just be able to take a little nap himself whilst his charge slept.

He hadn't slept for long when the narrow door crashed open. He opened his eyes in disbelief. The figure in front of him, staring down at Lieutenant Mond, was a character straight out of the pantomime which Emrys had seen as a child. He might be wearing a lieutenant's uniform, but he was immensely fat. He sported a highly polished Sam Brown holster complete with revolver despite being twenty miles away from any fighting. It was his face, however, which drew most of Emrys's attention. It was a bright florid red. The pantomime figure bellowed at Lieutenant Mond.

'Lieutenant Mond. Delighted to make your acquaintance. Charles Valadier at your service.'

Lieutenant Mond bellowed back.

'Boxer. Boxer. Boxer.'

Emrys rushed over. This wasn't going well. He grabbed Lieutenant Mond's hand once more.

'It's all right, sir. Calm down. This nice gentleman is going to help you.'

He turned to the man who called himself Charles Valadier.

'He doesn't like noise. With respect, Lieutenant. He's much better but you still have to talk to him quietly.'

Lieutenant Charles Valadier put his huge hand on Emrys's shoulder and whispered 'Thank you.'

Emrys hadn't been able to watch Lieutenant Mond's wounds being uncovered. It was too much for him. He hadn't even wanted to walk through that terrible ward full of despair and mutilation. He had to stride through quickly not daring to look to either side. He, finally, rushed through the front door and fumbled to extract a cigarette from its packet. He couldn't manage it. His hands were shaking too much. He had had enough. He couldn't go on any further. He looked up in despair.

In front of the terrible ward stood the most beautiful car that he had ever seen. He had on many occasions admired M.G. Roberts's car back home. This, however, was totally different. It was from another world. Perfect cream paint gleamed in the evening sunlight. The canvas roof was down, leaving the red leather front seat covers exposed to the sun. In the driver's seat slept the bored chauffeur gratefully accepting this opportunity to rest in the sun.

The back of the car was the most surprising. There was a single seat of green leather. Next to it stood something that looked suspiciously like the foot-powered dentist's drill that he'd seen in Swansea.

He jumped when a voice behind him said.

'Nice isn't it, soldier? It's a Rolls Royce Silver Ghost. Goes like a bomb.'

Emrys turned to see Lieutenant Valadier standing watching him studiously. The lieutenant continued.

'You did very well with Lieutenant Mond, soldier. It can't have been easy so you ought to be commended. I only hope that the Mond family will recognise it. Although I have my doubts.'

Emrys had never been talked to by an officer in such an offhand manner. This man was no ordinary officer, however. Still mesmerized by the lieutenant's bright red face and equally gleaming car, Emrys stuttered.

'Lieutenant Mond, doctor. Is he going to be all right? I mean he was so terrible at the aid centre. I thought he was going to die.'

Charles Valadier laughed.

'His face will be fine. It's not half as bad as most of those poor souls in there. We'll be operating on him this afternoon. Whether his brain will recover is another matter. He's pretty shocked, that's for sure. He seems to trust you, though. Why does he call you Boxer by the way?'

Emrys laughed back. His shaking hand had disappeared and he was, at last, able to light the cigarette that he had been so desperate for. He replied.

'It's a long story involving Billy Wells, the boxing champion. Nobody else calls me Boxer except Lieutenant Mond. Lieutenant? Why have you got a dentist's drill in the back of your nice car?'

Lieutenant Valadier smiled when he spoke. He had a strange accent, French, but not French.

'Well, soldier, when you called me doctor you were wrong. I'm no doctor that's for sure. I'm a dentist. When I'm not here helping to put faces and lives back together, I'm off to some rich man's manor house looking at teeth. Got all my own equipment in the back of the car. If you want a free consultation be my guest. Least I can do after all you've been through.'

Emrys couldn't believe it a few seconds later when he was sitting in the back of a Rolls Royce having his loose denture examined.

The following night, Emrys had slept remarkably well considering he was laying on an uncovered stone floor next to Lieutenant Mond's bed. His charge had slept well after his operation too. Indeed he was still sound asleep when Emrys awoke the next morning stiff from the cold.

Here was the opportunity to get out of this bloody ward, even if it was only for a few minutes. He was glad he had. The sun had just risen and he breathed the beautiful salty sea air deep into his lungs. It was going to be a lovely day, even if he wasn't going to be able to appreciate it stuck indoors looking after the lieutenant. A trip to the latrine and a quick wash down, the first he'd had since Bethune. He would be ready for anything.

He felt much better when he returned. Well enough to walk normally through the ward without rushing to get past the suffering. As he opened the front door the stench of rotting flesh hit him. By now, however, he was used to it. Today was going to be a good day.

Then he heard it. An excited scream was followed by the shriek of 'Boxer. Boxer. Boxer.' Emrys rushed down the narrow gap between the beds in the main ward. What on earth was happening to poor Lieutenant Mond? He shouldn't have left him for so long.

As he entered the room, a lady in a dark mauve coat with

fur trim around the neck turned and glared at him.

'And who do you think you are barging into an officer's room?'

The lady, standing on one side of the bed, peered down at the lieutenant. Next to her was a much younger lady, who was much more conservatively dressed in a brown coat and hat. Emrys had seen the young lady somewhere before but just couldn't place where. The nurse standing on the other side of the bed pleaded with them.

'Lady Mildred. Please. Can I ask both of you to come outside? You are distressing your son. Please.'

Emrys realised, at last, who these well-dressed people were. The older lady had to be Lady Mildred Mond, Lieutenant Mond's mother. The younger lady was none other than the lady with the long nose and green dress, who had mocked him in the recruiting hall. That seemed a lifetime ago. The nurse was getting even more persistent.

'Lady Mildred. I must insist. Leave the room immediately. I have summoned Lieutenant Valadier. He will be here to talk to you, shortly.'

The young lady talked in a much calmer fashion than her mother. The pomposity which Emrys remembered so well had disappeared. Like all of them, she had simply grown up.

'Nurse, we appreciate all that has been done for Henry. Mother is just worried about her son. We will wait over there for the doctor. But, nurse, we will be taking my brother home tonight. There will be no argument.'

She looked over at Emrys.

'You, young man, must be Boxer. He has been calling for you. We would appreciate it if you could see to my brother.'

She took her mother by the arm and led her to a chair in the far corner of the room. Emrys replaced them next to Lieutenant Mond and began to rearrange his bedclothes. The Lieutenant responded surprisingly calmly.

'Boxer. Boxer. Boxer.' And then. 'Eva. Eva. Eva.'

The young lady looked radiant. He had recognised her. Emrys felt a wave of unreasonable jealousy wash over him. He wasn't special anymore and that meant that he was less likely to get home. The door crashed open once more and Charles Valadier rushed in. His face was even redder than usual. He didn't look pleased.

'Charles Valadier at your service, Lady Mildred. I do wish that you had made contact before arriving. F ward is not a suitable place for ladies I fear. We will take you to another part of the hospital to discuss Henry's treatment. At present your son needs quiet after his operation. Please follow me. We can leave your son in the very capable hands of this young man. Your son knows him as Boxer.'

Emrys could sense that an argument was brewing. Lady Mildred didn't even deign to look at him before scowling at Valadier.

'I hope you, a mere lieutenant, are not telling me how I should look after my son.'

The young lady, Eva, intervened. She knew that with her mother in such a mood, things were unlikely to go well. Henry was after all still in the army and if this Lieutenant Valadier dug his heels in, there might be nothing that they could do.

'Lieutenant Valadier. First of all, we are most grateful for the care that my brother has received. I'm sure that he wouldn't have had better in Harley Street itself. But it is now time for us to take over, partly I have to say for Henry's psychological well-being. The Admiralty has been good enough to give us permission to travel over on a private steam yacht. We will be returning to England later tonight with Henry. It would be much easier with your cooperation.'

Lieutenant Valadier didn't look convinced when he replied.

'Madame, your brother needs constant nursing and perhaps further surgery. He has had two successful operations, one in Bethune and one here. He will have minimal scarring, but only if he gets the correct treatment. Treatment for both his physical and mental scars.'

Lady Mildred almost shouted at him making both Emrys and Lieutenant Mond jump.

'I can assure you that he will be going to the best place possible. The Queen Alexandra Hospital for Officers, in Highgate. Sir Alfred, my husband, is Chairman of Governors.'

Valadier looked as if he was trying his very best to maintain his fraying patience.

'With respect, Lady Mildred, Henry needs a specialist unit. If he has to leave here, I really do recommend my friend Gilles work in Aldershot. The unit there is first class.'

To avoid the angry altercation that seemed inevitable, the young lady intervened again.

'Lieutenant Valadier. As I have already said, we are most grateful to you for his treatment. It has, I'm sure, been exceptional. We do insist that he is looked after in a comfortable room in a private hospital. It would, undoubtedly, be the best thing for him. We know how pushed you are in the medical services. We would only seek to lessen that strain.'

Emrys could see that Valadier looked defeated. Valadier must know that Sir Alfred Mond was too powerful even for Army Regulations. He pointed at Emrys when he spoke in measured terms.

'This is the young man whom you need to thank. He has stuck to Henry through thick and thin for days and it would be in Henry's interest if he continues. If you insist on taking Henry from here, it is very much against my advice. I will not, despite my inclination, stand in your way. We will take Henry back to the dressing area shortly so that he is in optimal condition to travel. I must reiterate, again. It is against my advice.'

He lobbed a package over to Emrys, who juggled and then grasped it.

Valadier laughed.

'Don't drop it. It's your denture. I've had a bit filed down. Should be much more comfortable.'

Emrys sat down on the step outside the ward. Lady Mildred and her daughter had left and Lieutenant Mond carried off to have his wounds dressed. Emrys was just glad to have an hour to himself in the spring sun. He lit yet another cigarette. A few days ago he had been a non-smoker. He closed his eyes and relaxed for the first time in days. A large hand shook his shoulder. One of the orderlies from the ward was staring down at him.

'Hey, mate. Coming for a swim. The beach is gorgeous on a day like this.'

Despite living two hundred yards from a river and no more than two miles from a beach, Emrys had never learnt to swim. He'd never even been to the seaside. Whilst other boys of his age had risked the filthy water in the River Neath, he had never bothered. He supposed that he had never been encouraged to. In fact, his mam had always been so against it that he had never even tried. Here, however, was an opportunity. An opportunity that he might never have again. He had one problem.

'I've nothing to wear. These are all the clothes I've got.'

The orderly laughed.

'I'm sure we can find you something.'

The sea looked even more beautiful today than it had two days earlier. Despite the wind blowing down the channel, the sun was out and it was warm. Warm enough for Emrys's first swim. A large group of young men laughed loudly as they ran down the steps toward the wide promenade. This was a rare moment of escape from the horrors in the hospital. Another flight of stone steps took them down onto the golden sands. In the shade of the promenade, they all began to undress. All except one naive cyclist.

Then he understood why the orderly had laughed. The first man roared as he raced towards the sea, white buttocks gleaming in the evening sun. What the hell? Emrys wasn't going to drop out now. He quickly removed his dirty uniform and felt unusual freedom as he ran after the others. The wind was colder than he had expected as it blew on his naked skin. Not cold at all, however, compared to the first wave that hit him. He screamed.

'Fucking hell, boys. It's freezing.'

He dived head-first into the next wave as he had seen the others do. He got back on his feet, just in time to be hit by the next wave. The seawater stung his eyes and a strong taste of salt invaded his mouth. He spluttered with laughter. He must remember not to breathe in when underwater. He would have to keep moving. The water was, indeed, bloody freezing.

A few minutes later he trotted back out of the water. The rest had swum out away from the beach leaving him on his own. He was exhilarated but cold as he crossed the thin strip of sand to the point below the promenade, where he had left his pile of clothes.

Perhaps if he had not been screwing up his eyes, because of the salt water, he would have seen her earlier. Looking down on him from the promenade just a few feet above him was a woman, in a brown dress, holding her brown hat on her head in the wind. Emrys knew that there was only one person it could be. He silently cursed to himself as he turned his scrawny backside to her and began to pull his trousers on. He, finally, turned round still half dressed in just his trousers and vest. He looked up at the beaming young lady. His face had turned almost as red as Lieutenant Valadier's.

'I'm really sorry, Miss Mond. I didn't know you were there.'

The lady laughed.

'I've been seeing rather a lot of you today, Boxer. I rather enjoyed it actually. And it's Mrs. Isaacs, not Miss Mond. I'm married with a baby, so there's nothing I've seen today that I've not seen before. Now, quickly, before you catch your death of cold. Finish getting dressed and come up here.'

Five minutes later Emrys was standing on the promenade looking at the lady whom he now knew as Mrs Isaacs. His face was still red and she was still laughing. She, suddenly, became earnest as she began to speak.

'First of all, Boxer. My mother and I have to say how grateful we are that you have been with Henry since the accident. And looked after him so well.'

He could tell that she was about to say something not so pleasant. She hesitated before beginning again.

'The thing is, Boxer. We can't take you home with us tonight. I'm so sorry. I am sure that you had expectations, especially after what Lieutenant Valadier said. My mother feels it would not be beneficial for Henry in the long term. I have tried to persuade her but she is adamant. Apparently, my father was very definite about it. I am really sorry. You will be going back to the cyclists tomorrow.'

She shook his hand and turned to go back towards the hospital. Belatedly, Emrys began to speak.

'Mrs Isaacs. I hope you don't think I'm rude, but I want to say something about your brother. When he gets better, he will want to come back. Don't let him. Find him a nice job in London or something. He takes too many chances. If he comes back here he'll be killed for sure. And that would upset me.'

As Eva Isaacs looked at him, a tear ran down her cheek. She mouthed 'Thank you.' and turned back towards the hospital. She disappeared up the steps and out of his life, apparently forever.

When Emrys got down from the lorry, at Essars, everything had changed. The quiet little camp, that the cyclists had enjoyed previously, was now a bustling hive of activity. Soldiers and bicycles seemed to be going in all directions. He didn't even recognise most of them. Then one that he did know was walking quickly and purposely, toward him. What did Captain Davies want now? Emrys had hoped to slip in unnoticed. The captain welcomed him.

'Well. Well. Didn't expect to see you for a while. How is my friend, Lieutenant Mond?'

Of course, Emrys thought, he just wants to know how his friend was. The last time he had seen him, Lieutenant Mond was being carried off on a stretcher. Emrys replied.

'He's doing a bit better, I'm pleased to say. His mother and sister came over to France to collect him. Captain Davies, sir? Who are all these people?

Captain Davies had forgotten that the soldier, in front of him, had been away and wouldn't know what had gone on.

'Yes. You wouldn't know. All the cyclist companies have been amalgamated. You are now a proud member of C Company, the XI Corps Cyclist Battalion.'

A minute late, Ted and Gwyn were running over to question their friend about the previous few days. Emrys got the first question in, however.

'Where are Albert and Emelyn?'

Gwyn replied, quickly.

'Of course, you don't know. They've gone.'

Emrys's face dropped in horror.

'Gone. You mean they're dead.'

Gwyn laughed.

'No. You idiot. Joined the infantry. They said they were bored being a cyclist. They wanted more excitement.'

Emrys had had enough excitement to last him a lifetime. Bored would do him fine.

7

Mametz Wood The Somme, July 10 1916

David stood next to Captain Glynn-Jones waiting for dawn to break. Faint shards of light had appeared over the horizon, in the last few minutes. It wouldn't be long now. 6 o'clock. The moment for which they had trained so hard for the last year. The training that had started in Rhyl under the colonel all those months before. Everyone had said what a naturally gifted soldier David was. Naturally gifted enough to be a sergeant at the tender age of twenty. Well, now everyone was going to find out whether those complimentary predictions were going to ring true.

Despite it still being dark, they could see Mametz Wood in front of them easily. It was lit up magically by the continuous explosions. Missile after missile flew over their heads from the ridge behind them to add to the carnage. The noise was ear-splitting. God knows what it must be like for the gunners themselves. David needed to shout to be heard.

'Gerry's having a pasting, captain. Nobody could survive that.'

Captain Glynn-Jones answered in a surprisingly circumspect manner.

'Well let's hope so, sergeant. It's a long way across that bloody field. And there are woods on either side. If you please, sergeant, get over to our left to send Lieutenant Veneker my compliments. He may need some reassurance. I will need you back well before we advance.'

David walked quickly along the line towards the left. The boys were looking tense. Four months in the trenches had done nothing to prepare them for this. Occasionally a soldier would look up and acknowledge him. 'Sarg.' or one of the NCOs. 'Dai.'

He put his hand on the shoulder of a soldier who was weeping gently. God. He looked even younger than Emrys. No wonder he was terrified. He arrived at Lieutenant Veneker's platoon. The young officer had only joined them two weeks previously. Before that, he was probably still in boarding school. Now, he was in command of this bunch of gnarled men. No wonder he looked pale. He was visibly shaking as he stared forward not daring to look elsewhere.

David was worried that the young officer might piss himself. That wouldn't be good for morale. He lit a cigarette and handed it to the lieutenant. The lieutenant turned to look at David, who was shouting to be heard over the earthquake bombardment.

'Nothing to worry about, sir. Won't be a German left within two miles of us. Even if there were, we're in the third rank. It will be Major Mills and the front rank catching it not us.'

Lieutenant Veneker nodded his head and smiled a sickly smile. Neither of them was convinced that David's prophesy would turn out to be correct. David suddenly realised that this young man, who seemed so much more than two years younger than himself, was not worried about dying. He was just afraid of letting his men down. If he survived the day, he would change from a young boy to an excellent officer. David shook Lieutenant Veneker by the hand and, before turning to return to Captain Glynn-Jones, shouted.

'Good luck, Lieutenant Veneker. We'll have a good laugh about all this when we return to camp, tonight.'

As David got back to Captain Glynn-Jones's side, magically, the barrage ceased. Stopped except for one errant shot which fizzed overhead and slammed into the front of the wood. Then nothing. An eerie silence. Those soldiers who had been sitting slowly got to their feet. The captain waved his palm downwards as if to signal them to sit down again.

'Not yet, boys. There's still ten minutes to go.'

David remembered the detailed plan explained by Major Mills to the NCOs, the previous evening. A gap of five minutes without gunfire allowed Gerry to get out of his hiding place. Then, the barrage would restart and catch Gerry out in the open. David had wondered why they would need it if all the Germans had already been killed. He had thought it wise not to query it. To do so wouldn't have done his blossoming military career any good.

The silence was, suddenly, broken by an authoritative voice. It was Colonel Carden, commander of the next battalion, standing facing his men.

'Make your peace with God. You are going to take that position and some of you are not coming back. But we are going to take it.'

With that, the bombardment began again. Perhaps, David thought, Colonel Carden's injudicious words might not have had their desired effect on the men. In fact, he could palpably feel the drop in spirits. Formerly excited if also scared, their heads had dropped. They were now just terrified. He could see it in their faces. He wondered what his unflappable mam would do. He knew exactly. She would sing a hymn and he also knew which one. The ear-shattering explosions had become even louder, so he had no choice but to shout.

'Jesus, lover of my soul, let me to Thy bosom fly.'
While the nearer waters roll, while the tempest still is high.
Hide me o my saviour hide, till the storm of life is past
Safe into the haven guide. O receive my soul at last.'

By the end of the first verse, everyone had joined in. They were all singing to drown out the explosions and the sickening fear. Even Colonel Carden himself joined in, turning round to conduct with his walking stick.

'Other refuge I have none, hangs my helpless soul on Thee
Leave Oh leave me not alone, still support and comfort me
All my trust in Thee is stayed, all my help in thee I bring
Cover my defenceless head, with the shadow of Thy wing.'

David looked down at his watch. The watch that was his da's prize possession. Da had proudly given it to him when David had joined up. The watch read one minute to six. There would only be time for one more verse.

'Thou O Christ all I want. More in all in Thee I find
Raise the fallen, cheer the faint, heal the sick and lead the blind
Just and holy is Thy name. I am all unrighteousness.
Vile and full of sin I am. Thou art full of truth and grace.'

With impeccable timing, the bombardment stopped. For a few seconds, there was perfect silence. Then the shrill blast of Captain Glynn-Jones's whistle sounded in David's ear. The men struggled to their feet weighed down by their heavy packs, knowing that the moment had arrived. But the moment hadn't quite arrived. There would be a few seconds more before the front two ranks had moved forward.

Incredulously, David stared to his left. Colonel Carden was marching forward, waving his walking stick in the air with an orange and red handkerchief tied to it. David muttered not worrying if he was overheard.

'What the hell does he think he's doing? He might as well write shoot me on his chest.'

The inevitable volley of machine gun bullets began at that very moment. There certainly were still Germans in that bloody wood. A huge moan went up when the handkerchief dropped precipitously from view. The colonel was down. The moan was followed by an even bigger cheer as the handkerchief was lifted again. Despite his wound, Colonel Carden was back on his feet.

David's line, at last, began to shuffle forward. Their assault on Mametz Wood had begun.

David couldn't believe that he had made it to the wood in one piece. So many of his friends were lying dead in that bloody field. He was sitting on a shattered bough, surrounded by the scanty remnants of his platoon. All around was mayhem. Debris was everywhere. Shattered trees mixed up with ammunition boxes and a broken German machine gun.

An hour ago he had been certain that the attack was going to be a crass failure. A few of them had managed to get to the disused railway track, a hundred yards from the front of the wood, but no further. They had been pinned down there by the deadly machine gun fire. So much for all the Germans being dead. Captain Glynn-Jones had been the only senior officer left alive and he had just sent a runner to request another bombardment of the wood. The chances of the runner joining the piles of bodies in the field had seemed high.

Then a miracle happened. A large white flag had been waved from the front of the wood. For some incomprehensible reason, the Germans had decided to give up. A minute later, hundreds of Germans with bloody uniforms and bandaged heads were filing toward them. David had felt guilty about being jealous. Their war was over.

Now David's company was in possession of the front of the wood. Maybe they were behind time but against all odds, they had made it. Captain Glynn-Jones wandered towards him followed by Lieutenant Veneker. Emrys looked over at the lieutenant and smiled.

'You look better than you did if I may say so, sir. It must have been that stew we had last night. I shall take it up with the catering unit when I get back.'

Lieutenant Veneker grinned back at him. David thought that today might be the making of this very young man. His thoughts were cut short by the captain.

'Looks like it's the three of us. No more officers and precious few NCOs. Major Mills is dead, I'm afraid, and it doesn't look good for Major Gwyther.'

Lieutenant Veneker added.

'Colonel Carden didn't make it either.'

Why wasn't David surprised? Waving that bloody walking

stick, as if he was going for a stroll in the park. Now, when they really needed him he was dead. The captain began again.

'Sergeant, you take your people to the right. Stop when you get to the drove road. That's the border of our section. Veneker, you go the other way until you meet the 16th. And dig in, both of you. Soon as you can. Gerry won't take this lying down. There's bound to be a counterattack sooner or later.'

He waited for the other two men to comment but both were quiet. The captain continued.

'Right. Well done, chaps. Off you go. And, chaps, look after yourselves.'

David's men moaned when he told them that they were on the move again. After all, they had reached the target. Surely they deserved a rest. Instead, David made them struggle through sharp brambles and even sharper barbed wire. Not too far, however. In a few minutes, they arrived at the drove road.

They moaned again when David ordered them to get their shovels out. They were digging in. David, not being one to stand around supervising, began digging himself. He immediately hit a tree root. Digging in here was going to be difficult. He looked up and listened. The ominous sound of an incoming shot. Immediately, a shell exploded fifty yards away. David shouted at his men.

'Quick. Take cover. It's a bloody trap. They tempted us in here and now the bastards are going to try and blow us to bits.'

David lay down next to a large green bush with his arms shielding his head, as explosion after explosion crashed into the trees. He looked up sweating with fear. That's odd though. The fire was coming from the wrong direction. It was coming from the ridge from which they had started, only that morning.

Then he realised. The captain had sent a runner from the railway track asking for a bombardment. The runner, against the odds, must have got through. This was the artillery that they, themselves, had requested. It was just an hour too late. Then, as quickly as it had started the crashing explosions stopped. The bombardment had finished.

David slowly got to his feet and looked around. Astonishingly none of his men were dead. In fact, none of them was even wounded save perhaps for a few scratches from the brambles. All of them, however, just stared around, petrified by shock. Even David couldn't seem to pull his senses together after all the deafening percussions so close to him.

Something, suddenly, was enough to wake him from his trance. It couldn't be a noise as he still couldn't hear. It must be a movement. Too late he saw the phalanx of Germans, faces wreathed in contorted snarls, running towards them. They must be taking advantage of the bombardment and were already just ten yards away. David screamed at his men, oblivious to the fact that they still couldn't hear him. Then he grabbed for his rifle. But where was it? He must have dropped it at the first sign of an explosion.

Unarmed, David turned back towards the onslaught. He was hit in the chest by a flying figure. He found himself lying on his back straddled by a heavy German in a shabby grey uniform. He looked up at the contorted face of his enemy, as he felt the barrel of a revolver being thrust into his belly. Then the most massive punch in the guts rocked him backwards. It was the revolver discharging.

Despite or perhaps because of the shock, David realised that his bayonet was gripped in his hand. The same bayonet which he had carefully sharpened the evening before. As his life inexorably drained away he drew it, slowly, across his attacker's throat. The young German opened his eyes in startled terror and surprise. Gurgling, he desperately tried to pull the gash in his neck together. Finally, the German collapsed on top of his killer. As he drifted into unconsciousness, David said a silent sorry to his mam. His final thought before dying was 'Will I go to Hell for murdering this young man?'

Despite her guilty thoughts about grieving German mothers, Harriet was happy working at Taylors. It took her mind off worrying about her two boys. With Evelyn working there as well and with only three at home, they had never had so much money. That was despite the men at Taylors making more for the same work as the women.

Josiah wasn't working, of course. His chest had finally given up and he spent much of the day just sitting in the corner, smoking cigarettes. It was hard to remember what she had ever seen in him. Then she remembered what a dashing figure he cut as a well-healed miner, flashing his money. Then of course they had their accident. It wasn't really correct to call it an accident because that accident was now called David. The quick marriage to someone her da hadn't approved of had followed. To be fair to Josiah, he had provided well enough for them until recent years and they did have three wonderful children.

Harriet and Evelyn were working opposite each other on the hand-powered conveyer belt. This was Evelyn's favourite job at work. It was well away from the hot furnaces and involved lifting the shells into crates. She had started working there as a skinny adolescent, who had struggled to lift such heavy weights. She had since grown into a beautiful young lady. She was now taller than her mam but had inherited her clear fair complexion. Working so hard had given her beautifully sculpted shoulders. Her da had joked that she had shoulders like Billy Wells, Emrys's erstwhile boxing mentor.

They were fortunate that Mr Glen Taylor had kept a close eye on them. They were good workers and an asset to the company. It was unfortunate that Mr Newman had also kept a close eye on Evie and not only an eye. He frequently brushed past with his hand held inappropriately. But what could you do?

Harriet looked up because her chatterbox daughter had gone unusually quiet. All the colour had drained from Evie's face as she stared at something over Harriet's shoulder. Harriet looked round and saw her husband standing there wheezing uncontrollably. In his hand was a sheet of paper and floods of tears were flowing down this hard man's face. The two women ran over to Josiah and grabbed the piece of paper. Harriet read it and then disbelievingly read it again.

Royal Welch Fusiliers
Brecon

Sir

It is my painful duty to inform you that a report has been received from the war office notifying the death of
No. 19835. Rank Sergeant
Name. David Benjamin John
Regiment. 14th Battalion Royal Welch Fusiliers
Which occurred. In France

On the 10th July 1916
The report is to the effect that he was killed in action.

By His Majesty's command, I am to forward the enclosed message of sympathy from Their Gracious Majesties the King and Queen. I am at the same time to express the regret of the Army Council at the soldier's death in his Country's service.

I am to add that any information that may be received as to the soldier's burial will be communicated to you in due course. A separate leaflet dealing more fully with this subject is enclosed.

I am your obedient servant
W.G. Williams Captain.
Officer in charge of records

The three hugged each other, tears pouring down their faces. The other workers stared at them in unashamed dread. The next time it could be them. They came apart as Mr Glen Taylor approached. He put his arm around Harriet. He didn't know what to say. So he just said.

'I'm sorry, Harriet.'

Harriet stared at him still in shock.

'It says David's dead. They're wrong. I know they're wrong. I would know if he was dead.'

Glen Taylor ushered them to the door.

'Look. Go home. I'll find Reverend Hughes. Don't come back here. I'll come and see you in a few days. And Harriet look after yourself. And look after Evie.'

They staggered down Regent Street West, under the railway arch and into Regent Street East. They could walk only very slowly stopping every few yards for Josiah to catch his breath.

Beatrice Evans chose that moment to come out of her house. She looked at Evelyn with a terrified look on her face and said simply.

'Emrys?"

Evelyn replied through her tears.

'No. David.'

The two young girls had never liked each other at school but they now held each other tight and wept into each other's shoulders.

8

None of them slept that night. Harriet and Josiah clung to each other in a way they hadn't for many years, whilst Evelyn had convinced herself that it wasn't true. There must have been some mistake. It must be someone else. Anyone but David.

Reverend Hughes had been around with exemplary speed, to give the talk that he was finding all too familiar. Somehow even to him, prayer in these circumstances must have seemed painfully inadequate. When viewing the scores of black ribbons on the front doors, it was obvious that something major had happened to the 38th Welsh Division. It was equally obvious that whatever it was, they had paid a fatally high price.

Harriet and Evelyn got up early as any attempt at sleep was plainly futile. Josiah stayed in the comfort of his bed deep in thought. Neither of the women was hungry and none of them had eaten a morsel since the previous morning. Suddenly, Evelyn screamed from the front door.

'Ma! Ma! Da! There's a letter. A letter from David. He must be alive.'

Shaking, she rushed to the back room and handed it to Harriet. Harriet's heart raced and she felt so nauseous that bile rose into the back of her throat. The envelope mercifully was in David's precise handwriting. She tore it open just as Josiah reached the bottom step. She rushed to read the letter stumbling over her words.

France. 8th July 1916

Dear Mam,

   I only have a short time to write this note as we are very busy. I am taking this chance, while I can. I am not sure when I will next have an opportunity, as I think we will be taking part in an attack soon. You may have heard that the Ulster lot, from Ireland, had some work to do, last week, and although they did well, they had lots of casualties. It will be our turn soon and I think we will do just as well. Hopefully, we will have fewer casualties.

   You know that Colonel Davies has left the battalion. If he hadn't I might be in Officer's College in Rhyl, by now. I could have got home on the train to see you. Of course, that would have been nice. I certainly miss you all and the Ferry. June is my favourite month at home. You must have enjoyed going out to the river with no coat on. It is the thought of getting home with you all, including Emrys, that keeps me going. I am looking forward to the world's biggest party when we both come home.

   How is it going at Taylors? It's hard work for Evie. I know she's not a little girl anymore, but to me, she still is a little girl. Mam, look after Evie. I know you will, of course, Mam. You probably realise by now that the cyclists are no longer part of the 38th. I think that is lucky. I'm glad Emrys isn't any part of this business. I like my platoon even though most of them are from North Wales.

   Thank you for my parcel. Thank Aunty Vi for the chocolate. Many thanks to Evie again for the socks. I am ashamed to say being the sergeant that I am almost the only one of us who hasn't had trench foot at some stage. This has to be because I have so many pairs of socks that my feet are always dry.

   Colonel Davies was very good to me before he left to become an

MP. He has been talking to me about what I will do after this is over. He has been kind enough to say that I am too clever to be a rollerman and should go back to school. He says I should get some qualifications. It is very good of him to say so. None of us knows what will happen afterwards.

You will be glad to hear we had a church parade today. The problem was that it was in Welsh. Never mind, it was very good. I'm also sure that Jesus can understand Welsh.

Anyway, I have to go now. We will be as I said pretty busy for the next few days. I'm sure I will come through it in one piece, so don't worry too much. I'm just looking forward to some leave. Pass on my love to Aunty Vi and the rest. Obviously also to Da and Evie.

Love from your son David

Harriet grabbed the War Office letter to confirm what she already knew. The War Office letter said that he had been killed on the 10th. David's letter was dated the 8th. She slumped into the chair, head in hands finally reconciled to the fact that her favourite child was dead. By some viciously cruel twist of fate, David's letter had been delayed to such an extent that it arrived after the War Office one. He must have written it a matter of days or even hours before he had been killed.

Poor Evelyn was inconsolable. She had thought that her brother was alive, only to have her hopes cruelly dashed. She rushed upstairs and they heard the thump of her flinging herself on her bed.

Harriet heard the soft knocking on the front door. She stared at her motionless husband. It would be the first of a sea of kind people who just wanted to pass on their condolences. It was too early for her. For the first time in twenty years, she put herself and her feelings first.

Not daring to look at her husband again, she grabbed her coat and rushed out through the back door, into the narrow back lane. She urgently needed to talk with God. That is what she had been taught to do from a young age. She started to walk towards Rehoboth Chapel. She stopped. Rehoboth was the last place she wanted to be. All her friends would be congregating there. She couldn't face it. There was one place where nobody would dream of looking for her. Jerusalem Chapel.

Harriet found her way back along the back lane to avoid being seen. In better times this was the shortcut to M.G. Roberts' house. She quickly crossed the road and turned the knob on the large pair of oak doors of Jerusalem Chapel. She had prayed that the doors would not be locked, but then her prayers about David had gone unanswered. She sighed from simple relief when the left-hand door creaked open and she was able to creep in.

This was a building that she had never entered before. In fact, such was the venomous rivalry between the two Baptist chapels, she had never even dreamt of entering it. She took a seat halfway down the empty nave and surveyed her new surroundings.

She was surprised at how similar this was to Rehoboth. Similar even to the Ten Commandments written in large letters on the wall. She was beginning to feel uneasy and guilty. She felt guilty simply because she quite liked this building. She felt even guiltier for leaving her husband and daughter in their hour of need. It was so unlike her. She was the strong one. She would close her eyes for a few seconds before rushing home. She still hadn't opened them, when she heard the sound of a side door opening.

Standing in front of the altar table was the imposing figure of Elizabeth Powell, the pastor's wife. Mrs Powell seemed surprised to see who was sitting there. They were losing congregation not gaining them. She also seemed to sense that something must be gravely wrong. She quietly whispered.

'Harriet? It is Harriet, isn't it? Can I help you at all? But if you want to, just sit there. Just sit there with Jesus. I can leave.'

Harriet looked up with red eyes and replied.

'I have to go. David's dead. He died in France. I shouldn't be here. I have to be with my family.'

Harriet stood to leave but Elizabeth reached her first. Gently putting her hand on her shoulder she said.

'I'm so sorry, Harriet. We know that you usually worship elsewhere. This is God's House. You are always welcome. I am always here. If you need someone to talk to, I'm here.'

Harriet left quickly, hoping not to have been noticed and walked back down the road toward her home. Josiah would be in a bad place. He had gradually over the last year become so dependent on Harriet that he would be finding her brief absence intolerably difficult. It was Evelyn, who would have had to answer the front door to the frequent visitors, all wanting to express their sympathies to Harriet. A huge look of grateful relief passed over Evelyn's face when her mother, at last, walked through the back door into the scullery. She cried.

'Mam. Where have you been? Mrs Eynon said you went into Jerusalem.'

Harriet said nothing. She should have known better than to believe that she wouldn't have been noticed. The chances were that it would be Mrs Eynon. Indeed, every time anyone passed Mrs Eynon's house, her net curtains would flick open. It was only surprising that she hadn't come out to confront Harriet when she opened the chapel door.

The following two days were an endless stream of well-meaning, but tiring well-wishers. Late in the evening Evelyn had looked out of the front door and noticed a cooking pot. The pot contained a strange mixture of meat and vegetables. A note accompanied it.

'Dear Harriet, we have never spoken. You were very kind once to my son, Benjamin. I am sure you won't remember. It is part of our religion that you look after the bereaved by making sure that they are well provided for. It is important however not to intrude. We just leave food on the doorstep. My husband knew David and thought well of him. I am thinking of you. Ruth Reuben.'

Harriet tried to think who this woman, Ruth Reuben, was. She surely was the Jewish lady, living with her family in the cricket pavilion. They were refugees from Belgium. Unlike some, Harriet had always tried to be kind to them, particularly the children. What difference did it make if they were Jewish? Now her kindness was being returned.

The following day a third letter arrived. The dreaded letter that would finally extinguish any tiny hope that any of them might still be harbouring.

France July 1916

Dear Mr and Mrs John,

It is my sad duty to inform you of the circumstances of the death of your son Sergeant David Benjamin John. He was an invaluable member of the battalion and we don't really know what we will do without him. I know the late Major Mills thought hugely of him. It is really unfortunate that he was about to go back to England to become an officer. I'm sure he would have done well.

On the day he died, he was invaluable to me. I was in command because Major Mills had been killed and Major Gwyther wounded. Your son helped me stabilize the line, at a critical moment and then lead the advance to the target. It was there that the Germans counter-attacked and your son was killed. It was reported to me that his death was almost instant, so I'm sure he didn't suffer.

I have lost a good friend and colleague. I'm sure however it is nothing compared to your loss. God bless you.

Your servant
John Glynn-Jones. Captain

Harriet couldn't speak. She clung to her daughter for the hundredth time over the past two days and cried. Her thoughts inevitably drifted to Emrys. They had lost one son surely Jesus could not contemplate taking the other. Every day she expected another fateful letter. She just couldn't stand the confining pressure of being in her small home. The home that she had loved until a few short days ago. The home she now just wanted to run away from.

Overwhelmed, she grabbed her coat and wandered out of

the door. She knew just where she was going and this time she couldn't care less who saw her. She needed to see Mrs Powell in the hated Jerusalem Chapel.

She opened the door for the second time in her life and walked in. Mrs Powell was busily moving books in the pews with her husband. Mrs Powell looked up, saw Harriet and whispered to him. The Reverend Powell nodded and made for the side door leading to his tiny office. Mrs Powell walked over to Harriet.

'Harriet. It is good to see you. I'm pleased to see you decided to come back. Do you want to talk?'

Harriet looked embarrassed. She should really be at Rehoboth finding solace with her friends. Either that or looking after her husband and daughter. Hesitatingly she asked.

'Is it all right? I just need a few moments of rest. A rest from kind people saying that they are sorry. A rest from being the one who is always looking after people. A rest from worrying about Emrys. I don't want to disturb you. You and the Reverend are busy, Mrs Powell.'

Elizabeth Powell was well known for having time for everyone and anyone. She ushered Harriet to a seat.

'Firstly, I'm Elizabeth. Secondly, you can say what you like. It won't go any further. Or just say nothing. Just sit there while I collect all the hymn books up. We have a big meeting tonight.'

Harriet needed something to say. Something that wasn't about her or David. She asked.

'What meeting are you having? It looks as if you're expecting lots of people.'

Elizabeth looked embarrassed. Embarrassed that this mother of a dead son didn't know what kind of meeting they were having. Elizabeth spoke, quietly.

'We've got someone famous coming to speak to us. It's Sylvia Pankhurst.'

Harriet interrupted.

'I thought she was the person who jumped in front of the King's racehorse.'

Elizabeth smiled, patiently.

'That was Emily Davidson. She jumped in front of the horse. I also think that you were thinking of Emily Davidson's friend, Christabel Pankhurst. That's Sylvia's sister. Not that you'd know it. The two don't talk and Sylvia doesn't speak to her mother either.'

Harriet thought for a few seconds about this.

'She doesn't speak to her mam. I would hate it if any of my three did not speak to me.'

She, suddenly, realized just what she had said. Of course, there was no way David could ever speak to her again. She cried out and Elizabeth stopped arranging the books, looking up in pity and shock. Harriet recovered her composure enough to ask.

'What in Jesus's name could matter so much that she can't speak to her poor mam?'

There was some bitterness in Elizabeth's voice when she replied.

'The same as always these days. This dreadful war. It destroys families physically like yours. It also destroys them mentally like the Pankhursts. Mrs Pankhurst and Cristabel are supporters of the war. Sylvia and her other sister are against it. They have argued so much about it that they don't speak. I'd go as far as saying that they hate each other.'

Even in her grief, this attracted Harriet's attention. Were people actually against the war? Not ordinary people like her, who didn't know better and selfishly just wanted her boy back. No. Important people. Famous people from London were coming here to speak. Harriet asked.

'She's coming to our little town to talk against the war. Why? What interest does anybody have in us?'

Elizabeth whispered her answer.

'She was a friend of Keir Hardie before he died. She promised him.'

Harriet was unsure who Keir Hardie was. She was too embarrassed to admit that she knew exactly who Billy Wells, the boxer, and Dickie Owen, the rugby player, were, but not Keir Hardie. She began helping Elizabeth collect all the books together and store them in the cupboard. She suddenly decided she needed to get home, all be it with just a germ of an idea in her head. Elizabeth Powell, tentatively, spoke as Harriet began to leave.

'Look, Harriet. It's probably too soon. In fact, I'm sure it is. You won't want to be with a large bunch of chattering women. Not now for sure. Only if you were interested, you would be made very welcome. It's not just our people. We've got all sorts who say they might be coming. Even the Jewish, Belgian lady, Mrs Reubens.'

Harriet thoughtfully left the chapel.

Back home, Harriet was unusually quiet. Josiah and Evelyn could tell something was occupying Harriet's mind. Of course, they assumed that it was just David. That, after all, was excuse enough. Evelyn, however, was too similar to her mother not to recognise that there was something else. There was something that hadn't been present before she had gone out. Finally, Harriet decided to confide in them.

'Look. I've been thinking. I'm not sure that you will like what I have been thinking, but give me a chance. We've lost our poor David in a land we know nothing about. God forbid anything happens to Emrys. But what are the boys over there for? Our boys? All I want is Emrys home in one piece. Emrys and all his friends. And all of David's friends. There's a womens' talk tonight by Miss Sylvia Pankhurst.'

Evelyn interrupted.

'Didn't she jump in front of the horse?'

Harriet smiled and continued.

'I thought that too, but apparently not. She's talking about ending the war. She's talking about the working women ending the war'

Josiah, as expected, lifted himself out of the corner chair and shouted.

'No wife of mine is going to a talk like that. It is disrespectful to the King. It is disrespectful to David. It is disrespectful to Emrys.'

Harriet had been expecting and fearing the response. Josiah was a proud but old-fashioned man. He really hadn't moved on with the times. These of course were extraordinary times. She continued once more.

'I'm sorry. I'm going whatever you say. I would disrespect Jesus if it would bring Emrys home. It's in Jerusalem Chapel, tonight, and I'm going.'

Josiah and Evelyn looked shocked. Harriet was a deeply religious woman whose whole life had previously revolved around

Rehoboth Chapel. Now in a flash, she had taken the Lord's name in vain and was going to the despised Jerusalem Chapel. Evelyn surprised her mother when she spoke.

'I'm a working woman. I'm coming with you. I'm not having you go on your own.'

Two hours later the two women were walking rapidly towards Jerusalem chapel. Evelyn was trying to rush her mother as they were going to be late. Josiah had said nothing at all during their supper, his face wreathed in anger. For the first time ever the two women had ignored him. With not a single backward glance they had disappeared through the front door, leaving him in his corner chair. Normally Harriet was a stickler for good timekeeping. Tonight, she had intentionally planned to be late. She had hoped to creep in and sit at the back unnoticed.

She had not taken into account Elizabeth Powell, who was standing at the doorway, enthusiastically welcoming everyone. Jerusalem was already over three-quarters full. It hadn't held a congregation of this size for many years. Elizabeth probably knew that there had not been one this size since the summer of 1914 before the outbreak of war. The unusual feature of this congregation, Harriet realised was that it consisted entirely of women. Entirely women, except for a single pair of male plain-clothed policemen desperately trying to make themselves invisible. Two men in a sea of women could expect a difficult ride, even in this place of worship.

Elizabeth appeared shocked to see Harriet. She can't have imagined in a million years that Harriet would come, let alone bring her beautiful young daughter with her. They were led to the front pew and sat down next to the Jewish lady, Mrs

Reuben. Harriet was pleased that Jerusalem Chapel had no problem with allowing a Jew in. Of course, Jesus had been a Jew. Harriet hoped Rehoboth would have been similarly welcoming.

Harriet hardly had time to thank the Belgian for the food, before Elizabeth strode onto the raised podium in front of the alter table. She was accompanied by a striking woman, who looked in her mid-thirties. She had short, dark hair bunched on either side, under a large green hat. Obviously well versed in gatherings of women such as these, she knew to dress plainly.

Elizabeth stood and clapped her hands to attract everyone's attention. The chattering stopped, instantly, the only noise when one of the policemen dropped his pencil. Elizabeth began.

'Thank you, everyone, for coming. We welcome here tonight people of different denominations. We welcome here tonight people with no religion at all. We welcome at least one person who has a religion other than Christianity. You are all welcome, even the two policemen noting down everything I say.

Before I introduce our esteemed guest, I have two ladies here who are even more welcome. They are Harriet and her daughter, Evelyn. They are here despite Harriet's poor son, David, losing his life in France two weeks ago. In a moment we will give them both a round of applause. But our aim tonight is to explore options that will mean there will be no more Davids and no more grieving mothers and sisters, like Harriet and Evelyn.'

Elizabeth began to clap and soon everyone was joining in, even the striking lady with the large green hat. So much for creeping in at the back thought Harriet, flushing deeply.

Elizabeth continued.

'That's almost enough from me. It is now my pleasure to introduce our famous guest who is touring and talking all over South Wales. She will be well known to many of you but not all. So I will give a brief description of her career so far. This is Sylvia. Sylvia Pankhurst. Sylvia founded the Women's Social and Political Union with her sister and mother in 1906. She has worked tirelessly in a mammoth effort to bring about true political equality for women. With that in mind, she has been arrested fourteen times and undergone force feeding six times.'

Sylvia Pankhurst interrupted.

'Eight.'

Everyone, except the two policemen, laughed before Elizabeth continued.

'Sylvia left the Women's Social and Political Union because she felt it didn't represent ordinary people like us. She started the Women's Socialist Federation in the East End of London. She has tried to feed the poor in the East End with her cost-price food scheme. Now she is turning to this terrible war and its effect on women. She is working against the new Conscription Law.

She is visiting us and some other Welsh towns because of a promise made to the late Mr Kier Hardie, M.P. to Merthyr Tydfil. She is going to talk to us about the International Women's Peace Congress, in Holland last year, and her efforts for peace. Sylvia.'

Sylvia Pankhurst stood and smiled at the rapturous applause, before beginning.

'Elizabeth. Thank you. As ever, you are an inspiration to us all. Thank you all for allowing me to speak. I, particularly, want to thank all the people here who have sons and brothers in service abroad. Even more, I want to thank everyone like Harriet, who has lost loved ones to this terrible conflict. What I do not want to do is to diminish the sacrifices that all these people and indeed all of you have made.

What I want to talk about is the origins of this war and how those origins are based on the capitalist ambitions of all the countries. I was last here in 1913 when the world was a very different place. As women, as you know, we had significant problems. Now we have the once in a generation opportunity to change the world. If we do so we can put ourselves in a position that will never be diminished.'

She stopped to take a sip of water.

'As Elizabeth said I am here at the bequest of Keir Hardie. My heart was broken when I heard of his death last year. I am convinced that there will be a prime minister, one day in the future, who will have been named after him. That is the esteem I think he will be held in as the founder of our Labour movement. He knew my opinion on the part women can play in ending this idiocy. He also knew that I had attempted to attend the International Women's Peace Congress, in The Hague, in Holland.

One hundred and twenty-five of us wished to travel to join our sisters from all over the world, including America but more importantly from Germany itself. The only ambition any of us had was to try and find a solution to this terrible problem. One hundred of us, including myself, had our passports revoked. No reason was given. When the other twenty-five reached Folkestone, twenty-two were not allowed onto the ship. No reason was given. The three who went used their dual nationality to join the American delegation. The reason that we were not allowed on that ship was simple.'

She paused for a moment to emphasise her next sentence.

'The authorities knew that we had already written to the women of Germany and also knew what we had said. These are some of the things we said to the women of Germany.'

She paused again for dramatic effect.

'We asked them to hold on to all their faith in peace and goodwill between nations. Technically, we are at enmity in obedience to our rulers but we own allegiance to that higher law that bids us live at peace with all men. We asked them if they felt the vast slaughter of our opposing armies was a stain on civilization and Christianity. We asked them whether an even deeper horror was aroused in them at the thought of all those innocent victims. By that, we meant the countless women, children, old and sick, who are pursued by famine, disease and death, in the devastated areas, both East and West.'

Harriet could feel the anger, pent up in her for days, begin to rise up. She was just unsure who she was angry with. She was angry with this woman, but also with Field Marshall Haig and David Lloyd George. She was angry with Emrys and even David. Sylvia Pankhurst began to get into her stride.

'How strange. British transport workers- trade union men- are called to shoot down German transport workers. It is not so long ago in the time of our industrial war. I mean the great dock strike when we were fighting the large ship owners. We received with joy the news that these same men sent us five thousand pounds to help us with our fight for better conditions. We said that we would never forget their kindness. I have heard of rioting near here in Neath against German shops. Let us keep our word by treating all those German workers left behind in our midst with civility. Indeed we must treat German workers both in Germany itself and elsewhere with civility.'

Harriet was having difficulty fathoming why she should show any comradeship to these people who had killed David and taken her other son away from her. She was also surprised to find that her hand was tightly clasping the hand of the Belgian lady. Sylvia Pankhurst continued.

'In the East End of London, as here, I am surrounded by masses of poor women who have taken war work. Soldiers' clothes, equipment, munitions, whatever came as the sole means of keeping them and theirs from starvation. Inevitably, they passed to war work as peace employment failed. For these women, the fight against sweatshop labour must be maintained.'

Harriet was even more confused. This eloquent lady was surely making an attack on M.G. Roberts and Mr Taylor, who had done nothing but good to her family. On the other hand, she knew that some of the men at Taylors were less productive than she and Evie. She also knew that these men were being paid considerably more than either of them. For the next twenty minutes, Sylvia Pankhurst talked almost without stopping for a breath. Gradually, Harriet could feel her anger moving away from the speaker. The speech was coming to an end.

'To finish I wish to make the following points, which I believe should be the aims of the working women of this country. We should take whatever action is needed to achieve these aims.

First, we must empower our government and all governments to begin the dialogue which, with God's help, would surely bring this conflict to a rapid conclusion.

Second, we call on the government to take control of the food supply, in order that we all may feed or starve, together, independent of wealth or social position.

Third, working women to be consulted regarding the price and distribution of food.

Fourth, government committees should consult with the trade unions about wages and men and women should be paid at the same rates for equal work.

Fifth, the moratorium on debts above five pounds should be extended to those below. The poor will have debts below five pounds and only the rich above.

Sixth, any committees, either locally or centrally, dealing with food, employment or relief, should contain working-class women.

Last but definitely not least, a demand for votes for women.'

There were several cries of Votes for Women as Sylvia continued.

'This is undoubtedly a capitalist war. If capitalism ended there would be no more war. Indeed, there would simply be no need for war. Can we sit still and let the helpless die in their thousands, as die they must, unless, sisters, we rouse ourselves in the name of Humanity to save them?'

Sylvia Pankhurst sat down. Everyone else in the chapel stood as one and rapturously applauded. After two minutes, Elizabeth Powell stood and waved her arms so that she could speak.

'Sylvia has agreed to answer a few questions.'

There followed a series of uninteresting questions. In Harriet's opinion, they had obvious answers. One of the reasons Harriet had wanted to sit at the back was so that she could slip away unnoticed precisely at this moment. Evelyn stared in disbelief when her mother raised her hand. At last, Elizabeth Powell signalled for her to speak. Harriet asked her question in a voice laced with the anger that she had been feeling all evening.

'Miss Pankhurst. Thank you. I have a question for you. Did my David die for nothing?'

Sylvia Pankhurst answered immediately. This was a question that she must have been asked many times before. It was also a question that would have kept her awake at night, on numerous occasions.

'Harriet, you poor thing, thank you for asking that question. It is very brave of you to do so. It is I have to say probably the most important question that will be asked tonight. My answer has to be "No, David did not die for nothing." But I have to put a caveat on that. He will not have died for nothing, but only if we make sure that he didn't. To do that, we need to make sure that this country and indeed this world are very different places when this dreadful war is finally over.

This war was declared by politicians without recourse to public opinion. Any public opinion there was, had to be undemocratic because we women had been denied our opinion.'

She looked earnestly at Harriet.

'Do we really believe that if women had had a say in all this, that war would ever be even contemplated? If we could make employers lose rather than make profits we would swiftly bring this war to an end. So, Harriet, David will certainly not have died in vain, if we make sure that we come out of the war to a world entirely different from the one we have now. There are hundreds of changes to be made. We demand equal political representation for women. When I say women I mean all women, not just rich women. We also demand equal pay for women as men.'

Everyone stood again to clap whilst Mrs Reuben, Evie and Harriet hugged each other. Even the two policemen had stopped scribbling. After a few more questions everyone crowded around to shake hands with the reluctant heroine. When it came to Harriet and Evie's turn, Sylvia Pankhurst hugged them tightly. Harriet talked gently to her.

'Miss Pankhurst. There is something I would like you to do for me.'

Sylvia replied.

'Firstly please call me Sylvia. Secondly, whatever it is I will endeavour to do it if I possibly can.'

Harriet smiled.

'Miss Pankhurst. You are a very clever woman and lots of what you have said is true. What I want you to do is in some ways just as important. I want you to make up with your mam. Surely nothing can be so bad that you can't talk to your mam.'

Sylvia could do nothing but stare at her open-mouthed.

9

Northern France, July 1916

Emrys had never heard of Sylvia Pankhurst. Indeed he had so little interest in the suffragettes that he wasn't even aware that one of them had jumped in front of the King's horse. Had he been told, however, that his highly principled mother was listening to this contentious anti-war speech, then he wouldn't have believed it. If he had been told that it had taken place in the despised Jerusalem Chapel, then he certainly wouldn't have. But, then again he also didn't know about his poor brother's fate, at Mametz Wood. Perhaps once he did, his attitude to lots of things might radically change.

He was cycling happily with the rest of C Company, oblivious of his brother's death. The cycling was the good part. It reminded him of back home cycling along the Tennent Canal, on some errand for M.G. Roberts. The gunfire was away in the distance. It wasn't going to bother them on this fine July day. Not for the moment anyway.

As they approached their destination they were getting closer to the front. The crash of a discharging gun shook Emrys back into reality. The war hadn't gone away but at least they were better off than Albert and Emlyn in the infantry.

Laventie was a pleasant enough place. It was built around the usual picturesque town square and church. The boys laughed at an elderly clergyman cycling in a cassock. Emrys couldn't imagine Reverend Hughes doing that. Even the thought of it made him chuckle even more. There was surprisingly little war damage. Then again, the Divisional Headquarters was housed in the ancient Hotel de Ville occupying one side of the square. They all knew that the top brass always stayed well away from danger. If the cyclists were working around here then they would have an easy time.

They lined up in columns, neatly holding their bicycles on their left sides. Their rifles were strapped tightly to the bike frame just above the pedals. Sergeant Marshall stood out in front glaring at any miscreants. The officers were grouped around Captain Davies, chatting gaily as if at some cricket match. A military policeman marched smartly out of the headquarters straight towards the captain, saluted and began to talk. Emrys whispered to Gwyn.

'Don't like the look of that bloke. Keep your head down.'

Captain Davies looked very serious when he came over and whispered something to Sergeant Marshall. Marshall nodded and said almost to himself.

'Yes, sir. Our four best cyclists for a special assignment.'

Emrys tried to make himself unnoticeable. He had had enough of special assignments. There was, however, a certain inevitability to what was about to unfold. Marshall first talked to Corporal Jackson. Then walking down the rows of men, he laid a hand on the shoulder of Flinty and then Ted. Finally, he pointed to Emrys, before he walked back to the front. Gwyn seemed to think it was hilarious. Emrys less so.

Marshall had turned to address them all.

'You four go off with the sergeant here. You are running messages for the brigadier. The rest of us have the wonderful job of carrying poison gas canisters away from the front. It will be hard work, men. And remember your gas masks.'

It was Emrys's turn to laugh at Gwyn. Running messages for the brigadier sounded a much better prospect than lugging gas canisters around.

It took barely two minutes for the four cyclists, led by the military police sergeant, to arrive at the ruined farmhouse, where the brigadier had his headquarters. They had expected to have to travel to a place nearer the front. But no. This brigade commander must like the quieter life just half a mile out from the village.

Blocking the narrow lane, however, was the largest artillery piece that any of them had ever seen. It towered above them as they failed to squeeze their bicycles past. The police sergeant recognised it.

'Twelve-inch howitzer. Massive shells.'

The howitzer was completely blocking the lane to all transport despite the efforts of a team of twenty, rather bedraggled mules. Even to the boys, this looked like a serious situation. This must be one of the main routes to the front and a large roadblock had already developed. If the Germans up on the overlooking ridge spotted it through the morning mist, then they could expect some unwanted attention. Of course, what you need in a roadblock is a policeman. That was exactly what they had.

The police sergeant put the four cyclists to work. They pushed while the mules and sappers pulled the hulking giant. Emrys wondered whether they had actually chosen the short straw after all, as he strained his stiff, grinding back. His grimacing face was flat against the back of the gun. Gradually, the howitzer began to move. Suddenly, they realized that it had gained too much momentum as it began to accelerate down the narrow incline. The cyclists stopped pushing and jumped back. They grabbed the two ropes trailing behind and pulled as if their lives depended on it. Their quick action had prevented the howitzer from ploughing into the mules. After all, the cyclists had an affinity for the mules. Both of them were always given the dirtiest, shitiest jobs. They needed to get this giant into its rightful place in the prepared battery, fewer than a hundred yards from the Brigade Headquarters. One moment there were cries of Put your shoulder into it. The next they were desperately hauling on the ropes.

When they had finally positioned it in its rightful place, they flopped exhausted onto the ground. Ted breathed heavily.

'Hey, Emrys. The way you were kissing it, you'd have thought it was your girlfriend. What's her name?'

The answer came to Emrys from nowhere. The back of the howitzer, somehow, reminded him of his Aunty Lil's ample backside

'Elizabeth. Yes, that's it. Elizabeth. We can call her Laventie Lil.'

The sappers looked on approvingly. Laventie Lil was an excellent name for this troublesome bitch of a gun.

They were still sweating profusely when they, at last, arrived at the farmhouse. It might now be cloudy, with the occasional spot of rain, but it was still a warm July day. They were looking forward to removing their jackets. The sergeant whispered to them.

'It's the APM. Provost Marshall. Senior police officer. My boss. Best behaviour, please.'

In front of them stood an immaculately dressed officer. Emrys had never seen so much gold braid on a single person. The officer looked at his watch and then glared at them. He was not used to being kept waiting. He snarled at them.

'You are now part of 184 Brigade. Behave as such. Timekeeping is of the essence. Now, listen carefully. If the phones are down you will be our next method of communication. To division, in Laventie, behind. 183 Brigade to our right. 15th Australian Brigade to our left. Easy job. Reasonable tracks. Three-mile journeys maximum. As I said easy job. Any questions.'

He left without leaving any time for questions. The sergeant produced a set of maps and indeed the journeys appeared simple enough. Now, this was a job more to Emrys's taste. Lounging around until needed and then a short cycle ride. Even then, they would only be called into action if the phones weren't working. They were led into the farmyard outside the makeshift headquarters and just left to smoke their cigarettes and talk. Perfect.

The farmhouse was a hive of activity with officers rushing here and there, with strained looks on their faces. Something was going on but the cyclists would be the last to find out what. A pristinely dressed major appeared at the back door. He needed a messenger.

Corporal Jackson pushed Emrys reluctantly forward. He had been enjoying his cigarette in the sun. The major ushered him in through the side door into the main living room of the farmhouse.

Inside, even to Emrys's inexperienced eye, there was a palpable feeling of panic. In the middle was a general shouting angrily. Emrys had never been this close to a general before and this general seemed to be staring directly at him. He wasn't, though. The eye seemingly focusing on him wasn't real. It was false. A glass eye. Emrys had heard of them but had never seen one.

The well-dressed major calmly handed Emrys an envelope and whispered.

'Right, boy. You're to get to Le Trou and hand this to General Elliott. He's commanding the Australian brigade next door. General Carter insists you hand it to him personally and wait for a reply. Hand it to him personally.'

He was led to the door and back into the farmyard. The first thing to do was discover where he was going. The four cyclists crowded around the map. Le Trou was a first aid centre and command post. Unlike General Carter's HQ it was only three hundred yards back from the front line. Emrys would need to take some care as he approached the end of his journey.

He set off in the bright sunlight but with a pleasant cooling breeze. The journey looked almost exactly two miles. It should take no longer than fifteen minutes. That of course depended on good roads and no obstacles. The beginning of the trip was indeed straightforward. If the route was more on a track than a road it was at least a well-maintained track. It gradually, however, became more and more potholed. More obstructions appeared. A burnt-out cart here and a charred branch of a tree there. There was more personnel as well. Soldiers making their way back to their units. Fully laden mules carrying supplies forward.

There was no question of cycling the last six hundred yards. The road had become unmanageably muddy and he was getting too close to the front for comfort. A man on a bicycle would be a tempting target even at this range. Unable to strap it to his back, as prescribed by the designer, he had no choice but to put his bicycle over his shoulder and stagger the final few yards.

The first indication that he had reached his destination was a small but attractive cemetery. Somehow, it seemed to have come through the ravages of war untouched. It was a tiny area of tranquillity in a sea of madness. Conveniently, it was next to the first aid centre. In front of both were a number of battle-scarred bunkers built from concrete and earth.

Inside one of the dark buildings lit only by a single candle, he found a tall, bareheaded captain staring studiously at a map. When Emrys clicked his heels smartly to attention the captain looked up.

'Who the hell are you, Sonny?'

Emrys was shaken. He had never been sworn at by an officer before. Certainly not one with a rank as high as captain. Plenty of times by NCOs such as Sergeant Marshall but never by an officer. He regathered his wits enough to stutter.

'Beg your pardon, sir. I have an urgent message from General Carter for General Elliott. I've been told to emphasize that it's urgent.'

The captain's mood lightened.

'Well done, Sonny. Leave it on the table and I'll see that he gets it when he returns.'

Emrys was anxiously persistent.

'Can't do that, sir. My orders are to give him it myself. Personally, sir. And I need to wait for a reply.'

The captain looked irritated.

'Pompey's up at the line showing some bloody English major round. You'll either have to stay here or go up to find him yourself. He could be some bloody time though.'

Emrys intended to get away from these strange people quickly. They were unlike anyone that he had ever met before. The wisest course of action might be to make his way forward. The sooner he could get back to the relative safety of 184 Brigade HQ the better. He was confused, however, about who this Pompey was. That confusion only increased as he was leaving. The captain shouted after him.

'Funny bugger, Pompey. You can call him a fucking bastard and he won't blink an eye. Don't salute him and all hell will break loose.'

Emrys went outside and lent his bicycle against a gatepost, secretly worrying that one of these people would have stolen it by the time he got back. After all, according to Corporal Jackson, they were all the sons of convicts. He began making his way down the communication trench toward the front line. Despite being keen to get away quickly, he had learnt to take his time. Nobody would thank him if he tripped over a box of bombs.

Nearing the front line, he stopped a sergeant to ask whether he had seen General Elliott. He was surprised by the reply.

'Pompey is at the observation point about 50 yards down. He's got Wiercky with him and some English bloke. Seemed pretty intense, mate. I should leave em alone if I were you.'

Pompey again. Who on earth was this Pompey? Was he Captain Pompey or even Major Pompey?

Emrys walked around a sharp corner of neatly positioned

sandbags. In front of him, standing beside a massive bunker, was a dishevelled Australian major talking to a smart English one. Behind them, listening intently, was the largest man Emrys had ever seen. Large in every way. He was tall with huge shoulders and a sizeable belly jutting out in front of him. The two majors were sensibly wearing helmets. The large man wore a large floppy hat like those Emrys had seen cowboys wearing in the moving pictures.

Emrys coughed to attract attention and received a quizzical look from the Australian major. Emrys began tentatively.

'I've got an urgent message from General Carter, sir. I'm to give it to General Elliott personally and wait for a reply.'

The major turned to the large man.

'Pompey. This kid has a message for you from Cyclops. Says it's urgent.'

Emrys was still confused when the large man began to tear open the letter and read it intently. He had, at last, discovered that the large man was indeed General Elliott and everyone seemed, for some reason, to know him as Pompey. Who on earth was Cyclops? Then it came to him in a flash. A Greek mythology book he had read as a child. Cyclops only had one eye.

He waited for General Elliott to digest the message and giving his smartest salute, as advised by the captain, interrupted.

'General Elliott, sir. General Carter has ordered me to wait for a reply.'

Pompey Elliott looked at the young man and snarled.

'I have a reply for General Carter, Sonny. The message is simple. Tell him to fuck off.'

Emrys plaintively looked at the major who just laughed.

'I dare say that would not the best message for you to give to General Carter. We are all a bit fraught here, as you can see, and you haven't picked the best moment I'm afraid. Stay with us and I'll get something in writing for you in a while.'

Emrys was positive that if he was ever to get a sensible reply from this irascible general, then the only policy was to not let him out of his sight. So he would just have to blend into the background and wait. Of course, Emrys being Harriet's son would listen.

The British major was a Major Howard who had been sent by Field Marshall Haig himself. They seemed to be studying a massive concrete structure nicknamed the Sugarloaf, at least four hundred yards across No mans land. The Australians would attack this side and General Carter's men on the other.

They all began to make their way back towards Le Trou. General Elliott sent his major ahead. Perhaps he wanted to have a quiet word with Major Howard alone. They didn't seem to notice the young cyclist listening in the background. General Elliott shoved a pamphlet in front of the British officer.

'Look. This is the accumulated knowledge of two years fighting out here. It's a British document. It clearly states that no attack should take place where No mans land is more than 200 yards wide. My brigade will have to cover over double that. I don't think that this attack has a hope in hell. Strictly between ourselves, what is your assessment?'

Major Howard chose his words carefully.

'My assessment is that it will be bloody murder.'

General Elliott shook the major's hand.

'Please go straight back to Field Marshall Haig and tell him what you have seen.'

It was only then that they seemed to notice the cyclist. General Elliott growled menacingly at Emrys.

'And you, Sonny, make sure you keep that fucking trap of yours shut.'

They walked purposefully back to Le Trou with Emrys trailing behind. He was relieved to discover that Major Wierk had already put pen to paper and written a hopefully more diplomatic reply. The general briefly looked at it and laughed gently.

'When this is all over, you'll have to go into politics, Wierky.'

He turned to Emrys and shook his hand.

'Godspeed, Sonny. Keep safe.'

Emrys remembered to salute smartly and left. Perhaps he had been a trifle harsh on these people. He was not surprised to find his bicycle exactly where he had left it.

There were times near the front when everything seemed to slow down. The artillery seemed to stop almost as if neither side could be bothered. This was one of those moments, while he was first walking and then cycling back up the same track which he had come down earlier that day. The sun had come out and there were even a few birds singing. Unlike his mam, he knew nothing about birds or plants. Maybe after the war, he would take more notice of her when she tried to teach him.

The journey was perfect. There was very little traffic on the bumpy track so progress was rapid and pleasant. As he approached his destination the peace was dramatically broken by Laventie Lil barking into action with an ear-splitting roar. It was almost as if his girlfriend was welcoming him home to reality.

He swung into the farmyard and winked at Ted, who hadn't seemed to have moved for the whole three hours that Emrys had been away. He presented himself at the side door. The lieutenant took the message that General Elliott had recently signed and turned to re-enter the house. He, suddenly, turned back again and muttered to Emrys.

'You took your time. The general has been waiting for this. You'll need to do better next time, soldier.'

Emrys sat down next to Ted, who clapped him on the back. He had been dying for a cigarette for some time and gratefully put one between his lips. He joyfully took his first drag and closed his eyes. The comparison between the two HQs could not be starker, even for such a low-ranking observer. The Australian one was near the front and they calmly seemed to have their finger on the pulse. Here, they were considerably further back and there was the atmosphere of toxic panic, which had been so pervasive earlier. Still, who was he to comment? He kept his eyes closed and looked forward to eating. As usual, he was hungry.

They did nothing more, that day. Just before dark, they found their billets, in a low-ceilinged building, which smelled like a pigsty. That was because, as they soon discovered, it was a pigsty. Ted boasted to all who would listen what an easy time he had had. Emrys said nothing. He felt exhausted. His thoughts began to drift back to the man known as Pompey. There was a man you could follow.

They were woken as the sun rose above the German lines. There had already been an urgent call for a messenger. The easy times had ended. The following few days became frantic for the four messengers. The impending attack was imminent. It looked as if Pompey Elliott's appeal to the Commander in Chief had fallen on deaf ears.

Emrys was the one always sent to Le Trou. He would never admit it to his friends but he liked going there. There was a definite calmness. Despite the discipline and authority, there was none of the blatant bullyings that Emrys had sometimes experienced in the British army. He didn't mean Sergeant Marshall, the devout chapelgoer whose language had gradually deteriorated over the past six months to that of a sewer rat. Marshall underneath it all had a heart of gold. At Le Trou, however, if anyone got above themselves they would immediately be brought back down to ground level. Emrys felt that that might even apply to General Elliott, who he just couldn't manage to call Pompey. That was despite everyone around him doing so.

He had just delivered yet another message from General Carter, known here as Cyclops, to General Elliott, known as Pompey. Yet again it was about sally-ports, whatever they were. Cyclops was for them. Pompey would rage against them until calmed down by Major Wieck, known as Wiecky.

Then all of a sudden, they decided that it was time for something to eat. They just decided to sit down, talk and eat. Subconsciously, any discussion about the war was banned. Women and sports, even with these senior officers, seemed to be the topics of conversation. Emrys stopped for a moment to listen to the idle chatter about cricket, rugby and footie before making his way towards the door. He was immediately stopped by Major Wieck.

'Where the hell do you think you're going, Sonny? Come back here and have something to eat.'

Emrys sat back down. Even with Lieutenant Mond, this was definitely not a situation he had been in before. He was grateful for the food, of course. He was always hungry. But these were senior officers. He was now intent on staying deathly quiet. General Elliott had other ideas.

'We can't go around calling you Sonny even if you do look about thirteen. What's your name? You're Christian name, I mean.'

Emrys told them his name only for the general to exclaim loudly.

'Emrys? What sort of name is that?'

Emrys replied.

'Welsh, sir. I'm from Briton Ferry in Wales.'

The captain whom Emrys had met on his first visit laughed.

'Well, that's a relief. At least you're not bloody English. Can't get my mouth around Emrys though. We'll have to just call you Reece.'

He turned to the general and continued.

'Hey, Pompey. You rejected my brother because he looked too young. Reece here looks about thirteen and he got in. Why's that?'

General Elliott thought about it for a moment before replying.

'I've told you before your brother is a bloody awful liar. Perhaps Reece isn't.'

They all dissolved into laughter. Emrys kept quiet. He wasn't going to tell them that his mam had taken him to the recruiting centre. These officers had more important things to think about. The attack was planned for the following day.

Emrys was woken, in Leventie, by the pouring rain. He was fortunate enough to be under one of the only parts of the roof of the pigsty to be intact. It did mean however that the rest of the cyclists crowded up to get as much cover as they were able. It turned out to be a cold, wet and cramped night for all of them.

They got up, early the next morning, freezing and soaked. It not only continued to rain but was misty. The mist all but obscured the Aubers Ridge in the distance, behind enemy lines. The four young men knew that they would be needed. The sudden change in the weather was certain to lead to a change in the plans.

At Brigade HQ, Laventie Lil was ominously quiet. The vision was totally obscured so there would be very little point in continuing their range finder shots. It would just be a waste of ammunition. Emrys was immediately sent to visit his Australian friends to make sure that they knew that the attack had been postponed. The journey was the easiest yet despite the driving rain. It was almost as if both sides had decided not to bother for the day. It certainly seemed like that when he arrived at Le Trou. Pompey Elliott was nowhere to be seen. After days without sleep, his team of officers must have insisted that he rest. Apart from anything, it would give them a chance to rest too. The only person there was Major Wieck. When Emrys walked through the narrow door, the major smiled.

'Reece, mate. Good to see you. And what can I do for you?'

Emrys handed him the sealed order. Of course, everyone at the British HQ knew what was written in it, despite Confidential being written on the envelope. They always did. Emrys felt confident enough to ask a question.

'The rumour is that the attack is being called off, sir.'

Emrys still couldn't get out of the habit of not calling an officer sir. The major replied.

'Yep. Rumour is correct, mate. That's why Pompey is still

in his bed. Postponed. Hopefully, bloody well forever. We knew already though. Corps HQ let us know already. Good of Cyclops to make sure, though.'

Emrys interrupted.

'I don't think it was ...' he suddenly thought it wise to stop, before finishing. 'I think it may have been Major Jepp, sir.'

Major Wieck thought about this for a moment.

'I dare say you're right, mate. Jepp seems a good sort.'

To Emrys's acute embarrassment, the major made him a cup of tea before ushering him on his way back to the 184 Brigade.

That evening, the Provost Marshall complete with gold braid appeared to read an Order of the Day from Field Marshall Haig. He coughed loudly, while Major Jepp stamped his foot for silence. They wanted everybody in the crowded farm yard to hear, even the cyclists craning to see from the back.

'As you know we were going to have a fight on Monday, but the weather was so thick, that our artillery could not see well enough to produce the accurate shooting we require for the success of our plan. So I had to put it off and GHQ said to do it as soon as possible. I then fixed zero for Wednesday and I know you will do your best, for the sake of our lads, who are fighting down south.'

Emrys thought about Major Wieck's wish for it to be postponed forever. He had only been granted two days.

He had hoped that on Wednesday it would be raining again. It was not. There had been enough rain to make everything slippery, but the sun was now out and there can't have been any question of any further postponement.

The massive artillery bombardment, which was to smash the Sugarloaf defences to matchsticks, began at 11.00 hours as planned. The cyclists knew because it was begun by Laventie Lil herself. Before long all three hundred British pieces were dropping their mayhem onto the German dugouts and trenches. The question on everyone's lips was whether it would be enough. Emrys knew what Pompey Elliott thought about it. Of course, the German artillery wouldn't sit around doing nothing for long.

When it came, the response was both fiercely intense and frighteningly accurate. One of their prime targets seemed, inevitably, to be Laventie Lil. Near misses for Lil might be all too close for comfort to the four cyclists. Emrys knew from his Australian friends that the attack itself was due to begin at 6 p.m. sharp. Seven more hours of these percussions and the risk of being hit by artillery shells was dreadful enough. They could only imagine how bad it was down in the trenches themselves. They had to think themselves lucky. For the time being anyway. At any time they might be summoned to venture forward.

On the face of it, things seemed to be going perfectly. The telephone lines must have still been working because the cyclists were not called up to do anything. If it wasn't for the noise, this was going to be the easiest day ever. 6 p.m. came and things seemed to subtly change. Although Lil was still barking into action with ferocious regularity, there were no shells exploding near them. With the attack going ahead, the German artillery must have juicier targets.

Despite their boredom, the boys couldn't concentrate on anything. Flinty produced a pack of cards but none of them could think. Then, some action at last. Ted was sent with an order for the Buckingham Regiment, the Bucks. The telephone lines were down again.

The earlier confident looks on all the staff officers' faces were beginning to be replaced by ones of anxiety. Emrys was sure that anxiety would have increased fourfold inside the small farmhouse. It was obvious that they were very far back compared to Pompey Elliott, who Emrys was confident would be close to the front. He was unsurprised when he was summoned by a lieutenant to the farmhouse door and ordered inside.

He had been correct about the anxiety. The irascible General Carter, who Emrys secretly always now thought of as Cyclops, was shouting again. Major Jepp also looked at the end of his tether as he approached Emrys.

'Get this message to General Elliott. Are you positive that you know where to go? It's all written down, but it is most urgent that you get it to him as quickly as possible. Impress whomever you see that the Bucks will be attacking the enemy position at nine. They will be in urgent need of support. Do you understand, private?'

Emrys understood exactly. He had seen the Sugarloaf with General Elliott and the two majors only a few days previously. He replied calmly, saluting at the same time.

'I understand completely, major. You can rely on me. I know exactly where to find General Elliott.'

Emrys could feel his heart beating rapidly as he mounted his bicycle and rode quickly past the mammoth Laventie Lil. This was certainly quite a responsibility for someone of his lowly rank. On the other hand, the telephones were down. He would be the swiftest way of getting the message to the general, who would either be at Le Trou or, more likely, in the front line itself.

The first mile was easy and it was paying dividends having

a cyclist rather than a runner taking the message. Then more evidence of the ongoing battle began to appear. A deep crater obstructed the precarious track and Emrys was forced to dismount simply to go around it. He remounted but was only able to cycle a few hundred yards farther before meeting a disconsolate gaggle of walking wounded, clutching make-shift bandages to their bleeding bodies. He felt duty-bound to help these poor, disconsolate men. He couldn't. He daren't stop even for a moment.

The closer he got to La Trou, the more pitiful men he was forced to pass. At last, he arrived at the HQ. He was glad that he had been there before. In the midst of this mayhem, it would have been impossible to find otherwise. He was relieved to see the hulking frame of General Elliott leaning over a map. He had half expected to find that the general was on the front line or even leading some attack on the Sugarloaf himself. Saluting, he handed over the message and spoke calmly.

'Major Jepp asked me to emphasize that the attack will be at nine and would need your support, sir.'

Pompey Elliott showed the order to Major Wierk before replying.

'Thank you, Reece. Get back to Major Jepp and tell him that we are still unsure of the situation here but he will have our closest support. He can be sure of that. We will send in our last reserve at nine exactly.'

There was no hanging around for a cup of tea, today. Emrys saluted again and marched back out of the door less than a minute after entering. Grabbing his bike, he began weaving his way through the lines of wounded soldiers. This was definitely not going with the ease that he'd heard talk about around

184 Brigade HQ. The defences were supposed to have been smashed to pieces by Laventie Lil and all her friends. The infantry was going to march in almost unopposed. Well. There was little evidence of that on this pock-marked track.

The message was important. He had to get through. He shouted and swore to clear the way. The response was just an angry retaliatory torrent of abuse. Who could blame them?

After the interminable age struggling through the endless stream of wounded, he was pleased to be able to cycle the last few hundred yards to the farmyard. He threw down his bike and ran to the door. It opened immediately. Ted was coming in the opposite direction clutching a message. Ted stopped, momentarily, to speak to his friend.

'Christ, Emrys, you've been bloody ages. We were getting worried. I'm off to the Bucks again. The attack's been cancelled. They are not very happy in there.'

Ted picked up his bike and disappeared around the corner. A sense of foreboding swept over Emrys. He had just taken an order for the attack and now he had heard that it had been cancelled. Where was Major Jepp when he needed him? The major seemed to have disappeared towards the front. To make matters worse, no one else seemed remotely interested in speaking to him. At last, Major Jepp was striding towards him. Emrys didn't even have time to salute, before blurting out.

'Major Jepp. I've just returned from General Elliott. He says that he will be sending in his reserve battalion at nine. Rumour around here, sir, is that the attack has been cancelled. Pardon, Major. I know I shouldn't.'

Major Jepp looked pale.

'Do you know if any of your people have been sent?'

139

Emrys replied.

'Ted has gone to the Bucks, but none of us to the Aussies.'

Major Jepp was normally so polite and calm. This time he shouted.

'Jesus Christ! Stay here. I'll be back in a minute.'

He was actually back in less than a minute and looked even more harassed.

'Right, soldier. Well done. You need to get back to General Elliott immediately. Nobody seems to have had the sense to tell him except you. Damn it. You need to get to Elliott as quickly as you can. I'll try the telephones again. You've only got twenty minutes. Can you make it?'

Emrys picked up his bicycle as he spoke.

'I can try.'

Major Jepp shouted after him.

'God's speed, boy. And remember to deliver the message even if you're late. They might be delayed for some reason.'

Emrys was going to try his level best to get there in time. In his heart of hearts, however, he knew two things. Firstly, getting to Le Trou in twenty minutes, today of all days, was impossible. Secondly, no unit of Pompey Elliott's was ever going to be delayed, even for a second.

Emrys cycled his heavy bike imagining that he was on the main road to Neath working for M.G. Roberts. For a few valuable minutes, he made excellent progress. Nothing, now, seemed to be making its way towards the front. A few stragglers were, painfully, making their way back towards Laventie but not enough to slow him down. Perhaps he would make it on time.

Then, rolling towards him was a tidal wave of despair. The track had taken several direct hits since he had last been there.

The already wounded desperately making their way back from the front had taken the full blast of some vicious explosions. The acrid stench of blood and cordite was everywhere. Emrys would see the faces of pleading wounded in his mind for days. Of course, he could do nothing but leave them to whatever fate beheld them. His task was more important than showing comfort to these poor souls. However, he couldn't help thinking of his bible teaching as he passed them on the other side of the road. He was no Good Samaritan.

The next thirty minutes were perhaps the longest of his life. At least up there with when his little sister had died from measles. He struggled past deep shell holes and tumbled down walls. All around him were wounded soldiers, valiantly trying to help each other. There was just no other aid. There were too many of them. The mass of people got worse as he approached the dressing station at Le Trou. Of course, he was struggling to get to the Brigade HQ nearby. He never actually got there. In front of him stood the captain who had talked to him on his first visit. Emrys managed to mumble breathlessly.

'I need to find General Elliott or Major Wieck. It's urgent. The attack is off. I need to deliver the message.'

The captain answered angrily.

'Too fucking late. I'll take you to Pompey but it will be no bloody use. The boys attacked bang on nine and there was no sign of a bloody Tommy anywhere. They were hung out to dry. Got a telephone message from the division five minutes ago. Now you. I tell you you're too fucking late.'

Emrys was worried that the captain was about to punch him. He could only say that he was sorry, but that he had tried. He waited for the captain to continue his rant but the anger seemed to have turned itself off, like some resistant tap. The captain spoke calmly.

'Come on, Reece. We'll go and find Pompey. He is in a bit of a state I can tell you. I need to get him back here anyway, before he does something fucking stupid, like becoming a stretcher bearer.'

They found Pompey Elliott halfway down the communication trench, barely a hundred yards from the front line, still peppered by enemy artillery and snipers. His face was white with distress and anger. He was trying to shake hands with each and every soldier who hobbled towards him.

'Boys. Boys. This is no fault of mine.'

He was surprised to see Emrys patiently standing a few yards away and said, in a trembling voice.

'Reece, you back again? What do those bastards want me to do now?'

Emrys knew he would have to tread with the greatest care when he spoke. This man was capable of anything in his state of mind.

'I tried my best, general. They cancelled the attack and I came as quickly as I could to tell you. I knew it was too late but I came. I really did try, general.'

Even with disaster surrounding him, Pompey Elliott's eyes softened and he whispered softly.

'I'm sure you did, Reece. We have all tried our best. It's those bastards who didn't.'

Emrys wasn't sure who those bastards were. He and the captain led the broken man back towards Le Trou, past the red-stained sandbags and the shattered bodies. Emrys knew he ought to be making his own way back to Laventie, as it was beginning to get dark. That journey would be difficult and treacherous enough in the light let alone in the pitch black. Despite the danger, however, he felt compelled to stay where he was. Pompey Elliott soon confirmed that this was the correct decision.

'Stay close to me, if you please, Reece. I may be in need of your services. I dare say I will have to contact General Carter during the night.'

They arrived at the entrance to the HQ, to find a mud-spattered lieutenant impatiently awaiting their return. He handed a scrap of paper to the general.

'From Major Denehy, general. It's not good.'

Pompey Elliott's pale face grew even paler and a tear appeared in his eye as he read the message aloud.

'Men of all battalions are coming back from No mans land and fully expect them to gradually drift back to our original line. Many men are wounded, many not. Very many officers are casualties, including Majors McCrae, Elliott and Hutchinson, all of whom are reported dead. It seems impossible to reorganise without them. Not a single man of the 15th Brigade is now remaining in the enemy's trench, as enemy flares are coming from the whole of the front allotted to this Brigade. I am trying to organise the defence of our original trenches.'

Pompey Elliott slumped to the ground as the lieutenant added.

'Major Denehy told me to tell you that at present the front line could not be held against any counter. He says the damage is too great and he has too few able-bodied men. He actually said a bunch of bloody women could knock us back as far as Paris, the situation is so severe.'

The general sprung back into action. At least there was something which he could actively do. Emrys faded into the background as he watched this intriguing man working at the height of his powers. The telephone lines temporarily functioning, Pompey Elliott was talking to his superiors, demanding reinforcements and pleading for more stretcher-bearers. He then seemed to conjure up small groups of men from nowhere to send forward into the darkness of the front line. A machine gun company here, a platoon of sappers there. He forgot no one.

He only stopped for breath two hours later, when a second and more welcome message arrived from Major Denehy.

'Pompey. The situation has stabilized. Am confident that we could hold against any counter. The men are knackered and need relieving as soon as possible, but will hold for the present. Need ammunition and stretcher-bearers.'

Relief flooded Pompey Elliott's face. Dawn was only a few minutes away and it had been essential to be organised by then. As the light began to seep over the horizon, he got to his feet. He must have decided that it was time to search out what remained of his command. He needed to see for himself what he already feared. Turning to the captain and Emrys he said. 'Are you coming?' and strode out into the mayhem outside.

They walked slowly down the communication trench. Pompey Elliott seemed impervious to any danger. Despite being at least six inches shorter, Emrys and the captain ducked low. Dawn would mean an increase in interest from the jubilant Germans. The general just stood to his full, considerable height. He shook hands here and talked to a wounded man there. He patted the shoulder of some bleary-eyed private. He missed no one. He bent down to a lieutenant, with a shattered leg, crawling along the trench. He immediately shouted.

'Stop. Stretcher-bearers. Here.'

The lieutenant's life had just been changed forever. He whispered through the pain.

'There are thousands back there who can't even crawl. Let the stretcher-bearers fetch them first.'

Emrys decided that he ought to help this wonderful, brave young man. He bent down without looking at the general.

'Come on, lieutenant, I'll give you a hand. I've got nothing better to do.'

General Elliott clapped him on the shoulder as he and the lieutenant started staggering back towards the dressing station. Emrys had already experienced the dressing station at Givenchy and the casualty clearing station in Bethune, but nothing on earth would have prepared him for this. All he could do was dump the lieutenant outside the entrance to the first aid station and hope that someone would see to him. The lieutenant was just one more in a sea of wounded surrounding the doorway. Emrys needed to find the general again and maybe manage to get away from this hell hole.

The general was standing in front of his HQ watching his men trudge past. He stopped a captain with a bandage around his head and exclaimed.

'Good God. What have I done?'

He could stand no more and rushed into the HQ, quickly followed by Emrys. Inside, Pompey Elliott burst into tears. Automatically, Emrys put his arm around his massive shoulder but then pulled away in horror. This was not how you behaved to an officer, let alone a General. Pompey Elliott looked up and smiled briefly as he said.

'You're a good bloke, Reece. Might even mistake you for an Aussie. Now off you go to your general and tell him the situation here.'

Emrys waited for the order to be written and for Pompey Elliott to hand it to him. A massive hand was shoved out towards him and grasped his. Tears blurred his vision as Emrys whispered.

'He's not my general. You're my general.'

Emrys quickly turned away and out of the door before he could embarrass himself further. He somehow knew that he would never meet this amazing man again.

He was relieved to find his bicycle just where he had thrown it down, in a panic the previous evening. There was no real rush. He was sure that Major Jepp would be aware of the situation by now, even if Cyclops wasn't. He made his way painstakingly back and pushed his bicycle into the farmyard. Ted shouted out before grabbing him.

'Emrys. You're alive. We'd given up all hope. We were bloody sure that you were dead.'

Emrys replied.

'Not quite but I've been to a terrible place. It must be worse than hell itself, I can tell you. Are you all right?'

Ted nodded.

'Yes. I'm all right too. Thank God. It was pretty bad with the Bucks, as well. I don't want to see that again, that's for sure.'

Emrys remembered the message. He pushed himself towards the backdoor of the farmhouse, where Major Jepp was smoking a cigarette. He was escaping the ranting inside. He looked up at Emrys.

'Good God. You're alive. Who'd have thought it? When you

didn't come back your friends were sure you were dead.'

Emrys handed the major the note with a huge sigh of relief. Major Jepp smiled at him and turned to walk back into the farmhouse. That, hopefully, would be the end of his time as a messenger.

Emrys had noticed during his travails in the past that you seemed to somehow sense when you had, at last, managed to come out the other end. This seemed to be that moment despite all the stress around him. Laventie Lil was totally silent as were the rest of her friends. Even the Germans seemed to be leaving them in peace, to lick their wounds. For the cyclists, things were at last calming down.

That afternoon they made their way back to Laventie and then on to join the battalion at Essars. Emrys couldn't care less if he never saw this bloody place again in his life.

The cycle ride should have been a pleasant one. The sun was out and both sides seemed to be licking their wounds. The lack of artillery fire almost seemed unreal. All they could think about, however, were the horrors that they had left behind. Emrys just couldn't get the lieutenant, with the shattered leg, out of his head. The lieutenant whose blood was still smeared on his sleeve.

They were relieved when they finally arrived back at Essars. Some proper rest at last. They were quickly enveloped by their mates, who immediately began telling them how lucky they had been. Lucky not to have been lifting gas canisters.

Emrys was quiet. He didn't say a word. Something must have happened. Gwyn could tell. They knew each other too well. Emrys passed it off as nothing. He was not ready to talk or even think about what he had just experienced.

Gwyn then remembered that he had picked up a letter for his friend, the previous day. It would surely pick his spirits up. Letters were important. They were their only attachments to real life. Life away from the explosions, mud and rats, not to mention the blood and suffering. They were a memory of home and what they would eventually go back to. God willing. Gwyn handed it to Emrys.

'I think it's from your mam.'

Emrys opened it. It would be such a boost to get some good news. He was surprised when he pulled out a single piece of paper and a small rectangle of cardboard. Mam normally wrote reams. Reams of total inconsequential nonsense but just what he needed. He began to read.

Dear Emrys,

I am sorry I have to tell you the terrible news that David died somewhere in France on July 10th. We were praying that it was wrong, but today we got a letter from his captain confirming it. We are all at the end of our tether. We can think of nothing but poor David and of course you. You must make sure nothing happens to you. Your coming home is all we live for. I will write again soon when I can get my thoughts together. The lovely card is a wonderful thing from Evelyn.

Love Mam, Da and Evelyn.

Unable to speak, Emrys handed the letter to Gwyn and picked up the card. It had a blue and black surround with a small picture of David glued to one end. There were three paragraphs of print at the other end.

Far away from his home and his loved ones
Laid to rest in that faraway land
Never more shall our eyes here behold him
Never more shall we clasp his hand.

His cheery ways, his smiling face
Are a pleasure to recall
Though there's nothing left to answer.
But his photo on the wall.

We miss you when morning dawns
We miss you when night returns
We miss you here we miss you there
Dear brother, we miss you everywhere

Gwyn put his arm around Emrys who was only able to stutter two words.

'Fucking war.'

10

Jerusalem Chapel, Briton Ferry, July 1916

Harriet could tell that Evelyn was worried about her. As they began to make their way towards the door Harriet turned to hug Mrs Reuben and thank her again. She knew that their presence at Jerusalem Chapel would have been deemed shocking enough in normal circumstances, but so soon after David's death might just be unforgivable. On top of that even associating with, let alone hugging a Jew would certainly be frowned upon in certain quarters. She didn't care.

Harriet was clutching half a dozen pieces of paper surreptitiously handed to her by Sylvia Pankhurst. She felt her daughter tugging on her arm, to get her away before they were accosted, by the eagle-eyed policemen. Harriet would have much preferred to have stayed longer, talking to her new friend Sylvia.

An anxious, but elated Evelyn pushed her through the front door. Da had already taken himself to bed. What a relief. There would be no more confrontations that night. Evelyn took one of the leaflets off Harriet and began to read it aloud.

'REPEAL THE ACT

Fellow citizens

Conscription is now law in this land of free traditions. Our hard-won liberties have been violated. Conscription involves the subordination of civil liberties to military dictatorship. It imperils the freedom of individual conscience. It divides the people of all nations.

We cannot assist in warfare. War, which the people didn't seek, will only be made impossible when men and women stand true to their convictions.

We strongly condemn the monstrous assumption by Parliament that men are deemed to be bound by an oath that they have never taken.

Repeal the Act. It is your only safeguard.

If this is not done militarism will fasten its iron grip upon our national life and institutions. There will be imposed upon us the very system that our statesmen affirm that they set out to overthrow.

What shall it profit the nation if it should win the war but lose its soul?'

Harriet's, quietly, commented.

'Matthew sixteen.'

Evelyn stared at her mam as she continued.

'The last sentence is from Matthew chapter sixteen. I remember it.'

Evelyn was perplexed.

'But what does it mean? Will it bring Emrys home? It can't bring David home. That's really all that matters now.'

Harriet was confused enough herself without having to

explain it to her sixteen-year-old daughter. She tried her best.

'It's obviously not going to bring David back. More's the pity. It probably won't even bring Emrys home. The thing is though if someone like your friend Asher doesn't want to fight the Germans, then nobody should be able to order him to do so. The Act says that the Government can order him to fight. Even if you think Jesus doesn't want you to kill Germans, they say you have to. Miss Pankhurst and Mrs Powell think that's wrong. You know I think I do too.'

Evelyn struggled to find the right words.

'If they make Asher go to France and he helps bring Emrys home then that must be good. You know we could get into trouble if you get caught with these. Mam, we have enough problems already. We really have.'

Harriet knew that her daughter had had to grow up quickly over the past few days. She was incredibly proud of her. As much as she was of her boys. She was emotionally exhausted and said as she got up to go to bed.

'We'll think about tomorrow. It's just that if I can do anything to end this war I will do it. I don't want any other mams going through this. I really couldn't bare it.'

She felt her daughter's arms wrapping tightly around her. Evelyn whispered.

'You've got me. And Da. And Emrys. We'll do it together.'

The lorry was slowing, almost to a halt. In the back, Emrys could not see anything. He could smell the sea air and hear the shrieks of the seagulls above. He was on his way home. All he knew was that he was accompanying Captain Davies, back for his wedding. But why him? It wasn't his turn? Perhaps the captain had heard about David and was just being kind. It certainly would be in character.

The lorry finally ground to a halt and Emrys jumped down onto the quayside, next to a large ship. Strangely, it all looked surprisingly familiar. Then Emrys realized. He was in Boulogne. It was the same Boulogne that he had been to a few weeks previously. Hopefully, this time he would succeed in getting home.

Emrys was already, worrying about the prospect of another sea journey. He had had nightmares about the horrendous stormy trip over on the dilapidated paddle steamer, called The Maggie. It was not a name he would forget easily. Captain Davies began to speak.

'This place is called Boulogne.'

Emrys answer surprised the captain.

'Yes, sir. I've been here before. I was in the hospital up on the cliffs. I was there with Lieutenant Mond.'

Captain Davies belatedly recalled the trials and tribulations that Emrys had had to endure, caring for Henry Mond. He laid a gentle hand on Emrys' shoulder.

'At least this time you'll finally get home.'

Emrys was pleased to be woken by the early morning chill. They would arrive in Folkestone for the next leg of their journey in about an hour and he was awake before Captain Davies. Captain Davies appeared on deck soon afterwards for a cigarette and some fresh sea air, away from his cramped cabin. Emrys carefully lit the captain's cigarette as they both stared at the rapidly approaching cliffs of Southern England. It was almost a fantasy to be returning home, away from the stress and squalor. A fantasy especially for Captain Davies returning for his wedding and brief honeymoon.

Captain Davies reappeared from breakfast just as the ship was tying up under a monster-like steam crane, in Folkestone docks. Emrys had to decline the captain's offer to help with the bags. After all the sole reason that he was here, was to carry them. In the back of his mind he hoped that if he performed his duties well, Captain Davies might take him again the next time he had special leave.

The inevitable woman volunteer with her overburdened maid appeared with more tea, but also some cake. Whatever time of day it was, these women always seemed to provide a cake. Anyway, he was starving and could have happily eaten the whole plate.

Emrys listened to Captain Davies as he gave his next and deadly serious instruction. Pointing to a large clock tower at one end of an ornate two-storied Italianate building he said.

'This is important, private. We are not returning here on the train together. We will meet at seven in the evening, next Monday, underneath that clock. Do you understand? Seven in the evening next Monday. If you miss the boat we both might be shot, me figuratively and you actually. For God's sake don't be late.'

The two-hour journey to Charing Cross Station passed quickly, rolling through the pretty Kent countryside. Emrys was in Third Class having deposited Captain Davies in the palatial First. Third was fine, by him. The occupants of the carriage were to a man in a buoyant mood. They were all going home. Charing Cross, then Paddington and finally Briton Ferry. He couldn't wait.

Emrys had never been in a taxi. He was sitting next to the driver on the way to Paddington Station. A question, suddenly, came from the seat behind him.

'Are you looking for a promotion? Two stripes would look good on that shoulder.'

Emrys looked horrified. David had warned him that taking extra responsibility might mean more pay but also had risks attached to it. Maybe David should have heeded his own advice. He replied quickly.

'Definitely not, captain. I'm happy staying as one of the boys.'

Captain Davies laughed. This boy was only about eighteen and had yet to earn the respect of some of the older soldiers, despite his boxing prowess.

'First class to Aberystwyth. Change at Carmarthen for Aberystwyth, sir.'

The inspector looked with less interest at Emrys.

'Third class to Briton Ferry. No changes.'

They made their way to the first class carriage and Emrys started to haul the cases on board, whilst Captain Davies found his seat. He saluted the captain.

'Sir. Will you manage on your own at Carmarthen? I thought you would be going to Swansea.'

Captain Davies replied.

'The wedding is near Aberystwyth tomorrow. So I need to get there tonight. Thank goodness there haven't been any delays. Mrs Davies and I will be travelling back to Folkestone on our own. So are you sure that you will manage to get back on your own? It's just the opposite of what we did today.'

Emrys wished him good luck for the following day, before walking further up the platform to the overcrowded third-class carriage.

He excitedly looked out of the window as the train, trundled through Briton Ferry, hoping to catch a brief glimpse of home in the diminishing light. Then the train stopped and he was out of the carriage in the blink of an eye.

The front door was, as usual, unlocked and he walked through as if he had done so, just the day before. Inside there was a shrill scream. A tall young girl ran forward and jumped up at him clinging on tightly. He hardly recognized his sister. Behind her was his mam. She looked the same, except for a few wisps of grey in her hair. She looked so tired. She was trying hard but failing miserably to hold back the tears. In the corner, his da wheezed, as he got up to shake his son's hand. The tears quickly turned to laughter. They were all intent on these next few days being happy ones.

Emrys sat in his usual place at the table, with his mam next to him and sister opposite. Da, as expected, returned to the corner chair and lit a cigarette. Emrys's gaze stopped on the picture of the two brothers taken at camp in Rhyl, on the mantelpiece. It was decorated with black ribbon. Harriet noticed him looking.

'You saw him in France. Didn't you?'

Emrys realized that David must have written home about it.

'Well actually yes. Gwyn, Ted and I were in a place called Bethune. Who should be coming in the opposite direction but David? He took me out for lunch. Even paid for it. The last time I saw him was in the square in Bethune. He was smiling.

He was happy.'

He then took his three presents out of his rucksack. A packet of Woodbine for Da, some French chocolate for Evelyn and a tiny bracelet for Mam.

'It's from Bethune, Mam. Just along from where I met David. Think of it from both of us.'

Harriet hugged her son.

'Thank you, Emrys. You know I will never take it off. Never.'

The four of them talked into the small hours. They were careful not to discuss the war. Not tonight. Maybe Emrys would want to talk about it tomorrow. But not tonight. Instead, he told them of all the wonders he'd seen. Oxford. Salisbury Cathedral. The Druid Stones. The paddle steamer which made him sick as a dog. Evelyn listened in awe. There was a huge and exciting life outside Briton Ferry.

Emrys eventually wandered off to the bedroom which, in a former life, he had shared with David. Comfortable in bed for the first time in weeks, he quickly slipped into a deep, untroubled sleep.

He had slept so well that he overslept. By the time he woke his mother had already gone to her shift at Taylors. Whilst Mr Taylor might have given her some time off, Mr Newman was the manager and definitely wouldn't. So when Emrys entered the small back room, his da was sitting in the corner chair as if he hadn't moved since the previous evening. Evelyn was busy in the scullery, cooking eggs, from Asher Crocker's dairy. They were really pushing the boat out. Eggs for breakfast were an unheard-of rarity in this household.

Josiah lit another cigarette and offered one to his son. To his father's surprise, Emrys accepted it, lit it with a match and took a long satisfying drag. He explained.

'It's the only thing that soothes your nerves at the front.'

Emrys just wanted to rest. Maybe later he might wander around the town and see if any of his mates were there. Most of them, of course, would be away. He knew that Albert had been badly wounded, but was probably still in some military hospital, in England.

Evelyn had other ideas. Her brother might only be home for five more days but they were going to be action-packed. For today, they would go to Neath on the tram. Why they needed to was a good question. There was nothing in Neath, that they didn't have here in Briton Ferry. Evelyn took control.

'We need to be off soon. We won't have much time. Mam will kill me if you are not here when she gets back from work. She said to get your uniform off you to put to soak. She's put some of your old clothes out for you to wear.'

Ten minutes later he appeared fully dressed in his old clothes. They certainly felt and looked strange. The scrawny adolescent who had left had returned as a muscular young man. Evelyn looked enchanting in her Sunday best. Having given Da a brief kiss, they went out through the front door and happily walked down the road towards the tram stop.

They had had a lovely day. Emrys couldn't help but notice the sideways glances that his sister received from many of the men, both young and old. She herself seemed completely oblivious to it. She acted like she was. Still a young girl. Emrys was enjoying her company and doing what he had always done according to Mam. Spoil her. In the afternoon, Emrys decided that they needed to get home. As Evelyn had said there would be all hell to pay if they were not back before Mam got home.

Evelyn was looking in one last shop window. Emrys was fed up with shops. There was nothing to buy in them and, even if there had been, they had precious little money. Instead, he would wait for her in the busy square. He was in a world of his own, as a smartly dressed middle-aged woman walked towards him. He looked down as she pushed something into his hand. It was a small white feather. In an acidic voice, she screamed.

'You should be in uniform. A strong lad, like you. Your friends are over there getting killed while you are swanking around here with that pretty girl on your arm. Stop being a coward. Join up today.'

Emrys was still open-mouthed when Evelyn returned. She noticed his pale face immediately and asked.

'Is something wrong?

Emrys opened his palm and showed her the white feather. He pointed to the woman.

'I can't believe it. That bloody woman called me a coward.'

It is normally the elder brother who looks out for the younger sister. Not today. Without stopping to catch her breath, she stormed off towards the woman and grabbed her arm viciously.

'What do you think you're doing, you bloody bitch? Calling my brother a coward. He only got back from the front yesterday. I work in a munitions factory. Our brother was killed less than a month ago. You bloody bitch.'

She raised her other arm to strike the lady with her fist when Emrys grabbed her by the waist and pulled her away.

'My God. Where did you get that temper from? And the language. My Goodness. You sound as bad as an Aussie soldier.'

They began to walk towards the waiting tram when Evelyn turned, once more, to the woman and snarled.

'Bloody bitch.'

Emrys was laughing loudly.

'What would Mam say if she could hear you? Or the Reverend Hughes?'

Evelyn transformed back into a little girl from a belligerent tiger.

'You won't tell them will you?'

The following day was calmer for Emrys. The wonderful but exhausting Evelyn was at Taylors, while Harriet had Emrys to herself except for Josiah sitting in the corner. She hadn't blinked an eye when she heard that her son was now a smoker. Secretly she also suspected that he drank alcohol as well. And did she care? No. If it got him through to the end of the war, that was fine. Things that were so important just a few weeks ago were now unimportant.

She was itching to take her son to her favourite place, the woods rising high up the hill behind the house. Maybe there they could talk. As she had hoped, Josiah insisted on staying behind puffing on his cigarette.

Emrys suddenly understood what a clever woman his mam was and how funny. They laughed the whole time that they marched up the steep slope. An hour later they reached the clearing that Harriet loved so much. It was the place she went to when times were difficult and had never shared it with anyone before. Not even Josiah before his breathing had deteriorated. They sat down and Harriet opened an inevitable packet of cake. She had something to say.

'Evie told me what happened in Neath, yesterday.'

Emrys laughed.

'I bet she didn't tell you about how she reacted. I don't think the woman will ever recover from it. The trouble is, Mam, that nobody here really understands. You can't unless you've been there. I might tell some of it one day. Not now though.'

They just stopped and looked at the view for a few moments before he continued.

'I met a German once. Young boy, like me. Terrified out of his wits because Lieutenant Mond was questioning him. The thing was I really liked him. You know he wore a crucifix. He was a Christian. I just don't understand a thing these days. Sometimes I think that I should be playing football with him not shooting at him.'

He couldn't say any more. It would have been too painful. They walked quietly back to the house to find Josiah still in his corner chair, smoking another cigarette.

Emrys sat at the table to drink his cup of tea. Absentmindedly, he rummaged through a small pile of papers while Mam was busy. His eye stopped when he saw a plain brown leaflet. Bold print read REPEAL THE ACT. He picked it up and inquisitively questioned his da.

'Where did this come from, Da? Are you becoming a conchie?'

His father replied, smiling.

'No. It's your mam's. She goes to meetings every Thursday about it. At Jerusalem Chapel, as well. Evie goes too sometimes. Anti-conscription, anti-war, anti-everything as far as I can see.'

Emrys looked seriously at his da.

'Thing is Da. I think I agree with them.'

His father smiled again.

'Thing is Emrys. So do I. I had an idea. We hire the Cardiff

Arms Park and put all the generals and politicians, from both sides, on the pitch. Then we let them fight it out. We can sit in the stand and cheer. Then afterwards we can have a cup of tea with all the ordinary Germans. What do you think?'

Emrys chuckled.

'Brilliant, Da. And I will go around the stands selling carbonated water to the crowd. I'll make a small fortune. Next time I'm in London, I'll drop in on Mr Lloyd George and tell him.'

Harriet had returned to the room, delighted to see her husband and son getting on so well. She looked quizzically at Emrys regarding the carbonated water. Emrys explained.

'That's what I told Lieutenant Mond I was going to do after the war. Sell carbonated water. And that is definitely what I'm going to do. No tinplate works for me.'

Harriet was secretly elated that her son was thinking about after the war. She thought for a moment before speaking.

'We need a name for the company and I think I have one. Our boys back from the front.'

Emrys had half-expected disbelief and disdain. But he had received the opposite. Hugging his mam he said.

'Wouldn't fit on the bottles. But Our Boys would. We'll call it Our Boys.'

Harriet took the opportunity to ask Emrys an important question.

'Emrys. Do you mind if I try to get the war to finish early? I know little me can't do much. But if I can help a bit I want to do it. I will stop if you say so.'

Emrys smiled at his mam. He had seen so much more of the world than she had, but she was so much worldlier.

'Mam, if you can shorten the war by two seconds then I'm all for it. Only don't take any risks. I don't want to come back to a destitute household.'

Harriet only realized then that her little boy had gone forever. He had been replaced by a grown man.

The rest of the few days passed in a beautiful flash. So much fun and laughter, but also so much sadness. David always seemed to be present. Emrys went up to see M.G. Roberts in the big house. M.G. Roberts was still enthusiastic about the war and how it was soon going to end in victory. Emrys kept quiet.

Mam was only slightly disappointed when Emrys decided not to go to Rehoboth on Sunday morning. He said that he wasn't up to all the questions and all the people saying sorry for his loss. In truth, his faith of two years ago had disappeared on the track to La Trou.

Harriet and Evie walked, once more, up the road, this time accompanying Emrys to the train station. Harriet had promised Josiah that there would be no tears. Again, it was a promise she knew she wouldn't be able to keep and all three of them ended up blubbering on the platform. Emrys watched his mother and sister fade into the distance as the train gained speed. Next to him lay a huge pile of food, from Mam, some cigarettes from Da and some more socks from his sister.

That was the difficult part of the journey back to France over with. The rest was surprisingly easy. Captain Davies' concerns over his capability to negotiate the journey were proven to be totally unfounded. At ten to seven in the evening, he was walking towards the Clock Tower on Folkestone dockside. With her back to him stood a thin lady in an inappropriately beautiful blue dress, with a matching hat. Emrys enquired.

'Mrs Davies?'

There was no response. Emrys tried once more.

'Mrs Davies?'

The lady turned round with a radiant look on her face.

'Oh goodness. I'm sorry. I'm just not used to being called that yet.'

She turned towards a figure in uniform queuing at a desk beneath the clock tower and shouted.

'Percy. Percy. He's here. He's made it.'

She looked at Emrys and laughed.

'He's been worried about you all day. I've told him he worries too much. Now, I've got something important for you to do for me. When you get back over there you make sure you look after him.'

Emrys dissolved into the background, aware that these were the last few moments of the Davies' brief honeymoon. The lovely Mrs Davies would soon be returning to her hotel room on her own, having just sent her new husband back to war. She would watch the ship disappear from the port, waving furiously, but secretly wondering whether she would ever see her husband of five days again.

Captain Davies and Emrys silently stood on the upper deck, watching Folkestone disappearing into the distance. Eventually, Captain Davies took a slug of whiskey from his hip flask and said.

'Well, that's that then.'

11

November 1916

Whilst Emrys's leave had been wonderful and a blessing, for Harriet it had also been unsettling. On the one hand, she wanted to support her son and would continue with her contribution to the war effort. On the other, for David's sake, she knew that she had to do what she could to end this dreadful war. Occasionally at Rehoboth, she even felt like walking out. She could not stand it when anyone pontificated about the war. She had seen and understood the look in Emrys's eyes when they had been sitting together in the forest clearing. He had been correct. Nobody had the right to give their opinion unless they had been there.

The next big event was fast approaching and Harriet was dreading it. The Briton Ferry at the Front Committee, comprising of all the great and good, was giving commemorative watches to the widows or mothers of the so-called fallen. The recent battle around the town of Albert had been particularly costly and there would certainly need to be a lot of watches bought.

When the invitation arrived it had been disposed of straight in the bin. With infinite patience, Evelyn had fished it out. She had secretly written back and began working on her mother to attend. To not do so would look ungrateful. The watch would replace the one that Josiah had given to David.

Eleven sad women lined up in a neat row in the icy town hall. Six mothers, four wives and one sister. A smattering of well-wishers faced them in the audience. Evelyn was feeling very nervous. She knew her mother had not wanted to come. She hadn't wanted to share her grief with strangers.

Harriet was also aware that, the previous week, there had been a presentation to some of the boys back from the front by Mr Eccles, the committee chairman. She was secretly ashamed that she felt slighted by this presentation. These poor bereaved women only seemed to merit the deputy chairman, Mr H.A. Clarke.

The women waited in silence for the appearance of the members of the committee. They were the factory owners and town councillors together with their overdressed wives. Thank God that neither M.G. Roberts nor Mr Taylor was amongst them. They had been good to her. She would really hate to embarrass them.

She had insisted on still wearing black. In fact, it was her only presentable dress but anyway today black seemed to be appropriate. They had been told that this was a celebration of the soldiers' lives but it didn't seem so to Harriet.

Harriet waited patiently fifth in line. She began to feel guilty about what she was planning. The other women were bowing their heads respectfully to the dignitaries and thanking them for their watches. They arrived in front of Harriet, smiling. The clerk boomed out.

'David Benjamin John. Sergeant. Fourteenth Battalion Royal Welsh Fusiliers. Killed in action. France. July tenth 1916.'

Mr Clarke turned to the lady beside him and took the box

166

containing the soldier's watch off her. Harriet hesitated before she interrupted, raising her voice for everyone to hear.

'Mr. Clarke. I am sorry if you think me rude. I'm sorry if I seem ungrateful. I know you all mean well. Your watch won't bring our David back. He's gone forever. It won't even bring my Emrys back. We should be putting all our money and all our efforts into bringing all our poor boys home.'

There was a shout from a lady sitting near Josiah, whose daughter Harriet knew was a nurse in France.

'And girls.'

Encouraged, Harriet continued.

'Aye. Boys and girls. We must put all our efforts into ending this dreadful war and bringing them home. Too many rich people are becoming richer because of the suffering of the working people and the deaths of people, like my David.'

Harriet turned and ran out of the side door quickly followed by a startled Evie. Josiah was left sitting, wheezing, and feeling self-conscious on his own. The response inside the hall initially of stunned silence was quickly replaced by a strange combination of applause and boos. The reaction to Harriet's outburst just illustrated perfectly the differences of opinion within the town and indeed the whole country.

Evie reached her mother outside. Harriet was sitting on a wall, hyperventilating with anxiety. What had she just done? She had never, previously, done anything remotely militant. She had certainly never been seen to be disrespectful to her betters. Evie put her arm around her mother and whispered quietly.

'Well done, Mam. That was brilliant. You should have seen the look on Mrs Clarke's face. I thought she was going to hit you. Look. I shouldn't have made you come.'

Harriet looked at Evelyn through her tears.

'Yes, you should. You are proud of your brothers. You wanted it recognised. I'm just sorry if I spoiled it for you.'

The two women sat quietly waiting for Harriet to compose herself before Evelyn asked.

'Mam. What's a Bolshevik? Mr Jones shouted out that you were a bloody Bolshevik.'

Harriet was already worrying about the effect all this might have on her family. Despite her good looks and vivacious personality, Evie could sometimes be very vulnerable. Harriet held Evie's hand and looked into her eyes.

'I'm truly sorry, Evie. I know this is difficult for you. I just couldn't bare it if Emrys was killed too. It would be my fault. I could have stopped him.'

Evie put her arm back around her mother and they both slowly walked back down the road towards home.

The atmosphere, in the house, could be cut with one of Harriet's exquisitely sharpened knives. Josiah was giving the two women the silent treatment. You just didn't talk like that to one of the bosses. Not only was it discourteous but, more importantly, these things tended to come back and bite you when you least expected it. Whilst Josiah possibly admired his wife's stand, Harriet knew he wouldn't say so. He would rightly have concerns about how this might affect their family. After many years of struggle, they had, at last, got back on their feet. Then the devastating blow of David's death had come. They wouldn't be able to stand anything more. It wasn't worth risking.

Why hadn't she talked to him about it first? Of course, he must know. She had realized he would try to talk her out of it.

Harriet could stand it no more. She got up and marched out of the door leaving Evie glaring at her father.

Harriet knew immediately where she was going. There was little point seeking solace with the Reverend Hughes. He wouldn't be impressed with Harriet's mutinous actions earlier. It would reflect poorly on both himself and the rest of his congregation. Instead, she would search out Elizabeth Powell or even her husband, the Reverend Powell.

Harriet knew that Jerusalem Chapel would be closed and soon found herself in Cwrt Sart Terrace searching for the Powells' house. She had never been there before and didn't know in which of the neat terrace houses they lived. Knocking on the wrong door could prove disastrous in the circumstances. Harriet swallowed hard. Thank God. She saw Elizabeth Powell marching down the road towards her. Elizabeth smiled at her and spoke gently.

'We wondered whether we would be seeing you.'

Harriet laughed.

'You've heard. How did you hear? It only happened a couple of hours ago.'

Elizabeth laughed too.

'Why are you so surprised? You have lived here long enough. You can't keep anything secret here. I expect it took no more than ten minutes to reach me. Anyway, you could do with a cup of tea.'

Harriet was ushered through a nearby front door and into the back room, where Elizabeth's husband was reading his Bible. He looked up as she came in.

'Look who we have here. The person all the talk is about. The new heroine of our cause. You look as if you need a cup of tea.'

To Harriet's surprise, he stood up and went into the scullery where she could see him filling the kettle and beginning to prepare the teapot. That was definitely a woman's work in her household. Elizabeth sat her down and said exactly nothing. She knew that Harriet was holding everything in and it needed to come out.

It all then came out in a gush. Years ago Josiah had been the strong one making all the decisions. Not now. He had receded into the background leaving her to take all the responsibility. She had to be the one supporting him and Evelyn when David died. It was just like when baby Mary had died from measles. She had never really been allowed to grieve, herself. Even Rehoboth, for all its virtues, was more interested in the children than her. She just talked and talked and cried and cried, while the Reverend crept in with the cup of tea and then out again. Elizabeth still said nothing.

Eventually, Harriet ground to a halt stunned by how much she had revealed. Blushing, she said.

'I only came to see if you had any more leaflets to hand out. Now all I've done is cry.'

Elizabeth Powell smiled and at last, spoke.

'Harriet. You are an incredibly strong woman who has been climbing a mountain for years. We all admire you for the courage you have shown today. Of course, I will give you some leaflets. But I will also counsel you. Be careful. Think of all the repercussions of any actions you take. Think of the effect they may have on your family.'

Half an hour later Harriet was walking through her front door in a far calmer mood. Evelyn got to her feet and ran to her mother, handing over a piece of paper. She excitedly exclaimed.

'Mam. It's from Emrys. You weren't here, so we opened it'

France 14/11/16

Dear Mam,

Many thanks for the letter, which I received today. I was pleased to hear that Evie didn't have such a bad time on 5th of November. I should have really liked to have been there too and to have seen you all. We did not have such a bad time on the 5th. We seen quite a lot of fireworks but the worst of our fireworks is that if a stray one happens to catch you across the nut, you would not have much of a chance of seeing the end of the show. So Evie is not the only one to have fun that night.

Thanks very much for the chocolates and candles, which I received in the parcel. It was very thoughtful of Aunt Mary to suggest putting them candles in. They will come in very handy at night when we go out to kill. I don't mean Fritz this time, I mean rats and lice. I am sure things must be looking very strange in the Ferry, now they have to put all the lights out, by eight. I have never seen a lamp in the street lit out here. In fact, I have never seen a lamppost. I don't know how people manage in peacetime.

I will conclude now with love to Da and Evelyn. Your loving son Emrys xxxxxx

It was always lovely but had become worrying to receive a letter from Emrys. David had always written in such a clinical way to subtly dampen any fears. Emrys just told it as it was, rats, lice, fireworks landing on your nut and all. Still, it was nice to know that he was safe. At least, he had been safe on the 14th. Walking back home, Harriet had been considering the few words that Elizabeth Powell had said. Perhaps any paltry actions that she would be able to take would be so futile and the effects on her family might be so damaging. She had decided to toe the line. She would work hard at Taylors, keep her big mouth shut and pray hard that Emrys would come home in one piece.

Now, she was in turmoil once more. Why should her wonderful son put up with rats and all sorts of things? Why should he be in danger just because of the whim of politicians and the orders of some general? Those generals, whom neither of her sons had any time for. Except for some General Elliott, who Emrys had kept on about and said was his friend. As she got into bed next to Josiah, that night, she knew she would not sleep. She had too much on her mind.

She had thought deeply for two days about her plans. She knew that two men had been arrested and given sentences of hard labour, for distributing the very pamphlets that she had secreted away in her large bag. She had read both leaflets thoroughly time and time again. She knew that the first one was the one that had really caused concerns for the Authorities. It was cleverly phrased, by the anonymous writer, to cause maximum controversy. Anyone distributing it would be courting serious trouble.

The other pamphlet interested her much more.

An early conscience objector.

In the year of Our Lord 295, a young man called Maximilian turned the age of twenty-one. That was the age that he was compelled to join the Roman army. He would have to wear the tablet around his neck that professed his total loyalty to the Emperor, forsaking all others.

The recruiting officer threatened him. Maximilian said to the recruiting officer.

'I cannot fight.

I cannot do evil.

I cannot engage in earthly warfare.

I am God's soldier.'

The recruiting officer said.

'You must serve or die.'

Maximilian replied.

'I will never serve. You can cut off my head, but I will never be a soldier of this world as I'm a Soldier of Christ. My army is the army of God. I tell you I'm a Christian. You will say to me that other Christians serve and I will reply that that is their business.'

The recruiting officer said.

'If you don't serve I will condemn you to death.'

Maximilian said.

'I will not die. If I go from this place, I will live with Jesus, My Lord.'

Maximilian knelt on the floor and with one stroke the recruiting officer smote his head off.

Maximilian's views nicely mirrored her own. Surely nobody could object. Without telling either Josiah or Evelyn, she wandered the few hundred yards to St Clements's Church. Like both Jerusalem and Rehoboth Chapels it was next to the main road but was a far more prestigious building. Only built about sixty years previously it had large, imposing windows.

Harriet had never been in the church itself and didn't intend to do so now. She knew that there would be lots of people milling around outside, at midday after the service. They would be Christian people as well.

She stood on the pavement just outside the church gate. When Garnet Waters and William Davies were arrested here a few months previously, they had actually been on the church grounds. Josiah had laughed about how stupid they had been. They had not been handing out a Christian pamphlet. What she was doing was surely different. Nobody could object. In the back of her mind, however, she remembered that both of them had received a sentence of one month's hard labour.

She stood outside handing out pamphlets to the occasional passer-by. The first person glanced at her, smiled and put it in his pocket. The second made a great show of tearing it up. The third refused to take it and growled.

'You should be ashamed of yourself. You should be supporting the boys not undermining them.'

At that moment, the doors of St. Clements Church flew open and organ music could be heard booming out from inside. The Reverend Jones was shaking hands with each of his congregation as they queued to leave. Harriet considered how similar but so different it was to Rehoboth. As people milled around the gate and Grandison Street beyond, Harriet walked amongst them talking freely and offering pamphlets.

She was well known and everyone seemed to know about her loss at Mametz Wood. She felt guilty that she was being treated sympathetically simply because of David's death. She knew that she might have been dealt with far more harshly otherwise. The people were actually pleasant. Some were arguing with her of course. They simply disagreed.

Suddenly, her arms were grabbed tightly and pinned to her side. She turned to face the two police constables who were holding her. Very politely one of them said.

'I am arresting you as you are in contravention of The Defence of the Realm Act 1914. Please come with me.'

There was a faint round of applause as she was led away. Perhaps in retrospect, St Clements Church was not the most sensible place to make her demonstration. The police station was less than fifty yards away.

A few moments later she was pushed through the front door and deposited into a small room containing just a plain oak table. Nothing further was said. The only communication had been the initial one outside the church. Contravention of the Defence of the Realm Act. It sounded so serious. She had never previously even dreamt of having dealings with the law. She could only wait in agonizing trepidation. What would Josiah say? What would Reverend Hughes say?

After a few lonely minutes, the door flew open. The last person she wanted to see marched in. Inspector Hugh Morris. Not only was he a high-ranking police officer but a lay reader and deacon at Rehoboth. He was a large man with imposing shoulders. His jet-black beard bristled as he stared furiously at Harriet and snarled.

'You have brought disgrace on the chapel. You have brought disgrace on your family including David. And now I'm going to have to stick my neck out to help you.'

He produced the leaflets which had been taken off Harriet and placed them in an ashtray on the table. He then made a theatrical show of lighting a match and gleefully lit the few remaining pieces of brown paper. Harriet began to cough but

Inspector Morris didn't even notice the smoke. He watched the last embers extinguish themselves and then painfully grabbed her arm. Seconds later she was being manhandled down the road towards her home.

Inspector Morris pushed Harriet through the unlocked door and into the back room. Josiah and Evelyn sat stunned as the inspector brandished the last remaining pamphlet. He shouted angrily, his red face held a few inches from Josiah's.

'Josiah. I suggest you keep control of your wife in the future. She's been handing out these blasphemous things. If she wasn't a member of the chapel, whose good name I will do almost anything to protect, she would be looking at a criminal record and a large fine. Of all the places to do it. St. Clements. Reverend Jones has had enough of it I can tell you. Next time I won't be able to help. Josiah, get that belt off and teach her who is the boss in this house. Then maybe there won't be a next time.'

Inspector Morris stormed out the way he had come. Josiah, Evelyn and Harriet gazing after him. For once, Josiah was the first to react and it was a very surprising reaction. He began to laugh.

'In God's name, Harriet, what have you got yourself into now? And don't look so frightened. I've never laid a finger on you and I'm not going to start now. Certainly not at the say of that pompous idiot. The only thing I'm cross about is that you didn't feel you could talk to us.'

Josiah put his arm around her as she whispered.

'I thought you would tell me not to do it.'

Josiah laughed again.

'Absolutely right. I would have definitely stopped you from

going to St Clements. I'd have told you to go to Salem Chapel or even the Catholic Church, in Neath, before St Clements. I could have told you that you'd have problems with that Reverend Jones. Morris was at least right about him. He's done it before and given the chance he'll do it again, I dare say. Now, Evelyn, make your mother a cup of tea while I give her another hug. She looks as if she could do with both.'

The next day, Harriet and her daughter were walking through the entrance to Taylors for their next shift. She had been conscious of people looking at her. Everyone must know what had happened the previous day and would be talking about it. At least she was paranoid that they were. They would be saying how incongruous it was that she was objecting to the war while she and her young daughter earned good money, making shells. How two-faced was that?

Mr Newman was waiting for them. He ushered Evelyn into the factory, patting her lower back with a hand suspiciously close to her buttocks. At the same time, he snarled at Harriet.

'Boss's Office. Now.'

Harriet made her way slowly to Mr Taylor's small office. Before the war, the office had been much more palatial, but now every inch of space was being used.

Harriet felt guilty. She liked Mr Glen Taylor. He had been good to her. She still felt fortunate and grateful that he had taken Evelyn on, even though her daughter had paid him back handsomely. Despite Mr Newman's unwanted attention, Evelyn had proved herself a real asset to the company. Harriet knew what was coming. She only hoped that it wouldn't involve Evelyn. Mr Taylor stood grimly behind his desk. He was almost sympathetic as he spoke.

'Harriet. I have been contacted by Reverend Jones about what you did outside his church. Several other works owners have talked to me as well. I'm afraid I'm going to have to let you go. I can't have you working here anymore. I'm sorry. I know how difficult it's been after David.'

Harriet was about to ask about Evelyn when there was a knock on the door. Without waiting for a reply in walked a man from the shop floor whom she was barely on nodding terms with. His wife Jane Evans, however, she knew well. Jane worked for M.G. Roberts. Tom Evans began talking confidently. He seemed to have been in this position before.

'Mr Taylor. You shouldn't have been talking to this worker on her own. With respect, we all know what went on yesterday but that was outside work. You have no right to take any action against her.'

Glen Taylor replied succinctly. Tom Evans seemed to be a problem that he had had to deal with before.

'Look, Tom. I can't have a war objector working in a munitions factory.'

Tom Evans looked sternly back.

'Mr Taylor. She is an exemplary worker. She has done nothing wrong. If you dismiss her the workers will need to take action.'

Mr Taylor was now beginning to get angry.

'Tom. You know the Munitions of War Act 1915 prohibits you from striking.'

The conversation was becoming heated. Tom Evans didn't like being threatened and said so.

'There are other actions which we can take that will still make life most uncomfortable for you.'

It was gradually becoming a furious shouting match. It,

undoubtedly, would need the calm temper of a woman to intervene. Harriet interrupted.

'Look, Mr Taylor. I am truly sorry that you have been pulled into this. I certainly don't want to cause problems between you and Mr Evans. If you let me stay I will work hard for you. If I am going to do anything else like yesterday, I promise to tell you first and if you want I'll leave.'

Tom Evans joined in.

'That seems more than fair, Mr Taylor. Let's just call it a final warning.'

Glen Taylor was, by nature, a non-confrontational man who was just delighted to simply be able to smooth everything over. Reverend Jones and a few others might think him weak, but he didn't see it that way. He looked at it as being compassionate. He spoke with a relieved voice.

'Right. Very last warning. Now back to work both of you. I'm not paying you to stand around chatting.'

The two workers returned to the factory floor past Mr Newman. He had been confident that he had seen the last of Harriet, who always seemed to be hovering close by whenever he got anywhere near the beautiful, young Evelyn. As she took her place at the conveyer belt Harriet mouthed a thank you to Tom Evans. He replied with an exaggerated wink.

Emrys was having a difficult time in France and not just from the feelings of his own mortality, brought on by his brother's death. The new ambitious battalion commander, Major Watson, was the problem. Like Lieutenant Mond, he needed to be leading the charge from the front and that wouldn't happen with these easy-going cyclists.

Normally this wouldn't be a problem for ordinary soldiers like Emrys and his friends. Unfortunately, they discovered, all too soon, that the major's solution was to race around just behind the front line in the sidecar of a motorbike. He seemed to be spying on them. Not only did he attract the attention of the enemy artillery but he had the tendency to suddenly jump out when a group of cyclists had stopped to have a quick cigarette. As Gwyn put it, he could stand the Whizzbangs, but the major suddenly appearing was driving him crazy.

Things were no better when they were back at their base headquarters. The only difference was Major Watson's mode of transport. Somehow the major had managed to swap two of their much-needed transport horses for two fine, but useless cavalry mounts. The officers would spend many hours riding joyfully between the widely spaced groups of soldiers and then finding complaints about something.

To make matters worse, whilst the men were stuck in leaking tents, they knew that the officers were comfortably ensconced in a bright freshly whitewashed farmhouse. A farmhouse complete with an attentive farmer's wife and an even more attentive daughter. They would walk past the nice little stable housing the two horses. The horses had infinitely better accommodation than the men.

Emrys had a solution, which would come as a surprise to everyone. They would become machine gunners. It was such a surprise because David, of course, had always been very definite about him not volunteering to be one. True the pay rate would be a welcome three pence a day more. You were not paid for doing nothing, however. It was well known that the risk was much higher. They all knew that the safest thing was to just be an ordinary soldier and not take on a special skill, such as a bomber or machine gunner. Even if they stayed poor.

Emrys had met a corporal on the train back to Folkestone and they had got chatting. Emrys had been moaning about not going home again for an age. The corporal, however, had no such worries. He was going to join the Royal Flying Corps as a machine gunner. After every twenty-four hours flying you got two weeks of home leave.

What could be simpler? Regular home leave, out of the mud and even better out of the enveloping clutches of Major Watson. Glyn and Ted were dubious. Emrys always had plans and schemes but they often seemed to inadvertently get them either into trouble or danger. They would think about it. Emrys stormed off in a temper. He was cold and wet. His trip home, which was now fading into the past, had made him just miss home even more. His answer was simply to write another letter.

France

Dear Mam

Thanks for the letter which I received safely today along with the chocolate and the rest. We have been having some very bad weather over here now, nothing but rain from morn to night, these last few days. If it will keep up till Christmas, I see us having a fine time. I'm afraid there's not much hope of us getting home for Christmas. Things have not been going as good as what we expected them to. They are not going to send any more chaps from our company until the 16th. So by the time our turn will come around the New Year will be well in. It will probably be Easter before I to go up and wish M G Roberts a happy new year.

As you know we have not got too much time for writing. We are up in the trenches six days out of seven and the day we have off we generally use for cleaning up, so you see we have got all our work cut out.

I think I will dry up now. I have nothing special to report this time. Everything is very much the same with us. The war is still on and (I think) we are winning and all the rest of it, you know. Thank Evie for the mittens. It is definitely a nice change from socks. It is lovely to have such a thoughtful sister. Love to you, Da and Evie. Emrys XXXXXXX

Harriet read the letter for the tenth time as she prepared to go out to her regular Thursday night meeting which was normally at Jerusalem Chapel. It had become such a regular occasion that the gossip had moved on to some other pointless topic of conversation. The fact that Mrs Eynon had stopped talking to her at all could even be perceived as a blessing, rather than a detriment.

She knew that she would take her regular place next to her strange new friend Ruth Reuben. The difference tonight was that this was at the town hall. It was likely to be a noisy affair and tempers could be frayed, in this so-called Peace Meeting. She was going to be careful. Even so, Josiah had forbidden Evelyn from accompanying her. For one of the family's bread-winners to be courting controversy was one thing. To have both of them could be perceived as foolish.

Harriet arrived at the front door of the town hall early and was surprised to see how many people were already pushing their way in. No longer would she sidle in at the back. This time she was delighted to see that her new friend Ruth Reuben had managed to reserve a seat for her in the very front row of the expectant crowd. She had been worried that she would be packed in at the back, with all the baying, sweating men who had just come off a shift at the steelworks.

She and Ruth were an unlikely pair. Religion was important to both of them, but their religions were different. Ruth wanted to get back to her homeland whilst all Harriet wanted was her son back. Ruth always insisted that they kissed each other, on each cheek, as a sign of friendship. Harriet, irrationally felt awkward, especially when those around them laughed. Tonight she didn't care, as they began chattered about what the evening might bring.

The evening would be controversial. The speaker was Mrs Ethel Snowden, wife of MP Phillip Snowden, proposing a lasting and honourable peace. Harriet mused how petite and stunningly beautiful this lady, sitting quietly at the front, was. Harriet could not believe that this famous firebrand, who had previously lectured all over America, was in her little town.

The evening started badly. There was a massive audience so different to the sedate gatherings in Jerusalem Chapel. There were so many people that there was ill-tempered jostling to get in. Not a good start. At last, Harriet watched as the doors were forced shut. She could hear the crowds locked outside screaming angrily. Definitely not a good start.

A tense atmosphere prevailed, as Elizabeth Powell rose to introduce the speaker. That atmosphere only increased as the diminutive Mrs Snowden also got to her feet and began. Her turns of phrase were immediately electrifying. She was an eloquent, experienced public speaker compared with the street fighter, Sylvia Pankhurst.

'I have read enough history to prove to me the folly of war. All of this has never clouded my appreciation of the fact that war may be evil and yet by reason of vicious policies and agreements over a number of years, become the lesser of two evils for many good women and men.

I have never tried to influence the judgement of the young man called upon to fight. If he is purely motivated, he is entirely honourable, whether he chooses prison or the front.'

Harriet became mesmerized as the speaker continued.

'The young men have gone to fight for a thing that I believe cannot be achieved by fighting. But as a woman, who cannot be called upon to go into the trenches, it is peculiarly my business to seek to end this war as soon as possible. End it for the sake of the gallant lads who had no choice, consistent with their sense of duty.'

The first indications to Harriet that trouble was about to begin were the angry murmurs from the back punctuated by a single shout of 'traitor'. Ethel Snowden looked up but continued speaking serenely almost without taking a breath. She must have been in this exact situation many times before. It was, perhaps, predictable in this volatile little town. Grim men and scowling women screamed to make their voices heard.

Suddenly, everyone rose to their feet and began pushing forward towards the speaker. This was becoming dangerous. Somebody was going to get hurt in the crush. Harriet pulled Ruth towards the little used door at the back of the hall.

What a sensible decision that seemed to be. But no. Looking up, she belatedly realized that she had pulled them straight into the path of the tide of angry objectors. In fact, they were directly in front of Ethel Snowden herself. They were in effect acting as her bodyguards just as the sea of aggression was about to hit her. Confusion led to panic and panic inevitably to violence. A flying fist caught Harriet on the cheekbone whilst an accidental elbow caught Ruth on the eyebrow.

Panicking themselves, they pulled each other roughly towards the rear door, desperately seeking an escape from the terrifying danger. Harriet felt her dress sleeve rip as they propelled themselves precipitously through the door to welcome safety. She slammed the door shut behind them.

They took a few seconds to catch their breath. Harriet already had swelling coming up on her cheek while Ruth had blood dripping from a small cut above her left eye. It was a true boxer's cut. It was only then that they realized that there were more than two of them. They had not been pulling each other. Inadvertently they had each been tugging on an arm of Ethel Snowden. Whilst Harriet had a ripped dress and a bruised face and Ruth looked like some defeated prize fighter, Mrs Snowden didn't have a hair out of place. She looked as well manicured then as when she had gone for lunch at the White House in Washington.

Harriet looked from Ruth, whose blood was seeping down the side of her face, staining her white dress, to the immaculate Mrs Snowden. She began to laugh. Ruth looked shocked. Then she could do nothing but join in. The MP's wife cried out.

'What in God's name is so funny? I could have been killed in there.'

Ruth chuckled in her thick Belgian accent.

'It's just we look so ridiculous. I didn't get a scratch getting out of Belgium. Now, look at me.'

Mrs Snowden was worried about what on earth they should

do next. They certainly couldn't go back into the hall. She was the one who normally took charge. Not tonight. Even in the presence of this famous woman, Harriet seemed determined to take control. She could see how shaken the lady standing in the dark behind the hall truly was.

In front of them lay a large expanse of parkland and that was where Harriet was going to take them. She was going to guide the three of them to the large house two hundred yards away across the pitch-black park. Emrys had been right. The Ferry did look strange without street lights switched on.

Harriet carefully led the two other women across the muddy grass. Despite the dark, this was a journey Harriet knew well. She had made it on many occasions. Normally, Mrs Snowden would undoubtedly be worried about the state of her shoes but not this time. She was just glad that this woman was taking her away from the bedlam that could still be heard in the hall behind them.

They found the driveway that stretched up from the main road through the park to the large sparsely lit house. From there it was only a short walk around the back of the house, past some sinister Greek statues towards the two doors to the house. Harriet automatically made for the door she was accustomed to. The tradesman's entrance. Then she thought better of it. Surely Mrs Snowden was of sufficient stature to deserve the front door. Harriet was certain that the owner of Bay View, M.G. Roberts, would see it that way.

She banged hard on the brass door knocker, secretly praying that M.G. Roberts was in.

A chink of light appeared as the door was cautiously opened. Peering out through the narrow crack was Mrs Jane Evans, the housekeeper. She recognized Harriet, of course, but was taken aback by the lady in the fine clothes and the other lady bleeding profusely. All she could utter was.

'Harriet. What on earth has happened?'

Harriet had no time for niceties.

'Jane. Is M.G. Roberts's home? We need to speak to him urgently. We need to speak to him now.'

Jane was aware of all the problems that Harriet had had over the previous months. She was, after all, married to Tom Evans who had helped Harriet at Taylors. She was, however, worried about what her accommodating but fiercely pro-war boss would say.

She whispered 'Wait a minute', before shutting the door firmly.

A few moments later, M G Roberts appeared. Despite liking Harriet, he would have nothing to do with anti-war activities and was about to say so. His eye then fell on the dainty figure standing to one side. Once seen the exquisitely beautiful Ethel Snowden was not easily forgotten. M G Roberts had seen her before and definitely not forgotten. Smiling now, he said.

'Mrs Snowden. We met in Westminster last year. I had a meeting with Phillip and you were present. Please come in immediately.'

He turned to Jane Evans, before continuing.

'Jane. I'll show Mrs Snowden into the Drawing Room. Can you take Harriet and this other lady to the kitchen and sort them out? You may need to call Dr Murphy.'

Jane Evans was now in her element. She knew that Tom liked Harriet and it would have hurt her deeply if she had had to turn her away. She had a large number of active children and lots of experience with cuts and bruises. The Jewish lady just had a small cut, but in an area which always bled profusely. There was nothing that Dr Murphy could do that she couldn't. The answer was simple. A clean dressing and some pressure, while Harriet looked on. The cook had been in the middle of cooking dinner for M.G. Roberts. That would have to wait.

Harriet had been in this kitchen many times. It was about as modern as you could get in South Wales. There was no old Victorian kitchen for M.G. Roberts. That was despite the fact that he was rarely seen there and Mrs Roberts had died a dozen years previously. The daughters came in sometimes but less so now that they had grown up. This was the domain of Jane Evans and cook, with the help of a legion of occasional help, such as Harriet.

M.G. Roberts was indeed so rarely seen there, that Harriet was surprised when he walked through the door that evening. He was of course just following Ethel Snowden, who having rapidly recovered, was insistent on attending to the welfare of her two erstwhile rescuers. M.G. Roberts quickly discovered that Mrs Snowden was not someone you could say no to. She turned to M.G. Roberts while pointing to Harriet's face.

'Have you any raw steak to put on that?'

Harriet couldn't believe her ears. Wasting expensive meat. Meat that she could not even dream of being able to buy to feed Josiah. She was even more surprised when the cook actually appeared with a large slab of succulent beef and Mrs Snowden pressed it firmly against her cheek. Mrs Snowden then turned her attention to Ruth. Interfering with Jane Evans's excellent treatment, she immediately told M.G. Roberts that a doctor was needed. After all a cut like that, despite being small, would surely scar.

Ruth was having none of it. Jane's ministrations had been magically effective and Ruth was starting to get a headache. All she needed was to get home to her husband and her bed.

Mrs Snowden was then, of course, insistent that the two heroines were in no fit state to make their own way home in the dark. M.G. Roberts would have to insist on Ivor getting the car out. So, Harriet found herself, passenger, in a private car for the very first time in her life, bizarrely holding some steak to her face.

They dropped Ruth off first, at her cricket pavilion home, and then needed to pass the town hall to reach, 11 Neath Road. Ivor drove carefully. The anger of earlier had still not abated. Shouts could be heard from the doorway. Arguing men and women were spilling out onto the pavement. Harriet wondered whether they had, even, missed Mrs Snowden.

Harriet walked into their back room. Josiah immediately stood and breathlessly ran over to her.

'What's happened to your face? Where have you been? We expected you home hours ago.'

Harriet produced the large piece of beef from her side and said.

'I've been to the butchers.'

12

Northern France

Emrys could tell that Gwyn was elated. Predictably, Emrys had got his own way and they were again party to one of his madcap ideas. They had become Lewis gunners. Finally, Gwyn had found something that he was good at. His ability was in dismantling and repairing the bloody things. So, when one of the buggers jammed, it was invariably brought to him.

Emrys also noticed that whenever he brought up joining the Air Corps, his friend changed the subject. Eventually, he could stand it no longer. Gwyn was patiently sitting, with a Lewis gun spanner in his hand, when Emrys approached him.

'Gwyn, mate. You don't fancy flying, do you?'

A look of relief spread over Gwyn's face as he replied.

'Can't stand heights, mate. I'm sure I would just throw up. I'm just better off with two feet firmly on the ground.'

Emrys could see that his friend was making a wise choice. He had just been too embarrassed to say.

'It's the right decision, Gwyn. I'm sure it is. It's just we'll miss you, mate. I mean you're a pain in the arse most of the time but I'll still miss you.'

Gwyn looked sad when Emrys and Ted submitted their written applications to Captain Wiggins, the Adjutant. Wheels turned slowly in the cyclists and they knew that they wouldn't hear anything for some time.

They were, in the meantime, pleased to receive three pieces of excellent news. Firstly, Captain Percy Davies had been mentioned in dispatches by Field Marshall Haig and on the back of that had been deservedly promoted to major.

The second piece of news was the one they were really hoping for. Major Watson had been granted his unpublicised request to be moved to something more exciting. With no warning and no goodbyes, he was gone. Where nobody knew. Not that anyone cared. Of course, everyone wanted to know who his replacement might be. Would it be some ghastly Guards officer? Major Watson certainly had his faults, but you could never tell. Perhaps the new man might be even worse.

Then came the third and most welcome piece of news of all. The replacement would be none other than the newly promoted Major Davies. Definitely celebrations all around.

The next day, Major Davies and Captain Wiggins arrived to talk to Emrys and Ted. The two men saluted smartly. Major Davies was unusually unsure of himself. He looked reluctant as if he was about to give them some bad news.

'Look, boys. I understand that you have applied to be gunners in the Flying Corps. I believe that Major Watson has given his blessing. The thing is, chaps, I'm in charge now. I just couldn't say anything previously, but I would look at it as a great favour to me personally if you would reconsider.'

Emrys knew that Ted would be more than happy to reconsider. That very morning, he had said the Flying Corps sounded like a thoroughly dangerous occupation and the main reason to leave the cyclists, Major Watson, had literally disappeared.

Compared with even being in the infantry a cyclist was an undemanding occupation. Emrys didn't give Ted the opportunity to reconsider. He replied for both of them.

'Sorry, Major Davies, we can't do it. We both need to get home on leave and it doesn't look as if that will happen any time soon around here. In the Flying Corps, you get leave after twenty-four hours of service. That means every couple of weeks. With respect, sir, that's too good a deal to turn down. Even for you.'

Major Davies looked at them sadly. He always hated giving bad news and there was no way of letting these two down lightly.

'What you have to consider, unfortunately, is the reason why they promise you leave after just twenty-four hours of service. I'm sorry to tell you that nobody gets to twenty-four hours. They are all killed well before that. Look. I'm not just saying that. You know me. I only have your best interests at heart. If you change your minds let Captain Wiggins know.'

They watched the two officers wandering off, probably discussing how they could rid themselves of the two amusing but useless cavalry horses. They needed their transport horses back.

Ted piped up immediately.

'Well, that's that. We'd be bloody bonkers to go anywhere near an aeroplane.'

Emrys could see the relief on Gwyn's face when he said.

'Sorry, Gwyn. Not only we won't get our bloody leave, but now we are bloody machine gunners.'

Secretly, Emrys knew that Gwyn liked being a machine gunner.

Life in and out of the trenches quickly became a monotonous norm. The trials of winter, the mud and the cold had moved on to the trials of summer. Not as much mud but infinitely more Whizzbangs and other nasty surprises. More risk of Fritz getting through the wire and suddenly appearing in the middle of the night.

The platoon was lined up for Major Davies and Second Lieutenant Williams to inspect them. They knew that it was Williams's first time having his own independent command. He looked pale and nervous. It was also the first time that the newly trained machine gunners would take their new baby into the front line. So they were also feeling nervous. They had enjoyed the extra pay and now were going to have to work for it. Major Davies looked at Emrys and broke into a broad grin.

'Remember you're attaching to the Berkshire regiment. Posh boys from near London. Best behaviour for Mr Williams, if you please.'

A totally exhausted team of cyclists finally rode into the flattened village of Cambrin on the far side of the canal. Cycling with a Lewis gun was a lot more taxing than with a rifle. They were still breathing heavily, as they watched Lieutenant Williams disappear into the headquarters of the second battalion, First Berkshire Regiment.

Cambrin was disappointingly similar to the hated Givenchy, where Emrys had had such a bad time. In fact, he could see Givenchy just a few hundred yards away plainly visible through an area of brick smokestacks and then across the wide canal. He could also see that this area had exactly the same problems as Givenchy, too much water and overlooked by Gerry, on Aubers Ridge. They couldn't see any front line. Instead, there seemed to be a series of well-fortified outposts jutting into No mans land. Each outpost was reached by a single dark damp tunnel. Emrys could not help thinking about his last experience of tunnels, with Lieutenant Mond, over a year previously. That was certainly a performance that he was keen not to repeat.

Hopefully, they would just join the rest of the platoon in filling sandbags and repairing trenches. If you kept your head well down you were unlikely to have any problems. It was on the fourth out of six nights, there, that their luck finally ran out. The Lewis gun team were ordered up to the smallest and most dangerous of the outposts for the night. As Second Lieutenant Williams unhelpfully commented, closer to the Gerry line than their own.

The Berkshires had taken casualties over recent weeks. They seemed pleased to welcome some old hands, like the cyclists, while they bedded in their quota of raw recruits. The Lewis gun team felt embarrassingly fraudulent as they were definitely not old hands with the Lewis gun. Still, when they finally arrived at the tiny outpost, having slowly dragged their weapon along the low tunnel, they were enthusiastically received.

The young officer, in charge, was a new boy. He had only recently come out to France and this was only his second day in the trenches. The cyclists had been severely warned, under no circumstances to mess him around. It would get back to Sergeant Marshall, left behind in Essars, and that would not bare thinking about.

When he saw the officer a few yards away, Emrys could tell that he was not only new but also utterly terrified. No wonder they had been read the riot act. The officer was also the most immaculately turned-out soldier that Emrys and Ted had ever seen. His tunic was perfectly cleaned with all the brass buttons glistening. He was wearing a full Sam Brown holster, something the experienced officers had ditched years before. It drew too much attention from Fritz. His perfect hair was swept back on either side of a fashionable central parting. On his upper lip, he displayed a wispy moustache, valiantly attempting to grow it in an effort to look older.

Disturbingly for Emrys, he was sure that he recognised him from somewhere. He just couldn't place where.

The young officer saw Emrys and his eyes lit up in a smile. A smile that had come simply because he had himself, at last, recognised someone. Forgetting himself, he rushed over and grabbing Emrys's hand almost shouted.

'Emrys. Good God, what chance? Emrys it is you isn't it?'

Emrys suddenly realised whom he was talking to. Someone he hadn't seen since before he had even enlisted. The last time he had set eyes on him, Emrys had helped take his heavy trunk off the carriage in the driveway of Bay View, in Briton Ferry. This was Matthias Roberts, the youngest son of M.G. Roberts himself. If he was being honest Emrys had always taken a bit more notice of Matthias's four glamorous sisters than the boy himself. And now, having previously not passed more than a dozen words between them, he was being greeted like a long-lost brother. Second Lieutenant Mathias Roberts continued excitedly.

'Good God. What good fortune. Wait till I write home and tell Father.'

Emrys could see the sniggering grins of some of the veterans of the Berkshire Regiment. They had patently already taken an instant dislike of this frightened schoolboy. Some of them would have been over in France even longer than Emrys. A few may have even come over with the original BEF in 1914. Why logically should he be giving them orders? Emrys decided that if only for the young officer's father's benefit, he ought to show the greatest of respect. Standing to attention and giving his smartest salute he said.

'Lieutenant Roberts, sir. Thank you for remembering me. I would be most grateful if you would send your father my kindest regards. Thank you, Lieutenant Roberts, sir.'

Matthias Roberts would need to earn the respect of these old soldiers and the sooner he learnt that the easier time he would have. Had he been a cyclist, then their easygoing nature would have eased him into things. This lot, however, were what Ted called proper soldiers. He was going to have to work hard at gaining their trust. Almost hugging a derided cyclist would be treated with the utmost scorn. Emrys's show of respect might just mitigate it to a certain extent.

Emrys and Ted started their spell of guard duty at 0200. They were already exhausted. They had not slept in the cramped bunker waiting their turn. They knew, of course, that falling asleep whilst on duty in such a forward position might be punished by the most extreme of measures. It was likely to be a long two hours.

Emrys had just finished a spell on the periscope. He jumped when he felt a hand on his shoulder. Grabbing for his revolver he turned quickly to see the young features of Matthias Roberts. Emrys theatrically grabbed his chest and whispered.

'Lieutenant Roberts. Please don't do that. I'm sure you've given me a heart attack.'

Second Lieutenant Roberts replied.

'Good God. Sorry. I don't seem to do anything right. I couldn't sleep, so I thought I could keep you awake by having a chat.'

He took a cigarette out of his silver cigarette case. Emrys put his hand out to stop him.

'Not here, lieutenant. We're a bit close to Fritz to be smoking at night.'

The lieutenant put his case back into his top pocket and started to speak.

'See Emrys. I know absolutely nothing. What use am I? I'll tell you. None. I'm worse than useless. I'm a bloody liability. I was top of the class in the cadet corps at school. I was top of the class at officer's training at Balliol. I come out here and it counts for nothing. I'm just a little boy in a man's world.'

At that moment a sharp whine was followed by a loud explosion about a hundred yards away. Emrys didn't move a muscle, with an air of nonchalance and disdain. Matthias Roberts ducked involuntarily and gave out a scream. Emrys looked at him pityingly. He remembered how he had been that first time when Lieutenant Mond had taken them near the front. Soothingly he whispered.

'Mini wafer. Just listen carefully to the whine. It was going away from us. It was going to the left. You will get used to it in no time. It's the Whizzbangs you have to worry about. Ted, over there, hates them. No warning. They just get you. I don't mind. If they get you they get you. That's that.'

Matthias Roberts looked at him in amazement.

'That's that. How can you say that's that?'

Emrys laughed.

'Well, that just is how it is. You listen for a Mini wafer. If you get it wrong you can be in trouble. At least with a Whizzbang, you've got no choice.'

Matthias Roberts just shook his head.

'I can't see myself ever being used to it. I'll always be ducking at every bang. I see those men laughing every time I twitch.'

Emrys was beginning to feel very uncomfortable. He shouldn't be hearing things like this from an officer. With trepidation, he decided to talk further.

'Look, sir. It's difficult. Those men know it's not easy. They went through exactly what you're going through. We all did. It's what one of our officers, Captain Lucas, calls a rite of passage. Lieutenant Williams, whom you met, will probably not thank me for saying that he was reduced to tears when he first came out. Look at him now. Tough as nails and been given an independent command. I just think you're trying too hard. Relax a bit and rely on your sergeant. Sorry, sir. I think I've said too much.'

Matthias Roberts faintly smiled for the first time since he had been in France.

'No. Don't worry. First bit of sense I've heard since leaving school. Mind you, Father always said how bright you were. He said you would make something of yourself one day. I have tried too hard I know. I knew it but I just wanted to be a success. I wanted to look the part and this is how they all dressed in Balliol. I just want my father to be proud of me. You know Father. He desperately deserves a son to be proud of with all those women around.'

Emrys was surprised and elated to hear that M.G. Roberts, the man he had always looked up to, thought that he would make something of his life. He decided to continue his advice to this young man who had stopped shaking for the very first time.

'Can I give a bit of advice about your appearance? Tell me to shut up, sir, if you think I'm being impertinent.'

Second Lieutenant Roberts opened his arms wide as if to invite Emrys to do his worst. Encouraged, Emrys pointed to the Sam Browne holster.

'First thing to do is get rid of that thing. The second thing is to get rid of the moustache.'

Matthias Roberts had already unholstered his revolver and removed his Sam Browne before Emrys was able to finish.

'The thing is that you're just too clean. Smear some mud over your face and that tunic and you will look as if you have been here for years. Lieutenant Roberts, sir, don't wear anything that makes you look like an officer. No bright buttons. No revolver. If Fritz sees you like that, he will love it. You'll be mincemeat in no time. Your boys won't like it either, because you'll attract attention to them. That's half the reason they're giving you a hard time. So no holster, no shiny brass and lots of mud. You'll be more than fine.

One last thing. My mam would kill me if she knew I was saying this. Do something about your hair. It's much too nice. Sorry.'

Emrys stopped, waiting for the backlash. Why on earth had he said so many terrible things to an officer? Lieutenant Roberts was in fact beaming widely. He clapped Emrys on the back. Then he ruffled both his hands through his hair turning it into an unruly mop, before smearing his face and tunic with rancid mud. He turned to Emrys.

'Better?'

Emrys laughed as he said.

'Much better.'

Nearing the end of their two hour guard duty, Second Lieutenant Roberts moved towards Emrys again. The sun would start to appear soon and then there would be a general stand to. Dawn was in theory the most dangerous time, but everything seemed quiet. Roberts was noticeably less agitated. Maybe it was the talk with the cyclist or perhaps he was just getting used to things. Emrys smiled at his tousled hair and mud-stained face. Matthias Roberts smiled back.

'Seen anything, Emrys?'

A bleary-eyed private replied.

'Nothing at all. Can't see em coming tonight, but you never can tell, Lieutenant Roberts, sir.'

At that moment, another Minenwerfer shell landed a hundred yards away to the left, in No mans land. Roberts ducked instinctively but laughed.

'Mini wafer. I think I can see what you were talking about. You can almost feel where it might land. My name's Matt by the way. I'd like you to call me Matt when we're alone.'

Emrys immediately replied.

'That would be a very bad idea, Lieutenant Roberts, sir. Bad for morale Sergeant Marshall would say. With respect, you're an officer and I'm a simple private. It has to stay that way. After the war things will change, but not now.'

Matthias Roberts could see that he had, perhaps, become too familiar and now tried to make up for it.

'After the war. I've only been here four days and that already sounds good. What are you going to do afterwards? Are you going back to the tinplate or steelworks?'

Emrys replied again.

'Naw. I've seen too much out here to go back to working for someone else. I'm going to work for myself. I'm going to be just like your da. A self-made man. And I've got a plan too. A good plan. I'm going to make sweet carbonated water and sell it by the gallon. I'm going to build a factory and sell to the whole of Wales. Maybe the whole of England too. What are you going to do, Lieutenant Roberts? I expect you'll be off to Oxford. I've been through Oxford on a train, once. It looks like a magical place.'

Emrys stopped, realising that he had again said too much. It was just that he was so enthusiastic about his fizzy water company that when he found a receptive listener he just couldn't stop. Lieutenant Roberts was much more considered with his reply and yet seemed uncertain. He was about to divulge something that nobody else knew. Nobody at home or even at school.

'Well, it's like this. Father says I'm going to be a doctor. I even have a place in medical school reserved for me. St. Mary's in Paddington. Wonderful place. I know I could be a good doctor. The thing is I want to do something else. I really want to be an Archaeologist. It's a passion. You might even call it a calling.'

Emrys said nothing. He didn't have a clue what the lieutenant was talking about. Firstly, to actually be a doctor would be such a fine thing that he really couldn't imagine turning an opportunity like that down. Secondly, he had absolutely no idea what an archaeologist was. He said nothing and let the lieutenant continue.

'We had Lord Carnarvon talking to us in school. He talked of wonderful things. He's looking for ancient tombs in Egypt, with fantastic treasures. Until the war came, he was digging up all parts of Egypt. He says there is a valley full of tombs of kings. He's going back after the war. It's so unbelievably exciting.'

Emrys considered this. Seemed a pretty madcap idea to go around some Arab country searching for dead bodies. He'd seen enough dead bodies in France. It was easy to see, however, the passion that exuded from every pore of this vulnerable young man. He chose his words carefully.

'Lieutenant Roberts. When I was home, I told my mam and da about the fizzy drinks factory. My da said I would need a proper man's job as my brother had. My mam, however, said that everyone should follow their dreams. She said I could always become a rollerman if things didn't work out. Do you know that Da seemed to change his mind slowly? In the end, he was even more enthusiastic than Mam and me.

With the greatest respect, I know your father. He might just surprise you. You never know.'

Dawn was about to break. Stand to was imminent. Second Lieutenant Roberts wandered off to check the other guard posts before the rest of the men arrived for the beginning of the day. Emrys watched him go and, after waving to Ted, got back to surveying No mans land through the periscope.

Two days later, the cyclists' period at the front was finishing and they were due to return to Essars, for a well-earned rest. Emrys was not looking forward to dragging that heavy gun back across the country. Second Lieutenant Williams seemed to be looking for him, while he was joking with Ted. Tentatively

Lieutenant Williams asked.

'I think you know Second Lieutenant Roberts? I have some very bad news for you. He was killed this morning together with two of his men. Hit by a whizzbang leaving the communication trench. Didn't stand a chance. By the time we got there, there was nothing we could do. Sorry. Another brave man gone.'

At first, Emrys failed to comprehend what he had been told. Then he whispered.

'Poor Matt. He only arrived in France last week. And poor M G Roberts. I remember when Mrs Roberts died years ago. And now his son.'

He looked at Ted, ignoring the lieutenant.

'Just because they're rich doesn't mean they have an easy life. I think he probably had a difficult time trying to live up to expectations. No mam and four sisters. Well as I said to him a couple of days ago. That's that.'

He turned back to Second Lieutenant Williams.

'Should I write to his father, do you think?'

Lieutenant Williams put a hand on his shoulder.

'That would be very kind of you, private. I'm sure it would be appreciated. Just leave it a week or so. Let the official stuff get there first. Now mount up that Lewis gun. We need to leave in five minutes.'

That really was that. Matthias Roberts was dead, but life just had to go on.

Harriet decided to keep a low profile. She had courted trouble several times and had been fortunate enough to have suffered nothing worse than a black eye. By the time she had returned to work, the next day, the eye was nearly closed, with a large blue swelling over the cheek below. Inevitably, there were a plethora of comments, only some in jest, about Josiah having hit her. Only Tom Evans, Jane's husband, knew the truth and from him, she just received a broad smile and an inevitable wink.

That night Harriet, Josiah and Evelyn had the tastiest meal that they could remember. They had never before eaten meat of anywhere near the quality of the beef that had been slapped on Harriet's face.

She continued to go to Jerusalem Chapel every Thursday to listen to the various speakers. That surely couldn't do any harm. She always looked forward to seeing Ruth there. They had become such good friends and, if Harriet was honest, it was the main reason she attended. That was actually ridiculous. They, already, saw each other most days.

Harriet had used all her meagre savings to build a tiny memorial to David near the back of Ynysmaerdy cemetery. In fact, her savings were so meagre that they needed to be supplemented by Mr Glen Taylor. Harriet had taken to visiting the memorial every day and talking to David. Josiah thought it an unhealthy occupation which had perhaps become an obsession. On the positive side, she usually dropped into the cricket pavilion where Ruth still lived, on the way back. There, they would gossip and drink tea. Very occasionally Harriet might even laugh.

Her other new friend, of course, she needed to be a little more serendipitous about meeting. That was Elizabeth Powell. Still enjoying being an active member of Rehoboth Chapel, which had been such a large part of their family's life, she couldn't be seen in Elizabeth's company. After all Reverend Herbert Hughes had been more than patient with her, despite her anti-war sentiments. He and all her friends even tolerated her weekly Thursday excursions to Jerusalem.

She was surprised, just as she was leaving one of the meetings, to be approached by a man she recognised as a member of the Independent Labour Party. Josiah had never had much time for the Unions and was disparaging of this newly formed political party, which he dismissed as troublemakers. That was despite his liking of Joe Branch, the chairman. The man who approached her, she only knew from a distance. She thought that he might be a rollerman who had once worked with David. She also had seen him a couple of times talking earnestly with Joe. He seemed to know all about Harriet's encounter with the law, however. Carefully ensuring that they couldn't be overheard, he whispered.

'We have been tipped off that the IPL office is going to be raided again. We wondered if you would take some of our pamphlets. Just for a few days. It's quite safe. You're not a member so nobody would dream of looking in your house. Please though. We're desperate.'

Harriet thought about the proposition briefly. She had been becoming increasingly frustrated at not being able to have the courage of her convictions. Almost daily she was hearing of more grieving mothers and widows. This would be a start maybe. Just a small, safe start. She wouldn't have to tell Josiah or Evelyn. She didn't want to get them into trouble. She replied, carefully.

'If there's truly no one else, I'll do it. Don't want Josiah involved though. Just me. Can you do that?'

They met later that evening, in the dark passageway behind her house. The man was carrying a large box and silently helped her to hide it in a convenient recess behind the outside toilet. They shook hands gravely before he disappeared back into the darkness. Harriet had no idea of when he might return to retrieve the stash. She took one pamphlet to read. She was already beginning to regret her precipitous and foolhardy actions. She would read the pamphlet and if it was too seditious, she was considering burning the whole lot.

Harriet stayed in the back room, long after both Josiah and Evelyn had made their way upstairs. She carefully waited until she was sure of not being disturbed. Guiltily, she took out the pamphlet and began to read.

TWO YEARS OF HARD LABOUR FOR REFUSING TO DISOBEY THE DICTATES OF CONSCIENCE.

This was the sentence passed to Ernest Everett.

Everett was a teacher and had been opposed to war since the age of 16. He appealed as a Conscientious Objector. The Tribunals treated him very badly and recommended his dismissal from school. They only recognised his claim to have a conscientious claim against combatant service, but that he should do non-combatant service. As the purpose of that service was to release others from the trenches he couldn't accept that service.

He was taken to Warrington Barracks and forced to put on a uniform. He was placed in the Non-Combatant Corps, which is part of the army.

He adopted consistently a policy of passive resistance to all military orders saying 'I refuse any order given by any military authority.'

Everett was brought before the Colonel who read aloud Section 9 of the Army Act.

At his Court Marshall, he said that he was prepared to do work of National Importance, which does not include military service and doesn't release another man to do the work that I am not prepared to do.

The sentence was two years of hard labour.

Everett is fighting the old fight for liberty and against religious persecution in the same spirit in which the martyrs suffered in the past.

Issued by the non-conscription fellowship.

Harriet didn't know what to think. On the one hand, she wanted the end of the war to be as soon as possible. Tomorrow would be idea! On the other hand, why shouldn't this man Everett at least do something to help Emrys at the front? Even if he wasn't going to work for the Red Cross or something similar. She decided that she just couldn't risk having these leaflets in the house. She was being selfish putting Josiah and Evelyn at risk.

She went to bed intent on getting rid of them, first thing next the morning.

She hadn't slept at all when, at six o'clock the next morning, there was a loud hammering on their front door. Harriet jumped out of bed before Josiah had even awoken. Evelyn had got to the door first, wearing only her nightdress, a few seconds before her mother. There must be some terrible news about Emrys.

In front of them stood Inspector Morris accompanied by three burly constables. Inspector Morris was not in a mood to be trifled with. He had not wanted to get up at this early hour. Nor did he really want to be in this household. Ignoring Evelyn, he shouted at Harriet.

'I warned you last time and you have taken no notice. You have blatantly disregarded my advice. Now, go and get Josiah.'

By this time, Josiah had been woken by the commotion and joined them, wheezing, at the doorstep. Inspector Morris continued.

'Evelyn get some clothes on immediately. Josiah, we are searching your house under the Defence of the Realm Act 1914. We believe that there is subversive literature being stored here.'

Josiah was about to say that the Inspector was being ridiculous. Then he looked at Harriet. As the policemen pushed past him, it finally dawned on him that they were in trouble. He could see the disbelieving look on his wife's face. He walked over to gently take her hand. They would face it together. They would face it together for Evelyn and Emrys. And also for David's memory.

The policemen seemed to know precisely what they were looking for and where to look. The Inspector and one constable marched straight in, through the back room and back door, into the small backyard. The other two stayed with the couple in the back room. There, joined by the now-dressed Evelyn, they listened to the activity in the small toilet. The toilet was shared by three families but had running water and was kept spotlessly clean by the mothers. All three of them used the hiding place behind the panel, at times. It was a good place to put things temporarily before a better place could be found.

Inspector Morris walked through the back door followed by the constable holding the heavy box. Josiah made to speak but the Inspector held up his hand to stop him. He then turned to Harriet.

'Harriet John. I am arresting you under the Defence of the Realm Act 1914 for the spreading of subversive literature, which is disloyal and treacherous to your country and King.'

He ushered Harriet out of the front door and, followed by the constable with the box, began to make their way up the road past both Rehoboth and Jerusalem Chapels, to the small police station. Despite the early hour, lots of people were preparing to go to work. The arrest of a female was certainly an event worthy of gossip. Especially when the person was an upstanding member of society such as Harriet.

Two hours later, Harriet was being marched out of a small room in the police station and into the lobby. She was relieved to find Josiah sitting there with Tom Evans next to him. Why Tom was there, she had no idea. But where was Evelyn? Tom must have read her mind, managing to speak even before Inspector Morris.

'She's fine, Harriet. She's with my girls. They'll be spoiling her.'

Inspector Morris was not used to being interrupted. He growled at the two men.

'We have charged her under the Defence of the Realm Act. She will be appearing at Neath Magistrates Court on Tuesday the 22nd. This is serious, Josiah. She could go to prison.'

Harriet rushed over to Josiah and hugged him tightly. All she could do, through her tears, was say that she was sorry. Tom

Evans tapped them on their shoulders and whispered.

'We're going to fight this. We've got a solicitor who will do it at cost and we're going to raise money for it. This is a bloody outrage. A mother of two soldiers. We will fight it and bloody win.'

Harriet, Josiah and Evelyn were sitting on a narrow bench, outside the Neath Magistrate Court. Harriet hadn't wanted her little girl to attend, as she had a quiet foreboding regarding what was about to occur. She knew that Evelyn would have other ideas.

They were not only waiting for the case to start but also to meet her barrister for the very first time. Considering that neither she nor Josiah was a member, the Independent Labour Party had been very generous. As Josiah had said, however, it was the IPL's pamphlets that the police had found. Anyway, they could easily have set her adrift with no support. That, they certainly not had done. They were paying for the prominent lawyer, whom the previous year had defended Joe Branch himself for a similar offence. The fact that Joe had received a large fine was, to say the least, disconcerting.

Josiah kept anxiously taking a furtive glance at his pocket watch, which had replaced the one which he had given to David. Time was passing and there was not much left when the barrister, Mr Llewelyn Williams MP finally made a hurried appearance.

There was only time for brief introductions before they were summoned into the court. Evelyn immediately began to sob loudly. Harriet hugged her tightly, aware that she might not be allowed to hug her again for some time. She was ushered into a separate chair, giving Evelyn a final squeeze as she went. Evelyn and her father disappeared to the back of the room.

Harriet had never been in a courtroom, before. She'd expected wigs and gowns like she had read about in murder trials. Despite everyone just wearing ordinary Sunday best, it was a forbidding place. Three magistrates sat on a raised podium at the front, looking grim and menacing. In the middle was the presiding magistrate, Mr Thomas, who seemed to just stare at her.

The prosecutor was a large pompous man, who seemed intent on getting one over his more illustrious opponent. He began slowly, reading carefully from his notes.

'The defendant is charged with having by word of mouth and circular made false statements, likely to prejudice the recruiting, training and discipline of the forces. At the time of her arrest, she had hidden in her property at 11 Neath Road, Briton Ferry, without lawful authority, documents in contravention of Regulation 27 of the Defence of the Realm Act. This Regulation makes a person liable if they spread reports which are intended to or likely to prejudice the training and discipline of His Majesty's Forces. These were the same documents which were brought to this court, only last year.

I will ask the court to consider how the conduct and the literature of the defendant would affect the ordinary man in the street. Would they prejudice recruiting? Would they interfere with the training and, indeed, the discipline of those who had already given service to this great country, including her own son? I say they will.'

He then began to call his witnesses. The first was Mr H. Clarke who relayed in graphic detail Harriet's refusal of the watch in Briton Ferry town hall. Harriet was amazed at the skill of her famous barrister, who magically seemed to turn it to her advantage. He painted a desperate grieving mother, forced to attend the presentation totalling against her will.

The second witness explained everything that Harriet had been trying to work out for weeks. How had the police known that she had the leaflets and exactly where to find them? The witness was Mrs Sarah Eynon, the busybody from just along the road. It turned out that she had inevitably spied Harriet and the man carrying the box down the narrow passage behind the houses and entering the toilet. She had immediately hot-footed to the police station to relay the news.

Mr Williams seemed to have telepathically worked out the witness. He couldn't deny the evidence, so he had to try a different tactic.

'Mrs Eynon. Do you have or have you had any children in any of the services?'

He seemed to know that the answer would be no. He continued.

'Do any of your family do any work directly beneficial to the war effort, such as munitions?'

The answer again was no. He then went in for the kill.

'Are you aware that the defendant's son, David, gave his life at Mametz Wood, last year? Are you also aware that the defendant's other son, Emrys, is at this very moment fighting in France? Are you aware that both the defendant and her daughter work long hours in a munitions factory?'

Mrs Eynon could only reply yes before Mr Williams dismissed her.

'I would suggest that the defendant has given everything,

I repeat, everything for the war effort. You I suggest have the bare-faced cheek to sit there making vile accusations, when you, yourself have given less than nothing.'

The last witness was infinitely more impressive. He was Inspector Morris and wasn't going to be dismissed in the same fashion as the previous two. He stuck to the facts, both of the arrest and the previous episode, outside St. Clements church. There was very little that the barrister could do.

Next, it was the turn of Harriet and despite her nervousness, she was determined to give a good account of herself. Josiah had repeatedly told her to be contrite and not to get involved in any political arguments. Even he knew that it would not go down well with the magistrate. The beginning, of course, went easily. Mr Williams asked her about her work and about Emrys. Then he moved on to how David's death had affected her. Finally, he asked about the circumstances of the night that she received the pamphlets. They were difficult answers. She certainly didn't want to implicate herself in anything that she hadn't done.

The prosecutor was surprisingly brief. The facts were plain for everyone to see and he spent little time going over them, yet again. His final question was the one which Harriet knew Josiah feared if only because of the probable answer.

'What course do you think the war, the war your son is fighting in, should take?'

Harriet could almost hear Josiah holding her breath, as she carefully considered her reply.

'I think Mr Lloyd George and King George should immediately go to Berlin and negotiate peace with the Kaiser. To negotiate is not to give in. It is to use reason in place of force.'

Josiah sighed audibly. Harriet knew that it wasn't the answer that he wanted. Even the charismatic Mr Williams briefly looked at his feet.

The prosecutor stood and looked directly at the Magistrates. As he began to talk, the sense of foreboding returned to Harriet.

'The law and government of this land have been most considerate towards those who are genuine conscientious objectors. But, sir, are you going to allow people to go around out in towns encouraging others to acquire a conscience? Are you going to allow what you might even call a war against the war or even a crusade of conscientious objection? There are those amongst us whose natural being or upbringing has denied them the qualities needed in a soldier, namely courage and endurance. Shouldn't we protect these people from persons such as the defendant and so-called literature such as this?

The defendant wishes simply to infect those who have yet to join the army with an imaginary conscience. It is to give those people a loophole through which they can squeeze. Worse than all this, if that is possible, is to spread seditious thoughts to those already in the army. What, I ask you, will our boys think as they valiantly fight their way to victory if they feel that they don't have the support of those at home?'

Mr Llewelyn Williams began his reply.

'Members of the Bench, since the days of Magna Carta, every person tried simply for the expression of opinion, has had the right to be tried by their peers. For the first time, and I do not complain because it is law, that is not so. So, sirs, I suggest to you that, as you stand in a position which ought to be occupied by a jury, you need to approach the questions in a broader manner as a jury might.

I suggest that this lady has, if she has indeed been guilty of any offence at all, it was solely a technical one. I suggest that she was unaware that she was doing any wrong.

It has been laid down by the present Home Secretary that meetings for the purpose of advocating the Repeal of the Conscription Act are legal and writings of the same character are not to be liable for suppression if there was no violence. There has been no violence.

If we consider the first manuscript, the so-called Everett pamphlet. The language of it was for one purpose. It was not to prejudice people against the army. It was simply an appeal to the moral sense of the general public to see fair play and that decent punishment is accorded to genuine Conscientious Objectors. The fact that Mr Everett's term has since been reduced greatly on appeal, confirms that this was indeed a savage punishment, which is the only conclusion that this pamphlet comes to. The rest of the pamphlet is simply pure facts.

The prosecutor has reminded you that Mr Bertrand Russell, grandson of one of our greatest prime ministers, has been fined for writing this leaflet. It is however fair to remember that that judgment is under review and therefore cannot be taken into consideration.

I now draw your attention to the Maximilian pamphlet, which the defendant is said to have distributed outside St Clements Church, to the distress of Reverend Jones. The story of Maximilian is the literal translation of the death of an early Christian. It is a story which has been told in Christian homes for fifteen hundred years. If this is the kind of language that is aimed at by Section Twenty-Seven, then the sooner the Bible is suppressed the better. There are passages in the Bible for more dangerous to recruiting than that.'

He rested for a moment before continuing.

'I say to you as men of the world that the spirit and language of the pamphlets is not the spirit and language contemplated by the Act. As such, the defendant was not only not conscious of doing something illegal, but that in truth and fact, was not acting illegally.

I finally have to present to you a woman who has given everything. She has three children. The first rose to the rank of sergeant and was killed last July. The second is at this very moment in a trench, in France. The third, the young lady over there who is literally shaking with fear for her mother, went to work in a munitions factory aged fifteen. Finally, the defendant herself works alongside her daughter in the same factory. Her sole aim is to look after her family as best she can. I ask you to take all this into consideration.'

Mr Llewelyn Williams sat down, looking exhausted. Despite only being able to arrive at the last minute, this case meant a lot to him. He was deeply concerned that he was about to witness a gross miscarriage of justice. He smiled at Harriet and sat back as the Magistrates quietly discussed the case. After barely five minutes, the Chairman started to speak.

'It seems to the Bench that the Defence of the Realm Act leaves to them, rather ambiguously, to judge the likely effect on the interests of the country. The Act has undoubtedly changed the relationship between the people in this country. It is no longer possible, in the interest of the country, for people to always be able to freely speak their minds. The pamphlets quite clearly come within Clause Twenty-seven.

We do, however, wish to take a common sense view. We do

not wish to persecute the defendant for her views but by example will make sure that this isn't repeated. We are disappointed that the defendant took no heed of the similar case heard in this court, in the recent past, or the warnings of Inspector Morris.

We would normally be considering a sentence of three months of hard labour. However, out of respect for your brave son, who died last year, we will reduce the sentence to one month's prison or a fine of £50.'

Harriet slumped forward in her chair. Mr Llewelyn Williams grabbed her to stop her from falling to the floor. There was a loud piercing wail from the back of the court, as Josiah tried to console his daughter. There was also a general rumble of discontent from the sparse audience, ignored by the magistrates. Harriet rose to comfort her distraught daughter. A gentle hand on her shoulder restrained her. It was the elderly policeman seated next to her. He smiled as if to say that he knew it was unfair, but he couldn't let her go over to her family.

The clerk of the court led her to the little side door in the courtroom. As she went she glanced over her shoulder at her disbelieving husband and daughter.

Harriet was guided, gently, into a small room which doubled as a cell and left alone except for the policeman. She couldn't believe the injustice and the brutality of what had just happened. How had she got herself into such a mess? She just felt so guilty about inflicting this on her already bereaved family. Her contemplations were quickly broken by the appearance of Josiah, accompanied by Tom Evans and Mr Llewelyn Williams. Harriet's immediate concern was.

'Where's Evelyn?'

Mr Williams replied.

'She's fine. She's just not allowed in here because she's under the age of twenty-one. She's outside with one of your friends. I'm truly sorry that the outcome wasn't better. I think whatever the evidence had been it wouldn't have swung it. They were intent on this, the minute they walked into the room. They were determined to make an example of you.'

He then looked at Tom Evans, before continuing.

'The easiest option now would be to just pay the fine of £50 and be bound over for a year. Is that going to be possible?'

Tom looked apologetically at Harriet and said.

'Sorry, the Independent Labour Party does not have the funds to help, at the present time. What I am going to do is go around the members and people at Taylors and try to raise the cash. The trouble is that money is thin on the ground these days and £50 is a lot of money. We'll not be able to raise it quickly.'

Josiah must have already stated that they were in no position to pay the money, as Mr Williams said.

'The alternative is that we appeal. You would go home today and come back to court in a few weeks. I have a concern about that action. I think it would be hard to win. I am also worried about the length of your sentence. They reduced it from three to one month. Under this Law, if you lose the appeal, they would be able to increase it back to three. It is my opinion that this is indeed the stance that they would take.'

Harriet was by now calm enough to ask.

'So what do you recommend?'

Mr Williams was very firm in his reply.

'I recommend that you don't appeal. It is too risky. I am afraid that I believe that you should accept the sentence and hope that Tom Evans and your husband can raise the money and get you released early.'

The clerk of the court, who had slipped into the room almost unnoticed, interrupted.

'If that were to be your decision, then the Chairman insists on you going immediately into custody. That would mean staying here overnight and then being taken to Swansea by train, in the morning. From there we don't know. You might be transferred somewhere else. Maybe even England. I'm truly sorry.'

The clerk did indeed look sorry and even more so when Harriet asked him.

'Can I please see my daughter?'

The clerk's reply was the one she expected, in this uncaring and unchristian place.

'I'm sorry. She's underage. It's just not possible. The best thing would be for her to go to the train station in the morning.'

There was indeed only one possibility. Harriet would have to go to prison. Hopefully, it would be for just a short time, but the worst scenario was for a month. She just hoped that she would be kept in Swansea.

Harriet was soon sitting on the chair, alone. Josiah had wanted to stay but her greatest wish was for him to take Evelyn home. Mr Williams and the clerk had disappeared to discuss particulars, while Tom Evans was already trying to raise what he mischievously called the ransom. Harriet could only contemplate how things had gotten this far.

The clerk and the policeman soon returned to move her down the corridor to a small windowless cell. The walls were covered in profane graffiti. Harriet realised of course that they were the scribblings of some deeply traumatised men and women. Traumatised in exactly the same way that she was. She lay down on the only piece of furniture there, a hard creaking bed, and closed her eyes.

She wasn't asleep when disturbed, the next morning, by the rattle of keys in the lock. The elderly policeman appeared with a large cup of hot tea in his hand. Just what Harriet needed. They would be leaving for the station about an hour hence. All Harriet could do was wait, listening to the building coming to life once more, for another day's work.

The train station was only two hundred yards away. It was going to be easiest to just walk there. That was a worry. Her concern was simply the reaction of all the people near her. It was undoubtedly going to be a walk of shame. To make matters worse, when the sergeant came to escort her, he was carrying handcuffs. The kindly old policeman immediately objected.

'Is that really necessary?'

The sergeant glared at him and replied in one word.

'Regulations.'

Harriet was just pleased that it was such a short distance. Although she really didn't want her daughter to witness her like this, it would be reassuring to at least see her. She exited the front door quietly holding her handcuffed hands in front of her. The sergeant held her on one side and a young constable on the other, with the elderly constable trailing behind. She looked at her feet as they passed a poorly dressed woman, coming in the opposite direction. The lady said.

'God bless you, Harriet. I wish the rest of us had your courage.'

Harriet looked up in surprise. The woman gave her a beautiful smile. At that same moment, a middle-aged man wearing a leather apron was crossing the road. Judging from the angry look on his face, he was going to make his point vociferously. He was unlikely to be as complimentary as the woman. Harriet was wrong again. The man looked straight at the sergeant and said loudly.

'This is a bloody outrage. The court was a complete joke. We apparently live in a free country. My opinion on conscription is different from hers, but for God's sake she is entitled to that opinion.'

Unlike Harriet, the sergeant had half-expected trouble. He knew the man and simply replied.

'Out of the way please, Mervyn. We are just doing our job.'

The man, called Mervyn, stepped out of the way and also gave Harriet a smile. The rest of the short journey was the most surprising of Harriet's life. It was a journey full of smiles and shouts of encouragement.

It was at the railway station itself, however, that Harriet got her biggest shock. The platform was packed with people. Surely they couldn't all be going to Swansea. A murmur started up when she arrived. A few seconds later the applause began, quickly amplified by loud cheering. She couldn't believe it. They were cheering little old her, the nobody from Neath Road. The policemen fought their way to the edge of the platform, with men and women struggling to clap their prisoner on her back and wish her well.

In front of them stood a beaming Josiah and a tearful Evelyn. Despite the sergeant's command not to touch her, Evelyn immediately threw her arms around her mother and gave her the biggest of hugs. Evelyn struggled to speak through her tears and all the noise.

'Mam. I'm so proud of you. Have you seen all these people?'

Harriet only had time before being pushed onto the train to say.

'Look after your da, Evie. I'll be home in no time.'

The next thing she knew she was being eased into a seat in the train carriage, flanked by the two policemen. Her friend, the elderly policeman had been left, on the platform, beaming next to Evelyn. Harriet waved to him gratefully. The train slowly pulled out of the station with the crowd clapping, cheering and waving.

Still handcuffed, Harriet watched the sombre archway tower above her. The massive brick entrance to Swansea Prison was flanked by even bigger towers. The large doors crashed shut behind the carriage, which had brought them from the station. This was a dark place, with appropriately black clouds, above, threatening rain. The only relief came from the seagulls screeching. They must be near the sea and Harriet liked the sea. On further inspection, however, this place was about as bad as it could have been, even in her very worst dreams.

She stood motionless in front of the warder's table as he surveyed her carefully. She was very different to their normal clients. She was still wearing her best black dress that she had thought wise to wear to the court. Very different from the usual array of filthy rags or the bright clothing of some of their more questionable guests. Despite her posture, clothing and education, she could not be from anywhere but the working class. She listened to him carefully.

'The problem that we have is that you were not intended to come here. You were due to go to London. Unfortunately, there has been a logistical problem and you have been sent here instead. We are going to keep you just until this is sorted and transport is arranged. You will be leaving us tomorrow or the next day.'

Harriet looked disbelievingly at the warder and immediately said.

'I can't go to London. I have a daughter who needs me.'

The warden sneered back.

'We have rules here. Firstly only talk if you're talked to. Secondly, we say what is going to happen to you. I can promise you if you don't obey the rules, I will make sure you'll more than regret it. You are going to London and you can do nothing about it.'

Harriet realised that her only way forward was to say nothing more. Further appeals would only be futile. So, she just sat quietly while the reams of forms were painstakingly filled out.

She was then led into the hands of a scowling woman, dressed as a nurse. The next stop was a dark room and she was, loudly, ordered to undress. The nurse, if that's what she was, looked like another one not to take issue with. Despite the crowded homes that Harriet had always lived in, she was unused to being seen undressed. Even by Josiah. So, to take her clothes completely off and being stared at by this woman, did not come easily. She already knew that she had very little choice. She carefully folded her clothes and placed them on the table.

Naked, she turned to face the grinning nurse to see that she had a hosepipe aimed at her. A powerful jet of freezing water hit her in the chest. The nurse was as painfully rough, as she was rudely abrupt. Neither of those mattered to Harriet. It was the embarrassment that overwhelmed her. Finally, a cup of acrid white powder was thrown over her before she was handed her replacement clothes, made from an itchy material normally reserved for sacks. She coughed, violently, from the toxic fumes. It seemed as if she was a million miles away from the cheering crowd at the train station that morning.

By now disoriented, Harriet was led through two sets of locked doors into the single women's wing. She might have thought, given the reaction at the train station, that she would have a sympathetic hearing amongst the inmates. She was quickly disabused of that. A tall muscular woman barged into her almost knocking her down.

'Fucking conchie.'

Harriet hadn't appreciated, until that moment, that many of these unhappy women had sons and husbands at the front. Many of them didn't have the education to think of her other than fucking conchie. Then again she might have thought the same a few months previously, without the profanities, of course.

She was guided up a set of metal steps to a row of cells and pushed into one. It was tiny, seemingly no bigger than her scullery, even when empty of people. It contained a set of bunk beds on either side of the door with a bucket at the far end under the window. This tiny cell could accommodate four inmates and three of the bunk beds showed signs of already having occupants. She had no choice but to place her blanket on the unoccupied upper bunk. She looked sceptically as to whether she would actually be able to climb up there.

Harriet suddenly realised that she was ravenously hungry. She had hardly eaten for the previous forty-eight hours. She had fortuitously arrived just in time for the one meal of the day. As she walked back down the stairs towards the tables in the ground floor corridor, she could hear a sudden murmur from the gaggle of women below. What she couldn't understand is how they all seemed to know about her. Indeed the large, muscular woman had called her a conchie, within seconds of her arrival. She had quickly learnt that nothing was private in the prison and there were certainly no secrets.

All she could do was meekly line up with her battered metal plate, to discover what the large food pot contained. Nobody talked to her. A few women simply glared but most just diverted their gaze and ignored her. She arrived at the front of the queue and nervously thrust out her plate. A large gluey mass was unceremoniously dumped on her plate. Despite the way it looked, the food smelt surprisingly appetising.

She turned and walked back towards a near-empty table, grasping her plate in one hand and a rough wooden spoon in the other. Whoever had washed them had made a bad job of it. Not to the standard that Harriet would expect at home. But, she reminded herself, she wasn't at home.

She sat on the bench at the table only containing a thin gnarled old lady and a chubby young thing who looked even younger than Evelyn. Harriet closed her eyes in a quick prayer. Looking up, she introduced herself pleasantly to the other two.

'Hello. I'm Harriet.'

This was received with marked indifference. In total silence, she began her surprisingly nutritious stew. It was so different from home, where the meals were usually eaten with a cacophony of noise. She closed her eyes again and told herself that she could get through this. Whatever they threw at her she could get through it. She had to.

Immediately after the food had been finished and plates and spoons inefficiently cleaned, it was time to return to their cells. They were returning, despite it only being seven o'clock. They would be stuck, locked four to a tiny cell, for the next fourteen hours. This, for Harriet, would be her worst nightmare.

She was pleased to see the innocuous young girl already lying on the other upper bunk. She was dismayed, however, when the large muscular woman barged past her and sat, menacingly, on one of the lower bunks. Harriet felt obliged to smile at her and repeat.

'Hello. I'm Harriet.'

The muscular lady replied.

'We know who you are and we know what you done. We all got brothers in France, so we're not happy with you bloody do-gooders.'

Harriet feared that this would be a conversation she would repeatedly have over the next long month. She spoke calmly, knowing that saying the wrong thing might have dire consequences.

'One of my sons died in France last year. The other one is over in the trenches right now. I haven't seen him for nine months. I'm no do-gooder. I work in the production line in a munitions factory. So does my daughter. I'm no different to you. I've known hardship.'

The large woman snorted and ignored her. Harriet thought it wise to scramble up to her place in the top bunk, arrange her meagre blanket and stay out of the way. Despite being so early she would try and sleep. About an hour later, she was surprised when the young girl addressed her.

'Harriet? Can you write? Can you write a letter for me? To

my man. He's just gone to France a couple of months ago and I can't write good. None of us can write good.'

Harriet was surprised that the girl had even remembered her name. She took the single sheet of paper off the girl and waited for her to start.

'Dear Carwyn. I hope you are doing good and haven't been wounded or anything. I have some important news which I think will surprise you. I hope it will make you happy. I am going to have a baby.'

The two women in the lower bunks shot up and simultaneously exclaimed.

'What? Are you sure, Megan?'

Megan burst into tears and Harriet reached over and held her hand. Her being a conchie was, temporarily, forgotten and the four women excitedly began to chatter into the night. Harriet was the only one to have had children herself but the others all had younger brothers and sisters. While the others started telling the most gruesome of tales, Harriet talked in her calm, reassuring voice. Her pregnancies had all gone perfectly.

By 2 o'clock in the morning, Harriet had fallen into a deserved sleep. She had written letters to Megan's boyfriend and parents. More importantly, she had carefully and painstakingly written a letter for Megan to the prison governor, asking for clemency. Harriet had quickly become one of the girls. Being a conchie had been forgotten. She was happier and more confident about her situation, despite the nauseating odour from Mary, the muscular lady, defecating noisily into the bucket in the early hours.

The next morning they were disturbed early. The time was only 8.30 and cells were not normally unlocked until 9.00, for

227

slopping out and some much-needed nourishment. The warder pointed to Harriet and growled.

'You. Out now. You're leaving.'

Harriet, slowly, got down from her bunk. This nightmare was never-ending. She had secretly hoped that by some miracle she would be staying in Swansea. She had already surprisingly bonded with these three very different women. Even Mary hugged her and Megan tearfully thanked her. Harriet was also tearful as she was marched down the corridor and back through the two sets of doors. She really didn't want to go to England.

Back in the small office on the same shelf, which had the day before contained her uniform, lay her black dress. Without saying anything, the warder signalled for her to get changed. From there she was pushed into the windowless office next door. A scowling warder sat at the table. They patently didn't like their well-rehearsed morning routine being disturbed. He looked up and thrust a piece of paper towards her.

'Sign here. You're being released.'

Harriet looked dumbfounded and could only stutter.

'Pardon?'

He growled at her. He was not used to not being obeyed without question.

'Your fine's been paid, you lucky bitch. Now get out before someone changes their mind.'

Harriet rushed between the two towers and through the small portal in the main gate. The quicker she could get out of this sad place, the better. Her problem now, which she hadn't thought about until the door slammed behind her, was how on earth she was going to get home. She didn't have a penny on her and she felt too weak from hunger and emotion to walk the long distance back to the Ferry. She wasn't going to worry about that yet, though. She took in a huge breath of sea air and looked up at the gulls swooping above. She was free.

Out of the corner of her eye, she noticed a car parked across the narrow lane. It seemed strange to see a car, at this early hour and, certainly, in this part of Swansea. She looked twice in disbelief. The man leaning nonchalantly on the bonnet was Ivor, the chauffeur of M G Roberts. Ivor turned and opened the car door. Out appeared the short round figure of M.G. Roberts himself. He waved his hand calling Harriet towards the car. Ivor incongruously held the door open for her.

She felt embarrassed to sit in the back seat of this fine car, undoubtedly smelling of the acrid powder that had been thrown over her the previous day. M.G. Roberts was having none of it. She was going home in style. M.G. Roberts started by apologising.

'I am sorry I didn't manage to pay the fine yesterday and you wouldn't have had to go through all this. I was in London, until last night, and had other things on my mind, I'm afraid.'

Harriet was mystified but had recovered her senses enough to ask.

'You paid the fine for me, Mr Roberts? But why? Fifty pounds is a fortune. I mean thank you with all my heart, but why?'

M.G. Roberts had a desperately sad look on his face as he took a sheet of paper out of his jacket pocket.

'My poor son, Matt, has been killed in France. That makes us brother and sister when you think about David. He wrote this to us two days before he died. I would like you to read it.'

France

Dear Father,

Just a short note to tell you how it's going. I am up in the trenches for the first time and have very little time. I will write fully when I get back to headquarters in a few days' time. You will not believe how stressful the last few days have been. For a start, it is very scary to hear enemy artillery firing and wonder where it will land. Scarier is that I feel so young and inexperienced amongst these men, who have all the experience in the world. How am I supposed to give them orders? My biggest worry is that I will let you, but more importantly them, down.

I have therefore been most fortunate to meet someone who has put me on the straight and narrow. He's not an officer. He's just a simple private although he is by no means simple. You will not believe it but it's Emrys. You will, I'm sure, remember him. You gave him my old bicycle to run errands for you. Anyway, he and I had a wonderful chat last night.

He is a very clever chap and told me how it is. He reassured me that if I listen to the sergeant and behave well with the men, that I will be fine. Don't force it and earn their respect. Such good words. I wish he would be around all the time but he is only with us temporarily.

He told me his plans for starting a mineral water factory after the war. I think I would like us to help him if we can. We also discussed my plans. This might not please you, Father, but just as he has plans for after the war, so have I. I would like to give it a go travelling to Egypt, with Lord Carnarvon, as an archaeologist. I could always go to Medical School, later if it didn't work out. What do you think?

Anyway, I have to sign off now. I am due to go on duty soon. You know now that I will make you proud.

My love to you and the family. Matt

Harriet looked stunned. She turned to M.G. Roberts and said.

'I'm so sorry, Mr Roberts. Master Matthias was such a nice, gentle boy.'

M.G. Roberts replied.

'They're all nice gentle boys, Harriet. Now you see. I couldn't leave Emrys's mam languishing in that place, could I?'

They were both silent during the long journey back, lost in thought. She thought about David and Master Matthias. She thought of Megan, back in prison and what life might hold for her. She especially thought of Emrys, her son who unconsciously had saved her from a month in prison.

There were a few surprised looks when the car drew up outside 11 Neath Road and the person that they all thought to be in prison, got out. Not looking to either side she walked straight through the front door. She opened the inside door and both Josiah and Evelyn looked up. Within a fraction of a second, Evelyn was on her feet screaming 'Mam' and wrapping her arms around her mother.

13

March 1918

Harriet looked up from her knitting. She had been studiously labouring away for the past few hours, only stopping each time the train ground to a halt at a station. Most of her fellow travellers were just enjoying watching the countryside pass by. Enjoying, despite the hard wooden seats in the third class carriages. That wasn't in Harriet's nature. Four hours gazing out of the window was four hours wasted.

Now, the bustle of people getting up from their seats and looking for their belongings suggested that they were nearing their destination. She, carefully, packed her knitting away delighted to have almost finished all the repairing that had piled up at home. She sat, patiently, as the train began to slow. This was her first time out of Wales. In fact, she didn't know anyone else who had ever been to England. Except for M.G. Roberts and his family and the Taylor brothers. And Sir Alfred of course. And the soldiers.

She missed the Taylor brothers and missed working at their foundry. She had enjoyed the camaraderie and working with her daughter. She understood, however, that there was no way that they could continue to employ her. After all, she had been convicted under the War Act. Still, she needn't have been so worried about Mr Parfitt and Evie. She had discovered that her daughter was more than capable of looking after herself, particularly when it came to the likes of Mr Parfitt.

Harriet's problem, although she would never have admitted to it, had been being stuck at home alone except for a recumbent Josiah. She no longer had a growing family to bring up. In fact, for the first time in her life, she had been bored. Perhaps sensing this, M.G. Roberts had requested her presence more and more at Bay View.

So she had felt her hands shaking when she had been summoned to speak to M.G. Roberts, in the large opulent drawing room. Obviously, he was being pressurised to also dismiss her. She was, as she reminded herself frequently, a convicted anti-war protester. She knew that he might have no other choice. Indeed, he looked very serious, when he turned away from the bay window to talk to her. She stood waiting for him to begin, sure that in a few moments, Evelyn would be their sole remaining breadwinner. M.G. Roberts began.

'Harriet. I have received a rather strange request. Sir Alfred Mond wishes to meet with you. You remember Sir Alfred?'

Harriet remembered his hand on her leg.

'He is busy in Parliament, of course. So, he wants you to go to London to his house. He has asked me to give you the train fare and expenses. You might even have to stay the night.'

Harriet was taken aback. The conversation had taken a completely unexpected turn. She wasn't out on her ear. In fact, incredibly, she was going to London. She managed to regain just enough composure to reply.

'Mr Roberts? Have you any idea what this is all about? I mean he hardly knows me.'

M.G. Roberts hadn't been able to help.

'Sorry. It was his secretary that put the request to me. I did ask her but she didn't seem to know. Just said that Sir Alfred would see you at his house at 1 o'clock on Friday. He's always said how attractive and pleasant you were, you know. Perhaps he wants to offer you a job. Or, maybe, it could be something to do with Emrys. Emrys was in his son's platoon in 1916. You never know but he might even want to help get Emrys home.'

That certainly had made Harriet stop in her tracks. Help get her son home. Surely not. There must be some ulterior motive. He said that she was attractive. It couldn't be that either. After all, she was an old lady of thirty-nine with a few strands of grey hair. If he was that way inclined, he could surely have the choice of many eighteen-year old servants in London. Eighteen year old servants who hadn't had four children. People of that class liked kittens, not cats. Her thoughts were interrupted by M.G. Roberts.

'You are fully aware that I will support you whatever. Give you a reference. Or anything else he might want. You, also, know that I would do anything for you to get Emrys home.'

Harriet had only been half listening. Her mind was elsewhere. She too would do anything to get her son home. Absolutely anything. She might be damned to the Eternal Fire but he would be home.

Even Josiah had seemed to notice how attractive she looked when she left for the train station early on Friday morning. Apart, of course, from the large bag of knitting to be done during the journey. That sat incongruously from the arm of her cleaned Sunday dress. Her hair had been washed and carefully combed. She had even borrowed some perfume, preciously secreted from Belgium by Ruth.

She hoped that she looked more like Evie's sister than her mam. Harriet was arming herself for every eventuality. As she had reminded herself every hour, she would do anything to get her son home.

As she dismounted the carriage at Paddington Station, her courage began to fail her. She took a deep breath and looked around the teaming metropolis, which was so alien to her. Her courage returned as suddenly as it had left. She was ready for anything.

36, Lowndes Square, Belgravia. Somehow, she had managed to get there. The large clock on the church tower told her that she had arrived with ten minutes to spare. She was sweating profusely, half from anxiety and half from walking so far in her thick dress. It was, indeed, a grand house. Even larger and more palatial than Bay View. The porch, jutting out into the square, was bigger than the whole of her house and flanked by large, imposing stone columns. This obviously wasn't meant for the likes of her. There must be another entrance.

Carefully avoiding the thick layer of coal dust, she descended the narrow staircase leading to the basement. Taking yet another deep breath, she quietly knocked on the door. She stood, still sweating, waiting for it to open. A stern lady finally appeared and, not bothering to speak, looked quizzically. Harriet nervously stuttered, worried that her thick Welsh accent might not be understood.

'Is this Sir Alfred Mond's house? I'm supposed to be here at 1 o'clock.'

The stern lady growled at her.

'Name?'

Harriet hardly had time to reply before the door was firmly shut in her face. She stood there mesmerised. What on earth should she do now? This was certainly a strange place. The door, suddenly, flew back open again. This time, the lady stood with a very different look on her face. Indeed, she stuttered, nervously, as she spoke.

'You are expected, Madame. You have come to the wrong door. Mr Richards is waiting for you at the front door.'

She stopped before tentatively continuing.

'Madame. I must apologise if I appeared rude. I didn't mean to be.'

Harriet had never been called Madame before. Why should she be? Like this woman, she just worked in the house of a rich man. She smiled and laid a reassuring hand on the woman's arm, before turning to climb back up the stairway. Staring down at her was a balding man, in a long tailored jacket with matching trousers. This must be Mr Richards. He politely enquired.

'Mrs John. I trust you had a pleasant journey. My name is Richards. If I can be of any service, while you are with us, please ask.'

By this time, Harriet had climbed the narrow stairway and was mounting the far more opulent steps in the ornate portico. To her acute embarrassment, Richards gave her a shallow bow as she entered through the wide doorway. She turned to Richards.

'It's lovely to meet you. Please could you call me Harriet? What is your Christian name?'

Richards looked shocked.

'Mrs John. I couldn't possibly call you by your first name. Sir Alfred wouldn't approve. You must call me Richards.'

Richards showed her into a large room with yellow, button-back chairs and small mahogany tables. The walls were covered with ancient paintings. Above the ornate fireplace, with a roaring log fire, was a more modern portrait painting. A severe man, who looked like an older version of Sir Alfred, stared down at her menacingly. Richards began to talk.

'Mr Ludwig. Sir Alfred's father. A very good likeness I believe. Now, Mrs John. Please take a seat. Sir Alfred has not returned from the House as yet. He instructed me to make sure you were comfortable after your long journey. Can I get you a drink? A sherry, perhaps.'

Richards was surprised to see the look of horror on her face as Harriet, tentatively, took her place in one of the majestic chairs. She answered, softly.

'Mr Richards. I never drink alcohol. A nice cup of tea would be lovely. And, Mr Richards? Whose house is Sir Alfred at and will he be long?'

Harriet felt so ignorant when Richards replied.

'The House is The House of Commons. I can't say how long he will be. Depends on how long things go on, I suppose. I will bring the tea shortly. I think you might enjoy Ceylon.'

Harriet watched him bow again, before turning gracefully through the door, shutting it carefully, behind him. Harriet was left alone in this huge opulent room. She realised that she didn't like it. Perhaps she was acting above her station. Or perhaps she was, indeed, a Bolshevik. Nobody should have this amount of wealth.

The real reason she didn't like it was that, despite the blazing fire, it felt cold. It had no family warmth, a lived-in warmth like her tiny back room, at home. Apart from the austere painting of Sir Alfred's father, there was nothing personal. It was more like the museum that she had read about. She sat examining the old pictures. She even recognised some of the Old Testament stories, but each of them was festooned by a worrying amount of nakedness. The naked figures seemed to be of all ages and sizes. What odd paintings to liven up your best room with.

Harriet jumped to her feet when the door suddenly opened, surprised that Sir Alfred had returned so early. It wasn't Sir Alfred. A young girl, even younger than Evelyn, pushed the door with one hand while holding a tray with the other. Harriet leapt forward to help her. The young girl looked at her with shock. She was the lowest rank in the household. Nobody normally helped her. Certainly, nobody sitting in this room. The tray held an exquisite teapot with a matching floral pattern hot water jug, even more intricate than those in Bay View. A single cup and saucer were made from the most delicate of porcelain. But something was missing. The young girl seemed to read her mind.

'Lady Mildred refuses to let milk be served with tea. She says it's common.'

The young girl left again, curtseying to Harriet as she went. Harriet was left alone once more to study the paintings. She noticed a small plate of thin biscuits. Despite not having eaten since the early hours she wasn't hungry. She was too anxious to be hungry. She, carefully, emptied the plate into her coat pocket. Evelyn and Josiah would enjoy eating them when she got home.

She was nearly caught in the act. That would have been embarrassing. A moment later, the door flew open once more. This time it was not the young girl. It was a short rotund gentleman with a large bushy, black moustache. His hair was receding at the front but swept long behind his ears. It was Sir Alfred Mond. Harriet, immediately, shot out of her chair and curtsied. Sir Alfred waved her back into her chair.

'For goodness sake sit down. You are a welcome guest at my house. I am only sorry that I wasn't here to greet you, myself. The Prime Minister was going on a bit so I couldn't get away.'

Harriet's face had gone bright red with embarrassment thinking about the stolen biscuits in her pocket. What would happen if they were discovered? Sir Alfred continued.

'My dear lady, we are most grateful for you coming all this way. You will be wondering why we have summoned you. It's about your son, of course. My daughter, Mrs Isaacs, will be here shortly and may have some more news.'

More news? What could that mean? Had something happened to Emrys? Something terrible? She, surely, couldn't be kept waiting and began to speak.

'Sir Alfred. Has...'

She didn't manage to finish her sentence. The door swung open once more and a thin young lady rushed in and kissed Sir Alfred on the cheek.

'How are you, father? Lloyd George not working you to the bone I hope.'

Sir Alfred pulled his daughter gently by the arm over to Harriet, before speaking.

'Eva, I don't believe you have met Mrs Harriet John, Boxer's mother. Mrs John, this is my daughter, Mrs Eva Isaacs.'

For once Harriet was silent. Who on earth was Boxer? The young lady smiled directly at her while replying to her father.

'Actually, I have, Father. I was at the recruiting hall when she came in with Boxer. Or should I say Emrys? It must have been way back in 1915. I remember how young he looked.'

At least that explained one thing. For some unfathomable reason, they knew her son as Boxer. But it didn't explain what she was doing there. At least, she could now be sure that Sir Alfred had no ulterior motive. Indeed, she felt stupid to even have imagined it. He was now looking expectantly at his daughter.

'Well, Eva. Have you any news for Mrs John?'

Eva Isaacs beamed back.

'I absolutely have. They're in Italy. They went down there to help fight the Austrians. But there's been almost no fighting, so they've been lucky.'

Harriet could stand it no longer. She almost shouted with frustration.

'Who, on earth, are you talking about.'

Eva Isaacs smiled again, this time at Harriet.'

'The cyclists, of course. The XI Corps Cyclists. Emrys and his friends. He's not in France at all. He's having an easy time in Italy.'

Sir Alfred was becoming visibly more excited.

'The point is can we get him home? At least he's not in Flanders but can we get him home?'

Harriet noticed that Mrs Isaacs was still beaming when she continued.

'You know how fond Sir Rufus is of Henry. So, it wasn't hard to get him interested. Sir Rufus has been in contact with General Haking's ADC. Emrys is quite safe. As soon as they're back in France, we'll get him leave. Then, we'll not let him go back. Do anything to keep him here. Get him a job in the

Ministry of Defence or something.'

Trembling, Harriet kept quiet. This was mad talk. It had nothing to do with her surely. It had to be though. They were talking about her son. At that moment, Eva Isaacs looked over at their guest, sitting silently, on her face a look of startled incredulity. She continued, addressing Harriet this time.

'My dear Mrs John. You don't understand. We're going to get Emrys home. We must. Sir Rufus is my father-in-law. The Attorney General, Sir Rufus Isaacs. He can get whatever he likes. Mind you, we had a bit of trouble when we found that you had been convicted under the Act. That nearly threw a spanner in the works. The Attorney General helping an anti-conscriptor. Wouldn't do, would it? So you must promise not to tell anyone. Not even your family.'

Harriet finally summoned enough courage to stammer.

'But why? Why now? We've never done anything for you. Emrys hasn't even seen your brother since 1916. It must be two years now. And after what I've done.'

Mrs Isaacs looked very solemn for a moment, scrambling through her handbag to produce a piece of paper. She read it slowly herself, before handing it to Harriet. She whispered.

'It's a poem. It's written by Henry. It explains a lot of what we've been through for the last couple of years.'

Harriet looked at the neatly written poem.

Lord keep us safe this night
From evil and from harm
And may we dream aright
Lord let our sleep be calm

Lord make our darkness light
Lest in the dark we see
Unbearable before our sight
The things that must not be

Let nothing near us stray
No doubtful smell or sound
But let us feel as though we lay
Quite safe deep underground

Lord keep us safe this night
From evil and from harm
And if we dream we dream aright
Lord let our sleep be calm

Despite tears pouring down both cheeks, Harriet didn't understand. This young man was obviously very troubled but none of it made any sense. She looked sadly at Henry Mond's sister who gently questioned her.

'Did Emrys say anything about helping Henry? Perhaps something about giving him some blood? A blood transfusion?'

Harriet shook her head.

'We had an agreement not to talk about the war. Particularly, after David died. Even the time he came home with Major Davies. When Major Davies got married.'

Eva Isaacs nodded sagely as she continued.

'Well, we knew nothing about it either. Not till last week. You see when I got over to the hospital in France to visit Henry, he couldn't say a word. Nothing apart from 'Boxer', which is what he called your son. In fact, he didn't say a word for months. Not at all in the Officers Hospital. He just woke up screaming or couldn't sleep at all, just shaking. He was suffering something known as Shell Shock. In fact, if truth be told, he is still suffering from it. He still wakes up screaming, poor thing.

Eventually, we got him home and he improved. He began to talk and even, occasionally, laugh. Only, he wouldn't say anything about what had happened. The psychiatrist tried to get him to talk.'

Harriet noticed the disapproving look on Sir Alfred's face when he interrupted.

'Psychiatrist. Bloody charlatan, if you ask me.'

Eva Isaacs laughed for the first time.

'Father, for a scientist, you are remarkably old-fashioned.'

Harriet winced, expecting an explosion of temper from Sir Alfred. Certainly, it would have happened if Evelyn had dared to speak like that to Josiah. The young lady had stopped smiling, as she continued.

'In fact, Henry, despite everything, decided to go back to the front. It was then that I remembered the advice that your son gave to me on the beach, in Boulogne.'

Harriet looked up with renewed interest but uttered in disbelief.

'You met Emrys? On a beach? I remember him talking about Boulogne.'

Eva Isaacs replied.

'Yes. It was on a beach in Boulogne. The beach by the hospital. He gave me some very good advice. We managed to keep Henry home. It was, definitely, excellent advice.'

Harriet still didn't understand. This must have happened way back in 1916. The best part of two years ago. She could only sit listening patiently, as the young lady continued.

'And then Gwen happened.'

That look returned to Sir Alfred's face. He seemed to think the same about this Gwen, as he did the psychiatrist. Eva Isaacs, definitely, wasn't going to laugh this time.

'Father, I know you disapprove of Gwen but even you must admit that she has done wonders for Henry. Mrs John, you don't need to know the details. You might have read about it in the newspapers anyway. Henry is living with Gwen and he, at last, seems to have turned the corner. She has, actually, got him to speak about what happened. Two weeks ago, he started talking to her about the explosion. That's how we now know what your son did for Henry in 1916. We are just mortified that we didn't know before.'

Harriet could just look on, unusually quiet. She had nothing to say. Emrys hadn't mentioned a thing about Henry Mond, on any of the few occasions he had got home. He certainly wouldn't have worried his mother by discussing an explosion. She sat, with hands grasping each other tightly, waiting for Mrs Isaacs to continue. It was Sir Alfred who spoke first.

'Yes. I suppose you don't know that your son and Henry were in a tunnel when there was an explosion. The Germans blew up a mine and the tunnel collapsed. Your son dug Henry out and then accompanied him back to the dressing station. Henry was so unwell that they were just going to leave him to die. Emrys wouldn't let them. He made them take him back to the casualty clearing centre'.

Harriet turned to look at Eva Isaacs as she took over from her father.

'But this is the amazing bit. They took a pint of blood off Emrys and gave it to Henry. Saved his life.'

Harriet looked shocked as she interrupted.

'Took blood off Emrys and gave it to Henry? What in God's name are you talking about?'

Eva Isaacs was smiling once more.

'We were surprised too. Yes. They took blood, with a tube, out of Emrys's arm. Then they put into Henry. It's called a blood transfusion. Henry was lucky. Transfusion, apparently, is a North American thing and his doctor was Canadian. All in all, it saved Henry's life.'

Harriet could only whisper.

'I don't know what to say. We didn't know anything about it. Nothing.'

Eva Isaacs looked at her father.

'Father. Mrs John's tea must be getting cold. Shall I call for some more?'

Surely, they weren't about to stop the conversation simply for another cup of tea.

Harriet was relieved when Sir Alfred replied.

'I'm sure Mrs John would prefer to hear the end of your story. I mean you've nearly finished. We will have tea while we discuss what to do next. Perhaps we will have some sandwiches too. Mrs John must be starving. Look, she's eaten all her biscuits.'

Eva Isaacs started again, looking back at Harriet.

'Well. Father is probably right. There isn't much more to tell, anyway. After the transfusion, Emrys accompanied Henry to the hospital in Boulogne. Henry had an operation on his jaw. Mother and I went over to collect Henry and bring him home.'

For some unfathomable reason, she was chuckling when she spoke next.

'That was when I met Emrys. As I mentioned he was having a swim in the sea. Anyway, we brought Henry back to The Queen Alexandra Hospital for Officers, which Father is chairman of. I'm ashamed to say that we left Emrys at the beach to make his way back to the battalion. We are truly, truly sorry. If we had known, we'd have brought him home too. And not let him go back. But we are determined to try to make up for it now. We'll get him home this time.'

Harriet hadn't done any knitting or repairing, on the last train home that night. She just couldn't concentrate. In fact, she wouldn't have had any knitting, at all, if Richards hadn't raced after the taxicab, clutching the forgotten bag. She could only look out as the lights flashed past and think about her amazing day. The house and the paintings. Sir Alfred and Mrs Isaacs. But mostly Emrys and how he was coming home.

She quietly let herself through her front door, hoping not to wake anyone. She jumped in shock as a fully dressed Josiah got up from his chair. She shouldn't have been surprised that he would have stayed up waiting for her. A second later, a figure in a long white night dress flashed into the room. Evelyn might have gone to bed but Harriet knew she would also be waiting, unable to sleep.

Harriet was surprisingly calm when she spoke.

'He's coming home. They are bringing Emrys home.'

14

The next day, Harriet was sitting in front of the cricket pavilion. It had become a regular part of her life. Ruth had become such a good friend. Sitting here, away from the traumas of home, had been a lifeline. Ruth was the only one of her friends that she could truly confide in without it immediately becoming common gossip. Today, she had disclosed everything that had happened the previous day. Even the things that she was not supposed to.

Ruth spoke dreamily with a heavy Belgian accent, despite four years in Wales.

'I wonder if he's been to Florence. I've always wanted to go to Florence. Never shall now.'

Harriet replied.

'Yes, you will. When this is all over.'

She stopped for a moment, before continuing.

'Ruth. Can I tell you something?'

She didn't give her friend the opportunity to reply.

'When Sir Alfred called for me. I would have done anything to get Emrys home. Anything. That's terrible, isn't it? What sort of person am I?

Her friend was quick to reply.

'A mother. It makes you a mother. Don't you think I would do the same for my boys? Mind you, unlike you, I would never have the opportunity.'

Harriet grabbed her friend's hand.

'Don't be ridiculous. You, always, do yourself down. Anyway, Sir Alfred might like a nice Jewish lady.'

They both laughed loudly. They said nothing else for a few minutes, just enjoying the spring sun. Ruth still had a dreamy look on her face. Harriet asked.

'Ruth. You're thinking happy thoughts. Share them with me.'

Ruth smiled at her friend.

'Actually, I was thinking about Emrys. How lucky he is going to be. He'll have a lovely train ride back from Italy. The Alps, Avignon, Lyon and, then, Paris. The Rhône is supposed to be spectacular in the spring, with the blossom on the almond trees. Then he'll be home forever.'

Harriet felt a glow of optimism wash over her for the first time in years.

Emrys was sitting on the filthy floor of the cattle wagon with his back to the wooden side, looking out of the open door. It was indeed an idyllic train journey. That was despite the overpowering stench of horse manure emanating from the rear carriages. They were sharing the train with The King Edward Seventh Horse.

Every stop seemed to be prolonged by the horses being taken out to stretch their legs, by the pompous South African troopers. Still, it had meant that the cyclists had been able to get out themselves, breathing in the crisp air of the Alps, which had been their snow-covered friends for the previous months. The Alps were, now, disappearing behind them, signalling their dreaded return to France.

The slow movement along the single track and repetitive clunkedy clunk was making him feel tired. He was exhausted from having done nothing for three days. He looked down at the letter, only half written, and read it once more. He wasn't going to tell his mam about two things. Firstly, he still hadn't told her that they had become machine gunners, despite David's stern advice, all those years ago. The second reason was related. They had needed the extra 3d per day to pay for the Vina Rosa that they had become very partial to. As Major Davies had warned them before Christmas, the Vina Rosa was much stronger than the watered-down Vin Rouge, which they had drunk in France.

Dear Mam,

Sorry I haven't been able to write to you for some time. We were not allowed to because we have been in Italy and nobody was supposed to know. Now, we are returning to France we can tell you.

Italy is a wonderful country. Not like France. Mind you, we had a real bit of luck. Our company was cycling up to the front when we got called back. Nobody, not even the major, seemed to know why. We got the best job ever. All we did, for two months, was act as guards at the headquarters of General Haking. It was the prettiest place you ever seen, with a stream running through it. The town square was huge with really old houses. We spent our time off there. Up above us were the biggest mountains you ever seen. The tops are covered in snow, even in the summer. You would love it.

We are upset we are coming back to France. Mind you I had a nice surprise. As soon as we get back, I am coming home on leave. It's not even my turn but I'm not arguing. Somebody must have messed up because Gwyn should have been home before me. He's pretty upset but he'll get over it. Major Davies said something odd. He said that I must have friends in high places. No idea what he's talking about. Never mind I'm coming home. I might even be home before this letter.

He put the letter down and closed his eyes. He would finish it later. He had plenty of time. He had days, the rate that this train was travelling at. Now, he just needed to sleep. He just prayed that the return to France would not also signal a return of the dreams. The terrible dreams, which had seemed to have melted away, like the snow, in Italy. He fell into a deep sleep, still sitting with his back wedged painfully against the side of the carriage.

The dreams had returned. Only worse than ever. He was back in the tunnel with Lieutenant Mond. The tunnel roared with the roof crashing and shaking crazily. He opened his eyes, the only way to end the vivid vision. Only this time it didn't end. The side of the carriage, behind him, continued to vibrate as the one in front fractured viciously into jagged splinters. Then, nothing. For a few seconds, there was complete silence. Emrys looked around him. Everyone did the same. Even the ones who had been thrown to the floor. Remarkably, despite the ruinous condition of the carriage, Emrys couldn't see any injuries. Except for cuts and bruises. There were plenty of those. Gwyn held his hand to his head, blood seeping through his fingers.

Blind panic forced Emrys to bolt for the open doorway, unashamedly leaving his friends to manage for themselves. If a Whizzbang had their range, another round could be expected in close order. Then, he remembered. It couldn't be a Whizzbang. They were hundreds of miles from the front.

As he jumped down beside the track, a ghostly figure raced

past, missing him by inches. It was a large grey cavalry horse with blood splashing from a wound on his neck. The blood now covering his tunic was horse rather than human.

A French station master ran in the opposite direction towards the back of the train, waving his arms madly. The noise from shouting people, whinnying horses and discharging steam, was deafening. The odd thing was that the whistle of steam was coming from the rear of the carriages. Their engine, surely, was at the front.

Before he could look any further at the carnage around him, Emrys felt his arm being tugged. Major Davies must have got out of the first class carriage, towards the front of the train, at breakneck speed.

'Jump to it, men. Let's see what aid we can be. Be careful of the horses.'

Emrys found himself jogging behind his leader, swiftly followed by Ted and a handful of other members of the platoon. Those who were not either staunching their wounds or shaking from shock. Emrys couldn't get over how calm he felt. Perhaps after the tunnel and the time with the Australians, this was easy. The cyclists had undoubtedly been fortunate. Their carriages were mostly undamaged, apart from a few extra holes. It would be cold, if and when they got moving again.

The carriage behind was still on the rails but the whole of one side had been ripped off, as if by some malignant giant. A dead horse lay with its head draped over the edge, dripping blood and saliva. Behind two troopers comforted a wounded comrade while screaming frantically for stretcher-bearers.

Major Davies led them to the next carriage back. Only some of its wheels seemed to be on the rails and it had been, viciously, split down the middle. Nothing could be seen through the closed door, but Emrys could hear a high pitch wail and an intermittent crashing against the side panel. He looked at Major Davies, desperate for reassurance, as he tentatively opened the door and peered into the dark. He could see another horse, this time black, struggling in a vain effort to get to its feet despite a shattered leg. Each time it failed, it let out a wail of fear and pain.

Emrys and Ted, carefully, got up into the carriage. The poor beast was suffering terribly and could kick out, at any moment. He seemed to look Emrys straight in the eye, pleading for help. Emrys knew what he was going to do. What he had to do. Discharging a weapon, when not ordered to, was a great offence but he didn't care. He was next to the horse's head, stroking its ear in a forlorn effort to comfort it, when he drew his revolver, from its holster. Machine gunners carried revolvers, rather than rifles. Too late, Ted shouted.

'Emrys. No. You can't.'

The shout was cut short by the deafening reverberation of the discharge in the confined space. Emrys jumped back, automatically, his ears ringing, as the dead horse convulsed violently. Finally, it was motionless, out of pain at last. Despite the cold weather, Emrys was sweating profusely as he stared down at his handiwork, still clutching his revolver. Momentarily deaf, he couldn't decipher Ted's moving mouth. Then he could.

'Fucking hell, Emrys. What do you think you're doing?'

Through the smoke, they could see an angry face staring at them from the doorway. It was the cavalry major, who had shouted at them back in Milan station. What had they been up to? Getting in the way, probably. His gravely South African accent sounded even angrier this time.

'Did you shoot that horse, boy?'

Emrys knew that he was in trouble. The smoking revolver was still in his hand. He had used his weapon without permission. This bastard would want full retribution. Emrys stuttered.

'Yes, sir. It was me. Had to, sir. Really did. He was suffering. I couldn't stand it. He's at peace, major. Sorry, major.'

The major's reply surprised him.

'Boy. Never apologise when you are correct. You have put that poor beast out of his misery. All I can say is thank you. You are a credit to your unit. Now, look around this carnage and see what else you can find.'

Making sure that he wasn't heard by the major, Ted whispered to Emrys.

'Horse stew, tonight.'

They jumped when a pain-filled voice whispered from behind a pile of rubble.

'That's my fucking horse. If you eat him, I'll fucking kill you.'

Emrys and Ted, frantically, pulled away the rubble to expose a pale, pain-racked trooper. The cause of the pain was obvious. His thigh was bent at an angle which could only be caused by some horrendous break. The trooper looked up at Emrys.

'Are you the bastard who shot my horse?'

Emrys was too embarrassed to reply. The poor man, whose life had just been permanently changed, whispered again.

'Thank you. You're a mate. That horse was my life.'

They had to be careful. Two French ambulance men had appeared as if from nowhere and were waiting expectantly for a client. The two cyclists waited for the ambulance men to jump up but they weren't coming anywhere near this wreck, inhabited by some idiot, with a revolver. On top of that, only one set of wheels was still on their tracks, while the others were twisted at outrageous angles. It seemed as if a gust of wind might blow the whole thing over.

They were on their own. Ted grabbed the trooper under the armpits. Emrys stopped at the legs. He just couldn't do it. He knew what agony he would cause if he moved the shattered thigh. Through teeth grinding together in a vain attempt to kill the pain, the trooper whispered.

'Come on, boy. You have to do it. If I can stand it, you can. Now, get me out of this fucking place.'

Emrys screwed his eyes up as he lifted the two legs, trying to cut out the screams. He could feel the two ends of the thigh bone grating against each other, as they placed the trooper carefully in the arms of the awaiting Frenchmen.

Emrys felt Ted tugging on his sleeve and pointing him in the direction of the far end of the carriage. In the dark corner, sat a single silent figure. His eyes were firmly closed. He could have been sleeping. He was, however, deathly pale. Emrys and Ted slowly cleared a path, through the debris, and finally stood next to him. A large stake protruding viciously through his chest fixed him to the side of the carriage. He must have died instantly. Emrys was sick of dead bodies. He'd seen more than his share.

'Poor bugger. Came all this way to fight Gerry and he gets himself killed in a bloody train crash.'

He shouted over to the cavalry major.

'Major, sir. There's a dead corporal back here. We will need some help getting him out. Sorry, sir.'

The major answered calmly.

'Thank you, boy. Help is coming.'

Emrys and Ted were sitting against a fence at the side of the track. Having been helped to lever the dead trooper off the stake and lift him carefully into the hands of the ambulance men, they had clambered down from the carriage. Emrys bent over and wretched. Ted put his arm around his friend's shoulder and led him away from the track.

They were, at last, able to survey the bedlam in front of them. As the troop train had slowed to enter a station the civilian one behind it had not. It had slammed into the back of their train with the force of a jackhammer. The rear carriages, which had housed the cavalrymen and their horses, had been reduced to matchwood.

Dead horses seemed to be everywhere. Every so often, a single shot signalled that another had been added to that number. The civilian train continued to belch black smoke noisily, while its passengers spilt out onto the track, gesticulating irritatingly about the inconvenient halt.

Emrys had his eyes closed. He was trying to cut as much as he could out of his memory. He felt Ted's gentle hand lifting him to his feet. He looked up. Major Davies was striding purposely towards them. What on earth could he want now? As he got nearer, he waved his two men back to their seats.

'Major Macdonald, from King Edward's Horse, has asked me to thank you. As you can imagine, he has too much on his plate to do it personally. So, well done, lads.'

Emrys closed his eyes once more. Normally, a compliment from the battalion commander was a cherished event. It could result in a bonus or extra time off. This time, Emrys couldn't care less. He just wanted to go home.

Harriet looked over their small table and witnessed a rare event, these days. Josiah was beaming at their daughter. She didn't know why. Her mind had been elsewhere. It was still at M.G. Roberts's house, earlier that morning. She had been summoned for a second time into his drawing room. He had smiled at her this time when he spoke.

'Harriet. I have news. Sir Alfred has telephoned me. He has told me that I am able to inform you, as long as you promise not to tell anyone. Not even Josiah and certainly not Evelyn. Will you be able to do that?'

She already knew that it could only be good news. Excitedly, she had promised before M.G. Roberts had time to continue.

'The XI Corps are on their way back from Italy. The cyclists are with them. They'll be back in France any day. Then, Emrys will be coming home. Home for good.'

She looked over at Josiah again. A promise is a promise and she hadn't broken it. He seemed to know though. So, she asked.

'What are you two smiling about?'

Josiah smiled again at Evelyn, who spoke excitedly.

'Mam. Don't you know? You were singing. We haven't heard you sing for years. It was lovely, Mam. Just don't stop.'

Harriet laughed, for the first time, and all three, even Josiah, began to sing.

'My bonnie lies over the ocean.
My bonnie lies over the sea.
My bonnie lies over the ocean
So bring back my bonnie to me.'

A few hundred miles away, the cyclists were at last standing to attention, outside Bethune station. The train journey had been long and arduous. Emrys couldn't get the poor corporal out of his mind. He couldn't wait to get back on his bike after a week stuck in the cattle truck, fighting his memories. He would be pleased to be doing anything even if it was just to cycle back across the bridge to Essars.

Bethune was not the carefree town, which he had last visited a few months previously. The ornate ticket office of the station was now a hollow black shell. A direct hit from something. A small column of unshaven soldiers marched slowly past them. Emrys whispered.

'Look at that scruffy lot. Must be Italian.'

Gwyn coughed violently before whispering back.

'Naw. They're Portuguese.'

In the centre of the square, Major Davies was talking urgently to Captain Parry as he reread the contents of a small piece of paper. Something was up. Emrys wasn't bothered. Why should he be? He was off on leave, in a few days. Major Davies clapped his hands for silence.

'Men. We are, certainly, back in France. I have here an Order of the Day issued by Field Marshal Haig himself. It is an order to the whole British Army.'

Major Davies put his glasses on and began to read aloud.

'There is no other course open to us but to fight it out. Every position must be held to the last man. There must be no retirement. With our backs to the wall and believing in the justice of our cause each of us must fight to the end. The safety of our homes and freedom of mankind alike depend upon each of us at this critical moment.'

He took his glasses off before looking up at his men.

'We seem to have arrived back here at just the right time.

We have to be alert and ready, at all times. That means that you will be confined to camp in Essars until further notice. All home leave has been cancelled.'

15

April 9 1918

Emrys was not in a good mood, as he cycled alongside the rest of the battalion. He would have been at home if it wasn't for Field Marshall Haig and his bloody Order of the Day. The Lewis gun, strapped precariously to the side of his bike, felt even heavier than usual. David had been right about being a machine gunner. It should, of course, have been pitch black at that early hour. The horizon in front of them, however, had been lit up by violent explosions, for hours. Gwyn muttered to him.

'Some poor bugger is catching it up there.'

Emrys didn't reply. Up there was exactly the direction that they were heading. At that moment, there was a cry from Major Davies.

'Stop, men, and off your bicycles, quickly.'

Perhaps up there was not where they were heading. As they began piling up their bicycles at the side of an incongruously worrying cemetery, Emrys looked over at the other side of the narrow road. Long files of soldiers were piling out of a row of lorries. Heavily armed soldiers. Their officers were strutting around in jodhpurs. A cavalry regiment. A cavalry regiment with no horses. He thought he recognised them. They were, surely, none other than The King Edward VII Horse, whom they had shared a train with coming back from Italy.

Then, he knew he was right. Marching towards him was the major who had talked to them. What was his name? That's right, Major Macdonald. The major must have recognised him because he stuck out his hand and shook Emrys's firmly.

'Good luck, soldier.'

Emrys looked pointedly at Gwyn and Ted. This really must be serious. Cavalry officers didn't normally go around shaking an ordinary soldier's hands. They watched the officer also shake hands with their own major. Major Macdonald unfolded a map and pointed.

'Good morning, Percy. I think we may have pulled the short straw this time. We are guarding the bridge behind us. Place is called Vielle Chapelle. I understand you are going to cycle to this bridge, at La Couture. If one is overrun the other will be outflanked. You agree I presume?'

Major Davies answered confidently.

'Absolutely correct. Spot on, except we will leave our bicycles here with you. They will only get in the way otherwise. We will march to La Couture. It's less than a mile away.'

Almost 24 hours later, Emrys was sitting on the muddy floor of the strongpoint trying to rest. His trousers were soaking wet but what did it matter? That was the least of his problems. The atmosphere wreaked of despair. Despair and blood. Thinking back, he had had times during this dreadful war, which had been unbelievably horrendous. The tunnel in Givenchy, the Australian trench in Le Trou, and the train in God knew where came to mind. This strong point in some God-forsaken place, called La Couture, beat the lot.

He closed his eyes again and tried to think of home. He couldn't. His head ached continuously making him feel sick. He was deaf in his right ear and blood trickled from it. The continuous crashes from his Lewis gun must have damaged something.

He thought back to the previous day with anguish. It was strange that three years into the war, he had been able to convince himself that he had never killed anyone. Not now, that's for sure. The fact that they were not even Germans made matters infinitely worse. The previous morning, God help him, he had killed men from his own side.

The cyclists had waited all morning peering into the ghostly fog, which lay on the far side of the bridge. They had, eventually, begun to relax. Perhaps this was just another false alarm. Suddenly, hundreds of men were sprinting towards them. For a machine gunner, this was a present sent from heaven. All four guns and scores of rifles had opened up on the juicy target. They couldn't miss. Suddenly, Captain Lucas had rushed in with a look of panic on his face.

'Cease fire. For God's sake, stop. They're on our side. They're Portuguese. They're retreating.'

He still remembered the looks of anger on the faces of the survivors, as they struggled towards the rear. He had not been able to look at them. Despite telling himself that someone ought to have told them about the Portuguese, he still felt guilty. That feeling of guilt seemed to dominate all the other dreadful feelings he had endured. The sheer terror, caused by the frequent German attacks dispersed by even more terrifying bombardments. The feeling of claustrophobia from being in this confined space and the all-encompassing gas mask. The mask must have a leak because he was sure he could smell the eye-watering stench of gas.

He looked around the dark inside of the strongpoint, lit up by the frequent flashes of explosions in the distance. They had been left alone since just after midnight. No attacks. No shell bursts. It would not last forever. Dawn was drawing inexorably nearer. Their troubles would quickly return. He could hear the chatter of Lewis guns further up the road. The cavalry regiment was definitely not having such a quiet time. Emrys hoped that the charismatic, if scary, Major Macdonald was still in one piece.

At that precise moment a messenger, from the King Edwards Horse arrived. He looked around and saw Major Davies sitting a few feet from Emrys. Saluting as if on parade ground he began.

'Major Macdonald's compliments, sir. Major Macdonald wishes to know if you will continue to hold the bridge. If you do not then he will have to withdraw from Vielle Chappelle. He also wishes to inform you that many of your bicycles have been stolen.'

Major Davies looked at the trooper incredulously.

'Stolen? What do you mean stolen?'

The trooper couldn't suppress the smallest of smiles when he continued.

'Portuguese, sir. The Portuguese have pinched most of your bikes and buggered off. Beg your pardon, sir.'

Major Davies recovered quickly and authoritatively.

'Thank you, soldier. Tell Major Macdonald that we will hold for as long as we can in the morning. Also, tell him that we are getting short of ammunition. If we get no supplies, we will not be able to hold for long.'

Emrys watched the cavalryman disappear out of the small opening in the back of the strongpoint. He looked around him. Ted sitting next to him couldn't sleep either. They just smiled weakly at one another. Gwyn was watching the bridge, through the narrow aperture. Gwyn coughed frequently as he grasped his beloved Lewis gun. He had insisted on coming despite being ill. Bloody idiot.

Also keeping an attentive guard was a fierce-looking man with a large bushy beard. Emrys was ashamed that he didn't know this fierce fighter's name. He was one of the Portuguese who had turned to fight with the cyclists. They all looked grey-faced, with bloodshot eyes from the continuous smell of cordite in this confined space.

Major Davies had promised that they would hold but he must know that one more Gerry attack and that would be it. They would all be killed or captured. That was a sobering thought.

Emrys turned to look at Major Davies, the most positive man in the world. He was shocked by what he saw. The major was staring at him a tear running down his cheek. He whispered.

'Sorry, soldier. I was just thinking of your mam bringing you into the recruiting station, all those years ago. Make sure you get back to her.'

Captain Lucas sat down next to his friend.

'You all right?'

Major Davies nodded slowly.

'I'm just worried about these boys. I honestly don't give a damn about myself. It's them I always worry about and Margaret, of course. Did I tell you she's going to have a baby? I'm going to be a father.'

Captain Lucas asked the question which everyone already knew the answer to.

'We must be able to get out of here somehow. Get you back to be a dad.'

Major Davies shook his head.

'Afraid not. There's a hole in the line the size of Swansea. We need to hold that damned bridge for as long as we can in the morning. Give the general a chance to plug that gap.'

Captain Lucas looked over to Emrys and the rest, who were furtively listening to everything that was being said. He needed to lighten the mood.

'You know who we need. We need Henry. Henry Mond. He'd be on the top of the barricade alongside some mad Portuguese bloke.'

Percy Davies smiled as his friend continued.

'Have you heard anything of Henry? It must be almost two years since he was wounded.'

Percy Davies looked over at Emrys and Ted, once more. He didn't normally talk in front of the men. Then you could see the look change on his face. What the hell? They will probably all be dead in a few hours.

'You obviously haven't heard the rumours involving Gilbert Cannon, the writer. He writes novels. Not much good if you ask me, but Margaret likes them. Anyway, Henry crashed that bloody motorbike of his outside this chap Cannon's house in St. John's Wood. Cannon's eighteen year old lover rushes out and takes Henry into the house to nurse him. God knows why. Rumour is that Cannon and Henry now share this girl. Gwen Wilson her name is. They apparently tell everyone that they are a threesome. There was even a rumour going around that they all sleep in the same bed, but that might well be an exaggeration.'

Captain Lucas looked on in awe.

'No. You've got to be bloody joking. Where did you get all that nonsense from?'

Emrys and his friends were pretending not to listen as they stared out into the darkness. Certainly, this was a totally alien world to anything that they had ever even imagined, in Briton Ferry. It was Lieutenant Mond as well. Such an upstanding man. Their commander laughed as he continued.

'No, it's true. You know my father is in the newspaper business. He says it's fact, so it probably is. Good luck to Henry I say. He's certainly a lot better off there than here. Don't know what Sir Alfred Mond thinks about it though.'

Major Davies seemed to have recovered. The moment of light-heartedness must have rescued him. He was back to his efficient self. Emrys looked at Ted and shook his head. These people definitely lived in a totally different bloody world. In his house, back home, there were frequently three or even four sharing a bed but not for the same reason.

Another bombardment began. There were more cries from the wounded outside. Those who could be moved were laid against the back wall of the strongpoint or in one of the ruined buildings. Those who could not were just given a blanket and some morphine.

A further two figures staggered in. Their friend Flinty, Private Horace Flint, was supporting the pale figure of Captain Wiggins, with blood streaming from his shoulder. They slumped against the back wall as Major Davies rushed over to help his friend. Emrys had never liked Captain Wiggins, finding him pompous and overbearing. Today, however, he could not fail but be impressed. Despite his obvious pain, Captain Wiggins just closed his eyes and sat back never complaining. He quietly turned down the offer of morphine. Other people's needs were likely to be greater than his before the night was over.

At the very front of the strongpoint, Emrys and the rest manned every aperture, in case another attack followed the bombardment. Flinty came over to lend whatever help he could. He looked down at the meagre supplies of ammunition and raised an eyebrow at Emrys. One more attack and they would be defenceless. Flinty was one of those quiet types, whom nobody had a bad word for. His lyrical Birmingham accent sounded incongruous amongst all these Welsh ones. He just quietly encouraged and calmed everyone while keeping a careful eye on his self-appointed charge, Captain Wiggins.

The night slowed down until every minute felt like an hour. The bombardments had decreased markedly and the furtive movements outside had ceased. The long-awaited frontal assault just hadn't materialised. Emrys contemplated how fortunate they had been as they didn't seem to have sufficient resources to resist even one determined attack.

The worst thing was the raging thirst. All the water had run out many hours previously. All the water except the tempting bucket, which had been saved to cool down the Lewis guns. At that moment, the guns took priority over the men. They had not slept for over twenty-four hours and, even the officers hadn't eaten since the previous evening. They were all exhausted.

Dawn would soon arrive and at that stage, their problems would certainly return. Emrys watched Major Davies call

Flinty over. Flinty nodded grimly and disappeared through the entrance. Just a few minutes later, Emrys heard a loud cry 'Don't shoot. I'm coming in.' He laughed. No Gerry would talk with an accent like that. It could only be Flinty returning. Seconds later, Flinty stumbled through the doorway. He was waxy pale and sweating when he stood to address the Major.

'No good, Major Davies. Gerries everywhere. The only way out will be to fight our way out. Unless someone is sent to get us. Lots of noise up the road too. The King Edwards sound like they're are having trouble.'

Major Davies nodded grimly. They all now knew that there was no way out. Hold here until the ammunition had run out and then who knows.

It was perceptively becoming lighter and not only from the flashes of artillery but from the faint rising sun. The attack still hadn't arrived. They just couldn't fathom it out. Surely, now would be the ideal time to finish them off, at dawn but shrouded once more by fog. A glimmer of hope went through Emrys's mind. Maybe a relief force had been sent, after all. Ted was the first to hear it.

'Something happening, Major Davies. I can hear some rumbling down the road. And some people talking.'

At that moment, a large party of German soldiers appeared marching smartly along the road out of the mist. Behind them came the rumbling. A battery of six field guns was being pulled down the road towards the bridge, each by four emaciated horses. A rider rode on the right-hand horses, laughing and joking with each other. Incredibly, the Germans didn't seem to know that the cyclists were still there. They must have thought that they had all escaped during the night.

What an amazing opportunity. Major Davies quietly whispered the plan. Two Lewis guns and any rifles left would deal with the infantry. The other two would take out the first and the last field guns. The four guns, in the middle, would then be trapped. Major Davies calmly shouted.

'Fire!'

A sudden look of panic replaced the smiles on the faces of the artillerymen, as the British machine guns began their venomous chatter. The two riders on the back gun fell to the floor, mortally wounded, while their friends on the trailer sprung down urgently searching for cover. Two of their horses had already been hit. One was stone dead, a neat hole just above his eye. The other was spurting copious amounts of blood from its neck as it sank to its knees. The remaining two, still in their harnesses reared up in a panic. A stray hoof hit a retreating artilleryman directly on the head killing him instantly.

Gwyn was taking measured bursts with his precious Lewis gun, scattering the infantry as they scrambled for even the smallest piece of cover. Before there was any time lost, the sights were turned on the other four guns. The riders immediately jumped down from their mounts and also rushed for cover. The poor horses had become easy targets and were panicking. The second team, without any humans to control them, raced in the only direction that was clear. That was around the first gun and towards the bridge. As they raced across the bridge the gun flying behind them slewed through the parapet and into the river. The horses were pulled to a juddering halt. The cyclists cheered irreverently. The quiet of a few moments earlier had turned into joyous pandemonium.

The fire from the cyclists began to decrease, despite this

still being a prime opportunity to cause even more murderous carnage. Gwyn's Lewis gun still had one spare magazine but Emrys's was empty. Not a single round left. Emrys rushed around the confined space desperately searching the wounded for a few spare 303 bullets. He returned to Ted with fifteen rounds, enough to barely fill half a magazine.

A few well-aimed shots persuaded even the Germans that retreat was the wisest course. They staggered back down the road to the safety of a thick wood. Had they had time to notice, they might have observed that they had done so unmolested. They had no way of knowing that the cyclists were now out of ammunition and helpless.

The strong point was full of smoke and coughing men. Major Davies must, surely, be aware of the position that they were in. In front of them was a scene out of a Bram Stoker novel. Dead horses and men were everywhere. The horses which weren't dead were still attached to their trailers and whinnying frightfully, drowning out the screams of the wounded soldiers. A massive victory, but retribution would surely be swift and severe.

As the smoke began to clear Emrys was able to open his stinging eyes. Approaching the mayhem was something extraordinary. An extravagantly moustached German officer was marching down the road towards the bridge, followed by a single soldier vigorously waving a large white flag. Emrys tried to break the tension.

'It's Kaiser Bill and he's surrendering.'

They all laughed nervously. Major Davies told them to shut up. This was not a time for jocularity and Emrys was soon to regret his comment. So much for Major Davies remembering his mam. The major pulled a remarkably clean white hand-kerchief out of his pocket and handed it to Emrys. He must be joking. He couldn't be being asked to go out there into the fog and smoke.

He felt a firm shove in the back, as he was pushed out of the side of the strongpoint, frantically waving the handkerchief. He turned to look at Major Davies, who was standing next to him with an absurdly confident smile on his face.

They nervously walked towards the bridge where the German officer had stopped amongst the carnage. Emrys frantically waved his makeshift flag, the feeling of terrified nausea rising in his throat. The German had carefully positioned himself well away from the poor horses which were still fighting to free themselves from their harnesses. Emrys stared at the German flagbearer, who winked at him. Perhaps this bloke had been daft enough to make some stupid comment too.

Emrys watched Major Davies march smartly up to the German officer. Unbelievably, they saluted each other as if they were on Horse Guards Parade. It suddenly came into Emrys's mind from nowhere that now was the time that they really did need Henry Mond and his perfect German. But no. The German officer spoke English with the precise accent of an English aristocrat.

'We are asking for a brief truce. We wish to remove our dead and more importantly our wounded. We also wish to release these poor beasts, who are suffering so much.'

Major Davies pleasantly asked the German.

'What do you need? An hour?'

The German immediately replied.

'Forty-five minutes will be more than adequate. I'm afraid I cannot allow you to evacuate your wounded, but if you surrender your position then they will be well looked after.'

He signalled his men forward and there was suddenly a flurry of activity around the two officers from opposing sides. Emrys could just stare in disbelief. The two officers had started to discuss cricket. They had something in common. They had both been fast bowlers. In a world beyond his comprehension, the German had gone to a school called Rugby. That's why his English was so perfect.

Emrys tried to furtively attract his boss's attention. He had noticed that the Germans were using the truce to bring guns up to the edge of the near wood. They would be firing over open sights. The end, when it came, would be both rapid and brutal. The German officer talked earnestly to Major Davies.

'I can give you the opportunity to save your men. You can see that they have no chance at all. They will all be killed and for nothing. You are surrounded.'

He repeated.

'You are surrounded. You have no chance. You have done your duty. You can do no more.'

Major Davies looked straight at the German.

'I'll talk to the men.'

Emrys walked in the wrong direction towards the river. He bent and carefully, filled his empty water bottle. He turned and held out his hand for the Major's bottle.

'Boys are parched, major.'

The two cyclists walked slowly back to the strong point, clutching their full water bottles. Emrys continued to wave the handkerchief vigorously. He trusted the German officer but not some of the men, who were tending to their friends.

The looks that they had on their faces were those of sheer hate.

He, finally, released his held breath. He was back inside the relative safety of the stronghold. He took a swig from his water bottle before handing it to Gwyn. He turned to listen to Major Davies. This was going to be interesting.

'Our position is quite hopeless. Even if we had enough food and ammunition, I cannot ask you to give up your lives needlessly. I am ordering you to surrender. I have no choice. It is my duty. I need you to quickly destroy the breeches of all your weapons.'

Major Davies looked at Gwyn.

'Especially the machine guns. I don't want our own guns used against any of our friends.'

There was a loud murmur of discontent from the men. It was the very first time that an order from the Major had been received with such insolent discontent, bordering on mutiny. He continued this time raising his voice to make himself heard.

'There is no shame. This is my order.'

Outside the German officer was getting impatient. His column of men had been held up long enough by this motley crew.

'We need to have you coming out immediately. I can give you just ten minutes more before we start firing again.'

Ted shouted irreverently.

'Can you give us half an hour, we're just having a nice cup of tea?'

Even Major Davies laughed. Emrys only hoped that the rather straight-laced German would see the funny side too. The tension broken, the men set about disabling their weapons. The expert at mending Lewis guns, Gwyn, was also the expert in breaking them. Two minutes in his hands and the gun would never fire again.

Emrys looked at Ted, wondering what to do with their revolvers. It seemed such a shame to destroy them. They might yet come in useful. Ted had an idea. Major Davies might not approve but it was an insurance policy. Grabbing a spade he surreptitiously dug a shallow hole in the corner, carefully placed the two revolvers in and then covered them roughly with some rocks.

It was time to surrender. Major Davies had said that there was no disgrace so why did they all feel so ashamed? The major had already left to talk again to the German when they began to file out, Emrys and Ted bringing up the rear. The sun had, at last, come out. It was actually turning out to be a lovely spring day. Flinty supported Captain Wiggins who grimaced silently, with pain.

They all stood hands in the air, in front of their strong point, patiently but nervously awaiting the arrival of the grim-faced Germans. All except Flinty, still supporting his wounded officer. The Germans crossing the bridge indeed looked grim-faced. In fact, they looked bloody furious as they ran up towards the motionless cyclists. They were the same crowd that Emrys had noticed at the bridge. This didn't look right. The German officer broke off from talking to Major Davies and screamed at the men.

'Nein. Nein.'

The cyclists had begun to scatter even before the first bomb had been thrown at them. Emrys and Ted were already back in the strongpoint, frantically scrambling for their buried revolvers. The bomb landed short and there was not a single casualty. They were not so lucky with the second.

Most of them had already reached safety but Flinty was still struggling with Captain Wiggins. A cloud of shrapnel caught the captain on his right hip, causing him to cry out for the first time. Flinty vainly tried to lift the stricken captain back onto his feet, once more. A bullet caught the soldier in the back of his unprotected skull. Wordlessly, Flinty dropped the captain and crumpled to the ground.

Inevitable panic took over the strong point, once more. They were shut back in the concrete coffin but this time they were all defenceless. A cry emanated from near the window.

'Bastards. They've killed Flinty. They fucking shot him in the head.'

Just as Emrys had succeeded in uncovering his buried revolver, a large German wielding a rifle complete with an enormous bayonet appeared at the doorway. Emrys leapt to the side as the bayonet was thrust at him. He only just jumped in time, as the bayonet sliced through his jacket and the skin at the side of his chest. Three inches to the right and it would have been his heart. Emrys had only actually fired his revolver once before and never in anger. He blazed away indiscriminately in the direction of the mighty German. He could be sure that if the German lunged again, he wouldn't be so fortunate. There was a scream of pain and the German staggered back out of the door.

Firing three shots in close succession in this confined space had left Emrys shocked and deaf. This hand-to-hand fighting was something he had never experienced before. It wasn't something that he was looking forward to experiencing again. He glanced down at his chest momentarily. He would worry about his wound later.

All was suddenly quiet apart from the distant artillery fire. The Germans had withdrawn to the river bank and been joined by Major Davies and the German officer, who was red-faced with anger. Listening carefully the cyclists could hear some faint scratching at the bottom of the door. Captain Wiggins had crawled five yards towards safety despite his injured leg and shoulder. Ted pulled him roughly inside. The situation was now a stalemate. The fact that the cyclists had just two revolvers between them was fortunately unknown to the Germans.

A few minutes later, Major Davies and the German officer were striding purposely towards the strongpoint. Standing in front of them, Major Davies pleaded.

'I know you feel betrayed. In fact, you have been betrayed. Some of you have suffered as a consequence. I'm sorry. The Germans who did this to you will face consequences. It is no excuse but they were artillerymen. They were upset about us killing their friends and horses. They have been moved away. They will trouble us no more. The colonel here has given me his word and I have accepted it. I want you all to walk out of there slowly but with your heads held high. I could not be more proud of you.'

Nobody moved. The disquiet had returned. Further murmurs of dissent began to be heard. From the corner, the pain racked voice of Captain Wiggins interrupted.

'You have been ordered by an officer. Now step to it immediately.'

The cyclists silently began to file out from the safety of the strongpoint, into the bright sunlight. Emrys and Ted quickly reburied their revolvers. They were still hoping to escape and come back for them. They then stooped to pick up Captain

Wiggins and gently lifted him. Outside they looked away from the crumpled body of poor Flinty, who seemed to be just staring peacefully at the sky. A few feet away Major Davies was shaking the hand of each and every one of his men as they quietly passed him and wish them well. He stopped Emrys and Ted to talk briefly to Captain Wiggins. Despite his pain, the captain smiled at his friend.

'See you in the Army and Navy club when this is finally over. Good luck, Percy.'

After a clap on the back from Major Davies, the two cyclists carried the captain down to the river's edge. All three of them were desperately thirsty. They had only had the meagre sip earlier. Emrys bent down, once more, at the river edge to refill his bottle. The slowly flowing water was, now, streaked red, with blood. It was impossible to know whether it contained human or horse blood. Looking at the nearby bridge it was probably both. Needs must. He sat down next to the captain handed him his bottle and, silently, awaited their fate. A German sergeant marched over and said quietly and soothingly.

'Tommy. For you, the war is over.'

It certainly didn't feel over. In fact, it felt like it was only just beginning.

In the small terraced house, the blood drained from Harriet's face when she heard her daughter's wail-like scream.

'Mam. There's a letter. Jesus Christ, there's a letter.'

There could be no doubt from the tone of the young girl's voice, exactly what she meant by a letter. Harriet rushed out and grabbed it from Evelyn. She frantically tore it open.

France April 1918

Family of 7647 Private Emrys John. 11th Corps Cyclist Battalion.

I am sorry to inform you that your son is reported as Missing in Action. The battalion was in action in an area which is now behind enemy lines. Much of the battalion was reported missing, including Major Davies, who we believe was taken prisoner. We have unfortunately had no similar report about your son.

You will be proud to know that the battalion performed so well that day that we have received personal thanks from Field Marshall Haig, himself. Your son's sacrifice has therefore not gone unnoticed.

With regards. Lieutenant Collins Acting Commander Cyclist Battalion

Evelyn looked up to see the grey sweating face of her mother. Harriet slumped into a chair, clutching her chest, while her daughter started to panic.

'Da. Da. Come quick. Mam's ill.'

16

Ted joined Emrys looking after Captain Wiggins. He looked worn out by worry and fatigue. Given Flinty's fate a few minutes before, he had good reason to be worried. Perhaps being close to an officer might give them just a modicum of security. Then again Flinty, himself, had been looking after the captain when he was assassinated. They looked over at their friend, Gwyn, who was deathly pale. He was coughing continuously and despite now being out of the smoke-filled strongpoint, was breathing rapidly. Emrys, for the tenth time, wondered why his friend had not called in sick the previous morning. They would, now, just have to wait patiently next to the river. He looked down at his side. His wound had stopped bleeding. He would leave it for the moment.

Out of the corner of their eyes, they could see parties of Germans methodically searching the exhausted cyclists and Portuguese. One would threaten them with a vicious bayonet while another, stopping only briefly to laugh at their captives, would rip their clothes open. No hidden bombs or daggers were discovered. Then, Emrys could have told them they wouldn't. Major Davies had ordered them not to. Even at this stage what Major Davies said was done.

Two soldiers approached their little group. The privates would be slim pickings. Some cigarettes perhaps. They were aiming straight for the captain. Captain Wiggins winced in pain as he was roughly pulled to his feet. Emrys sprang to his feet. Couldn't they see that the poor captain was badly wounded? Ted swiftly pulled Emrys back down again. It would benefit nobody to antagonise these bastards.

For the very first time, the cyclists heard Captain Wiggins complain. A weasel-faced German had, gleefully, ripped his ornate Hunter watch from his pocket.

'Please. My mother gave it to me. It is very precious to me.'

The German turned to his friend with a triumphant grin on his face. Looking back at the captain he spat on the ground and then walked away.

Captain Wiggins spoke quietly to his three aides.

'This is bloody wrong, boys. They're not allowed to steal from us. And they're supposed to move us away from danger. Our artillery will target this bloody bridge any time soon.'

He then turned to a passing German corporal.

'Under The Hague Convention....'

He got no further. A rifle butt was slammed into his wounded shoulder with a sickening thud. The three cyclists immediately sprung to their feet to protect their stricken comrade. In a flash, the corporal had turned his rifle round and was jabbing his bayonet towards Emrys's unprotected chest. He was thoroughly enjoying himself and would only need the slightest excuse to wound or even kill one of the cyclists. From his position, lying on the damp grass, Captain Wiggins intervened, his voice wreathed in pain.

'Bitte hör auf. Wir meinon keinen schaden. Wir werden ohne Frage tun, was Sie woolen.'

The corporal looked down at the captain, smiled malevolently and finally walked wordlessly away. Emrys breathed a long sigh of relief. Despite being in front of an officer he swore.

'Fucking hell, boys. I thought I was a goner then. Good thing the captain can speak bloody Gerry. Thanks, Captain Wiggins. We owe you.'

A few minutes later Captain Wiggins got his wish. He was going to be taken out of harm's way, but not by any Germans. He was carried like a corpse by four pallbearers. He was balanced on a duckboard from the bottom of a trench with a cyclist on each corner. Emrys looked worriedly at Gwyn. He wasn't well enough for this. Emrys, himself, winced as a rivet dug painfully, into his shoulder and his wound began to bleed once more. This was going to be a long journey.

Indeed, it had been a long and difficult journey. They were glad to get out of La Couture but where to? Four hours later, desperately struggling with the weight of Captain Wiggins they arrived. Every jerk had been greeted by a gasp of pain. There was never, however, a single cry of complaint to accompany it. They doggedly just walked on, until they arrived at a road. On either side of the road were lines of ruined houses.

It once must have been a thriving hamlet. Now it was just a shell. To the side of that shell were parked two lorries. At long last some relief. They would not have to continue this never-ending march. The final part of their journey, wherever that was to, would be infinitely less exhausting.

It finally dawned on Emrys that two small lorries would never be enough for all the bedraggled prisoners marching down the road.

'Christ, boys. They're for the officers. There's nothing for us.'

They watched in silence as Major Davies, Captain Lucas and the rest filed, guiltily, onto the two lorries. The last person was Captain Wiggins. He smiled at them and said, 'Thank you.'

The four soldiers lifted his stretcher onto the back of the lorry. They raised the tailgate and the lorries disappeared into the distance. They stood around staring at one another. They had been at the officers' beck and call for three years. They never had to make a decision for themselves. They just obeyed orders. Now those officers had gone.

Emrys turned to Gwyn, who had his hands on his knees and was wheezing noisily. Lifting Captain Wiggins, on his stretcher, had been the final straw for Emrys's friend. He seemed to have reached the end of the line. Emrys spoke quietly and emotionally. He and Gwyn had been best mates since they had been toddlers.

'Gwyn. You look dreadful. You won't manage much more of this. I'll get some help.'

Gwyn looked up.

'If you do that those bastards will just shoot me. Just give me a bit of a hand and I'll be fine.'

He looked again at Emrys.

'Have you looked at yourself, mate?'

Emrys looked down. The side of his tunic was covered in blood. His own blood. He looked back up, put one of Gwyn's arms over his shoulder and began to chase after the rest of his friends. Ted said nothing. He just grabbed Gwyn's other arm and the three friends staggered down the road, like some sick three-legged race. Emrys knew he couldn't manage this for long. He was hardly in a state to even look after himself. He would, however, manage for as long as he could.

Emrys's faith in God had disappeared many moons previously. If there was a God then surely, he wouldn't allow this hell. Then, some of his faith was perhaps restored. As they made their way down the road, a spire appeared out of the mist. As they approached the spire, they could hear the faint sound of a train and the smell of smoke. This church had a railway line near it. They were going to be put on a train. Maybe they were going to Germany.

They staggered past the front of the large church. Unlike the rest of the churches that they had come across in France and Italy, it was modern. Indeed, apart from the spire, it could have been Rehoboth's big brother. A large German captain stood outside, carefully monitoring the passing prisoners. Occasionally, he would grab an arm and gently push the soldier towards the door of the church. When the three friends limped past, he stuck out his arm. Emrys looked blankly at him. Saying nothing, the German pulled Emrys and Gwyn aside and pointed to the door. Looking at Ted, he pointed down the road where they could see the distant outline of a train. Emrys objected.

'Please, sir. Please. We need to stay together. We want to go on that train.'

Emrys was surprised to get a reply in faltering English.

'Your friend is not going there to catch a train. He is going to work and work hard. They will be taking the ammunition off the trains for it to be taken forward.'

He pointed to Emrys's blood-caked top and continued.

'You two are not fit for work. The German army is kind and valiant. You are going into the church, which is our hospital. You will be looked after.'

He pushed Emrys and Gwyn towards the door whilst Ted, after one final look over his shoulder, began to walk down the road. The two cyclists were on their own. No officers and no friends. They filed exhaustedly into the church which seemed to have somehow escaped the tribulations of war almost untouched. Some of the brightly coloured windows were even intact. The darkly stained wooden pews were still standing proudly. The two soldiers slumped into the seats and momentarily said nothing.

Emrys was the first to sit up and survey their new surroundings. Above the doorway was a large sign. L'Eglise de Salomé. The Church of Salomé. Irreverently, Emrys asked.

'Who the fuck was Salomé?'

Gwyn, who must have paid more attention in Sunday school breathlessly giggled.

'I think it's more a question of who did Salomé fuck? The answer I think was Herod. Salomé was the girl with the seven veils who got John the Baptist's head chopped off.'

They might all be wounded prisoners but there was still military discipline to maintain. A sergeant from the Seaforth Highlanders growled.

'You are British soldiers in a place of worship. You will show some respect.'

They were quiet again. Apart from occasional moans and sounds of activity from the front, where the altar was being used as an operating table, everything was quiet. Emrys looked at the ornate tiling on the floor stained red with blood. Looking around he realised that the blood belonged to many nationalities. German and Portuguese soldiers as well as British were patiently waiting for their turn. He was hungry again. They had the last of some hard bread many hours earlier.

Grinning, he removed his cap and rummaged in the lining. He removed two of his carefully concealed cigarettes and offered one to Gwyn. Gwyn shook his head wordlessly. He didn't have enough breath to drag on a cigarette. Gwyn smiled to reassure his friend, but the effort only made him cough violently, into his hand. They both looked in horror at the hand full of blood.

Behind them lay a British sergeant, unconscious and breathing noisily. Intermittently the breathing would stop and the sergeant would be motionless. Then with a loud sigh, the breathing would start again. An elderly captain, a doctor, sat next to him. Noticing Emrys watching, the captain whispered.

'It's called Cheyne Stokes breathing. Unnerving isn't it? It means the poor bloke won't be with us much longer. Your mate doesn't look great. You need to get those wet clothes off him. He'll catch pneumonia if he hasn't got it already.'

As Emrys started to help Gwyn take his greatcoat off, the captain took two blankets off the dying sergeant and threw them over to him.

'Dry him with these. And be quick about it.'

To Emrys's horror, the captain begin to take the sergeant's bloodied coat off and immediately objected.

'You can't do that, sir. He needs it.'

The captain replied without looking up.

'Poor bugger doesn't need anything now, boy. He might need a set of wings or perhaps a fork shortly, depending. He certainly doesn't need this coat. Matey there does.'

Within a few minutes, Gwyn was dry and wrapped in the poor sergeant's coat. When Emrys returned from scrounging some cups of tea, the sergeant's rasping breathing had stopped. The captain made a cross sign to the German orderlies and pointed at the sergeant. He was rapidly removed to make more room for the next needy customer. Emrys handed a cup of tea to the exhausted captain. This doctor had decided to stay with his patients rather than leave them when the German advance overran his dressing station. He didn't look as if he'd slept since.

It was surprising how quickly Emrys and even Gwyn began to feel marginally better. They had just needed dry clothes, some rest and warm drinks. Emrys had had his wound dressed with a paper bandage by the kind captain. Emrys suspected that he was really too well to be here and would probably be sent off to work the very next day. Leaving his friend for a moment in the care of the captain, he wandered out to the large, ornate porch. He had managed to save a last cigarette in his cap for just such an emergency. This seemed as good a time as any to smoke it.

The porch was guarded by a single very young German. He walked with a pronounced limp, with his right leg withered and shortened by some abnormality. Undoubtedly if it wasn't for his disability, he would be up at the front with boys of his own age. Instead, he was back here. The boy looked longingly at Emrys's lit cigarette. One of the older men would have stolen it, but he just sat down and watched. Something told Emrys to offer this young boy a drag. To Emrys's surprise, he gratefully accepted. Mam would be pleased. The German beamed as he handed the half-smoked cigarette back to his benefactor. How incongruous was this? Two boys, one German and the other British, sharing a cigarette.

The two new friends sat on benches on either side of the porch. Of course, the German boy spoke no English and Emrys no German. Emrys decided to try his rudimentary French.

'Je m'appelle Emrys.'

The German beamed as he replied.

'Emrys. Tres bien. Je m'appelle Henry.'

Emrys laughed loudly.

'You're having me on. You can't be called Henry. Vous ne vous appellez pas Henry. Fritz or Heinrich or some bloody name.

The German laughed back as he searched in his pocket.

'Non. Je m'appelle Henry.'

He then produced a grubby picture of a stern woman in a black dress.

'Mutter. Mere.'

Emrys examined it quizzically and then understood. He excitedly took a photograph from his own pocket and said.

'That's your mother. Mutter means mother. This is my mutter with my sister.'

Their loud laughing was, immediately, overheard by a sombre German sergeant. Emrys quickly disappeared back into the nave of the church, leaving his new friend to receive the angriest telling-off ever.

That night was dark. Drizzle beat against whichever glass windows was intact and came through those which weren't, soaking the wounded soldiers sitting underneath. If they needed any reminding that the war was still going on, they could still hear the gunfire in the distance. The captain was continuing his work aided only by a single candle held by Emrys. Then Emrys heard Gwyn shouting for him.

'Emrys. Emrys. I need you. Please quickly.'

He rushed over to see what his friend wanted.

'I'm sorry. I need to get to the latrine. I'm desperate. I've tried to get out myself but I just can't. I need help.'

Emrys looked quizzically at Gwyn. It was cold and wet. The latrine was a trench ten yards from the porch which he had sat in earlier. They would certainly get soaked again. He knew, however, that Gwyn, of all people, would not make unnecessary demands. He put his arm under Gwyn's armpit and together staggered towards the door.

There might have been some argument at the doorway if the guard hadn't been his friend Henry. The latrine was in full view, anyway, in the gathering light of the early morning. There would be no risk of escape. Smiling Henry signalled Emrys and Gwyn over to the latrine and sat at the entrance to the porch, watching. The two cyclists staggered over to their destination just in time for Gwyn to gratefully squat down.

At exactly that moment, they became aware of an all too familiar sensation. In coming fire. Shellfire undoubtedly coming in their direction and seemed to be coming from the British lines. Gwyn screamed as he desperately tried to pull his trousers up. Emrys ducked and put his arms over his head. As if that would help him. There was a loud explosion a few yards in front of the church followed by one on the far end. The final shot of the salvo landed directly over the altar, where the German doctors had been desperately operating all through the night.

One moment there was a beautiful building, the next a ball of fire. Emrys realised that if Gwyn had not desperately needed a shit then they might both be dead. His next thought was could he do anything to help any of those poor screaming souls inside the burning church?

He rushed towards the burning porch. Just inside a figure, with a flaming coat, was doing a strange panicked dance tugging at his clothing. Emrys pulled him out by his arm and threw him to the ground. He remembered what he had been taught whilst working in the furnace of Albion Steelworks, a lifetime before. Frantically he rolled the burning figure in the wet grass until the blazing inferno finally extinguished itself. Remaining was the smouldering remains of a German greatcoat.

Inside was the blackened, moaning body of a distorted human being. Emrys turned him over to help him breathe. Barely recognisable was the face of Henry, distorted by fear and pain. A German corporal ran forward to help Emrys. Together they dragged the figure away from the burning building. The two rescuers then collapsed face down on the ground, coughing frantically with Henry moaning between them.

Emrys got to his knees with tears still pouring from his reddened eyes. Tears from the acrid smoke but also tears of frustration and grief. He looked over to Henry who opened his eyes and smiled up at him briefly, before sinking into a welcome coma. Gwyn crawled over from the latrine, shaken and confused. He sat quietly next to Emrys, who cradled Henry's head in his lap.

Confusion surrounded them as if in a blur. Like some terrifying nightmare, people seemed to be rushing around aimlessly. Some of the former occupants of the church had somehow made their escape and were coughing and spluttering, next to the cyclists. Emrys looked down again. Poor Henry had stopped breathing. He was out of pain.

Emrys got to his feet and began to wander around the survivors, looking desperately for the kindly doctor. He was nowhere to be found. Unsurprisingly, the captain must have perished amongst his patients. He returned to Gwyn who was still lying next to the smouldering body of poor Henry. This was perhaps the ideal time to attempt an escape, but he had neither the strength nor the energy. He just sat, patiently, awaiting the next instalment of their sorry tale.

The corporal, who had helped Emrys a few minutes previously in his futile efforts, came over and clapped him on his back. He then offered the two cyclists cigarettes. Despite the poor quality of the German tobacco even Gwyn accepted gratefully. The three men were soon puffing away surveying the suffering all around them. The corporal began searching carefully through Henry's clothes. A smouldering photograph was removed from an inside pocket, amazingly well preserved. As the corporal studied it sadly, Emrys said.

'Mutter.'

The corporal replied.

'Ya. Mutter.'

To Emrys' surprise, even during the anger and confusion, he had become something of a celebrity. He couldn't work out why. Wasn't it something everybody would have done? The fact that the man he had tried to save from a horrendous death was German seemed irrelevant to him. The only thing that really mattered was that he had failed and Henry's mutter would soon be receiving the dreaded letter.

The senior Germans seemed to think otherwise. A clever-looking major, wearing prominent horn-rimmed glasses, even came over to shake his hand. The two cyclists had to just sit patiently, watching the efforts to douse the fires in the ruined church. Henry was eventually removed to lie in the increasing line of dead bodies. Emrys closed his eyes in a rare, but heartfelt prayer.

Several hours later, the major returned and began to talk, first to Gwyn.

'You are unwell. We are moving you to hospital. You will be sent to Germany.'

He signalled to two orderlies who gently lifted him onto a stretcher and started to carry him towards a waiting ambulance. No marching up a road this time. Emrys quickly got to his feet and grabbed his friend's hand. His voice breaking with emotion, he said.

'Look after yourself, mate. Get yourself well. I have big plans for us after this bloody war.'

He turned to the major and pleaded.

'Please, sir. We need to stay together. I need to look after him.'

The major meant to be kind, but it came out sounding callous.

'No. You are well. You must go to Lille, where you will work hard. He cannot work.'

The last Emrys saw of Gwyn was his stretcher being loaded onto a makeshift ambulance. Gwyn used the last of his strength to prop himself up and wave forlornly to his friend, as the ambulance disappeared down the road. Emrys stood speechless. All those friends who were on that first train from South Wales to Rhyl, over three years previously, were gone. He was now on his own. The corporal arrived to usher him to his transport. His next stop was Lille.

Josiah and Evelyn didn't know what to do when the second letter arrived. Harriet had been slow to recover from her heart attack, precipitated by the previous letter. That letter at least had left them with some hope.

Harriet had been confined to bed convalescing on the advice

of Dr Pegg. When she was eventually allowed downstairs once more, she was just a shadow of the beautiful woman who had seen Emrys off on that train in 1915. She had visibly aged ten years overnight, was breathless almost at rest and had thick swollen ankles. Worst of all she seemed to have given up. She just sat on a hard-backed chair, in the opposite corner to her husband, staring at nothing.

So what should they do? This letter might be the final straw. It might be the final shock that put this previously strong woman into her grave. Harriet herself made the decision. She turned to her daughter and spoke in a quiet kind voice.

'Evelyn, my love. I know you're not telling me something. I can see you have been crying again. You two are keeping something from me. You know you can't hide anything from me. Not knowing is worse than knowing.'

Josiah got up from his chair and took a piece of paper from his shirt pocket. He handed it to Harriet, who shook as she felt for her glasses.

France May 1918

Family of 7647 Private Emrys John. 11th Corps Cyclist Battalion.

Further to my previous letter, I am disappointed that I have further news confirming the death of Private John.

The information we have is from a soldier of the battalion. Corporal Coney escaped from captivity and has returned to us. He has been able to confirm that your son was indeed killed. According to Corporal Coney, your son survived the action, previously mentioned, and was a prisoner of war behind German lines.

He was being held in a church which was being used as a hospital. The church was near an important railway station. British artillery targeting the train station, unfortunately, accidentally destroyed the church. Corporal Coney has been able to confirm that there were no survivors, including your son. Corporal Coney escaped a few days later and brought us the news.

I am sorry to have to inform you of this terrible news. We have no way at present of knowing where your son is buried. You may get further information subsequently from the Authorities.

Lieutenant Collins. Acting Commander 11th Corps Cyclist Battalion.

Harriet looked up in despair and whispered.
'Poor Emrys. I only let him go because of his teeth.'
Her face went deathly pale as a realisation came to her.
'God help me. I might have killed him. It might have been one of the shells I helped make in Taylors that killed him.'

17

Emrys had never been infatuated with a female before. She wasn't even that beautiful and was considerably older than him. Well, four or five years was much older when you are still only nineteen. Her English was, as you would expect in occupied Lille, limited. She had something, however. Emrys couldn't say what but she seemed to glow. Glow in the same way as his mam did. To Emrys's disappointment, she also seemed to treat him like his mam did. Certainly not as Emrys would have wanted a prospective suitor. Then, he had to remind himself he was very young and looked even younger.

Despite his experiences in the war, she was so much worldlier than he. She had endured four years of German occupation and had become a widow aged twenty-one. Yes. She was Madame Vaillant not Mademoiselle. Her dashing Chasseur husband had been killed in the first weeks of the war and she didn't seem to have forgotten it. Deep inside her, very rarely exposed, Emrys sensed a deep loathing for anything German.

His first view of Lille had been inauspicious. Sitting in the back of the lorry, he gazed out blankly. He was already missing his friends. As he rode up the pock-marked street, between rows of ruined buildings, he looked out at the people.

On the one side, there were columns of German soldiers marching grimly and silently towards the front. The unwelcome sounds of the front could be heard in the distance. He was just glad that he was out of it. No more Lewis guns. He would be happy just to wait here until the war finished. His sole worry was that his family might not know that he was safe.

On the opposite side of the road were some French civilians. In fact considering the hour quite a lot of civilians. They all looked the same, painfully thin and with their eyes glued to the pavement. They were uninterested in the lorry or the columns of soldiers. Their only interests could be survival and their next meal. He realised that he might have another worry. At first sight, Lille seemed a desperate place.

The prisoner-of-war camp came as a complete surprise. He was first out of the lorry when it finally ground to a halt. He was stiff from being cooped up in the same position for so long. He wanted to get moving. He stood motionless, however. He could only stare upwards. Soaring above him was a huge stone gateway with an ornate coat of arms, above the pointed arch.

Bloody hell. As a child, he had read Ivanhoe. He had always wanted to live in a castle. Now, he might be getting his chance although perhaps not in the circumstances that he had imagined. He blinked again when he noticed the moat with a bridge over it. It indeed was a castle.

They had filed slowly, through the gateway into the square inside. Except it wasn't a square. One of the only things Emrys remembered from school was shapes and this was a pentagon. It matched exactly the vast stone walls of the castle. There were five of them. Disappointingly, there were no ancient medieval halls like they had seen in Italy. Instead, there were four identical brick buildings which looked like warehouses. In Emrys's inexperienced opinion, they looked cold and ugly. They were, however, likely to be home for the foreseeable future.

German efficiency had taken over. All these men needed

processing. While waiting patiently in the queue, a thought dawned on Emrys. Mam had always told him not to lie, but Mam had never been in a place like this. Messenger boy would not impress any German. When he finally reached the wooden table at the front, the bespectacled German corporal didn't even bother to look up.

'Name?'

'Emrys John.'

'Number?'

'7647.'

'Regiment?'

'Eleventh Corps Cyclist Battalion.'

'Occupation before the war?'

Emrys swallowed hard before replying.

'Motor mechanic.'

The German corporal looked up over his glasses for the first time. He seemed to study Emrys, intently, for an age, before looking down again.

'Good. We will, certainly, find a use for you.'

Emrys didn't discover what that use might be until the following morning. A group of them paraded in the pentangle, just after dawn. Emrys drew his greatcoat around him for warmth. Thank God he had put it on to help Gwyn, in Salome. He would be in a difficult situation otherwise. This multinational group of prisoners seemed as if they might be the chosen few. Those who had given the right answer to the final question. Or perhaps, it was the wrong answer. They would soon find out.

He jumped when a door behind him creaked open. This place was bad for his nerves. Out of the door filed ten solemn

French civilians. All of them looked intently at the ground, refusing to make eye contact with any of the curious soldiers. Emrys jumped again when a German captain shouted.

'For those of you who are new. Welcome to the Citadel. Take a second to look at the walls. There is no point in trying to escape. If you do try, we will take the gravest measures. I repeat. The gravest measures. You will be fed only if you work. You have been selected to stay in France, rather than sent to the rigours of a German coal mine because each of you has skills. Those skills will be useful to us. Use those skills to the very best of your abilities. So, soldiers, work hard and I will be happy. Slack, as you English say, and you will pay for it, severely.'

The great gate opened, slowly, exposing the city in full depressing view. Emrys realised, immediately, how wise he had been to lie about his profession. This was grim enough but the thought of the coal mines, in Germany, sent a shiver up Emrys's spine. They began to silently file through the gate, over the bridge and towards the city.

He decided to carefully take note of his surroundings. You never know when it might come in useful. He didn't have any plans to escape. You would be mad to even think about it. You never know, however. Circumstances can change quickly during a war. He took note that the moat, unlike in Ivanhoe, had no water in it. The far bank had four bunches of fresh flowers carefully placed. Very strange.

He was feeling faint from hunger. He had drunk the unappetizing brown water, which was in plentiful supply. He hadn't eaten, however, since poor Henry had shared half a biscuit with him in return for a drag on his last cigarette. He was dying for a cigarette as well. It was the first day that he had not had a Woodbine for almost two years. He walked slowly, between an ancient German guard and a Scottish corporal, who quietly whistled to himself.

They were led by the ten silent Frenchmen, who were no longer staring at the ground. They were laughing nonchalantly to the crowd who, also, said nothing but laughed back in encouragement.

A young girl, no older than ten, stood tall and gave a perfect salute. Before the girl's terrified mother could pull her away the ancient guard's rifle butt slammed into her skinny shoulder. A pitiful scream accompanied the crunch of a broken bone. Emrys swung round in alarm and instinct forced him towards the little girl. He was met by the muzzle of a rifle and the beaming smile of the malignant guard. This one had the shortest of fuses. Emrys knew that he would need to be more careful next time, as he got back into line, next to the still-whistling Scot.

Their destination, quickly, became apparent. From the end of the boulevard, they could smell the distinctive acrid odour of smoke. For someone brought up, as Emrys was, just a few hundred yards from a goods yard this could only mean one thing. Trains and lots of them. Perhaps, they were on their way to Germany after all.

But no. The wooden gates, topped with barbed wire, opened. They, at last, knew what work they would be doing. This was also a goods yard full of trains overloaded with ammunition, desperately needed at the front. They would be unloading the trains. Emrys, however, had his own job. He didn't need to be told. Premonition had told him already. He, the mechanic, was meant to mend any broken vehicles. He didn't have a clue.

Emrys quickly got into the routine of working. He had never

been any good at sitting around doing nothing. Secretly he enjoyed it, feeling only slight guilt for helping Fritz. Most days, he just mundanely lugged ammunition boxes off the frequent trains and onto the lorries and carts. Only occasionally was he called upon to help one of the other mechanics mend something. He had, quickly, learnt so much. So much that would be useful when he, eventually, opened up his own business back home. He couldn't really think about back home. It was still another world.

Life, in fact, might have been quite tolerable if it hadn't been for the hunger. He had been here for two weeks and hungry for two weeks. The tiny scraps of black bread did nothing to ease it. Then he knew from marching through the city twice a day that he was witnessing a whole city, gradually starving to death.

He couldn't get used to those marches led each day by the ten Frenchmen. When he finally summoned up the courage to ask who they were, he got a brisk reply. They were hostages. If anyone in the city made trouble, they would be shot. Shot, unceremoniously, in the moat of The Citadel where the fresh bunches of flowers seemed to appear each morning.

The flowers he was told were put there by the grieving mother of a seventeen-year-old boy executed there, in 1914. His mam was still putting flowers there four years later. Would his own mam do the same? He was sure she would. The thought, suddenly, made him worry even more. What if his mam thought that he was dead? Would she be putting flowers out like this poor French woman? The answer to that question was also yes. Beautiful flowers collected from her special place in the woods, behind their house.

Harriet was, carefully, arranging two bunches of flowers in her new special place in Ynysmaerdi cemetery. Against the back wall, she had placed two rough wooden crosses, one for each of her poor boys. In between was a small wooden chair, made for her by Josiah and Evelyn out of some old wooden planks that they had found on the riverbank. It had taken Josiah every last bit of his energy but they had finished it. He and his daughter had looked at it with pride. For all his faults, he wasn't a bad man. He must be suffering too but just not showing it. Then men just couldn't, could they?

She sat down on her special chair and did what she did every day. Every day, without fail, rain or shine. She talked to her two boys. Talked for hours. She knew that Evelyn couldn't imagine just what she talked about. But she knew and it gave her a modicum of tranquillity. Without it, the grief and guilt would have been unbearable. Each day she seemed to stay just a little bit longer.

Today, as usual, she feared the journey home. Since her heart attack, her legs had swollen up like pit props. Every step hurt a pain of retribution for allowing her sons to go to war. She was also ashamed to admit that she was almost as breathless as her husband. She might only manage to stagger twenty yards before she would need to stop. The cold wind today would make it even worse. There would be nothing for it. She would have to rest halfway, at the cricket pavilion, where her best friend, Ruth, lived. She would, again, need to beg for a cup of tea. Yes. Her best friend, Ruth, wasn't even a Christian. That was a turn-up for the books which she frequently discussed with her poor, absent boys.

Emrys sat, hungrily awaiting the bread which would make up his meagre lunch. There might, also, be some thin cabbage soup if they were really lucky. He surveyed the scene with interest. The sun was shining and at least he was warm. It wouldn't be so clever if they were, God forbid, still here in the winter.

In front of him, the woman was laughing with two German guards. She was not one of the hostages. She was a worker. He hadn't ever summoned up the courage to talk to her. He just watched her in barely disguised awe as she took orders from the Germans and then spat them back out at her fellow workers. Nobody seemed to argue with her. Nobody dared. Then she was walking towards him. Was that what he thought it was? It was an almost imperceptible wink. Without asking, she squeezed in next to him and spoke in faltering English.

'Bonjour. My name is Madame Vaillant. When we are away from those pigs, you can call me Madeleine.'

Emrys stuttered back.

'Hello. I mean Bonjour. Je m'appelle Emrys.'

She surreptitiously pressed something into his hand, got to her feet and walked away from him. He looked down at his hand. He saw something he hadn't seen for many years. My God. It was an apple. He looked up. As she disappeared around a corner, she looked over her shoulder and smiled at him again.

The next weeks proved a dichotomy. One moment, she was ordering everyone about. She was the Germans' lapdog. The next moment, she was sitting next to him whispering quietly and stuffing a half-smoked cigarette butt into his pocket. You don't get anything for nothing. She must want something. It didn't take long for him to find out.

He was sitting alone, once more, daydreaming. He had

always done it, but since arriving in Lille, the dreams had taken a darker tone. Today, as usual, he could almost see his mam opening the letter saying that he was dead. Sometimes it happened at Taylors as it had with David, but today they were all in the back room, in their terraced house. He closed his eyes as a tear trickled down his cheek. He felt, rather than saw, the two figures sit lightly down beside him. He opened his eyes to see Madame Vaillant gently smiling at him.

'Bonjour, Emrys. You look sad. More sad than usual. Have you had some bad news?'

Emrys suddenly had a brain wave. This lady seemed to be in cahoots with Fritz. Maybe, just maybe, she could help? Surely, it wouldn't do any harm to ask.

'Well. It's like this, Madame Valliant. I think my family thinks I'm dead. They don't know I'm here. It will kill my mam.'

Madame Vaillant became more serious as she nodded to the woman on the other side of Emrys.

'He's right. Those pigs won't have told his family. If they had, then the Red Cross would have shipped him right away from this close to the fighting. He wouldn't be of much use to them, then. Not as much as here.'

The other lady laughed back.

'Well, Madeleine, maybe we can help this young man. At a price of course.'

Madame Vaillant turned back to the bewildered soldier.

'Believe it or not, we might, just, be able to get a message to your poor mother. We have our contacts.'

Emrys looked at her in disbelief.

'But how? Fritz won't let you. I'm sure they won't.'

Madame Vaillant laughed again.

'Don't ask any questions. Just be sure that it won't be the first time we've done it. Now, quickly. Have you a scrap of paper? I'll need your address.'

Emrys's hand shot into his inside pocket and drew out a prized possession. He had paid a lot of money to have that photograph taken in Bethune, just a few weeks previously. He hadn't had time to send it home before all the trouble. Looking at it one last time, he handed it to Madame Vaillant who showed it to the other lady. She spoke quietly.

'You look so young. You are only a babe. Your address before the pigs come.'

She wrote quickly, as he spoke.

'Emrys John. 11 Neath Road. Briton Ferry. Britain.'

In a flash, the photograph disappeared behind the large wooden crucifix and down the front of her dress. She spoke more urgently now.

'We need you to join our fight against these bastards. We are secretly doing our best. We will call on you to help us. It will be exciting.'

Exciting, over the previous three years, had sometimes been a substitute word for dangerous. Lieutenant Mond and General Elliott could be described as exciting, but anyone caught near them would not stay in one piece for long. He had the sinking feeling that Madame Madeleine Vaillant might just be cut from the very same cloth. He waited in trepidation for her to continue.

'We wish you to.' She stopped for a moment to search for a word. 'Pisser. In the petrol tanks of some of the lorries that you are looking at. Only occasionally. And only when we are sure that those pigs aren't watching. Or any of our people. You cannot trust anyone apart from Anne-Marie and me. There are traitors everywhere.'

Emrys looked on in stunned silence. She wanted him to piss in the petrol tanks. He didn't know what it might do to the bloody lorries but, from the look on her face, it would be nothing good. And even worse there were traitors everywhere. She continued not waiting for him to object.

'That's settled. Another recruit. Don't worry. We've been doing this for four years. Nobody suspects us.'

She stood up and walked away, giving him another seductive smile as she went. Emrys still hadn't said anything. His friend, Gwyn, had always said that he was good at getting himself into trouble. Surely, neither of them could have foreseen anything like this. He was going to risk being shot for what? A chance that his mam might know that he was alive. That was true. The odd cigarette butt, a few extra morsels and, of course, the occasional smile. And you never know, perhaps something more.

That was how it had all started. He had adamantly decided not to do anything stupid. He was content to just see out the war here. In the first few weeks, the gunfire had faded away until it was barely perceptible in the distance. More recently, it had become more audible again. Surely, it could only be a short time before the British Army came rolling into Lille to save him. To do anything, now, to help the girl might be viewed as suicidal. He owed it to his family not to do it.

A nagging doubt, however, gnawed away at him whenever he tried to sleep. He could see his friend, poor Flinty dropping to the floor with a hole in his head. Maybe, just maybe, he should do whatever he could to fight back against these bastards.

The first time is always the most difficult but, in fact, it was easy. Anne-Marie had nonchalantly stood guard, while he quickly unscrewed the cap of the petrol tank and peed into it. He had been worried that he would piss his pants, before he even had a chance to complete his task, but no.

He had sighed quietly, as he screwed the cap back on and looked over in relief at Anne-Marie. He had sighed again as he watched the lorry being driven away. For it to break down before it had even got through the gates might have been a problem. His reward was a welcome small piece of bread and an even more welcome squeeze of the thigh from Madame Madeleine Vaillant.

It became a lethal addiction. Perhaps, it was just a replacement for the cigarettes, which had become such a necessity to him since his escapade with Lieutenant Mond. He began almost enjoying the racing heartbeat, sweaty palms and dry mouth, which preceded the events, quickly followed by the intense wave of relief which engulfed him afterwards. The secret attention given to him, by the two young Frenchwomen, was just an additional if wholly gratifying bonus. Particularly gratifying from the one whom he now called Madeleine.

He, gradually, began to recognise all the tricks that she had been getting up to. How she was getting away with it and still kept her trusted position with Fritz, he just couldn't fathom. Perhaps it was because of that trusted position that she could get away with it. No one would suspect her. Perhaps, because these old men guards were just the leftovers of the great German Army, they were happy with the easy life.

She also just didn't seem to care about anything. One moment, she was allowing some gross German to grope her. The next, she would be referring to the same German to Emrys as a disgusting, fat pig, before going off to secretly take the fuses out of a few shells. She was an intoxicating force of nature which Emrys seemed addicted to. He would do anything for her. At least, almost anything.

He had quickly come to the conclusion that he would have to do very little to the lorries. His lack of mechanical knowledge was enough. He would laugh to himself when the same vehicle would return for his care yet again. Perhaps he was becoming as good an actor as his erstwhile mentor.

He could, however, sense that Madeleine was about to demand even more from him. It was almost as if the approaching gunfire and the increasing despair, on the German faces, were encouraging her to take one more big hit at the oppressors. One more, big hit of vengeance before Lille was rescued and their war was over.

Emrys knew just what she was capable of as well. He had heard about it in an unguarded moment from Anne-Marie. Way back in 1916, Gerry stored all their ammunition under some railway arches, called 18 Ponts, in the middle of the city. Somehow, Madeleine had managed to blow it up. Half the district went up with it.

Gerry thought it was an accident but it wasn't. It was Madame Madeleine Vaillant. She hadn't cared how many of her fellow citizens were killed only how many Germans. Now she seemed to be planning some similar finale. Emrys knew who might be asked to play a leading role.

He realised something was up, the moment that he saw her. Her face was etched with anger. There were no smiles for Emrys this time. For the last few weeks, she had been encouraging him to escape. It would be easy she had assured him. He hadn't been convinced. Remembering the words of the officer in the Citadel, on his first day, he was convinced that any escape would end up in the moat, next to the flowers. He just wanted to stay put, until the war ended.

When she shouted at him he looked around. If Fritz was nearby, they would be in trouble.

'Pigs. They've shot Jean Leclerc. They say he was signalling to the British planes. Jean Leclerc of all people. The last person who would do it. He was scared of a mouse.'

Emrys tried to calm her down before someone noticed them. He grasped her shoulders and held her tightly. He could feel her shaking violently from anger and frustration. She opened her mouth to continue her rant. Looking at her in panic, he firmly placed his lips on hers and kissed her very briefly. Madeleine jerked her head away in surprise, her face transformed into an angry scowl. Emrys could feel the blush rising on his face. Mam had always been able to tell when he had done something wrong from the bright hue on his face. This time it was from embarrassment. A part amused, part angry look spread over her face as she began to speak again.

Then she heard it. Behind her, she could hear the loud wheeze of some breathless old man. She stopped speaking abruptly and turned around. A German guard was standing just two paces behind her. Emrys was smiling when he whispered.

'Only way I could get you to shut up. To ferme your bouche or however you bloody say it.'

He was delighted to imagine that he must have gone up immeasurably in her estimation. He wasn't a babe, some little child, anymore. Some child who would, unquestioningly, do her bidding. Maybe now she would listen to him and stop all these bloody escapades before it was too late. They walked away arm in arm.

The old guard gazed, jealously, at the young couple as they disappeared from view. Around the corner, they hugged once more and giggled with laughter. Emrys was the first to break the spell.

'That was close.'

His heart stopped when she began to speak. She was still consumed by that intense anger. Whatever he could say he realised that she was never going to listen. Not until there wasn't a single Fritz in the whole of France.

'Emrys, this is your chance. Your chance to really hit back at these pigs. You and I are going to make them pay for John Leclerc. I have a plan. It can't fail. We mustn't fail.'

She kissed him again. This time it was more a sister's, than the lover's kiss which he so desperately craved. She walked away, briskly and confidently. Her brief moment of weakness had passed. Emrys could almost see the cogs of her mind revolving as she plotted some audacious catastrophe.

He thought that she must have calmed down. It had been a week since Jean Leclerc's death and she had done nothing. She had sat with him, frequently, and they had laughed together. Their legs touched and Emrys imagined some magic chemistry between them. She wasn't even trying to get him to do any of the minor things like piss in the petrol tanks. He had, in fact, graduated to become a considerably more talented saboteur than that, anyway. There would no longer be the risk of literally being caught with his trousers down. He had much more subtle methods. Still, she hadn't asked anything from him which was encouraging. She was normally such a hard taskmaster. Maybe, she had had second thoughts and was content to wait for the British to arrive. Then, she put her delicate hand on his thigh and looked at him earnestly.

'Emrys, they've made a mistake. The mistake we have been waiting for. They have stored a load of hay in the shed. It's feed for the cavalry regiment. God knows why they need a cavalry regiment. Anyway, the hay is dry as tinder after the summer we've had. And this is the good part. The shed is next to where we unload the ammunition train. We will make some diversion, while you nip in and set the hay on fire. The blaze will set off the ammunition. It will be chaos.'

Emrys began to panic. Chaos it might be, but the chance of it coming off was minimal. The chance of him being caught in the shed with matches in hand was high. An image of him standing in the moat next to the flowers entered his head and wouldn't leave. He must have known that Madeleine Vaillant would never be put off. She was far too ruthless for that. She kissed him on the lips, perhaps this time a lover's kiss, and excitedly said.

'Emrys, You're so brave. Thank you.'

He was, as always, at the mercy of a pretty young woman. What could he say in response? Nothing. That's exactly what he said.

He ate nothing for breakfast, the next morning. Deep nausea, seated in the pit of his stomach, prevented him from devouring the slim slice of bread which would be their only sustenance until midday. It had never happened to him before. Even at La Couture and before the terrible cycle ride to La Trou, he had eaten ravenously.

He just stood in line, pale and nervous, waiting for whatever fate might bring later in the day. As they marched past the bunch of flowers in the moat, a cold shiver shot up his spine. Would he soon be standing next to them waiting to be shot? Would the ten poor French hostages, who were leading their column, be standing next to him pleading for mercy?

There seemed to be even more guards than usual at the gates of the goods yard. In Emrys's vivid imagination, Fritz was already aware of their vague plan. They were just watching and waiting. Madeleine looked nervously at him as he disappeared towards the train.

He secretly wished that there had been lorries to mend. That would have scuppered the plan before it had even taken shape. It wasn't to be. He would be toiling away at the train. He would, also, be available for whatever Madeleine had in store for him.

He looked, glumly, at the train where a morning of lifting heavy ammunition boxes lay in front of him. It would be back-breaking work. He knew, however, that he might be elsewhere at any moment. There would be no point setting the hay alight if the train had been emptied of shells. As if on cue, he felt a hand delving into his pocket. He turned to see Madeleine walking beside him not daring to look at him. Her hand left his pocket, leaving the obvious shape of a matchbox in its place. It was definitely happening. He would, now, just have to wait to see what form the promised diversion might take.

His nausea was becoming overwhelming. He struggled to swallow the bitter bile burning in his throat. He just couldn't do it. Panic was overcoming him and he knew that he just couldn't go through with it. He leant over and began to wretch violently. He could tell that within a few seconds that he would be running as fast as he could, towards the gates. That would be the end of it and Madeleine would never speak to him again.

Restitution came suddenly and from a strange place. Every time he had been in trouble, over the past three years, he had thought of his mam. For the first time, it was his da. The da whose brand of Christian parenthood mainly involved his belt. The da who had never tired of boasting to his friends about David. The da who Evelyn could wrap around her little finger but never seemed to care about Emrys. He was desperate to just do something which would at last make his da sit up and take notice. Da probably would never hear about it but it didn't seem to matter. He wanted to be the one that Da could be proud of. He stopped still for a moment, before turning and striding back towards the train.

A second later, the shouting started followed quickly by the unmistakable rattle of Mauser rifle fire. Could this be Madeleine's promised diversion? He hadn't been told what form it would take. He just was told that he would know when it happened. The rifle fire seemed to be aimed into the sky and panicked workers were running for cover. He looked up and couldn't believe his eyes. Surely even Madeleine Vaillant couldn't concoct such a diversion.

Two British biplanes seemed to be heading straight for him. Of course, in reality, they were heading straight for the train with its tempting load of ammunition. He had a vital decision to make. Given that the accuracy of planes was a standing joke amongst the soldiers, should he plunge on with the plan? Or should he join all the others who were scrambling towards safety? A moment of calm swept over him as he slid open the bolt on the shed door. He was going to do it.

The shed could not have been designed to make his task any easier. In fact, he wondered why the Germans had been so unusually lackadaisical. This place was just a fire waiting to happen. The fodder was dry as a bone and crammed tightly into the confined space. The tiled roof had collapsed in the middle. Once the fire had taken hold it would act like a chimney. Madeleine had been right again about the train. The shed was just a few feet away from a carriage load of ammunition. It would, surely, catch fire too and it would be wise to be well away from it when it did.

Emrys had regained his composure after his brief moment of panic. He stood still for a few seconds to catch his breath. He had closed the door behind him and the only light came from the small hole in the roof, through which grey clouds could be seen passing quickly overhead. There was a wind. That would help too. He felt unreasonably safe in this confined space with the sounds of shouting and shooting, in the real world somewhere outside. The only explosions could be heard far away in the distance. The aeroplanes were living up to their reputations.

He wanted to get out of there quickly. It had been foolhardy in the extreme to be part of it in the first place. It would be the last time. Definitely, no more. He shoved three old pieces of ancient newspaper into the dry hay. He struck the first match. His sweaty hands were shaking so much, it split in two, now unusable. He took two deep breaths and struck the next one, praying that it hadn't become damp in the recent rain. It sputtered into life and he quickly lit one piece of newspaper before the match had a chance to go out. The paper had been a godsend. It burst into flames even before he had struck the next match. He raced to light all three pieces of paper. It was going to work. The fire was already taking hold. He didn't need to hang around a moment longer. He needed to be far far away and quickly. He unlatched the door and got ready to run.

He looked up in horror. In front of him stood a German soldier, wielding a rifle and huge bayonet. It was the same fat guard who had hit the little girl during Emrys's first march from the Citadel. He stood motionless between the menacing German in front and the burning building behind. He was trapped.

Emrys was surprisingly calm. He looked directly into his adversary's eyes. The old man looked both shocked and afraid. Afraid enough to not take any chances. Emrys could tell that if he gave him the slightest excuse the guard would use his rifle and that would be it. He would be dead. If he didn't try something, however, he knew that he would find himself being marched towards that moat. The result would be the same. So he would have to try something and soon. Before the old man had time to summon help. He looked at the ground despairingly. These would, inevitably, be the last seconds of his life. Poor Mam.

He looked up when he heard the venomous grunt, just in time to witness the edge of a spade smashing into the cap-covered head. The guard seemed to stare at him, incomprehensibly, before crumpling to the ground. Emrys looked down at the twitching body, blood already flowing inexorably from the gaping head wound.

He looked up again to look at his saviour. A snarling Viking warrior stood there, bloodied hands grasping the spade like a great battle axe. A Viking warrior wearing a floral dress. The floral dress which Emrys knew so well. Madeleine Vaillant was grinning at him, her face covered in a spray of bloody spots. He couldn't speak. He was going to vomit. Madeleine spoke confidently as if she was enjoying herself.

'Quickly. Before the fire gets out of hand. We must throw this bastard in there before he's discovered.'

Emrys looked down in horror at the prostrate figure in front of him. It was breathing noisily as it continued to twitch.

'Christ, Madeleine. We can't. He's still alive. He will burn to death.'

He stared at Madeleine. At a click of a switch, she had changed back into a snarling devil bent on revenge.

'He's a pig. He's been touching me for months whenever he could. Thought I would fuck a stinking fat pig like him. I will enjoy the smell of roast pork when we let him burn.'

Her voice mellowed as she began to drag the figure towards the shed. They would only have a few seconds before they were, inevitability, discovered,

'He is as good as dead already. He won't feel a thing and we must destroy the evidence. If they think he has been murdered, the bastards will shoot the hostages. Now, quick. Help me.'

Emrys was still in a dream when Madeleine helped him wash the blood from his hands in a convenient water butt a few hundred yards away. His mind still hadn't registered the full horror of what they had just done. He stood there gaping at her through dilated pupils. Washing her own hands and face seemed to have almost washed her clean, like some demonic Christening. The only evidence left was a crimson smear of blood down the front of her dress and the large wooden crucifix, which hung between her breasts. The crucifix had looked so incongruous, as Emrys had helped her drag the moaning mass into the burning shed and shut the door.

Now, he couldn't even remember how they had gotten here. It was blank. She must have helped him. Without her help, he surely would have just stood there stricken by immobility. Now, they were able to listen to the shouts of 'Feu. Feu' from the trackside and watch the pall of smoke rising from the shed.

Back to her normal self, she spoke quietly to him. There was no sign of the vicious lioness of a few minutes previously. She spoke in a quiet and encouraging voice like a patient schoolteacher.

'Well done, Emrys. You did your job and did it well. We had no choice. We need to get away from here before the train blows up. Get away and clean up properly.'

He was still staring at the bloody dress and the crucifix. She spoke again, this time with renewed passion.

'Yes. The crucifix. It's what keeps me going. My husband, Pierre, gave it to me the day he went off to war. It was the last thing he did for me. Every time I touch it, it seems to give me his strength. Gives me the strength to put up with those pigs pawing me. The strength to fight back.'

He felt her hand grasp his and pull him, gently, away from the confusion. Her delicate hand was disappointingly rough and gnarled. They were working hands that had known a hard life. They were like his mam's. He recognised, suddenly, where they were heading. They were walking towards the entrance. Surely, Fritz wouldn't let them through daubed in blood, as they still were, and he in uniform.

He looked up for the first time. To his amazement, he discovered that they were by no means alone. The whole panicked workforce must have had the same thought as Madeleine. They needed to get well away from that train before it blew up.

The gate had opened to let the ancient fire cart through and, now, a sea of people were pouring in the opposite direction screaming as they went. There was a warning rattle of rifle shots but to no avail. This crowd was stopping for no one, not even the German Army. In the middle, unnoticed and with his head ducked low ran a khaki figure, hand in hand with a woman in a floral dress. Emrys was doing exactly what he had sworn not to do. He was escaping.

As they ran through the narrow lanes of Lille and crossed the wide boulevards, Emrys waited for the inevitable shout. Or, perhaps, feel a bullet tearing into his body following the crack of a rifle. It seemed impossible that they wouldn't be discovered. Perhaps all the Germans were too concerned about the fire raging behind them to carefully examine the throng of people. Or maybe, in this area of dilapidated, ruined houses, there were just no Germans.

In front of them stood a large church, with a tall tower and beautiful dome, mercifully untouched by the rigours of war. It must, surely, be their sanctuary. It would be a beautiful and welcoming sanctuary. With one last jerk on his hand, he felt Madeleine pull him through the tiny side entrance into the church. He stood with hands on his knees, gasping to inhale the incense-filled air and peered into the dark, interior of the ornate building. He was safe, at last, if only perhaps for a few moments.

For the first time since lighting the first match, he started to come to his senses. He had, never, really come to terms with these vast mediaeval churches with their painted screens and brightly coloured glass. It didn't seem part of the Christianity, which had been such a large part of his old life. So different from Rehoboth, where the only red was the 'EXODUS CHAPTER XX', above the Ten Commandments, painted on one wall. L'Eglise Saint Sauveur seemed somehow different. Perhaps it was just the tranquillity inside, compared to the turmoil outside. The quiet, compared with the screams of panic which had enveloped them as they ran. Even the incense, which had been so overpowering when he had arrived, seemed calming. He felt giddy again. There was nothing for it. He needed to quickly sit down in a pew, with his head in his hands before he fainted.

A few seconds later, he looked up to see where the voices were coming from. There were only two other people in the church, Madeleine Vaillant and a very old priest, wearing the brown cassock that had been so common when they were in Italy. Italy which seemed years ago, but was in fact only a few months.

The priest was very elderly, indeed bent at right angles by a crooked spine. He craned his neck upwards to talk to the lady. He didn't look happy. He was making his point by waving his arms and then pointing at Emrys. Madeleine waited for the tirade to finish and then seemed to respond calmly. She looked over at Emrys and smiled. He gave a half-hearted smile back.

He studied the large painting on the wall in front of him. Even he, who had normally slept through Sunday school, recognised the topic. It was Jesus calling the little children to him. He put his hands over his face, once more. He sobbed loudly, vainly trying to hide it from the girl.

18

Emrys examined the inside of the terraced house, once again, while the two women continued to argue. It was remarkably similar to their house, back home. Mam would like it. She would, probably, start to tidy it up. She would clear away so that all the surfaces were pristine and woe betides anyone who cluttered them up again.

He had stayed in the church, for several hours, with only the reluctant priest as company. Madeleine had left, quickly, only telling him that she would pick him up later. Later, when it was safe. When it was dark and the curfew was in place.

When she did eventually return she was tight-lipped. She looked tired and anxious. Things didn't seem to be going well for Madame Madeleine Vaillant. Without saying anything, she ushered him through the large front door. He could see why they had not attempted this in the daylight. They crept unseen, across a large open square and, gratefully, into a narrow, dark alley.

They only needed to draw breath for a few seconds as their destination in Rue Soltin was only a few yards away. They were, soon, in the safety of the terraced house. The terrace had survived the rigours of war, remarkably well. They had been lucky.

Waiting inside was a young woman in a tight black dress. Despite the red hair, there was only one person that she could possibly be. She had to be Madeleine's sister. She was not a happy sister, either. She scowled at Emrys before she launched a tirade of abuse towards Madeleine.

He sat down and patiently waited for her to stop. He couldn't understand a word but smiled for the first time. The two women were now yelling at each other, as only siblings can. It reminded him of Evelyn and himself. If he and his sister were typical then these two women would soon be hugging and making up, as if nothing had ever happened. Perhaps French women were made of sterner stuff, however. The redhead glared at Emrys once more, turned on her heel and marched upstairs, slamming the door as she went. Madeleine also looked over at him and just shrugged her shoulders. Emrys broke the silence.

'Madeleine, I'm sorry if I got in the way. I didn't really have any choice, you know. Your sister seems upset.'

Madeleine shrugged her shoulders once more.

'Yes, she is upset. Distraught, in fact. With good reason too. So am I. It's nothing to do with you. Well, only a bit. She's worried about being caught with you in the house, but I have explained that it will only be for a few more hours.'

She paused, wondering how much she should tell him.

'The German pigs worked out that the hut was set on fire. They don't suspect me. In fact, they, probably, think that it was you, the escaped British soldier. Despite that, they took the hostages to the Citadel and shot all ten of them. In cold blood. It's just terrible. One of them was Marie's lover. Her married lover, so she can't even be seen making a show of herself.'

Emrys looked on in horror. They had done nothing and been taken to that bloody moat and shot. They thought he had blown the train up. What would they do to him, if he was caught? So, he spoke, very quietly.

'I suppose they are not too pleased about their train being blown up.'

Madeleine laughed sarcastically.

'That's the joke. The train didn't blow up. Some traitor got into the train and shunted it out of harm's way. When I find out who he is, he is dead, I can promise you.'

Emrys had wondered why he hadn't heard the crashes of explosions while sitting in the church. Now, he knew. It had been a failure. The German guard and ten Frenchmen had died for nothing. He spoke, gently, again.

'I was wondering. How on earth did you get those aeroplanes to attack? Right on time, too.'

Madeleine looked surprised when she replied.

'You surely don't think that was anything to do with us. It takes us weeks to get information to the British. Through Holland. That's how we got the letter to your mother.'

Emrys's ears pricked up.

'You sent the letter to Mam? You think it actually got there.'

Madeleine smiled for the first time.

'Of course. I promised we would. And the photograph. We wrote in French. We can speak English much better than we can write it. She will just have to get someone to translate it.'

Emrys looked in amazement. The Belgian lady whom his mam knew came into his head.

'But how? And why? Why take the risk?'

Madeleine was still smiling.

'Can't tell you much. Marie works in the bar. She has contact with a Dutch diplomat. A very close contact. He takes things to Holland for us. It's perfectly safe. We have been doing it for years. If we have found someone like you, we just add a little note to the bundle. Add it to all the important stuff. All the information. As I said. It's perfectly safe. Just takes time. So, we couldn't organise the planes. We had another plan, but didn't have to use it.'

Emrys turned to see Marie flounce down the stairs. Marie the barmaid or waitress or prostitute or, most probably, all three. Despite the same pouty look on her face which he had been so used to Evelyn using, he had to admire her. She was risking a lot and had lost even more. She deserved the adulation. He looked over, solemnly, at her.

'Marie. I don't know if you speak English. I am sorry for your loss. I am grateful for everything that you are doing.'

Marie ignored him and talked straight to her sister. She spoke in heavily accented English.

'When are you getting rid of this fool? The pigs will be doing a house to house search for him once it's dawn. He needs to be gone by then. We all know that all you want to do is play mother to him, but he can't stay. It's just too dangerous.'

The back door opened on the word dangerous, making Emrys jump. In crept a silent figure, an extraordinarily young boy. His face was smeared with mud and his ancient jerkin torn in many places. Within seconds the room was filled with the smell of stale urine. The street urchin stood and said nothing. His face was expressionless. Madeleine disappeared into the kitchen and returned with a slice of bread. The urchin grabbed it, unceremoniously, his yellow teeth tearing into it. She turned to Emrys.

'This is your guide. He never speaks. The pigs think that he's harmless, so let him out during the curfew. In fact, he would slit his own mother's throat for another piece of bread. He will guide you out of Lille. Now, quickly, you must burn all your things in the fire. Any more photographs? Everything. If you are captured, it is vital that you don't let them know that you were in the Citadel. If you do, they will bring you back and shoot you. That is for certain I'm afraid.'

The fire was glowing in the grate. Emrys began sorting through his few remaining belongings. The picture of Mam and Evelyn disappeared quickly into the flames, followed by some letters from Aunty Jess. Why he had kept them he had no idea. Finally, he stared down at his paybook. His precious paybook, which you just couldn't lose. It was a cardinal sin. He paused for just a moment. Marie took it off him and, nonchalantly, tossed it into the fire. Everything had to go. He gazed for a second. His whole person seemed to have disappeared into that fire. He closed his eyes.

Bang. Bang. His moment of reflection was, rudely, broken. Someone was hammering on the front door. His eyes were now wide open in fear. Madeleine Vaillant was only able to confirm his fears.

'The Germans!'

Everyone stopped still just for a moment, except for the urchin. Emrys felt himself being pulled towards the back door. A second later, he was outside in the dark, the urchin's fingernails digging into his forearm. The urchin seemed to glide, effortlessly, while Emrys stumbled, uncontrollably. He hadn't even had a chance to say thank you or goodbye. He needed to be far away from Madeleine and quickly. He had the expert guide.

Seemingly, just a moment later, he was catching his breath, behind a wall a quarter of a mile away. All the houses were just grave-like shells of their former selves. Only rats could live here. He was safe, if only for a few moments. He looked down at his companion. The urchin had still said nothing. He looked totally unconcerned. This was his playground so why should he worry? Emrys, however, knew that there were less than two hours until sunrise. If he was still in the city then, there would be no hope for him.

Evelyn was perpetually tired. She was the only member of the household still working. Da was just sitting in the corner. Mam was half the woman that had spent that night in prison. Harriet's main effort of each day was the slow painful walk to the cemetery.

This was something that Evelyn could have really done without. They had been ordered to have spotlessly clean overalls and report at the tram stop, going to Neath. They would have the honour of parading for and being presented to the Prime Minister, Mr David Lloyd George. He was in Neath to open the Eisteddfod. As Evelyn closed the front door behind her, she wondered what her mam, if she had been fit, would do. Mr Lloyd George could not be said to be her favourite person.

The rest of the girls were already gathered around the tram stop, giggling with excitement. There were few men indeed still working at Taylors. Those who did, slouched at the back smoking their cigarettes. The women were identically dressed in brown overalls on top of blue trousers. Evelyn smiled breafly as she remembered being sent home for wearing trousers, on her first day. Life had changed in so many ways. On their lapels, they proudly wore their triangular On War Service Badges.

Evelyn said nothing on the tram journey. She was simply

overcome by her thoughts not to mention all her worries and responsibilities. Silently, she took her place alongside her friends in the column of workers. In front of them, she could see the steelworkers and in front again, the Boy Scouts. At the very front were the band of the Welsh Guards. The drum banged and they were off, trying but failing to march in time with the martial music. All the houses were covered in flags and the streets lined with laughing crowds.

Evelyn failed to break into another smile. There was nothing to smile about. The march finished at the Gwyn Hall, where they lined up patiently in five ranks, waiting to meet the Prime Minister. Mr Lloyd George was well known for admiring the female form even in the presence of his wife. It was therefore inevitable for Evelyn to be pushed, reluctantly, into the front rank.

They waited patiently in the sun. The weather was unusually hot for that part of South Wales, even in August. Someone above obviously liked Mr Lloyd George. The open-topped car drove slowly down the ranks of people and stopped in front of the Boy Scouts. A dapper little man got out, briefly stopping to raise his hat a few inches to the adoring crowd. He was followed by an elegant woman in a white dress and a large matching hat. They quickly walked down the line of scouts before reaching the rows of women in their overalls. He stopped in front of Edith Jones, one of the shift managers. Trying desperately to look interested, he asked.

'What do these women produce?'

Considering that she was talking to the Prime Minister, himself, Edith was very self-assured when she answered.

'High explosive shells, sir. Eighteen pounders. We produce five thousand a week.'

The Prime Minister looked more interested when he continued.

'And which firm do you work for?'

Edith Jones confidently replied.

'Taylor and Sons, Briton Ferry, sir.'

The Prime Minister was instantly delighted.

'Excellent. Do you know that Taylors was the first firm I dealt with when I was Munitions Secretary? Excellent?'

His gaze wandered along the beaming line of women and predictably stopped at Evelyn. The eyes of powerful men, like Lloyd George, always did. A pretty girl when she joined Taylors aged fifteen. At eighteen, she was stunningly beautiful. Even wearing khaki overalls, she was stunningly beautiful. He walked along the line until he got to her, smiled and said in his deep gravelly voice.

'And you, my dear. What do you do?'

At that moment, she was thinking about what Miss Pankhurst had said in her speech in Jerusalem Chapel all that time ago. In a flash, Evelyn knew what she was going to say.

'I know what I would like to do, sir. I would like to negotiate peace with the Germans. I cannot do that, sir. You could.'

Lloyd George looked unphased. It must have been quite a shock to hear this pretty young thing talking like a seasoned pacifist. He replied calmly.

'I can tell you. Only this morning I was given news of a great victory, near Amiens. We are on the road to final victory. We cannot negotiate now. It would be a betrayal of all the sacrifices that we have made.'

He seemed surprised when the young girl had the audacity of continuing, despite the urgent tugs on her sleeves.

'You cannot talk to me about sacrifices, sir. Both my brothers are dead. My mam is heartbroken. You have had the chance to end all this. You haven't had the guts to take it.'

Lloyd George was still calm when he replied.

'I am truly sorry for your losses. Be assured that they have been for King and Country. Please send my sincere condolences to your poor mother.'

Evelyn felt a hard grip on her arm, as she was pulled away. She looked up to see the strained face of Tom Evans urging her to come away. But Evelyn's blood was boiling and like her mother, she had never run from a fight. She tore her arm free and turned again to the Prime Minister. She ripped her On War Service Badge off her overalls and flung it at his feet.

'You can keep your fucking badge. I'm ashamed to wear it.'

The soldiers guarding the Prime Minister belatedly pushed in front of him, suddenly aware of the growing threat. Tom Evans had got there first, however. His large arms enveloped the young girl and calmly guided her through the stunned crowd. Lloyd George smiled, raised his hat again and went on as if nothing had happened. Tom led Evelyn quickly down a narrow alleyway. The sooner he got her away from that place the better it would be for both of them. Tom's son, Martyn, rushed after them, his face red with excitement.

None of them said anything on the long walk back to Briton Ferry through the streets festooned in flags, in the Prime Minister's honour. Furious as he was, Tom couldn't help but admire his young companion. Then again. Should he be surprised? She was her mother's daughter in more ways than just her looks.

An hour later they were walking down Neath Road, towards Harriet's little house. Two doors down was Mr Ivor Jones, the postman, a satchel slung over his shoulder. He immediately shouted out to Evelyn.

'Evelyn. There's a letter here. The thing is that it's addressed to poor Emrys. We think the postmark might be from Holland.'

Without saying a word of thanks, she grabbed it and barged through the front door, quickly followed by Tom and Martyn.

They rushed down the narrow passageway into the back room. Josiah was asleep in his chair as usual. Despite her physical limitations or perhaps because of them, Harriet had to keep busy. She was in the opposite corner to her husband knitting furiously. All thoughts of Mr Lloyd George gone, Evelyn knelt down quietly next to her mother. Gently, she whispered.

'Mam. There's a letter here. It might be from Holland and it's addressed to Emrys.'

Harriet frantically grabbed the envelope from Evelyn's hand and tore it open, taking so little care that it ripped across the neatly written address. Out fell a postcard with the same neat handwriting on it. Madame Vaillant. 2 Rue Soltin, Lille (Nord). On the other side was a photograph of Emrys looking very smart in his uniform. Harriet looked in shock first at her daughter and then at Tom Evans. Evelyn got up and woke her father as her mother removed a single piece of paper from the mangled envelope. It was note paper, the likes of which she had never seen before. It was a faint yellow colour but with coloured flowers gaily decorating the edges. It had plainly been written by the same confident hand.

Lille, Juillet 1918

A la Famille d'Emrys

J'ai le grand plaisir de vous informer que votre fils Emrys n'est pas mort. Il sojourner ici a Lille et je travaille avec lui tous les hours. Il est en assez bonne sante et il a l'air heureux. Il a maigri un peu depuis son arrivee ici parce qu'il y tres peu de nourriture dans la ville, dont les allemands prennent la plupart. Comme j'ai deja dit il va bien a part d'avoir faim. Il s'inquietait que vous ne sauriez pas ce que lui est arrive. Je prie pour la fin de cette bierre terrible et le jour ou vous vous unirez. Veuillez trouver ci-joint une photo de lui.

   Avec routes mes amities.
   Madame Vaillant

Harriet looked white as a sheet as she struggled to her feet. Evelyn rushed over to her mother.

'Mam, where are you going? We all need to stay calm.'

Unperturbed, Harriet wheezed as she made for the front door not bothering to stop for her coat. She turned her head around and shouted.

'I need to see Ruth. She can read it for us.'

A strange group of people slowly made their way up Neath Road, leaving Josiah, at last awake, in his chair, trying to work out exactly what was happening. Tom was relieved that Martyn was still with them. He could send him up to the cricket pavilion, to make sure that Mrs Ruth Reubens was in. Tom couldn't afford to have Harriet, in this state, walking all that way on a fool's errand. Despite being supported on either side by Tom and Evelyn, progress was painfully slow. Every fifty yards they stopped for Harriet to catch her breath only for her to quickly usher them to get going again.

As they turned the corner out of Neath Road, they met Martyn running towards them. Behind him, struggling to run in her long dress, came Ruth. They all crowded around Harriet as she breathlessly handed the piece of paper to her Belgian friend. Ruth stared at it in disbelief before screaming.

'Harriet. Praise God. He's alive. Emrys is alive. It says here. Emrys n'est pas mort. It means Emrys is not dead. Praise God.'

Harriet looked at her friend disbelievingly. She had been caught out like this before. She had been given false hope before with David, only for those hopes to be quickly dashed. She looked at Ruth and calmly asked.

'Is it dated?'

Ruth quickly replied.

'Juillet. July.'

Harriet slumped to the ground, tears of joy and relief brimming from her eyes. There could be no doubt. He was alive. The previous letter from the lieutenant had been dated May. They carried Harriet the rest of the way to the cricket pavilion. Normally fiercely independent, she really couldn't care less about the ignominy of being carried. All she could think about was that her son was alive. They sat her down next to Ruth, to catch her breath. Martyn produced a stub of pencil and a sheet of paper, from his pocket. They all crowded around as Ruth wrote down a translation, with a trembling hand.

Lille July 1918

To the family of Emrys

I am pleased to tell you that your son Emrys is not dead. He is living here for a while in Lille and I work with him every day. He is in reasonable health and seems happy. He has lost some weight since he has been here because there is very little food in the city and most of what there is goes to the Germans. Apart from being hungry, as I have said he is well. He was worried that you would not know what had happened to him. I pray for the day this terrible war is over and he can be reunited with you. I enclose a photograph of him.

With all my best wishes.
Madame Vaillant.

Martyn broke the silence.

'Well, she seems very nice.'

'For a Catholic,' said Ruth, chuckling.

They all broke into laughter for the first time in weeks. The fact that Ruth was Jewish was not lost on any of them. Tom ushered Martyn away leaving the three women sitting together. He was already planning how he would tackle Mr Glen Taylor to persuade him not to sack Evelyn. He didn't want that to happen on this day, of all days.

Harriet rose and beckoned her daughter and friend to follow her. Saying nothing, she slowly led them towards the cemetery. There was no rush now. They could take their time. Against the back hedge was the chair with a rough cross on either side.

Harriet bent down and firmly pulled one of the crosses out of the ground. Giving it to Evelyn she said.

'Hopefully, we won't need this for another fifty years.'

19

Emrys was standing with his nose pushed, firmly, against the farmhouse wall. It had been a very long three days, since he had waved goodbye to the urchin, on the edge of Lille. The urchin still hadn't spoken or even smiled, as he had signalled towards the gun flashes, in the distance. That was the way that Emrys would have to go. Then the urchin had disappeared, as quickly and silently as he had arrived. Emrys had been on his own for the first time in years.

He couldn't, now, believe that he had been so stupid. He had got to within a few miles of the front before he had been recaptured. Resting during the day, he had, stealthily, moved only in the dead of night. That morning, however, he must have dropped his guard, just for a moment, and been seen hiding, in the wood. Five minutes later, surrounded by bayonets, he had been marched unceremoniously to this ruined farmyard.

The discharge of a German gun reverberated loudly from close by. He had got so close, but not close enough. Now, what would fate bring him? A strange feeling of relief swept over him. He was no longer the master of his destiny. He didn't need to worry about how he could cross the front, without being shot. What would now happen, would happen?

He did have cause to be worried, however. His experience of Germans had, in general, been surprisingly good. There were exceptions, of course. That bastard, who had hit the little girl, and the artillerymen at La Couture came to mind. He would never forget them. Most, however, were just like him. Their main concern was simply when they would get their next meal. They just wanted this bloody war to finish and go home.

This lieutenant, however, was a different breed. Emrys could tell that even his men thought that he was a little shit. Perhaps Emrys hadn't helped himself. The lieutenant had asked him where he had escaped from. Madeleine Vaillant's warning ringing in his ears, Emrys had answered bluntly.

'Bugger off.'

A rifle butt had slammed into his shoulder.

The lieutenant now prowled, venomously, behind him as his nose scraped against the wall. In the British army, these young officers were the worst. It was almost as if they had something to prove. It appeared to be the same with the Germans. He heard a volley of orders from behind him. Two soldiers grabbed him by the arms. The left arm, which had been hit so violently by the rifle, screamed with pain. He was sure that it was broken, as he was hauled painfully through the farm gate into the field, beyond.

In years gone by, this field must have been fine pasture. Four years of war had turned it into a morass of mud and discarded rubbish. He tripped and fell awkwardly before being hauled back to his feet. Arriving at a clear space, Emrys looked up. In response to another curt order, from the lieutenant, a corporal reluctantly hurled a spade onto the ground in front of him. Emrys looked at the soldiers. They didn't look happy. The lieutenant, however, was smiling as he pointed to the spade. At that moment, Emrys finally understood. He was being told to dig his own grave.

A million thoughts went through his mind, as he began to

dig the hole. Was there any escape from this? He looked up. There was no way out. His six guards might disapprove of their officer's actions but what could they do? They wouldn't disobey him even if he was a bloody shit. Emrys's spade struck the dry ground once more, jarring his injured shoulder.

His life raced before his eyes. Not the life of the last three years but his former life. His life charging along the Tennant canal, on his old bicycle with some message from M.G. Roberts. His life, laughing about some disaster that had happened to him with Evelyn and Mam. Those disasters seemed so inconsequential now. Poor Mam. She would never get over this.

Not surprisingly, letters were met with a feeling of acute foreboding, particularly if, as with this one, it had a London Post Mark. Harriet's hands shook even more than usual, as she carefully opened it.

October 1918

Dear Harriet (if I can call you that)

I apologise profusely for never thanking officially you and your friend, Ruth, for saving me in Briton Ferry Town Hall in 1916. I met Elizabeth Powell, recently, who told me that you haven't been well. I am sorry to hear that and wanted to send my best wishes. She also reminded me of how you went to prison because of your stand, against conscription.

You will be interested to know that Phillip, my husband, used you as an example when discussing the Representation of the People Act in Parliament. He discussed how women such as yourself deserved the vote, having given so much. We are of course

*delighted that the Act was passed and you will have the vote when
we next have an election. You should be proud that you played a
part in the Act being passed.*

*I am just disappointed that your wonderful daughter will have
to wait until she is thirty to vote. We all heard of what she said to
David Lloyd George. Philip says he wishes he had had the courage
to say it himself.*

*Finally, I was delighted to hear from Elizabeth that your son
is safe as a prisoner of war. You must be so relieved that he is no
longer in significant danger. The mood, in London, is optimistic.
The feeling is that the war will soon be over. For the first time, I
believe that this might be correct and you will soon see your son
again.*

Yours faithfully
Ethel Snowden

Harriet read the kind letter again. Her eyes focused on no
longer insignificant danger and will soon see your son again.

He dug further down. He was waist-deep in the six-foot long
trench. He could dawdle to delay the inevitable, but what was
the point? He might as well get it over with. Rehoboth flashed
into his head. He prayed for the first time in a very long time.

Emrys had deliberately turned his back on the soldiers. The
final few seconds of his life were approaching. Some snarled
order in German, followed by the scraping of the rifle bolts
being pulled back, would give him some warning. He couldn't
watch, however. It was easier just to look away.

He closed his eyes when the angry, guttural German shout

caused his heart to momentarily miss a beat. This was it. The angry shouting continued. It didn't stop. There was no sound from the rifle bolts. He tentatively looked over his shoulder. Deep in thought, he hadn't heard the approach of the captain. It wasn't the lieutenant who was shouting. It was the captain and, to the amusement of the soldiers, it was the lieutenant who was being bellowed at.

Common soldiers, all over the world, enjoyed nothing better than witnessing a junior officer receiving a dressing down. Even though he spoke no German, Emrys could tell that the lieutenant was receiving an almighty bollocking and not enjoying it. The lieutenant looked at the captain defiantly and Emrys, disdainfully, before marching off.

Two soldiers rushed over to pull him from his self-made grave while another clapped him on the back, before handing him a water bottle. They seemed to be almost as relieved as Emrys that they hadn't had to shoot him. He felt the nausea start to fade as the captain began to speak to him in perfect English.

'On behalf of the Imperial Army, I can only apologise for your treatment. It should not have happened. Certainly, it shouldn't have happened in my battalion. The only excuse I can give is that he is young and his older brother was killed, in 1916. I suppose I have to admit that it is a reason, not an excuse.'

Emrys had finally stopped panting and took a sip of water before speaking.

'My older brother was killed in 1916, too.'

The captain seemed to be deep in thought, for a moment, before replying.

335

'Yes. In more ways than we would like to admit, we are all brothers in arms. Anyway, you are alive. That I suppose is the important thing. Although, when you experience the place where I have to send you, you may wish that I hadn't interrupted him. Your colleagues refer to it, I believe, as the Black Hole of Lille. I am only able, I'm afraid, to offer you a small share of our food before sending you on your way. I also proffer you my best wishes and the very best of luck, of course.'

Emrys had met some incredible people during the previous three years. Major Davies, Madame Vaillant and General Elliott immediately came to mind. This captain would certainly deserve a rightful place on that list. He was a Fritz, too. It said a lot about this bloody war.

When Emrys and his four guards, eventually, arrived at their destination, he could tell that his German friends were becoming more anxious. It had been a very long march, but the five had quickly become close friends. One thing was for sure, nothing would induce Emrys to try to escape again. Absolutely nothing. Sensing this, his guards had relaxed and they all had enjoyed themselves walking away from the front.

Only, now, as they entered the ancient high street of Mons en Baroeul, on the outskirts of Lille, did the glum faces and military posturing return.

Like the Citadel, this prisoner of war camp looked like a castle. The difference was that it was more like a modern castle. The moat was filled with water, but the concrete walls behind were squat and ugly. Even the doorway, in the middle of the wall, was uninspiring. The plain oak door creaked menacingly open, to reveal the next painful instalment of Emrys's odyssey.

Behind the door stood an outlandish character, whose reputation had obviously gone before him. His four guards appeared distinctly uncomfortable, their sole aim being to leave this place quickly. Before Emrys had a chance to thank them, they had gone and the door slammed shut behind them.

A German colonel was studying Emrys carefully. During the whole of his war, Emrys had never seen anyone returning to duty after such terrible injuries. The right sleeve was empty and pinned to the breast pocket of his immaculate jacket. The left breast was covered, in medals. This man had seen a lot of service and could only have led from the front. At some stage, his jaw had been shattered and expertly reconstructed. The Germans must have their own Lieutenant Valadier. His face was still, however, tilting towards the remnants of his right ear, making him look unfortunately lopsided. Despite the reconstruction, he spoke, with a barely audible slur.

'Welcome to Fort Macdonald. Your colleagues I understand have a far less complimentary name for it. I trust that it will live up to its reputation. You will be enjoying the facilities for about a week. After that, you will be moved to the Motherland to enjoy further rehabilitation. There will be times, while you are here, that you will wish that you were dead. That wish can easily be granted. You only need to think of escaping and you will be executed. It will perhaps not be a quick death. Are we of one accord?'

Emrys didn't reply, struck dumb by stomach-churning fear. The colonel's face broke into a lop-sided smile as he signalled for two guards to take their prisoner away. They were surprisingly gentle as Emrys found his arms pinioned behind his back. Almost apologetically, they led him towards a thick metal door deep below the outer wall.

The door creaked slowly open. The pungent stench of rotting faeces blasted him in his face, making him cough. A hard push in the back propelled him precipitously, through the doorway, into the darkness. His eyes were streaming as he tried to focus. Two narrow windows high in the far wall might sometimes give some light, but tonight the gloom outside meant that the room was pitch black.

His foot slipped on something and he just managed to keep his footing. To do otherwise would have been a mistake, judging from the squelching under his boots. His eyesight gradually became accustomed to the darkness. He could make out some figures. Lots of them and all were motionless. They were also strangely quiet. Not a sound. Were they human or devils?

His eyes had stopped streaming, despite the terrible smell, and he began to see just a bit more. The room was a huge stone cellar. Looking towards the far wall, it was as long as the nave in Rehoboth but it was cold and gloomy. Reverend Hughes would have loved the size of the congregation, however. Every space seemed to be filled by one of the motionless figures. The lucky ones were seated, shoulder to shoulder, on some narrow beds. The rest could only rest by sitting, on the fetid floor. He could make out their uniforms: French, British, and even Portuguese. There were soldiers of so many nations. It made no difference. None of them talked to him. None of them even looked at him.

There was a small space next to a copper bath, in the middle. Emrys pushed his way towards it. At least there would be some room for him to stretch out a bit. He, suddenly, understood his mistake, the reason why there was a space. The bath was overflowing with faeces and urine. He began vomiting. This place was hell. It was worse than hell. This was going to be a very long night.

The next morning began early. Sunlight began streaming through the two narrow windows. Emrys could, at last, see the true horror of the situation in which he found himself. How could anyone survive this even for a day? The veterans of that terrible room began to edge forward towards the doorway. Something was about to happen but what?

The silence was broken by the creaking door followed by the roar of a panicked stampede. All the prisoners seemed to be, at some unsaid word, storming the door. All but a few. The ones who were just too weak to join the rush and the ones, like Emrys, who just didn't know what was about to happen.

It was breakfast time. Four hard loaves of bread came flying through the doorway, flung by invisible, uncaring hands. The panic lasted just a few moments. The loaves disappeared quickly and violently. Emrys could only gaze on hungrily. There was no chance of him getting any. The door slammed shut and tranquillity returned. All the food had gone and everyone could rest again, leaving two motionless figures lying where they had fallen.

Lunchtime was more sedate. The old timers knew that there would be no rush, this time. It was just the new boys like Emrys who crowded towards the door. They had missed breakfast. They weren't going to miss out again. Only this time no bread was thrown in. The two guards silently signalled with their rifles and the prisoners filed out into the welcome light of the courtyard.

Emrys blinked in the sunlight before joining the orderly

queue. A grimy, wooden bowl was thrust into his hands along with an equally dirty wooden spoon. The bowl was half filled with a thin soup together with a lump of hard bread. The soup was lukewarm and stank of decayed cabbage. It was, however, at least some form of sustenance. Emrys devoured it ravenously, quickly overcoming the nausea. However bad this became he was going to survive.

He looked up and saw the one-armed colonel surveying his kingdom. Whatever this bastard threw at him, Emrys was going to survive. Unlike those two poor souls, whose bodies were being removed from the cellar while the prisoners were outside. Both of them must have lost their footing on the wet floor and had been trampled to death in the stampede for the bread.

Half an hour later, Emrys and the rest were being prodded by bayonets back into the dim light of the cellar. The door crashed shut again. The next time it would open would be for another bread fight in the morning.

Emrys didn't know how long he had been in that hellhole. It could have been just a few days but could have just as easily been a couple of weeks. As his strength gradually faded, his sense of time disappeared as well. He was no longer able to fight his way to the front to participate in the bread fight. He could only sit on the floor and watch enviously. He didn't seem to notice the rancid smell of human decay that had caused him to vomit, on the first day.

His initial determination had disappeared too. He was simply marking time, while waiting to die, with a brief respite each day from a few minutes in the courtyard. He continued to look up at the one-armed colonel. Surely, he must have some compassion. He must have enough heart to give them some more time. The answer was always the same. The prods of the bayonets pushed them back into the cellar.

Nobody in the cellar said a word. They were trying, desperately, to conserve their energy. The only noises came from the guards on the wall overhead and the sound of gunfire in the distance. Perhaps, it was just a mirage, but Emrys imagined that the gunfire might be getting closer.

The following night he was sure of it. Even in that terrible place, an air of expectancy seemed to grow. Something was about to happen. Maybe they were about to be rescued. Or more likely, they would be taken out into that courtyard and the demonic colonel order them to be shot. They could only wait to see what morning might bring.

When light eventually began to seep through the two narrow windows, Emrys didn't try to open his eyes. Even the faint light seemed to exacerbate his headache. It was a throbbing headache, which had started making his nausea worse, the previous evening. He was desperately trying not to vomit. His clothes were soaked by the cold sweat. He knew that, if he had been back home, Mam would have bundled him into bed with some sort of repulsive herbal treatment harvested in the woods. Here, he could just sit on the wet floor shivering profusely. He would not bother fighting for the bread when the door opened. He no longer had the energy or the appetite.

Even in his desperate state, Emrys realised that things were somehow different. The gunfire had disappeared to such an extent that each rare shot now made the prisoners jump. The bright sunlight could be seen outside, through the two windows. It must surely be later in the morning. The bread fight normally occurred just after dawn, in the semi-dark. The guards were either being unusually negligent or the food had just run out. It couldn't be negligence. The guards were as petrified of the colonel as the prisoners.

He could feel the tense anxiety in the crowded room, rising by the minute. He was, also, beginning to feel claustrophobic. It was a word, that he somehow remembered Lieutenant Mond using in that bloody tunnel. At the time, he hadn't understood what the lieutenant had meant. Now he knew. The sheer panic seemed to restore just a little of his waning energy.

He blindly pushed his way towards the doorway ignoring the multilingual curses thrown in his direction. He was going to get out. He had to get out. Stumbling over a body, unnoticed by all since the previous night, he crashed into the metal door. The shoulder, battered a few days previously by the cruel rifle butt, shook with pain. A loud gasp from behind him, however, brought him back to his senses. The door had opened. Just a few inches but it had opened.

Nobody moved. Emrys looked around. What should he do? The rising nausea of claustrophobia was forcing him through the narrow gap. What was on the other side? Was the colonel waiting on the wall above them along with a machine gun? He could stand it no longer.

Closing his eyes, he pushed the door fully open and crept out up the narrow flight of stairs to the courtyard, above. Every second he expected to hear the click of a machine gun bolt being pulled into place. It would be the last thing that he ever heard. The next thing would be the slamming of bullets as they struck him. Nothing. Nothing but the flutter of wind through some hidden trees. He stopped for a second and opened his eyes, squinting in the unaccustomed sunlight. Nothing. Still nothing. The courtyard was empty. No colonel. No machine guns. In fact, no Germans. They had gone.

He sat down with his head in his hands, as the rest of the prisoners began to file past him staring around in incredulity. One of the Germans must have had enough humanity to unlock the door before they left. Who would have believed it? Why had they left in such a hurry, though? There was only one logical answer. The British Army must be coming soon. Then at last they would be free.

Emrys was violently awoken from his stupor. The tell-tale whine of an incoming shell was followed by a deafening explosion. It must have landed just on the other side of the fortress wall. The second shot which followed was even closer. This was perhaps not the place of safety that he had envisaged for a few ecstatic moments. A place where they could simply wait for their saviours to arrive. The German guards may have shown compassion but their artillery was not.

This was still a dangerous place and common sense told him that he should leave. His head still ached and he hadn't eaten anything for at least twenty-four hours but he knew he had to get away. He would travel west, back towards Lille and the British Army. Difficult as it would be that is what he would do.

The first obstacle was the huge wooden gate, which had greeted him a few days before. Would it be unlocked too? Yes, it was. The moat outside was full of muddy water and he was able to drink his fill. It might taste of mud laced with shit, but he had no choice. He can't have drunk for twenty-four hours. He could hardly recall coming up this road a few days earlier.

Perhaps, it was a few weeks earlier. Everything was such a blur.

He looked up for the first time. Fifty yards down the road and striding towards him were men in khaki. Without a doubt British soldiers. His headache seemed to disappear, if only for a moment. He was saved. He was going to get home.

With perfect timing, the next German salvo landed somewhere between him and his erstwhile saviours. Perhaps he wasn't yet safe.

Two hours later, he was sitting at the side of a road feeling dizzy. Perhaps leaving the fortress had been a mistake. He had staggered away from the falling shells, ignored by the fighting men more intent on keeping themselves alive. He was now out of the fighting zone but had only exchanged one death for another. He was unable to take even one further step forward. This was the end.

He tried, valiantly, to focus on the battered lorry which had stopped on the other side of the road. Fresh soldiers were pouring out of the back keen to join the advance. They were welcome to it. The driver got out and lit a cigarette, glad to be ridding himself of his load. He looked over at Emrys, looked away and then looked back in undisguised amazement.

'Emrys? Is that you?'

Emrys studied the young driver with renewed interest. He recognised him from somewhere. Then, he remembered. The last time he had seen him was when crossing the River Neath, to get his teeth done, back in 1915. It was the dairyman who had been collecting the milk from the other side of the river, Asher Crocker. Emrys whispered.

'Asher. I'm glad to see you.'

Asher Crocker beamed back.

'Well, Emrys. I'm glad to see you too. We all thought you were dead.'

20

October 1918

Chocolate had never tasted so good. It was only two small pieces, which Asher Crocker had been saving. To Emrys, it was a banquet to be savoured with undisguised zeal. Asher kept on looking over at him, however, as he drove the lorry carefully along the pock-marked road towards the ruins of Lille.

'Christ, Emrys. You look grim. You're thin as a bloody rake.'

Emrys didn't reply. Fate seemed to be playing funny tricks on him. Fancy meeting Asher just at the right moment. Even more surprising was that Asher had actually recognised the emaciated, bearded tramp. It had taken very little for Emrys to persuade his friend to help him up into the lorry and drive him away from danger.

He gazed absent-mindedly out of the window, only partially revived by the blast of cold air. He said nothing. He was too tired to say anything, until the moment he shouted.

'Stop! Stop!'

Asher Crocker slammed on the brakes automatically, in response to the urgent scream. Surely, Emrys must have seen something that he himself had missed. Some unexploded ordinance, perhaps. Emrys's eyes were fixed on the tower and dome of a church, standing proudly in the middle of a sea of devastation. Emrys whispered.

'St.Saviours Church. I have friends there. They will look after me. I know they will.'

He turned to Asher while painfully scrambling down from the lorry.

'Asher. You have saved my life. No doubt about it. I will never forget it. Nor will my family. Look after yourself. This bloody war is nearly over. Don't do anything daft.'

The lorry disappeared into the distance. Emrys was alone once more. It was difficult to believe that he was in the same city. The houses were just as ruined, scarred by the constant trauma of four years at war. The streets, however, were no longer empty. They were overflowing with a jubilant throng of people. People who were still emaciated but now beaming. Smiling and laughing, they waved Tricolour flags for the first time in many years. They swigged liberally from bottles of red wine, uncovered at last from their secret hiding places. They acted as they felt, free at last.

Emrys crept slowly and painfully, towards the dome of the church. The celebrating mass parted in disgust, as the flea-ridden tramp pushed his way through. No welcome for a conquering hero this time.

Everything looked so different. All these people and not in the dark. He knew that Madeleine Vaillant's house must be very close but where? He had no idea. The tower of the church, which had previously granted him sanctuary, soared above. Perhaps, he thought, it would help him again. He staggered towards the doorway, pushing the last of the revellers firmly out of the way. What he would do if the church door was locked he had no idea. He imagined that he could hear a sound, from inside. Unbelievably, it sounded like singing.

As he swung the great door open, with the last of his energy, the singing seemed to increase in volume like some jubilant greeting. He staggered in and collapsed on the tiled floor a few feet inside. He knelt, wheezing noisily for a few seconds, and then looked up. His own gaze was met by that of a hundred worshippers, who had turned in shock to see the cause of the commotion. He had noisily crashed in on a church service. It must, surely, be a service to commemorate freedom.

Emrys didn't know what to do. He was on all fours, feeling faint and nauseous. He had no doubt that if this had been a church, back home, then he would have been swiftly and callously ejected. There would be no Good Samaritan there. Here, an elderly couple walked back towards him, with the kindest looks on their faces. Despite his rancid uniform, they gently lifted him by the arms and eased him into the adjacent dark pew.

A young boy placed a cup of water in his hands. Perhaps, Emrys thought, it might be Holy Water. That would be a turn-up for the books. Drinking Holy Water in a Catholic church. What would Reverend Hughes say? Emrys looked, momentarily, up at the painting of Jesus summoning the children and then closed his eyes. A moment's rest, overcome by the smell of burning incense and the tranquil sound of chanted psalms, would surely revive him.

He awoke suddenly and looked around him. All was quiet. He really must have been exhausted. The church was almost empty. He had slept so deeply that he had not woken, when the service had ended and the worshippers filed past him, into the reveries outside. The only people still in the church were the couple, who had eased him into the pew, and a priest.

Almost unrecognisable in all his finery was the elderly priest, whom he had watched talking to Madeleine Vaillant, only a few weeks previously. The three were standing, near the altar, talking intently. They must be discussing what to do next, with this filthy soldier. He coughed loudly.

The three French people looked around, in surprise. They, probably, had expected the exhausted figure to sleep for longer. They bowed to the altar, a gesture so alien to Emrys's upbringing, and strode towards him. These were, undoubtedly, kind people. People like his mam. In fact just like Mam. He took another sip of water before croaking, desperately trying to remember just a little of his woefully inadequate French.

'Bonjour. Merci beaucoup. Madame Vaillant. I need to find Madeleine Vaillant. Please. S'il vous plait.'

He was shaken by their silent response. They looked at each other with a look of embarrassment and then back at Emrys. God. She must be dead. The Germans must have shot her for helping him. He struggled to find the French for dead from the depths of his weary mind.

'Mort. Madeleine Vaillant is mort?'

The priest replied slowly and deliberately.

'Non. Non. Madeleine n'est pas mort.'

A wave of relief swept over him. He was surprised by the depth of the feelings which he still held for that young woman. The young woman who had nearly got him killed. The young woman, whom he had witnessed battering a man to death with a spade. He continued, his voice now louder.

'La maison de Madeleine Vaillant. I must find the maison of Madeleine Vaillant.'

The French people looked, again, at each other dubiously.

Then, after the inevitable shrug of his stooped shoulders, the priest signalled for Emrys to follow while the couple helped him to his feet.

Rue Soltin had changed very little since Emrys's previous brief visit. It was, still, remarkably undamaged, compared with most of the surrounding streets. There were, of course, so many people making their way down this shortcut towards the city square. Previously, there had been no one except himself and Madeleine, creeping through the nighttime curfew.

He was dismayed that the other changes were strangely confined to Number 2, Madeleine's house. All the ground-floor windows were smashed and red paint was liberally smeared on the front door. On the side wall, written in large red letters, was the word 'TRATTREUSE'. Emrys looked at the priest, who had his hands on his knees, recovering after his efforts. The priest said nothing. He just silently pointed to the door and mimicked knocking.

Emrys pushed on the door. None of the houses back home was ever locked. This one definitely was, not surprisingly, considering that they were in a starving city in the middle of a battlefield. He looked back at the priest who mimicked knocking, again. Emrys knocked gently on the wooden door. Nothing. Not a murmur in response. He knocked again, this time louder. Still nothing. Nothing, perhaps, except the slight flicker of the curtain in the upstairs window. He stood back and shouted up at the window.

'Madeleine. Madeleine. It's Emrys. I'm alive. I'm alive.'

Still nothing. He knocked again. The priest took his arm and began to pull him back towards St Saviours Church. Whatever was going on in that house, they wanted nothing to do with this waif and stray. Emrys would need to change his plans. As he trudged, forlornly, back down the narrow road, he heard a door swing open behind him. He turned when he heard his name.

'Emrys. It is you. Mon Dieu. We thought you were back with the British. Either that or dead.'

He stared in shock at the young woman, who last time he had seen her looked so marvellously young and alluring. One arm of her dress had a jagged tear, exposing the blue hue of a large, painful bruise. Her right eye was closed and swollen, crowned by a long gaping wound in her eyebrow. Her nose was, also, swollen and perhaps bent slightly to the side. Her lip was split and still seeping blood. Her previously long dark hair had been shorn, viciously, by some demonic barber, and all that remained were blood-stained tufts. Only briefly lost for words, he gasped.

'Madeleine. My God. What have they done to you?'

The young lady, gently, pulled him towards the doorway. She was only able to whisper.

'You think I look bad. Perhaps, I should give you a mirror. And you feel so hot.'

He staggered through the door, greeted by an equally ravaged face, topped with massacred red hair. The last thing Emrys remembered, before falling into welcome unconsciousness, was Madeleine's sister saying.

'Jesus. You're the last thing we need.'

His dreams were surprisingly vivid. He screamed out in terror at the malignant imp who was waiting round the corner of a dark tunnel, to jump out on Lieutenant Mond. A soft female voice, from above, seemed to be calming him. He felt himself jolt upright when the ghost of the cavalry horse jumped at him. Cool angel's hands laid him flat again.

He couldn't tell whether he was still dreaming. If he was then it was a good dream. He was in a soft bed, smelling of lavender. The whole room smelt like Mam and Da's room, back home. Lavender laced with tobacco. He didn't want to open his eyes. He was afraid of what he might see. Something that might wrench him from this exorbitant tranquillity. There was the reassuring sound of a woman talking quietly in the corner, interrupted by a gruffer male voice. He opened his eyes slowly.

He didn't want that bloody headache to return. The late autumn sunlight, filtering through the window, made him close his eyes again but just for seconds. Then he began squinting in the direction of the voices. Madeleine Vaillant was sitting with her bruised face screwed up. The man standing over her was concentrating deeply. He was dressed in the pristine British army uniform of a major, and talked quietly, in a melodious Scottish voice.

'One more little stitch, my dear, and it will be over. I only wish some of my soldiers were as brave as you. Not even a murmur. Very impressive, I must say. Wish I'd gotten to you a bit sooner, mind you. Still, patched you up enough to meet General Birdwood. That's the main thing.'

They didn't seem to notice Emrys as he began to slowly appraise the situation. He felt as weak as a kitten. Too weak to even murmur. How long had he been here? In fact, how on earth had he got into this bedroom, the like of which he had never even imagined? It oozed femininity, except for the photograph on the wall of a strapping cavalryman standing beside his grey horse.

The last thing he remembered had been the narrow hallway. Somehow, Madeleine and Marie, perhaps with the help of the ancient priest, had got him up the stairs to one of the bedrooms.

The coarse blankets covering him felt damp, from perspiration, and made his skin itch. He, carefully, rubbed his face as if to ensure himself that he was indeed alive. His chin was smooth. He remembered when sitting, patiently waiting, in St. Saviours Church, he had been sporting an impressive beard grown through neglect, in the fortress. It had gone. Somebody must have carefully shaved him.

The major had put the last stitch into Madeleine's forehead. He sat back to admire his handiwork and caught a glimpse of Emrys in the large mirror. The young soldier's eyes were open.

'Good God. Our young invalid is awake. Who'd have believed it?'

Madeleine shot up out of her chair and ran over towards Emrys. Despite the stitches, her face seemed a lot less bruised than he remembered. He must have been laying here for quite some time. He tried to speak but failed miserably. His throat was as dry as autumn leaves. Madeleine lifted a glass, carefully, to his mouth as the major continued.

'Back in the land of the living, I see. Absolutely nothing to do with me, I'm afraid. You can put it down to this expert nurse and her sister.'

Marie had, quietly, crept into the room to join Madeleine as the major turned to speak to them.

'I have been informed that you will be given an armed guard until things get sorted. The truth will be out, you know. You're both heroines. No doubt about it. As I informed you, on my arrival, General Birdwood himself wishes to thank you.'

He took out a stethoscope and briefly examined Emrys, before talking earnestly to him.

'You're a jolly lucky chap, soldier. This influenza seems to be extraordinarily powerful. Especially for chaps like yourself, weak and malnourished. As I said you would be in the cemetery by now if it wasn't for these two. Still could be if we move you now. If Madame and Mademoiselle will continue to have you, you should stay here.'

Madeleine interrupted.

'Leave him here. We will look after him. You care for the wounded in your hospital. All we will need is some food for him and ourselves. It is still not safe for us to step out of the door.'

Emrys was feeling tired and confused. He couldn't work out what was going on. The two women had obviously been badly battered by the Germans, but why? If they had been discovered surely, at best they would have been taken to Germany, at worst to that bloody moat, with the flowers. He slipped back into a deep but this time peaceful sleep.

When he eventually woke, he felt extraordinarily better. Still exhausted but much better. The feeling that he had had, almost continuously, for the last three years had returned. He was ravenously hungry. As if by magic, Madeleine Vaillant was sitting, patiently, next to him. In her hands was a bowl of soup. Soup. Mam would love her. She slowly began to spoon it into his dry mouth. With each spoon full, he could feel just a little of his strength returning.

She put the empty bowl down and began to rearrange his blankets. Emrys was only capable of an almost inaudible croak.

'Madeleine. Let me go to the hospital. You have done enough for me. More than enough. I can't ask you to do any more. You helped me escape and got beaten up by the Germans. Goodness knows what else you have done. Now you are looking after me.'

Madeleine put her fingers to the vivid row of stitches in her forehead, followed by her swollen nose, before laughing painfully.

'You think the Germans did this? It wasn't those pigs. It was our brave compatriots. Those bastards who did nothing for four years. Me, who blew up the ammunition in 1916 and took risks every day, and Marie who allowed fat Germans to paw her every night. Just to get information. Now they are accusing us. Of collaborating. Us of all people. We were lucky that they didn't shoot us.'

Emrys didn't understand.

'You mean French people did this to you. Your friends. But why? Everyone must know what you have done. Surely?'

Madeleine looked deadly serious.

'Some people lost a lot in the explosion, in 1916. It might have killed some Germans too, but my fellow citizens don't care. They can only see their losses. When you escaped and the hostages were shot, they suspected it was me behind it not you.'

Emrys couldn't believe what he was hearing. She hated Gerry so much. Her husband had even been killed by them, for God's sake.

'But Marie. She's done nothing.'

Madeleine spat back at him, her voice laced with venom.

'Jealousy. Just jealousy. They have seen her, dressed nicely, and they forget all the rest. Anyway, forget about it. Things are better now, mainly due to you. You don't realise it, but you've become our guardian angel. Those bastards wouldn't dare do anything while you are here and while the doctor is visiting.'

Well, this was a situation that his friends wouldn't believe. Stuck in the house and, indeed, the bed of two beautiful if bruised, young women. He had an armed guard, outside, and daily home visits from a doctor. A major, as well, not some young lieutenant. Emrys couldn't fail to grudgingly notice that the major seemed to spend far more time examining Madeleine, than himself. Perhaps, even majors were partial to the alluring attractions of Madame Madeleine Vaillant.

The previous three days had been like nothing that he had experienced in France, over the past three years. He had recuperated quickly, in the comfort of Madeleine's bed, perhaps only wishing that she was sharing it. The major had been as good as his word and produced the most food Emrys had seen, since last being home, eighteen months previously. Had it really been that long? He really missed home, now. For the last few months, it had been a question of simply surviving.

Despite the luxury that he now shared with these two ladies, his only wish was to get home. The worry, in the back of his mind, was that, as he was feeling so much better, some jumped-up little bastard might make him go back to the cyclists. If the cyclists still existed, of course, after La Couture. If not, then, some other battalion. The infantry, perhaps. That would be the bloody end.

It wasn't to be, thank God. The major had informed the girls that they were to be presented to General Birdwood, at the Freedom Parade. That might put an end to all the speculation and rumours. Emrys was told he would be going home. He had to make the major repeat himself. He just couldn't believe that it was true. It was. All prisoners of war were going home. That would mean Ted, Gwyn and all his friends, too. If they were alive.

Emrys said goodbye to his refuge in Rue Soltin and a thank you to the church of St. Saviour, which towered behind them. The two girls, Emrys and the major walked slowly up the passage, through the crowds, towards the main square. Emrys still hadn't fully recovered and stopped frequently to catch his breath. The other three waited, patiently, each time. They had plenty of time. The rushing of the previous years seemed to have passed as quickly as the war itself. The sound of artillery could still be heard faintly to the east. It was a long way away and wasn't going to bother them. It had gone forever.

The ancient and opulent square seemed to have survived the war better than many of the poorer areas of the city. Perhaps, Emrys thought inwardly, that was always the way. Tricolours flapped madly in the autumn wind, in dispersed with Union Flags and one solitary Welsh Dragon. It was cold in the wind, despite being blessed by some October sunshine and he began to shiver.

One side of the square was filled with tightly fitted rows of wooden chairs. That was where the undeserving dignitaries would, undoubtedly, sit to watch the parade, while the rest of them, those who had fought and suffered, would have to stand. Only, two of those ushered towards the seats, could neither be described as dignitaries nor undeserving. He watched Marie and Madeleine push their way along to their allotted places.

The Merci he had just given them had seemed painfully inadequate. He was pleased though. Even their fiercest critic would have to be quiet now. He watched jealously as a balding man lifted his hat and made a show of sitting them down next to him.

'Mr Churchill.' Muttered the major. 'Used to be First Lord of the Admiralty. Planned the Dardanelles, where my brother died. I hate to say it, soldier, but I have no love for Mr Churchill. Now, let's get you in a good place to watch the parade.'

Instead, Emrys shook the major's hand, before turning towards the railway station. He had seen enough bloody parades, for a lifetime. The last time he had shaken a man's hand, it had also belonged to a major. The cavalry major before they marched down that road to La Couture. That was immediately before this nightmare had begun.

21

He had slept all the way, on the train, not wanting to witness the devastation of war passing outside. He hadn't been fortunate enough to meet any of his friends, so his mood was surprisingly flat.

He wasn't even interested in the port of Boulogne, only briefly acknowledging the previous times that he had been there. He wondered, momentarily, how Lieutenant Mond had fared and whether Lieutenant Valadier was still working in the strange hospital, on top of the cliff. Soon, however, he was on board the large, modern ship and gazing towards the white cliffs and port of Folkestone. As for France, if he lived to be eighty, he was never going back. Never.

His stop in Folkestone, was remarkably brief, barely having time to recognise the ornate clock tower where he had met Mrs Davies, in 1916. He hoped Major Davies had survived. The two of them deserved to be happy.

The sole blot on the landscape was that the train which they were, unceremoniously, herded onto, was not bound for London and then home. They were to be processed in a place which he had never heard of, called Canterbury. Typical of the army. They couldn't just let them go home. They had to be bloody processed and a goods yard next to the station was where that would take place. He had no choice. Frustrating though it certainly was, it didn't really matter. After three years another few hours would make precious little difference.

If St. Saviours had seemed huge when compared to Rehoboth, the Cathedral near the station at Canterbury was beyond description. Some, perhaps those away from the front line, might feel that all the wonderful things they had seen, while away, made the last few years worthwhile. Emrys wasn't one of them. As he queued in that goods yard, he wished to God that he hadn't persuaded his mam to let him go. Call him a coward, but how he wished he had never left Briton Ferry.

He looked around at the men in the two lines awaiting processing. They all had surprisingly glum looks on their faces. There wasn't the raucous hilarity that he had expected. Perhaps, they were all having similar thoughts to himself or else they were just too tired.

His queue was the short one. It was the one for those, few in number, who had lost their paybooks. Their paybook had always been their most precious possession and Emrys remembered the difficulty Madeleine Vaillant had had to persuade him to burn it. It didn't seem to matter to the sergeants sitting at tables, however. They were just intent on getting these poor souls through rapidly and efficiently.

Word had, quickly, gotten around the soldiers that their rewards were going to be clean uniforms and back pay. Back pay from April before La Couture would be a fair sum.

The sergeant that Emrys stood before looked bored. He had done this same monotonous task, day in and day out for the past weeks, as the prisoners of war gradually trickled home. He was sick of it.

'Name?'

'Emrys John.'

'Unit?'

'Eleventh Corps Cyclist Battalion.'

'Number?'

'7847.'

The sergeant shuffled through a disorderly pile of paper on the desk in front of him. He began to study a neatly typed list before looking up at Emrys. The sergeant's look had changed. The boredom had gone. It was replaced by a stare of intent appraisal, peering over his half-rimmed glasses. Something was wrong. After three years in the army, Emrys could tell. The sergeant growled angrily at him.

'Name and Service Number, again if you please.'

'Emrys John. 7847. Captured in April.'

The sergeant shot up from the table and stood at his full height. A tall man, he stared down at the nervously perspiring soldier in front of him. With his index finger pointing directly at Emrys, he looked like a poor man's Kitchener, as he screamed for all to hear.

'You are a liar and a scoundrel. The soldier, you are wickedly pretending to be, was confirmed dead, in May. You are trying to misappropriate his money. You are a disgrace. Stand aside and let a proper soldier take your place. The military police will deal with you, soon enough.'

Emrys stared back in horror. He seemed to be stopped at every turn. When the police arrived they might think that he was a deserter. Then, he would be in real trouble. Well, he'd had enough. He had fought for three years and had nothing to show for it, except the stinking clothes that he was standing up in. He didn't have as much as a farthing to his name. He wasn't going to wait around for some officious bloody military policeman. Whatever the consequences he was leaving.

The tall sergeant was concentrating too hard on the next customer to notice Emrys, as he crept silently away. He took a deep breath as he trotted to the main station next to the goods yard. He was free even if it was only for a few hours. He opened the convenient door of the nearest train carriage. He had no idea where it might be going. He didn't care. He just wanted to get away from bloody Canterbury.

The train was full. Every seat was taken. The morose atmosphere of the goods yard had been replaced by an air of jubilation. They were, at last, going home. Emrys slumped down with his back against the carriage door, invisible to the platform outside. A few curious eyes gave him a second glance, but they didn't take much notice. They had too much else on their minds.

As the great tower of the cathedral faded into the distance, his eyes became heavy once more. The continuous chatter of the train passing over the rails induced deep sleep.

He woke to the sound of soldiers rising from their wooden seats and searching for their few scarce belongings. The train had begun to slow as it crossed a large metal bridge with a wide river flowing slowly below it. Emrys stood and shook the stiffness out of his body. Looking out, the skyline was dominated by the huge domed roof of yet another massive church.

A wave of elation swept over him. He recognised that church. He had seen it before while travelling with Major Davies. It was St. Paul's Cathedral. By good fortune, he was arriving in London. If he could walk from wherever this was to Paddington, he would only be one train ride from home. He may not have eaten for twenty-four hours and had no money, but surely that couldn't be too difficult.

The advantage of having slept against the door was that he now stood at the very front of the queue of jostling men. As the train slowed into the station, he just had time to read the sign. Charing Cross. Yes. He'd been here before. He'd been amazed by the underground railway that he had caught when previously returning from leave. Much as he would have liked to, there would be no underground today. Despite everything, he would have to walk.

As he jumped down from the still-moving train onto the wide platform, he knew where his first port of call would be. Surely, there would be the usual welcoming party of upper class do-gooders, handing out cups of tea and, with any luck, cake.

As he pushed past the throng of soldiers disembarking from carriages, Emrys caught sight of his target, a group of well-dressed women crowded around a table. Behind them stood rows of servant girls who would undoubtedly be the ones doing most of the work. No matter. The table contained a large tea urn, piles of cups and a plate full of cake.

He placed his last prized possession on his head, his filthily weathered cap, complete with his beloved rifle and wheel cap badge. He had been so proud of that cap back in 1915. He was leaving this place what he was, a proud cyclist.

Perhaps it was his delinquent condition which attracted the lady, in an elaborately expensive dress, to him. An incongruously chipped cup was, rapidly, placed in one hand and a welcome piece of cake in the other.

The lady studied the filthy young man intently. He was painfully thin and his face was etched with fatigue. Her gaze stopped on his cap and she spoke almost nonchalantly.

'You're a cyclist. My brother was a cyclist.'

She looked away towards the next expectant customer and then back again. Her tone, suddenly, changed to one of incredulity.

'My God. You're Boxer. You're alive. The last time I saw you, you were running out of the sea stark naked.'

Confusion hit Emrys like a wave. Who on earth was this patently well-off young lady, who claimed to have seen him stark naked? Then it came to him. The only person who had ever called him Boxer was Lieutenant Mond. This could only be his sister who had been on the beach that day in Boulogne when he and the orderlies had gone swimming. Regaining his composure, he spoke quietly.

'It's been a long time since I was called Boxer. How is your brother, Miss Mond?'

The lady laughed.

'It's a long time since I was called Miss Mond as well. I'm Mrs Isaacs and I even have two children. Henry's very well, thank you, considering all that happened. You, of course, know all about that. The tunnel and the transfusion. We are all very grateful and I'm sure he'd want to see you and say thank you himself.'

Emrys laughed, as well.

'Sorry, Mrs Isaacs. I'd forgotten, that you were married. Look. I just need to get home. Give me another piece of cake because I'm bloody starving. Beg your pardon. Then, I'll be on my way. Do send Lieutenant Mond my best wishes mind.'

Eva Isaacs took Emrys gently by the arm and led him to a chair. He began to panic. He, certainly, didn't want to give lice to this fine lady. He slumped down, only then realising how exhausted he really was. She smiled down at him.

'Were you there in April? Henry heard what happened. What happened to Percy and the rest of you. Henry still feels guilty about not being there with you.'

She sat down next to him and put her hand on his mud-spattered sleeve.

'We tried to get you home, you know? Your mother came up to London to see my father. Do you remember my father, Sir Alfred? That was when we first heard how much you had helped Henry. You were in Italy, by then. Once you got back to France, you were supposed to come home. We don't know what went wrong. All we knew was that you were either killed or captured.'

Emrys tried to get things straight in his own mind. It would explain a lot. Why they were suddenly pulled away from the front, in Italy, and given that cushy job guarding that general. Why he was going to go on leave when it wasn't his turn. God. If it hadn't been for that bloody General Order, he would have been spared the whole nightmare. What he couldn't fathom was what his mam was doing in London. She only even went as far as Neath, once a year. Mrs Isaacs patted his arm, again.

'It must have been terrible.'

Emrys let everything out. Sitting there on the freezing platform, in Charing Cross Station, he told her everything that had happened over the previous six months. Her eyes widened as he moved rapidly from Flinty's murder to Madame Vaillant and then to The Black Hole of Lille. By the time he reached his desertion, in Canterbury, tears had begun to stream down her face.

That was it. He would never talk about it ever again. Certainly not to his family. Perhaps to some disbelieving grandchild, when he was eighty. He looked at Mrs Isaacs with embarrassment.

'I'm sorry, Mrs Isaacs. I have upset you. I shouldn't have.'

Eva Isaacs wiped her tears away, with the cleanest handkerchief Emrys had ever seen.

'Boxer. Boxer. It has been a privilege, a true privilege, to listen to your story. Thank you. Now you are unwell. Father has converted Melchett Hall, our home in Hampshire, into a convalescent home. Fatten you up, with three meals a day and you'll be better in no time. My useless brother might even visit you.'

Much as three meals a day sounded like some unbelievable utopia, he knew he couldn't accept. He had to get home. He didn't know if Madeleine Vaillant's letter had actually got to his mam. If the sergeant, in Canterbury, thought that he was dead then surely his mam must too.

'Thank you, Mrs Isaacs. It is a very kind offer. I must get home, though. I must see my mam and make sure she knows I'm all right. So, if you could just give me another piece of cake, I'll be on my way. It looks like it's going to rain soon. I want to get to Paddington before it does.'

Eva Isaacs looked very seriously at Emrys.

'Look, Boxer. Neither my father nor my brother would ever forgive me if I made you walk to Paddington. Wait here, for just a short while, while I get organised. I will take you myself in the car. I will send the maid to fetch you some food. Something a little more nutritious than cake, perhaps.'

Emrys looked on, in disbelief, as Mrs Isaacs, marched off to find her maid. Things, at last, might be looking up. He had a few minutes sitting silently, watching more returning heroes as they limped past, stopping only briefly for a cup of tea. If this was indeed the last part of what Mrs Isaacs had described as his odyssey, then what an odyssey it had been. He, suddenly, thought of all the people he had had the opportunity to meet along the way. Lieutenant Mond, Major Davies, Lieutenant Valadier, General Elliott, Madeleine Vaillant and, even, Mrs Isaacs herself. Then there was that nurse and Canadian doctor, in Bethune. He couldn't remember their names. The wonderful people, in Italy. How could he have forgotten them? Yes. It had been a true odyssey.

The young maid, dressed in a severe black uniform, shook him by the shoulder and woke him from his thoughts. He couldn't believe the contents of the paper bag carefully placed in front of him. Pieces of cooked chicken. A delicacy he had not seen for years. He began to eat slowly, enviously surveyed by the passing soldiers.

Another touch of his shoulder made him look up again. It was Mrs Isaacs. After one final mouthful of chicken, he followed her out of the station. Towering above him, he recognised Nelson's Column and in front a dark green car, with shiny silver surrounds. A neatly dressed chauffeur stood next to it, holding open the back door. Eva Isaacs spoke, immediately regretting her banality.

'It's a Rolls Royce. I don't suppose you've been in a Rolls Royce before.'

Emrys laughed.

'Well, actually, I have. In fact, it was with your brother. It was an ambulance mind. Mrs Isaacs, I can't go in that. Not in the state I'm in.'

Eva Isaacs pulled him by the arm, once more, towards the car.

'Boxer. As I have said, it will be a privilege to have you accompany me in the back of my car.'

From the look on his face as he helped this vagrant into the car, the elderly chauffeur didn't agree with his mistress. Emrys sat, uncomfortably, on the pristine leather seats, next to this immaculately dressed lady as the car started on the journey. He stared out of the window, as they passed a massive stone building. Eva Isaacs smiled at his look of pure disbelief.

'That's Buckingham Palace. It's where King George and Queen Mary live.'

This time it was Emrys's turn to smile.

'It's how this all began. We paraded in front of Queen Mary the day before we sailed to France. It seems a lifetime ago.'

A few minutes later, they were drawing up next to Paddington Station. Eva Isaacs broke the silence.

'Boxer. Stay here while Michael goes to buy your ticket. Single to Briton Ferry, Michael. Would you like to travel First Class, Boxer?'

Emrys considered this, carefully. Imagine that. M.G. Roberts's messenger boy returning First Class. That might cause a stir. He replied, speaking gently to his benefactor.

'I think, Mrs Isaacs. It would be for the best if I was with my own kind. I'm grateful for the offer, of course, but it would be for the best. I just want to say thank you for everything.'

He remained in the car, as Michael disappeared to buy his ticket. Third class to Briton Ferry. Eva Isaacs began to talk earnestly.

'Boxer. You won't remember, but on that beach, in Boulogne, you gave me some advice. It was advice about Henry and it was good advice. I'm sure it saved his life. So, it is for us to say thank you to you. Now, Boxer, go home to that wonderful mother of yours.'

As he began to make his way towards the platform, he heard a voice call from the car, behind him.

'And Boxer. Go home and have a good life. Have a happy life.'

He was fortunate to wake, from another deep sleep, just as the train began to slow. He strained his head to see if he could steal a brief glimpse of his home as they glided along the side of the River Neath. Seconds later, he was out of the carriage and trotting down the platform towards the exit. He half expected a band to be playing. But why should it? Nobody knew he was coming and even if they did, they wouldn't have a band for him.

He crossed the main road, carefully. It would be ironic if, at this last moment, he was knocked over by a tram. A figure was limping towards him. They recognised each other simultaneously.

'Emrys.'

'Albert.'

'Emrys, when did you get back?'

'Just five minutes ago. Haven't even got home yet. Albert. I heard that you were wounded.'

Albert laughed.

'Yes. I was stupid enough to leave the cyclists and joined the infantry. Caught it at Mametz Wood. Still, I'm better off than some. You know that Emlyn was killed, in Belgium, last year. And, Emrys. I was sorry to hear about your brother. He was such a nice chap.'

The two old soldiers hugged, once more. Perhaps Emrys thought, they shouldn't really describe themselves as old soldiers. It was over three years since they first went to France. He was still only twenty and Albert even younger.

As he began to near 11 Neath Road his pace began to increase until he was nearly running. The door would, undoubtedly, be unlocked and he would let himself in. He would give them the biggest of shocks. At that moment, the door opened and a tall young woman came out. A woman he barely recognised. Evelyn screamed and jumped into his arms.

'Emrys. Emrys.' Followed by. 'God, you stink.'

22

Emrys stood at arm's length looking at Evelyn. He couldn't believe his eyes. His little sister had grown up and he hadn't been around to see it. She looked just like the pictures of Mam when she was younger. Just taller. Evelyn was now only an inch shorter than Emrys himself. He laughed at her and her wrinkled-up nose.

'It's not just the smell you need to worry about. It's the lice. The sooner I get rid of this lot and into my old clothes the better. Mam will want to mend them and keep them. Me. I want to take them and throw them in the furnace over there.'

He pointed over his shoulder at The Albion Steel Works. It was still belching the same red smoke as it had done the day he left, three years previously. He looked back at Evelyn.

'Where are you off to in such a hurry? Come in and watch Mam jump when she sees me.'

Evelyn stood still.

'She's not in. That's where I'm going. See where she's got to. She should be home by now, but you know Mam. She'll be talking to somebody. Probably having tea with Ruth or still at the cemetery.'

Emrys looked quizzically at his sister. Cemetery? What was she doing at the cemetery? A sudden thought came to his head.

'Da. Is Da all right?'

It was Evelyn's turn to laugh.

'Of course. Does nothing all day but sit in that seat. He doesn't change at all. Has Mam running round after him. I think that's why she goes up to the cemetery. She says it's to talk to David, but I think it's to get away from Da, for a few minutes.'

She paused for a second.

'Do you know something? She used to talk to you as well, until we got the letter from a Madame Vaillant, in Lille.'

Emrys interrupted.

'It got here. Thank God for that. She said it would, but I didn't believe her. I was sure you would all still think that I was dead. If you're going to find Mam, I think I'll join you.'

The two of them began to walk slowly back up Neath Road. Emrys was surprised at how unfit he was. The Black Hole of Lille and the illness must have really taken it out of him. As they passed Mrs Eynon's house the curtains flickered open. Emrys laughed.

'Somethings never change.'

Evelyn stopped and looked at her brother.

'Emrys. Lots of things have changed, including Mam. I think you'll be shocked when you see her. She's no longer the woman she was when you were last home. You know how much David affected her. Well. When she thought we had lost you, it was just too much for her.'

Emrys said nothing in reply. There was nothing he could say. They slowly made their way to the cricket pavilion, where Mam was almost certainly having tea. Emrys was amazed when he saw the building. Before the war, it was quickly becoming dilapidated from neglect. Now, the leaky roof had been repaired and the wooden walls painted. A holly bush grew to the side of the doorway. On the other side, a Chrysanthemum still grew in a rough stone pot, waiting for the first frost. Somebody must love this building.

Evelyn mounted the two steps to the door and knocked loudly, as she had many times before. A short lady with grey hair opened it and immediately beamed at Emrys. She shouted in an accent that Emrys recognised so well, from the three long years in Northern France.

'Emrys. You're home. Have you seen your mother yet?'

Emrys was surprised. He had never met this lady before but it could only be Ruth. She had recognised him immediately. She continued more calmly.

'I recognise you from the photograph. The photograph that the French lady sent. But where's your mother? Where is Harriet? I was expecting her hours ago.'

Evelyn looked worried.

'She must still be in the cemetery. I hope she's all right.'

Ruth grabbed her coat. She looked worried too. It was a cold day for Harriet to be sitting alone on that seat. The iron gates to the cemetery were only two hundred yards away and beyond them row upon row of cold stone gravestones. It wasn't raining but an icy wind was blowing up the valley from the sea. Emrys had forgotten how exposed it was up here. At the very back sat a solitary figure, surveying the graveyard in front of her. It was Mam.

This was the moment that he had been looking forward to since leaving Mrs Isaacs in Paddington. It was the thought of this moment that kept him alive when he was ill in Madeleine Valliant's bed. It had also stopped him from giving up in that dreadful dungeon. He wasn't going to think about that though.

It was too painful. Today was a happy day. He waved his arm vigorously and shouted.

'Mam. Mam. It's Emrys. I'm home. Home for good.'

There was no reply. Harriet was still sitting motionlessly. The two women began to run, sidestepping graves as they went. Emrys hobbled painfully after them, overcome by a deep sense of foreboding. When he arrived at the rickety chair, his mam was sitting with her eyes closed. Despite Evelyn's warning, she looked so beautiful. Serenely beautiful. The two women were knelt on either side of her.

Ruth whispered.

'May His great name be magnified and sanctified in the world that is to be created anew, where He will revive the dead and raise them up to eternal life.'

Ruth hugged Evelyn to her and then looked up at Emrys.

'She's at peace at last. She's with David, where I think she always wanted to be.'

Evelyn stared blankly at her brother with tears already streaming down her cheeks.

'You're too late, Emrys. Why didn't you come yesterday?'

Emrys muttered almost to himself.

'Fucking war.'

Epilogue

A land fit for heroes. Those were the words of Evelyn's nemesis David Lloyd George. The world didn't end in November 1918. This is what that land (and other lands) held for the people and places in this story.

M.G. ROBERTS became Mayor of Neath in 1922. A painting of him still hangs in Neath Town Hall. His son MATT is commemorated in many places, including a window, in Worcester Cathedral, where he went to school. His grave can be found in Sailly Labourse Cemetery Extension, grave B12. His Gravestone reads 'I sleep but my heart waketh'.

SIR ALFRED MOND served under Lloyd George first as first Commissioner for Works and then Minister for Health, whilst MP for Swansea. He was the first chairman of ICI, in 1926. He became 1st Baron Melchett in 1928, a year before his death. The paintings from his house in Lowndes Square, so disliked by Harriet, hang in the National Gallery

EVA ISAACS nee MOND was born into one remarkable family and married into another. Her father-in-law was Rufus Isaacs, the Attorney General and later Viceroy of India. She had been horrified by child poverty, when accompanying her father around his constituency, in Swansea. She became increasingly involved in child welfare charities, including being President of The Nursery Nurse Training Colleges. She converted to Judaism in 1933. Her brother, Henry, was independently doing the same thing, without telling each other. She became Marchioness of Reading, on the death of Rufus Isaacs in 1935. She became Vice President of the World Jewish Congress, in 1957, a year after being awarded the CBE. She died in 1973, two years after being awarded an honorary fellowship at the Hebrew University in Jerusalem.

LEVI GETHIN HUGHES was chaplain on the western front for four years, being mentioned in dispatches. He stayed in the army after the war. In 1942, he was appointed as Deputy Chaplain to the Forces and Honorary Chaplain to His Majesty King George VI. He was the first Baptist minister to be given that title.

BILLY WELLS. Bombardier Billy Wells was the British Heavyweight Champion from 1911 to 1919. He was the first Heavyweight to be awarded the Lonsdale Belt. He was due to fight World Champion, Jack Johnson, in London, in 1911. It was blocked by the then Home Secretary, Winston Churchill.

THE MAGGIE. The paddle steamer La Marguerite, which transported the cyclists to France, covered 52000 miles during the war, carrying 360000 troops to La Havre from Southampton. She was broken up in 1925. Her bell was presented to The London Rifles, the first regiment to sail in her. The bell still hangs in the Regimental Memorial Chapel in St. Sepulchre Church, in London.

TAYLORS FOUNDRY produced munitions during both World Wars. It is now listed by Coflein as a building of Archaeological interest.

CAPTAIN PAUL JONES, of the 9th Cavalry Brigade, describes the 38th Division Cyclists' concert in his book War Letters of a Public Schoolboy

NURSE BEATRICE ALLSOP, Emrys's nurse in Bethune, was one of the first females to receive the Military Medal. In August 1916, the Casualty Clearing Station, in Bethune was severely damaged by shelling. Despite being wounded herself, she helped move over two hundred wounded into the basement. There, she continued their treatment.

CHARLES VALADIER has been recognised as one of the pioneers of facial surgery. He was promoted to Major in 1917. He became a Chevalier of the Legion d'Honaire in 1919, a British citizen in 1920 and was knighted in 1920. His Rolls Royce Silver Ghost was sold for £800000 at auction in 2013.

CAPTAIN JOHN GLYNN-JONES, who held the line in front of Mametz Wood, won the Military Cross, in 1917. After the war, he became the welfare officer for the Ocean Group of Collieries. He noticed the multiple problems that the young colliery boys, often aged only 16, had. He founded the Boys Club of Wales to educate these children and give them holidays. Many boys and now girls have benefited over the years, including in more recent times, Joe Calzaghe, the boxer.

SERGEANT DAVID BENJAMIN JOHN. His body was never found. He is commemorated on Pier and Face 4A of the Thiepval Memorial. In the wonderful, Danzig Alley Cemetery, overlooking Mametz Wood, there is a stone seat commemorating the 14th Royal Welsh Fusiliers, his battalion. Nearby is a gravestone which says 'July 10th 1916. A Welsh Sergeant. Known only to God.' Perhaps?

SYLVIA PANKHURST didn't take Harriet's advice about reconciling with her mother, Emmeline or sister, Christabel. After the war, she immersed herself in left-wing politics, travelling to Soviet Russia. In the 1930s she veered away from British politics, after the Italian invasion of Ethiopia. She became a supporter of Halle Selassie. She and her son moved to Addis Ababa, as Halle Selassie's guest and advisor. She died there in 1960 and was given a state funeral. A talented artist, an exhibition of her work took place in the Tate Modern, in 2013.

POMPEY ELLIOTT. General Elliott was vociferous in his criticism of senior officers, after the failed attack on the Sugarloaf, now known as the Battle of Fromelles. Probably Australia's greatest soldier and despite heroics during the rest of the war, he was passed over for promotion, from then on. After the war, he returned to Melbourne to work as a solicitor. He mainly worked in cases involving returning servicemen. Probably suffering from what we now know as PTSD, he killed himself in 1931, by cutting his wrists. His coffin was pulled on a horse-drawn hearse, through the streets of Melbourne, followed by thousands of ex-servicemen. There is a statue of him in Ballarat.

ETHEL SNOWDEN also travelled to Soviet Russia, but became very critical of it, alienating her from other left-wing activists. In 1926, she was appointed as Governor of the newly established British Broadcasting Corporation. Her husband, Phillip, became the first Labour Chancellor of the Exchequer, under Ramsey Macdonald, MP for Neath. He became ill, resigned and was elevated to the Lords. Ethel became Viscountess Snowden, in 1931.

11 NEATH ROAD, BRITON FERRY AND 2 RUE SOLTIN, LILLE shared the same fate. Both were knocked down, one to make way for a bridge and the other a Hotel de Ville.

LA COUTURE was completely destroyed but has been rebuilt. Some of the defences are still visible, behind the church. A large monument to the Portuguese dead dominates the square. Both the Portuguese President and Prime Minister attended a Memorial service there, on April 9th 2018, to commemorate the centenary of The Battle of La Lys.

BLACK HOLE OF LILLE. Fort Macdonald, named after one of Napoleon's Marshalls, still exists. It is an attractive park and community centre on the outskirts of Lille. There is little trace of its grim past.

THE CYCLISTS. When they held muster, the evening after the action at La Couture, only 20% were present. The rest were casualties. They did, however, see action again just a few days later and were not finally disbanded until 1919. They and The King Edward's Horse were both mentioned in Haig's dispatches to the Prime Minister. This was one of the very few occasions that Haig mentioned a battalion, by name. The following are just some of them.

HENRY. Percy Davies's story about Henry Mond having a menage a trois with Gwen Wilson and the author, Gilbert Cannon, is for the most part correct and was the scandal of its day. Cannon travelled to America in 1919, to promote a book, for D.H. Lawrence. He returned to discover that Henry and Gwen had married in his absence. On moving into Mulberry House, in Westminster, they had a fireplace designed by Charles Jagger, called Scandal. It is made from iron and shows a naked Gwen and Henry, being surveyed by horrified Society Women. It is now in the Victoria and Albert Museum. Henry published a book of war poetry, in 1919. He became a talented financier and was the director of ICI and Barclays Bank. Like his sister, he converted to Judaism in the 1930s and became the chairman of The Jewish Agency for Palestine.

PERCY. Major D. Percy Davies returned to the bar, in 1919, having been released from captivity in Germany. He followed his heart and went into journalism. He became Editor of The News of the World and Constable of Glamorgan.

ALBERT joined the 16th Royal Welch Fusiliers and was badly wounded at Mametz Wood. He spent eighteen months in the hospital but lived into old age. He witnessed the unveiling of the Red Dragon Memorial, in Mametz Wood in 1987.

EMLYN also joined the 16th RWF. He survived Mametz Wood unscathed. He was killed by artillery fire in November 1917. He is buried in Cite Bonjean Military Cemetery, in Armentieres.

FLINTY. Horace Flint's body was never found, after his murder by the German artillerymen. He is remembered on the Ploessteert Memorial Panel 11.

TED Ted must have been next to Emrys in the recruiting centre in 1915. Their service numbers are consequetive. He returned from captivity, near Lille, in November 1918.

GWYN spent his captivity in the Dulmen POW camp, near Munster, Germany. His incarceration affected his health and he developed Tuberculosis. Donations, including an anonymous one from London, paid for him to go to Davos, Switzerland in 1935. The treatment failed and he died in Neath, in 1937.

EMRYS eventually did get his back pay, aided by the intervention of Sir Rufus Isaacs. Using this and the help from M.G. Roberts, which Matt had asked for in his final letter, he set up his mineral water business. As decided with his family in 1916, it was called Our Boys. Unsurprisingly, he never got offered a watch by the Briton Ferry at the Front Committee.

THE HEROINES. The women in this story are the real heroes.

ELIZABETH POWELL continued helping Reverend Powell at Jerusalem Chapel. In the 1930s, the family adopted an orphan, Maria, from the Spanish Civil War.

RUTH REUBENS Having lost her friend, she returned to Belgium, in 1918. She said goodbye to the cricket pavilion, which had been her home for four years. Unfortunately, she failed to get out of Brussels, in 1940, as she had in 1914. She died in Auschwitz, in 1945.

MADAME MADELEINE VAILLANT. Her photograph, along with her flowery notepaper, which she used to write to prisoners' families, is in the Imperial War Museum archives. She was still suspected in some quarters of being a collaborator and hated, in others, for destroying a part of the city, whilst blowing up the munitions dump, in 1916. She was reported as dying from influenza, in January 1919.

HARRIET Her funeral was one of the largest seen at Rehoboth Chapel for many years. At Evelyn's insistence, the Old Testament reading was read by Ruth Reubens and the New by Elizabeth Powell. In the seats in the second row sat M.G. Roberts and his family, as well as the Taylor brothers. Behind them sat Sir Alfred Mond, Eva Isaacs and Ethel Snowden. In the very back row were Tom and Jane Evans, with their family, including Beatrice, whom Emrys eventually married.

EVIE. Now that's another story.

ME. DAVID. On Charing Cross Station, Emrys told himself that he wouldn't tell his story until he was eighty and to some disbelieving grandchild. I am that grandchild.

Website for photographs harrietseternaltears.co.uk

ACKNOWLEDGEMENTS

The following books were very helpful to me in researching *Harriet's Eternal Tears* and are all well worth reading:

Pompey Elliott by Ross McMullin

Sylvia Pankhurst by Katherine Connelly

The Welsh in Mametz Wood by Jonathan Hicks

The Battle of the Lys by Chris Baker

A Political Pilgrim in Europe by Ethel Snowden

The following were absolutely essential:

Not in our Name by Philip Adams. It is a superb account of the anti-war activities in Briton Ferry. If you have read *Harriet's Eternal Tears*, you will recognise some of it. Philip Adam's book is about what really happened!

Neath and Briton Ferry in the First World War by Jonathan Skidmore

The Journal of Bill Tucker (late of the 11th Corps Cyclist Battalion), held in The Imperial War Museum.

I would like to thank the following.

The National Archives, Kew.

The British Newspaper Archive.

Kathy, obviously, for everything, including putting up with years of me talking about Henry Mond.

Helen, Abi, Rob, Andrea and Ros in my writers group. Your support has kept me going.

Andy Flint, Joyce Ruddell and Ian Pinker for their support

and for reading some or all of this book. Ian, you were right about the commas.

My Faber Academy reader and Sara Cox.

Grampa for that one conversation which started all this.